Sing One Song

By Helen Topping Miller

Historical Novels

SING ONE SONG

THE PROUD YOUNG THING

THE HORNS OF CAPRICORN

MIRAGE

TRUMPET IN THE CITY

SOUND OF CHARIOTS

SHOD WITH FLAME

DARK SAILS

Romantic Novels

APRIL TO REMEMBER

HOLLOW SILVER

FLAME VINE

CANDLE IN THE MORNING

SPOTLIGHT

WICKED SISTER

WILD LILAC

HUNTER'S MOON

Sing One Song

by

Helen Topping Miller

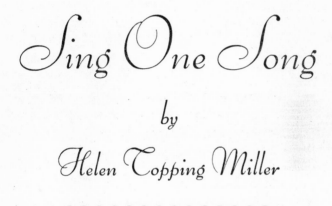

APPLETON-CENTURY-CROFTS, INC.

New York

TO CHARLES AND SIBLEY HOWELL

Sing One Song

1

A CROWD HAD GATHERED IN THE STREET AND THE PEO-
ple stood very still. There was no murmuring such as usually arises from a watching throng. Most of the faces were
set and some pale, eyes averted, mouths drawn down.

Two men slipped quietly away from the watchers and
entered a grocery store, carefully closing the door. One was
an important-looking small man in a good black suit and
high, tight collar that compressed his pink jowls, making
his prominent cold blue eyes protrude a little—a paunchy,
strutting little man with an air of dominance about him.
The other was leaner, sober, now apparently depressed.

The storekeeper stood at the rear weighing out salt for a
countrywoman, his face rigid with controlled fury.

"Dirty business!" he muttered out of the side of his
mouth. "Him an old man too. Must be past sixty."

The two men declined to answer but the woman blazed her eyes toward the street and turned shrill.

"It ain't the Yankees done it! It's them scoundrelly Home Guards they done enlisted. Scum and trash from everywheres. All het up about gittin' back at folks they got a grudge against. Like the pore old judge. Sent 'Lish McBride to jail for beatin' up his wife and young ones and now that's 'Lish out there totin' a gun with a blue coat onto him, grinnin' from ear to ear."

"You'd better hush, Martha," cautioned the lean man. "They've been sending women south through the lines, I heard. When people like old Governor Morehead and Henry Clay's own son ain't safe, there ain't anybody safe unless they think Abraham Lincoln is God Almighty."

The pompous little man turned at that. "You had better watch your own tongue, Ira. Disloyal talk can get you into plenty of trouble. Everybody knows that Judge Nesbitt had an opportunity to take the oath, and refused. He has two sons in the Confederate army, and worst of all, he's been drawing his wife's money out of my bank and investing it in Confederate bonds. If that's not treason to the Union I wouldn't know what to call it!"

"You'd know about money gettin' drawed out of the bank, wouldn't you, Harper?" asked the storekeeper. "I reckon you know every penny gets drawed out of that bank."

"It's my business to know," snapped Hume Harper. "I'm responsible to the depositors for what happens to the money in that bank."

The storekeeper and the woman looked at each other dryly, their mouths twisting a little. The woman grumbled, "Ain't that a disgrace! A pure disgrace to this town and the hull state of Kentucky. You-all mark," she threatened the banker and the other man with hot, angry eyes, "I ain't for Jeff Davis. I ain't for no war at all. I figure we ought to run both armies out of this state and fight to keep 'em out and run our own business. But I'm for what's decent and right and that ain't havin' no honorable, good old man like Judge Nesbitt that's done a kindness to most everybody in the country paraded through the streets roped up like an ornery steer! Weigh me a nickel's worth of snuff, Seth, and don't be too dum stingy about it."

Out in the streets was a somber thudding of feet, the clink of cartridge belts, the thump of canteens as the Home Guards under the orders of General Jere Boyle of the Union Command paraded Judge Horace Nesbitt off to the railroad to be shipped to some Union prison in the east as a "notorious and dangerous Confederate sympathizer and an inciter to rebellion."

Judge Nesbitt's long white hair lay on his collar under his beaver hat. His body was a trifle bent with years and from long leaning over the bench in courts of law but he held his shoulders as high as he could and his head was unbowed.

His hands were bound at the wrists with hemp rope but he held them proudly across his chest and stared straight ahead over his bonds with an aloof and scornful dignity that made the shambling rank of men in blue who guarded him look cheap and dogged in spite of the uniforms they wore. Some of the guard were obviously uncomfortable and shamefaced. A woman hissed at them from the sidewalk but she was swiftly and gently silenced with her husband's fingers over her lips. But most of the Home Guards wore a grimace of triumphant malice and carried their guns insolently, occasionally giving a sidelong glare at the silent, frowning watchers.

Behind a curtain in the big wooden house on the corner opposite the bank three people stood watching. There were two women who wept and a lanky boy of eighteen

3

with a pale, taut face and a forelock of soft brown hair hanging over his brow.

"He holds his head high. He scorns them, the poor darling—*le pauvre petit!*" choked the younger woman.

"They will never crush his spirit. Never!" declared the older.

She was Amalie, the New-Orleans-born wife of Judge Nesbitt. Her dark hair showed a touch of gray but her face was still beautiful with great dark eyes under dramatic brows and lashes.

"But where is it they will take him?" wailed her daughter-in-law, wife of the oldest Nesbitt son, Milo. "We will never know. He could die and we would not know." Like her mother-in-law, Denise Nesbitt had come from Louisiana and the piquant accent of the bayous still colored her speech.

"I heard them talking at the bank," said the boy. "The Adjutant General wrote Mr. Crittenden that these whole-sale arrests are alienating good Union men. At least two hundred men have gone south to the Confederacy in the last two weeks."

"Henri," said Denise, "Henri is one that went, and for that they arrest poor Papa! Why do you not go, William? Henri was your best friend."

"I can't," sighed William Harper, whose father was president of the bank. "Pa's already bought a substitute for me to keep me out of the Union army. If I went at all I'd have to go for the Union."

"You could run away like Milo," persisted Denise. "When John Morgan came through here last month Milo borrowed money from Maman and bought a horse and before daylight he was gone. To me he did not even say *au revoir,* to me his wife!"

"To protect you, *ma petite,*" said Amalie. "If they come

4

with their guns, if they say 'Where is your husband?' you do not have to lie. You say 'How do I know?' and that is the truth. William could not run away. Not with honor."

"I could! I might do it," flared William, his thin face flushing, "but not with John Hunt Morgan! I wouldn't be a raider, burning barns and robbing banks like Morgan. We all sat down in the bank with guns for three nights when Morgan came this way. I could slip down the river to join Braxton Bragg but it would about kill my mother and I reckon if I joined the Confederates Pa would never let me see her again."

"I am a mother too," sighed Amalie. "Two sons I have seen go away and only the good God knows if I'll ever see them return. And now—" she cried, desolately, "my husband. The poor Moreheads do not even know where their papa is and he was governor of Kentucky!"

"They got bail for James Clay. I heard Pa talking about it," said William.

"We have no money for bail," said Amalie flatly, not looking at him. "Bonds—bonds, all the time the judge buys the bonds. And who would help us? Who, in Kentucky?"

"I'd better get back to the bank," muttered William unhappily. "Pa was out when I slipped over here. I'm mighty sorry about the judge, Mrs. Nesbitt, mighty sorry!"

"Go out the back way!" ordered Denise, sarcastically. "Do not be seen associating with us! We are *canaille!* We are Confederate. Maybe also they will put Maman and me in their filthy bastille! At least then we will eat."

There were mock-orange bushes growing in the back yard and William Harper crept through them and out a rear gate into the alley where some whitewashed Negro cabins stood in littered yards. The Negroes were still slaves but it was in the air that Lincoln meant to set them all free, and one bold wench cut her eyes at William defiantly.

5

Kentucky's abortive neutrality had proven so soon ineffectual and been abandoned under Union pressure. All this hate and suspicion had fermented in Abraham Lincoln's birth-state so fiercely that Kentucky was distrusted everywhere—both in Washington and in Jefferson Davis's new capitol at Richmond.

The Union, the holy Union, his father prated. But slavery was to blame for the severance of the Union no matter how many phrases the politicians made up or how much pompous patriotism shuddered on the wind that blew south from the Ohio River.

"The slaveowners are to be reimbursed," his father was continually saying. "Three hundred dollars for every slave of a loyal Union owner, freed in Kentucky."

"You value Hessie at only three hundred dollars, Mr. Harper?" William's mother inquired. "My father bought her for me when she was only fourteen years old and the price he paid was far more than three hundred dollars."

"I can only remind you, Mrs. Harper"—Hume Harper always spoke crisply at home as though he tasted every word that issued from his smugly pursed lips—"that your Hessie could be set free without any recompense to us whatever. It can happen and it may."

"Would you leave me, Hessie?" asked Ellen over her breakfast coffee. "After twenty years would you leave me if Lincoln set you free?"

Black angular Hessie twitched a shoulder. "Dunno, Mis'-tiss. These bad times. Body dunno what he do."

William could not find it in his mind to reproach faithful Hessie for the turmoil that had all Kentucky seething in this sultry August of the war. But Hessie was part of the Cause that his friends Henri Nesbitt and Denise and Tom Findly talked about incessantly. Tom Findly was his sister Harriet's sweetheart. Tom had gone off too, with Morgan's raiders, and Harriet Harper was always moping and crying, putting cornstarch on her eyelids so that their father would not notice and ask questions.

Mrs. Harper knew that Harriet was in love with Tom Findly, but the alliance was kept secret from Hume Harper. The Findlys had a mortgage, and though the elder Tom Findly was fiercely for the Union, a mortgage could not be lived down. It clouded the respectability of any family in Hume Harper's estimation. And that young Tom was for the Confederacy put him forever outside the pale.

So Harriet had met Tom in secret, slipping out to ride with Tom in the farm buggy along tree-hung country roads at night. Hume Harper was deceived but William was not. Nobody paid much attention to William. He was the Harper boy who swept out the bank, cleaned the spittoons and lingered always on the edges of things. But in that obscure position he overheard many things not intended for his ears.

Left alone in the bank he saw papers and documents, sometimes even letters. Not that he planned to pry but he knew where some of his father's money came from, the sudden new prosperity that never went on the bank's books or into the safe, but was carried home and locked away in a stout steel box. He knew about the cotton that came up the rivers and the contraband goods that went down to the seceded states. And though he was only eighteen and vastly ignored by his father, William was shrewd enough to know that whatever transaction occurred, whatever illicit trading was done with the rebels, the name of Hume Harper would never be found on any document whatsoever. He knew this because on those days after the hairy, profane river captains came and went, he had searched, half in dread and half in reluctant admiration for his father's cleverness in making himself rich out of the destruction of war.

7

Out in the alley William walked boldly down a side street and across the courthouse yard and entered the bank as casually as though he had just returned from an errand. The elderly clerk, Mr. Merrill, looked up from his ledger.

"You go by the depot? You see him—the judge?" he asked.

"I saw him in the street. Not after that."

"Heard they were taking him to Boston. No telling who'll be next. Might be me. I've got two nephews riding with Turner Ashby. Anybody with kin south of the Cumberland or in Jeff Davis's army is a suspect. Be harried and watched and like as not dragged out of his bed at night. Even your pa could be, big man in the town and state like he is. They could find out about all those hides and the pork that went down river."

"You shut up!" snapped William. "My father is an honest man and loyal to the Union."

The clerk nodded, scratching behind his ear with his pen. "William," he said paternally, "you stay blind and deaf—and dumb, like you are, and likely you'll live through this war!"

"He's safe to live," drawled the cashier, a narrow-faced man in his forties who spoke so seldom that people usually jumped when any sound issued from his dry, colorless lips. "He ain't stopping any bullets or minie balls!"

William glared at the pair of them in affronted dignity. Someday, he was thinking, he would be president of this bank himself and then listen to what came out of their mouths! "Yes, Mr. Harper, sir. No, Mr. Harper, sir."

Now he shouldered some heavy books and carried them into the strong room. This chamber was built of brick with a ceiling of steel bars and a barred door with a heavy padlock. At the back of this space stood the shining new safe against the wall, the round eyes of its twin dials winking in the afternoon light. It was a handsome safe painted a glossy green with a colored view of Niagara Falls on the door. The steel door was eight inches thick and guarded by heavy bolts. His father always closed this door after the bank business was finished, shoving it to with a smug clang, twirling the dials importantly to lock it.

Take dynamite to break open that safe, Mr. Merrill declared. It had cost a lot when it was installed. William had seen the invoice on his father's desk one day and been appalled at the figure. A good house and lot could be bought for what that safe cost, he was certain, but his father was continually saying that the bank's money was the people's money. It had to be kept safe. It had to be loaned wisely; mortgages must be honored and the interest kept up or the people's money was in jeopardy. Fortunately the interest on the Findly farm was kept scrupulously paid up by Tom's grim old father. But there were other accounts in bad shape, the boy knew, Thad Briscoe's for one. The Briscoes were people he liked, Thad having a family of bright and pretty daughters.

Henri Nesbitt was in love with the oldest Briscoe daughter, Teresa, but the Nesbitts were in Harper's black book too, the Nesbitt mortgage having been neglected for more than a year.

William had heard his father complain about the Briscoes and say, "I shall have to take over that paper personally, I fear, to protect the bank. The Briscoe mortgage has been running on for years." Or, "I made that Nesbitt loan on the basis of personal friendship but if people have so little regard for their credit that they dispose of their funds elsewhere rather than meet their obligations, the supporters of the bank must not be made to suffer."

Hume Harper came into the bank now, going to his desk, hanging his hard hat carefully on the peg, pulling a pair of

9

paper cuffs over his sleeves. He leafed through a few papers, opened and shut a drawer, then moved over to Merrill's desk.

"Merrill, have you taken the oath?" he demanded abruptly.

The clerk blinked and swallowed. "No sir, Mr. Harper. I never have. Not that ironclad oath they talk about."

"Then go and do it," snapped Harper. "Go to the provost's office immediately the bank closes and swear allegiance to the Union. They say that Braxton Bragg and Kirby Smith are gathering forces down below Cumberland Gap. They may bring their abortive Confederate war into Kentucky and if that happens every man's loyalties must be made very clear."

"Fighting, Pa?" asked William excitedly. "You mean there'll be fighting up here?"

"General Buell certainly isn't going to sit still and let those rebels take Louisville and Cincinnati. There are plenty of turncoats over in the bluegrass who would welcome a rebel army but they will be dealt with eventually—and severely. I want no one under suspicion in this establishment, so be on your way, Merrill, as soon as I have locked the safe. And when you swear the oath let yourself be seen doing it, you hear?"

"I didn't swear the oath either, Pa," William reminded him.

"There was no need, William. Officially you are in the Union army, by your substitute. You don't mean that you have doubts in your mind, I hope? That defection, sir, I would not overlook nor condone."

"Well," began William uneasily, "I don't think they treated Judge Nesbitt right."

"He brought it upon himself—entirely! He had the opportunity to take the right stand and he refused. He has ignored his just financial commitments and wasted his money and his wife's money helping to support a scoundrelly rebellion that is doomed to utter failure. Complete and utter failure!" orated Harper. "Now, sir, get back to your work."

"But a man ought to have a right to his beliefs," persisted William recklessly. "Suppose the Confederates do come? Suppose they take Kentucky. They might be marching you off to some prison, Pa, with your hands roped up like you were a murderer!"

"Small chance of that. What do you think the Union forces, all the troops in Kentucky and across the Ohio, will be doing while the rebels are trying to take Kentucky? I'll tell you what they will be doing. They'll be annihilating Braxton Bragg and all his deluded followers! They will be wiping them out, that's what they'll be doing. Now, I'll hear no more from you, sir! Loose talk can be very unwise in these times, so watch your tongue."

As always near closing time, a number of people came in to cash small checks or make deposits. The cashier counted out money unsmilingly, not moving a muscle of his pallid face. The customers were glum too, the atmosphere of depression in the street seeming to come in with them. One or two directed hostile glances toward Hume Harper's indifferent back, and William caught those looks and his unhappiness increased. He knew that his father was not well liked. He was dreaded more than he was respected. A man who refused a loan was always undeservedly unpopular with the person who had requested it, William's mother had explained. But to the boy's mind there was more underlying the guarded remoteness of the people who did business with the bank, something almost verging on contempt. That cotton sent up the river, he was thinking.

In this town everything was known, no man had any

secrets regardless of how discreetly he operated. Servants listened, whispers ran on the inscrutable Negro grapevine up and down the alleys, carefully guarded matters leaked out through kitchen doors.

The bank was finally swept out and mopped clean and every cuspidor scoured and polished. William headed for home through the hot summer twilight. He noted the closed doors and drawn shades at the Nesbitt house. A house in mourning. She was there, Denise, with her hot liquid eyes and flashing temper, her softness and ivory roundness of arm and shoulder. Denise was a man's wife but for a long time she had troubled young William's dreams, making him wake sweating and uneasy and ashamed.

He had never touched Denise but he knew how her flesh would feel under a caressing hand. That she was now in trouble and might even be in need made William ache with indignant fury.

Milo Nesbitt, her husband, was with Morgan, and it was reported that Morgan and his men rode night and day, were often hungry and seldom paid. It was common gossip that the Confederate army was usually not paid at all. The thought that Denise and Mrs. Nesbitt might not have enough to eat tonight made William choke on his own supper.

2

*T*OM FINDLY HAD NOT KNOWN THAT IT WOULD BE LIKE this.

Like all young men grown to their majority on Kentucky farms he had spent long hours on horseback but never before had he lived in the saddle till both he and his sweated, jaded horse were ready to drop beside the trail.

At Nashville and at Murfreesboro there had been a touch of glory. Morgan's men were fresh then, untired, their plumes and sashes jaunty, their rifles polished and the officers' sabers gleaming. Tom Findly had no saber. That was another thing he had not known. That Morgan had made riflemen of his command, that rather than the wild exhilaration of the charge with flashing sword and galloping horse, much of the fighting would be on foot with horseholders guarding the precious mounts and troopers dragging through summer-hot woods or over rough hills and fields like so many plebeian infantrymen. Morgan's Lexington Rifles.

In Murfreesboro things had gone well. Morgan had passed his men off for Federal cavalry and been cheered by the Union watchers on the streets. Then at Lebanon everything had changed. Out of a hot, confused and furious battle in the streets had come defeat. Tom had pushed his horse up and down a little street firing at swarming troops in blue. He had seen men of his own company hurl burning torches into houses and chase terrified women with whoops of defiant glee. Then Basil Duke, Morgan's brother-in-law, had been shot from his horse and wounded and the bugle had sounded a sorrowful retreat.

Tears running down his face, Morgan had watched his wounded men stream past him, some dragging on foot with blood dripping from arms and bodies, some lashed inertly to their saddles. Night came and somewhere on the road back to Kentucky Tom slid from his saddle and lay face down in the dry weeds, shuddering with weariness and despair while his spent horse stood with heaving sides, too exhausted to stray.

A trooper roused him at last by beating on his shoulders with the butt of a rifle and Tom dragged his aching muscles into the saddle again, the leather chill and slippery with the mist of early dawn. The Morgan men who had been captured in Lebanon were being taken to Cave City in southern Kentucky on a train, they told him. Morgan planned to capture that train.

The railroad twisted through the ragged hills. Keeping well hidden in the rough undergrowth, the Lexington Rifles followed the right of way. Horses stumbled and reached hungrily for any green grass that grew on the shaly hillsides. When they halted to drink at little streams Morgan rode up and down shouting impatiently for them to be on the move. A train would not wait. There was no time to eat, no time for a man to rest his aching body, his loins, saddle-burned and agonizingly painful.

Tom snatched bites of the hard corn pone he carried in his pocket, choked on the crumbs for want of water. Thinking of the food that was undoubtedly being cooked on his mother's stove this April morning only made his stomach jerk in convulsive misery. Ham from the smoke-

14

house maybe, fresh eggs, their golden eyes upturned as they floated in the rich red fat. All the hens would be laying now with spring a delirium in the air. He could hear cackling in the distance as they skirted the farms. A detachment at the rear swung off to the east and came galloping back later with the limp bodies of dead poultry flopping on their saddles.

On a long curve they overtook the train, cut across country to head it off. But the cars in which the Confederate prisoners were locked were too well guarded. A hail of bullets came pouring out of every window. Tom saw two men of his company roll out of their saddles, their bodies hurling down a rocky incline into the cold roiling of a little creek.

He pulled his horse back into a willow thicket and waited. Ahead six men had leaped aboard the mail car and he saw three of them fall out, their arms upflung, their guns clattering down the slope of the roadbed. But the other three jumped, ducked and crouched against the bullets of the guards till the train roared on, then they came shouting back, carrying a heavy leather sack. Excitedly Morgan's command milled about them.

"Captured the Fred payroll!" one trooper shouted exultantly to Tom. "General's counting it now. All gold!"

Word came along the ranks later as they rode on. Eight thousand dollars! Morgan was heading back south now to Knoxville. Give the men a chance to rest, a chance to spend some money! Tom rode for two days sidewise in his saddle to ease his blisters. At a camp on the Cumberland where they rested two days he wrote a letter to Harriet Harper. Somewhere there would be somebody riding north who would mail it. On second thought he penned a note to his mother. Probably she would never see it, not if his father got the mail from the post office in town. The elder Findly would never forgive his son for taking sides with the Confederacy.

His mother was for the South too, but she in her husband's mind was only a woman full of the foolish vagaries of womankind, never able to forget that she had been born in Mississippi. A woman could be permitted to think nonsense but in a grown man of twenty-one it was treason!

He wrote, *Dear Ma, Well, they licked us at Lebanon but we won't stay licked. We will be back and when we come Kentucky will know that some real soldiers are fighting this war. I sure wish I had a piece of your dried apple pie this morning. We have meat but nothing good cooked up like you can cook it. I've about worn out my breeches. These saddles are sure plenty hard but the Gen. says we will all get new outfits when we get where we are going. Your loving son, Tom Jr.*

Marcia Findly never got the letter. If her husband took it from the post office she was never told and did not dare inquire. Tom Findly, Senior, wore a face like a thundercloud these days. The spring work was heavy and there was no help. He had never condescended to own slaves and the two Marcia had brought with her from Mississippi he had promptly returned, declaring that to own a human being was against God, and that to be bothered feeding and supporting one was extravagant folly.

"Ought to be here, helping me plow!" Tom Senior grumbled whenever he noticed young Tom's straw hat hanging on the peg in the kitchen. "Off tearing up the country with a lot of thieves and traitors. Well, he picked his side, let him live with it."

Later he came in jeering triumphantly. "Licked your Johnny Rebs down yonder at Shiloh, in Tennessee. I guess your brave Lexington Rifles never got there or the battle would have gone different. That is if brags are as deadly as bullets."

"If they were there Tom could have been killed!" Marcia cried. "If he were killed I don't suppose you'd be man enough to tell me, Mr. Findly, hard-set in your mind as you are!"

"He won't get killed," growled her husband. "That boy will take care of himself. I might drop dead out yonder in the furrow most any day but that wouldn't concern you, I guess, or your rebel of a son either."

Knoxville to Sparta and then northward into Kentucky. A raid, ran the word through Morgan's command. The rebel yell shrilling on the air. Union outposts driven in and slaughtered. Barns burning, horses driven off to be caught and haltered and geared later by the hard-riding men. June was hot and humid. Young Tom Findly's new gray uniform grew sodden and stank with sweat and his coat clung to his shoulders.

Tompkinsville and Glasgow. A shoe store entered there and some of the man shod from looted merchandise. Tom drew a pair of boots too small for his country-bred feet, traded them at the next town for a twist of tobacco, a little sack of sugar, and some sheets of writing paper. Night riding and dawn riding, heat and flies and always the aching weariness of body and bone.

At Russell Creek to the east there was a halt while the pickets watched and men bathed in the icy water and washed their shirts and whatever underwear they owned, spreading the yellowed garments on bushes in the hot sun. While their clothes dried most of them slept sprawled in the sedge grass under screening thickets but Tom wrote another letter. They would come to a railroad before long and there might be a chance to toss it aboard a northbound train.

The women in his life were being well fended against him, Tom knew. Hume Harper was a militantly loyal Union man. So far Tom and Harriet had been lucky enough to keep their love affair hidden from Tom's father and Hume Harper, but a letter from the south might never reach the girl at all. It was a chance he had to take. His pencil point broke and he sharpened it with his fine-honed knife. So little to say. *I love you.* But that would be enough if ever it came to her eyes.

Lying with the rough grass scratching his neck, Tom recalled every moment when he had held Harriet in his arms. She was always so clean and sweet-smelling, lavender or something, he didn't know what the fragrance was but he could smell it now over the gun-smell, the man-smell and death-smell of a mounted army. It made his fingers tingle and his hands tighten into fists. In a month, in two months at least, so ran the boasting in the regiment, they would drive all the Federals out of Kentucky.

Hadn't Buckner gone south already, taking five hundred men with him, turning a scornful back on the Union army? Wasn't young Tom Hines riding now, tearing up the rails of the lines that brought Union troops and more Union supplies south over the Ohio? Rumors of banks robbed and small Union detachments put to rout came drifting back, every report to be greeted with a defiant rebel yell.

On the thirteenth they were at Harrodsburg, only twenty-eight miles from Lexington. Women brought them pies and fried chicken, but horses were being driven into hiding by others. There was no attack. They were too many, too brash, whistling into the town like a noisy wind, Morgan waving his hat and saber and shouting his greeting.

"Kentucky men and women, we have come to rescue you from the oppressor! Strike for your altars and your fires. We molest no one who is not in arms against us. Strike for God and your native land!"

Always there were some who cheered and some who snarled at John Hunt Morgan's oratory. But always it sent a quiver of pride down young Tom Findly's spine. They rode on to Versailles and to Georgetown and there Tom Hines emerged from the woods to join Morgan. That night over the campfires the troopers whispered that Hines, the quiet-spoken, cold-eyed, dangerous young man, had found his father arrested and his mother ill. With the canny ability that for years enabled Hines to skip through the border states like a flea, the young captain had escaped all the Union patrols and informers set to trap him. Now he took over again his command of E Company.

Cynthiana, was the word that went down the lines as they formed before dawn. Captain Castleman's company to push in the pickets around Lexington and mask the movement of Morgan's main force.

Cynthiana was so near to home that Tom Findly debated slipping away through the woods and fields to see again his mother and Harriet. Useless and dangerous, that idea, he knew. He would be picked off by a Union patrol before he had gone ten miles, if he was not shot down by one of Morgan's own men as a deserter.

The regiment moved before dawn, heading for the ford of the Licking River. All was quiet and the men rode, relaxed and ready, holding their guns and ammunition high as they moved down to ford the swift stream. Then suddenly hundreds of men in blue appeared on the heights behind them. Regular Union troops and Home Guards. A withering fire blasted the Lexington Rifles as they plunged into the icy current. They held their arms and ammunition high over their heads, struggling to get across, but men slid from their saddles, sank silently or thrashed about

19

screaming in the rolling water. But the line did not waver. The two companies under Hines and Castleman held the bridgehead in spite of terrible losses.

Tom prodded his frightened horse into the stream, his rifle high. The current caught at them and the horse slipped on the moss-covered rocks of the bottom. As his mount rolled over and fought for footing, Tom twisted free of the saddle, making a grab for the stirrup. He felt a heavy blow in the middle of his back but kicked his legs furiously, keeping afloat, trying to pull himself back into the saddle. The other bank looked miles away but he kept his eyes upon it, the trees there, the milling men, the smoke and flashes of fire all running together in a tortured haze.

Then he was lying in the trampled mud, with horses' feet churning around him and his gun slowly sliding from his grasp toward the stream. He tried to reach for it but something caught at him like a red-hot claw and he fell back, his cheek pressing the cool slime of the shore, his arms covering his head to keep from being trampled.

Men were still dropping from the Union fire, horses screamed in agony, but Tom did not raise his head. He felt the thunder of hoofs as the command galloped away, the sun grew hot on his back and eased the tearing pain that had raged there. After a while he managed to pull himself up on an elbow and look around him. The sloping bank of the river was strewn with fallen men, both blue and gray. An abandoned canteen lay, blood-smeared and battered in a muddy pool, and he inched himself toward it and managed to unscrew the top and drink some of the warmish water. But the movement brought the pain again and he lay still, while the shadows moved over the ground and the sun struck silver fire on the river that had run red in the morning.

It was dusk when he felt the ground quiver again under

the tread of horses. Weakly he turned his head, glimpsed gray trousers above a pair of boots, feebly waved a hand. The horseman slid down.

"One of ours—alive!" he shouted. Gently he turned Tom over, felt his chest. "He's alive." Two others came up then and through the queer twisting mist Tom looked up into a face he knew.

"Milo!" he whispered.

"Good Lord!" exclaimed a voice. "It's Tom Findly. From home. Get his feet, Joe. Ease him up on my horse. Where you hit, Tom?"

"There—in his back," said another voice. "Better leave him lay, hadn't we, till the wagons come? Start that bleeding again and he might die on us."

"Milo—they beat us?" Tom managed to gasp.

"Lord, no!" Milo uncorked a flask. "Here, take a swig of this. Keep you alive till they can fix you up. No, they didn't lick us. We took the town and four hundred prisoners. Man, you should have seen those fellows from Texas charge! General's heading south now, going to cross the Cumberland at Monticello. They've got carriages and wagons to move all the wounded. Joe, ride back and send some kind of rig down here to move this boy."

"You—all right, Milo?"

"Sure. Never touched me. We counted a hundred Union dead before they lit out north. That fellow, Captain Hines, a wild man if ever was one. You lie still, Tom, they'll take care of you. I've got to ride on now, scout around to see if any more of our men are left alive along here."

The heat and the pain and the flies! They had put him in a carriage with a top but the sun bore in and the leather was as hot under his head as the top of his mother's cooking stove. He twisted and groaned while the patient horses jolted on at the urging of the grimy trooper in a torn and blood-stained jacket who drove them. Dust swirled chokingly in the trail of the pounding troop ahead. It made Tom cough and whenever he coughed that red-hot claw raked at his wound again. At times he could feel the slow warm creeping of blood down his flesh and smell the rawness of it.

They had packed the ragged wound in his back as best they could and given him opium pills and whiskey but these only made his head swim and his stomach heave sickeningly. When he retched and moaned the driver gave him an exasperated look.

"Keep your guts inside you, soldier! You'll need 'em before this here war is over."

Outside the town of Paris there was a halt and they brought him coffee and hot soup but he could not swallow. Tom was vague and delirious. They did not try to move him, but somebody, could be a doctor, put fresh cotton in his wound and gave him another pill. He was on a cot when he became aware of things again. He smelled chalk and opened his dazed eyes to see a blackboard. He was in a schoolhouse and there were other men there too, who lay still and groaned and coughed. The doctor was a definite form now, a brown beard and sunburned face, stiff with dust and weariness.

"You've got a ball against a kidney," he told Tom. "Can't probe for it, might tear a mortal artery. You lie on this pad so it will drain out clean, then I'll cauterize it. Hurt some, but you'll live. Never fight any more though, likely. How old are you, son?"

"Twenty-one," whispered Tom through dry lips. "Water?"

"Water, but no more whiskey. Start that hemorrhage again. Don't want any gangrene in there either. I've got a half dozen amputations already."

22

Tom lay still. This was the end of glory. This was the end of the war for Tom Findly. Maybe they would let him go home.

Go home! Did he have any home? His father had locked the gate against him when he left, forbidden him to say goodbye to his mother. Would he ever unlock that gate again? Would his son ever be permitted to come home?

3

SHE WAS, DECIDED HER FATHER, THE PRETTIEST THING alive. Thad Briscoe's child, his oldest daughter, whom they had named Teresa after her grandmother but who was always called affectionately "Little Tee."

She was almost eighteen now and her skin was fair and lovely, even with the sun burning down from a white-hot July sky. Her bright golden hair was tucked up under a sunbonnet and her small feet shamed by heavy, worn shoes, her slimness lost in the limpness of a faded calico dress. But even so she made her father's heart hurt because she was precious and because now he could do so little for her.

It was the war. This stupid, senseless chaos of a war that had disrupted every settled and comfortable aspect of living on the old Briscoe place. The war had taken his horses and cattle, requisitioned or pre-empted by both armies, and had led his Negroes to drift away one by one, intoxicated by promises and made irresponsible by the fever of freedom that hovered like a poisonous smoke in the air.

Because of the war Little Tee and her sisters were working like slaves in the fields and Thad suffered because he could not give them the fine clothes and good saddle horses and the nice things that should belong to girls raised on the rich plantations of the bluegrass country. Now he was hard pressed to keep them all decently covered and fed.

He wanted elegance for Little Tee and sixteen-year-old Clementine, called Clemmy, and Priscilla, ten, who had been called Baby till later Rowena came along. But instead they had hayrakes in their hands and were trudging behind the one-horse wagon trying to save the dusty hay that would keep their one remaining horse and two cows alive through the winter.

There had been no grain at all this year. No way to plow or reap with all his working stock confiscated by Anderson's soldiers, intent on building fortifications against the Confederate armies of Braxton Bragg. Thad knew that he was lucky they had left him so far unmolested. Many of his friends had been sent south through the lines or had vanished into Union prisons, but he had carefully kept from expressing his Southern sympathies too loudly.

The horse, fed on grass all summer, sweated too much and stopped too often. Thad looked lean and underfed himself as he jabbed a fork into a cock of hay and heaved it up to the improvised rack on the wagon where six-year-old Rowena danced on it. The hay would have to be dampened down before feeding or it would give the horse the heaves. Thad sneezed himself, as he flung it high, yelling at the horse.

"Git along, Joe!"

Ahead of the wagon the three girls, Teresa, Clementine and Priscilla, raked with perspiring desperate haste, snatching the mown hay into piles, their young faces flushed and grimy with dust.

"You go too fast, Pa," panted Teresa. "This stuff is snarly and heavy."

Ten-year-old Priscilla dropped her rake and ran to the wagon where a jug hung under the rear axle.

"I have to have a drink, Pa. I've swallowed so much dust I'm about to choke."

"Me too." Clemmy reached for the jug. "Don't you drink it all, Baby."

"If I do, it's your turn to take the jug back to the house and fill it." Priscilla tilted the cool jug and coughed as water ran up her nose and down her little round chin. "And fetch a tin cup. You can mighty near drown trying to drink out of this thing."

Thad leaned on his pitchfork, his shoulders sagging, his tanned face set in lines of weary patience. He was forty years old and until two years ago he had never lifted a hand in manual labor. There had been enough to do, riding these wide fields, the Young Master, ordering the plowing and the planting, heir to the acres that had been his family's home for four generations. Now everything was changed—he himself changed most of all. What was right, what was just in this turmoil of a war he had never been able to decide.

Fighting against the South had appeared to him to be a madness, and now Kentucky was a commonwealth torn asunder, neighbor against neighbor, distrust and suspicion rife, guerrilla bands riding to rob and destroy, important men disappearing not to be heard of again. Dejectedly Thad Briscoe had begun to lose confidence in himself. Almost he had lost confidence in God.

Clementine untied the jug and shouldered it with a

scowl of exasperation. "I don't blame the Nigras for wanting to be free," she grumbled.

"Anyway," remarked Priscilla, shaking the chaff out of her sunbonnet and retying it under her chin, "while you're after water you won't have to rake hay. Fetch me a cold biscuit and tell Mama to blow that dinner horn soon and loud."

"It's peas again," said Teresa. "Ceph picked 'em and Marshy shelled 'em, but Mama said if the young ones found any peaches left she might bake a pie."

"There are some peaches rotting on the ground," said Priscilla. "I looked. But the bees are so thick you can't get near them."

"If those young ones get stung you can hear them yell to Cynthiana." Teresa took up her rake again.

All his children were pretty, Thad was thinking, with their big flashing brown eyes and soft heavy hair, braided now into long plaits down their backs. Only Teresa and Rowena were blond like their mother, but Rowena's eyes were dark too while Lennie's looked faded and wept out. Ten children, born too fast, had made a frail, dogged ruin of the prettiness and gaiety that had made Lennie Ward one of the most attractive girls in Bourbon County when Thad Briscoe had wooed and won her.

Back in 'forty-four that was, with war only a distant grumble of discontent in the air and a growing anger of political dissension in men's minds. Eighteen years now since he had set yellow-haired Lennie Ward on a fine saddle horse with a new side saddle and brass-trimmed bridle, and ridden home with her from the church. All the young blades had whooped and fired their pistols that morning and the girls screamed and tossed old shoes and rice.

Eighteen years! The most fateful stretch of years in the history of Kentucky, Thad was convinced. Certainly never before had the proud been brought so low and men of no consequence set in such high places. He had brought Lennie to a rich upland farm tended by more than thirty slaves. Now the grass burgeoned where corn had marched up the gentle slopes and more than three fourths of the white-washed cabins were empty. Only the four oldest and most feeble of the Briscoe Negroes had stayed on, and they were liabilities mostly, too weak to do more than putter around stables and yard, just so many more mouths to feed.

It was the threat of enrolling Negroes in the Yankee army that had sent the younger slaves scurrying off. The controversy over enlisting colored troops in Kentucky still raged and because nothing was settled many younger slaves had slipped away as far as Canada. Congress had battled over the question, there was fury in Frankfort, and some of the newspapers in Lexington and Louisville stormed. Governor Magoffin had written endless letters to President Lincoln but now it was rumored in town that Magoffin was being forced out of office, that his resignation was imminent, any day.

Thad worked on doggedly, loading the wagon as heavily as he dared, then with the three girls trudging behind he slogged toward the big barns, leading the horse. Two years ago fat teams with red-tasseled harness had hauled great wains of hay into those barns, a Negro boy astride each off horse, bare lavender feet dangling. Thad had been jaunty himself then, bright brown beard fanning over his chest, boots shining, wide hat tilted as he supervised the haying. Now the old opulence was gone. This creaking wagon, this spiritless horse were all he had left to wring a living for twelve people from too many mortgaged acres.

But he did have a son. Ward was only four years old, the tenth child born to Lennie, the youngest of the six who had lived. Nine girls and then at last a son. Lennie, drained by too much travail, by the repeated anguish of standing beside little graves, had cried out when Ward was born, "Now you've got a boy, Thad Briscoe, and I'm telling you straight out that he's the last!"

When Ward's a man I'll be past sixty, Thad was thinking. He opened the gate and stood by while Tee led the horse through. Sixty and past if he lived and what would happen to Kentucky in that span of years?

The huge barns still stood, the white paint peeling. But the good cedar shingles that had grown a little mossy were intact. Only a few had blown off in the winter gales. Two cows drank at the green-edged pond beyond the rail fence. Once there had been a hundred, gold and white and red on the rich hills. He was lucky, the way things had been going, that he had even two left.

Some of the livestock that had been requisitioned had been paid for with warrants. Likely he would have to wait till the end of the war to collect on them. That is, if they didn't decide he was a Southern sympathizer and therefore entitled to no compensation. Thad still doggedly told himself that Kentucky was neutral and that he was neutral too, but now they were talking that Kentucky's neutrality was at an end. The Federal troops were in control, bearing down hard on anybody who was rated a rebel.

A slaveowner, Thad had nevertheless deplored slavery. There had been plenty of times when he had been ready to set them all free, with no urging from the black Republicans and abolitionists up north. Slaves cost too much to maintain on a place that did not grow cotton. He had inherited most of them, the rest had been natural increase. He had tried to feed them well as long as he could, and house them as decently as most owners, but with the first blast of upheaval and disruption they had vanished, one

28

family after another, leaving only old people like Lum and Marshy behind, and weak-witted Ceph and feeble Jericho, who had come to Kentucky from Virginia with Thad's grandfather.

Marshy groaned at churning a turn of butter now and Lennie grumbled that she was no use any more and fell asleep over any simple task.

Thad's daughters, his pretty children, working in the fields, hot and dirty and so tired that their young faces were pale under the graying dust! And there was the hay to get in yet, but he would make Lum and Ceph climb into the mow to drag it back and trample it. They would moan and complain about dizziness in the head and misery in the back, but he would lay down the law, work or not eat, and stick to it.

Lennie would bathe all the girls and put their clothes to soak in the big wooden tubs and likely insist on washing all their hair, no matter how tired she was, while the younger ones wailed at the suds from the homemade soap in their eyes.

Thad slid the harness off the horse, sloshed the foaming sweat from his shoulders and flanks with a tow sack dripping from the water trough, and turned the animal over to Ceph, who opened the gate into a yard where some long grass grew against the fence. Ceph was blind in one eye now, and walked sideways like a crab. Thad knew that somehow he had to get another horse. There must be a team to plow, not just an acre or two for garden truck but fields for feed grains, fields turned that had for two seasons now lain fallow.

The children were running to the house, shaking out their skirts. Teresa stopped at the mounting block to sit down gravely and take off her shoes, brushing the dust and broken grass from them with the sunbonnet, turned wrong side out. Suddenly he wanted white silk stockings for Little Tee, and red slippers with bows on them, and anger surged up in his throat like heartburn, choking him till he muttered a curse to ease the strangling pressure.

Old Marshy sat on a flat rock outside the kitchen door, sunning her black bony knees. She dropped her skirt with a senile giggle as Thad strode up.

"Rheumatiz git me too bad, Young Marse," she cackled.

In the kitchen Lennie was ladling out food into a row of fine china plates. The back of her cotton dress was sweat-soaked and her hair lay plastered against her high forehead from the heat of the stove.

"Why don't you make Marshy help you?" Thad asked in irritation as he came in.

Lennie shrugged impatiently. "She makes me so mad! I put her to shelling peas right after breakfast and when I went out an hour later there she was sound asleep sitting up straight on the chopping block and not a pint shelled!"

"She's old, Lennie," Thad placated. "I don't know how old—older than my dad, maybe, and he would be going on past seventy now if he was alive."

"She eats young enough! Between her and Lum they put away a dozen pones and all the pot liquor. Oh, my word, Tee—look at you! Get washed up. You can't eat with arms as dirty as that."

"Not much use to wash," Teresa sighed. "We've got all that load to mow."

"I'll make the Nigras help mow. It's no work for you girls," Thad said.

"You know they'll groan and not half do it, and you'll get sorry for them and send them away," said Teresa. "Why are we eating on the company plates, Mama?"

"Because I'm sick and tired of old worn-out things!" cried Lennie, with passion. "Saving all the best for you girls when you get married, and drinking out of old cracked cups. You can wash those hands and arms anyway. There's soap there in the gourd in the entry. Pour the water on my flowers. The sun is baking the life out of them and a body has to have one pretty thing to look at or go crazy."

"You've got me." Teresa pulled her skirt wide and did a dance step. "And Clemmy's kind of pretty when she's not mad."

"I meant something pretty—and clean!" Lennie gave her daughter a push, then a relenting pat. "I never thought when you were born that I'd see the day when I'd let any of you be dirty. Everything looked so nice and prosperous then, this house all painted new every other year and your grandmother's silver polished till it made you blink. And all the women in blue cotton dresses with clean white aprons in the afternoon, and somebody to pick up a chemise and wash it the minute you laid it down!"

It had been a happy dream then, her daughters coming down the curving stairs with trailing skirts of silk or muslin, and every eligible swain in the county come courting. She sighed over it now, shrugging her thin shoulders.

"Oh, you did bake a pie!" exclaimed Clementine, breaking the spell. "It smells good."

"Three pies—but we've got to divide with those old Nigras!" complained Priscilla. "And we won't dare let Marshy wash a dish for fear she'll break it."

"She would too," said Clementine, "but I reckon they get hungry as anybody."

"Hungrier. Lum would eat that whole pie in two slurps. Mama, could I have coffee?" begged Teresa. "I'm almost eighteen."

"Tee, you'll get bumps all over your face. I don't want you to spoil your complexion," Lennie protested, slowing between stove and table.

31

"If it's not ruined already it never will be," sighed Teresa. "Who's going to see it, anyway? Not a boy left that any girl would look at."

"Well, you don't want to look at anybody but Henri Nesbitt," teased Clementine, scrubbing her wrists and frowning at the streaks of brown water that ran up her arms. "Poor Henri, his father got sent off to prison for being a Confederate!"

"What are you?" demanded Teresa. "A Yankee? Anyway one thing is certain, I'd never look at a poor sissy like Willie Harper."

"I'm not a Yankee, I'm nothing," declared Clementine. "I'm against the war and Jeff Davis and Lincoln and everybody mixed up in it. So is Pa. And you too, Mama, if you'd admit it."

"Nobody could be for a war," said Lennie. "Not a stupid, destructive war like this one. No war ever settled anything. You stop picking on Tee. Nesbitts are good people and Henri is a good steady boy, and if he's off fighting he hates it as much as we do."

"If nobody would fight there couldn't be any war," insisted Clementine, with smug solemnity. "If they'd all refuse to fight then Lincoln and Jeff Davis could just shoot it out between them and I'll bet neither one could hit the other. It would be a draw and then Hettie and Jigger and Pride and all the rest of our people would come home."

"They say," said little Priscilla profoundly, "that Willie Harper's mother sews lace on his drawers."

"Baby, you hush!" admonished her mother. "William is a good boy too. The Harpers are fine people."

"And we owe Mr. Harper the mortgage," put in Teresa. "You have to speak well of people if you owe them money."

"Mr. Harper looks like a frog anyway," persisted Priscilla. "In church he looks like a frog with his eyes bunging

32

out and Willie looks like a shidepoke with that long neck sticking out of his collar."

"I want an end of this," said Lennie firmly. "Clemmy, you find your brother and 'Ria and get them cleaned up for dinner."

"He'll be up a tree or on top of the henhouse, filthy as anything," complained Clementine, "and probably his pants torn off him."

"He's tough, he'll get along." Thad grinned approval of his son.

"If you ask me," said Priscilla, "Ward's a mess!"

"Go call 'Ria. The last I saw of her she was making a tumblebug house down under the china tree."

"Bugs! They play with the nastiest things, Mama," Teresa said. " 'Ria even made a mud house for a toad down there by the trough. She named him Jefferson Davis and chased flies for him, till Ward dropped a rock on the house and smashed it. The toad got away."

"If those children get warts all over them you'll know the reason," supplied Priscilla. "Jericho can take off warts though. With spit. He mumbles words but they don't make any sense."

Rowena was only seven but she could give her father a softening jerk of the heart because every change of expression reminded him of the girl Lennie with whom he had fallen in love. Six-year-old Maria was darker like her other sisters, with flyaway brows and a quick, fiery spirit.

"Touchy as a hornet and as hard to catch," Lennie said of her youngest daughter.

Little Ward was sturdy, dark and reticent. He was an odd little monkey to his father's mind, always wandering off by himself, creeping into remote places, playing his small strange games alone. When his sisters teased him his temper flared into swift, silent reprisals. He could be deadly and

33

quick and he was amazingly strong for a tad of four, but he held no grudges and apparently forgot his defensive fury long before his victims did.

Thad admired his unpredictable little son though he had never felt really close to the boy. As a baby there had been an odd remoteness about Ward that shut out even his mother. It was as though he graciously tolerated affection and solicitude but had no real need of them.

"Turn that young one loose in the big road, he git along," old Lum had said dryly.

Ward ate rapidly and in silence. His dark, sleek head was bent over his plate, his brown bitten legs dangling from the high stool, bare dirty feet poking out of linsey breeches. A year ago Lennie had had to take him out of dresses and cut his hair. He tore off his skirts, discarded them and left them dangling from any handy bush.

"Men," he had stated then, "wears breeches."

When he had scraped the last of the peach juice from his plate and licked his spoon, he slid down from the stool. "Through," he announced, and was at the door in a flash.

"You say 'excuse me,' Brother," prompted Lennie.

He looked hard at her with his intent dark eyes, pushed the door wide.

"Somebody comin'," he said. "Horse and buggy."

Thad Briscoe got up, moved to the door. "Oh, God!" Lennie heard him mutter. She hurried to look over his shoulder and her heart gave a sick, downward plunge.

"What is it, Mama?" Teresa noted the quick change in her mother's face.

"Nothing. Just a man on business."

"It's Mr. Harper," said Clementine, at the window. "I know that buggy."

Teresa put her arm quickly around her mother's waist.

"Don't worry," she whispered. "Pa can always talk him down."

Lennie patted her daughter's cheek. Too old, too molded by adversity, this her pretty one!

"All I ever wanted was for you, Tee," she said. "For you and all the rest of them!"

"It's the war," cried Teresa. "This silly, senseless mess of a war! I wish somebody would shoot that old Lincoln and hang Jeff Davis—hang all of them!"

4

HARRIET WAS IN TEARS AND HER MOTHER HOVERING OVER her anxiously when William came home.

"Is your father on the way?" Ellen inquired uneasily, rubbing camphor on Harriet's temples and pushing back her heavy dark hair. "Harriet, you go up to your room. I'll tell your father that you have one of your sick headaches."

"What's the matter with her?" demanded William.

"She had some bad news," his mother told him.

"Tom's wounded," wailed Harriet. "He may be dead."

"Tom Findly's mother sent word by a neighbor," Ellen Harper explained. "There was a terrible battle over near Cynthiana. Some Union man who was captured in the battle escaped, and he told the Findlys that he saw Tom shot off his horse crossing the river but that he wasn't killed. They carried him away."

"He's dead!" Harriet shuddered. "They don't get any care after those battles. He's dead and his mean old father won't care. He hates Tom for joining the Confederacy."

"Come along, dear," urged Ellen. "I'll put you to bed. Don't mention this to your father, William. He surely must have heard about the battle downtown but he never even mentioned it."

"The Union must have got beat," remarked William. "If they had licked the rebs he'd have mentioned it, all right."

They went up the stairs, Ellen's long skirts swishing gently. She would come down again wearing the same calm, pale face she always showed to her husband. Her smooth hair would be brushed back in neat coils and the same cameo breastpin would fasten the ruffles at her throat. His mother, William was thinking, was better-looking than Harriet right now, old as she was. She must be middle-aged, anyway almost forty, but she still had a kind of placid freshness about her. That any repressed rebellion could lurk beneath would have amazed and frightened William.

Harriet had fair skin and heavy brown hair but her mouth was like their father's, only with more petulance about it. She was short too, like Hume Harper, and she had the same small hands and feet. Hands that William always thought had a look of cruelty about them. Her heavy eyelids could look cruel and condemning too.

He wondered how long Tom and Harriet were going to be able to keep their clandestine courtship concealed from his father. Tom was all right enough, William conceded, a farmer's son with no very exciting prospects for the future, and now he had thrown away those prospects by dashing off to fight with John Morgan. Blond, slow and amiable, Tom had always made friends easily, a gift that William, achingly shy and self-conscious, envied fiercely. Tom, William

36

decided, was really a nicer person than Harriet, who was prone to selfishness and to flashing a spiteful tongue.

It was certain that Hume Harper would never agree that Tom Findly was any match for his daughter. There would be one of those tense, dreadful family scenes that always left Harper triumphant and denouncing somebody, Ellen white and grim and silent, and William himself limp with misery and sunk even deeper into depression. William did not hate his father. His conscience told him that would be a mortal sin. But he did dread him and always caught himself flinching and withdrawing into himself whenever his father voiced one of his positive statements.

As they sat at supper Harper was defiantly displeased by Harriet's weakness and his wife's indulgence of it.

"You should have given her a dose of blue mass," he complained. "It's nothing but biliousness. She is a strong girl and should be intelligent enough to control it."

"Yes, Mr. Harper," agreed Ellen, "but Harriet was badly salivated the last time I gave her blue mass, and I don't want her teeth ruined."

"All nonsense! She ate something she shouldn't, some acid or other. I've taken blue mass all my life and I've never been salivated."

"Young people lack our experience, Mr. Harper. We can't expect them to be as wise as we are," defended Ellen.

"I never expect William to display any wisdom whatever," snapped Harper scornfully. "If he goes around taking up for traitors and Confederate sympathizers as he has been doing, you can expect to see him hauled off to some Federal prison."

"I wasn't taking up for traitors!" William got out in a strangled voice. "I just said it wasn't right to tie poor old Judge Nesbitt's hands up with rope and march him through the streets like that!"

"The provost ordered his arrest. I warned you to keep out of it."

"They did that?" gasped Ellen. "To an old man like the judge? How could you allow it, Mr. Harper?"

"I had nothing to do with it." Harper was testy. "Certainly I couldn't intervene in the case of a proven traitor to the Union and the Constitution!"

"But he used to be your friend," protested Ellen.

"There are times when a man must be careful of his friendships." Harper helped himself to hominy, spooning gravy over it with the same studied precision with which he did everything.

"I guess they haven't much money now," observed William meekly. "Maybe they won't even be able to pay their interest."

His father's eyes bulged and blazed coldly. "You will not discuss the bank's business here or elsewhere, sir," he ordered sternly, his eyes reminding William of those two dials on the safe. "And you will not examine any papers at the bank, understand? You will not even see them, and if anything is discussed about bank affairs you will not listen, you hear?"

"Yes, sir," gulped William, "but you said I was to learn the banking business."

"Learn your own duties then. Nothing beyond your assigned task concerns you in the least."

"But you've always said that you meant to train William to take over your place when you retire," Ellen suggested. "He has to learn while he's young, doesn't he?"

Harper's jowls reddened and swelled. "I am not senile yet! I am not even middle-aged as businessmen count age. If William can't learn to keep to his own concerns and practice discretion in his speech how can he be taught to take over responsibility? The first essential of the banking business is careful judgment and it is poor judgment to go about bleating half-baked opinions in times like these, when we could have an invasion from the south any day."

"An invasion?" exclaimed Ellen. "You can't mean that surely, Mr. Harper?"

"Am I in the habit of making wild statements, Mrs. Harper? Who can say what those lunatics down there may do? Braxton Bragg and Kirby Smith will certainly try to take over Kentucky and force the state into their so-called Confederacy. Governor Magoffin is the prime traitor in my opinion. He refused to furnish troops to Lincoln and he'll show his true colors if there should be an invasion. They are putting pressure on him to resign but it hasn't done any good. This state is practically in a state of civil war right now, so I say rash statements from William or anyone else connected with the bank could be like fire in a powder mill."

"Sounds like you're talking kind of rash yourself, Pa," said William boldly. "About the governor, I mean."

"I do not expect what I say at home to be repeated outside, sir."

"Yes, sir." William followed his mother as she left the room. "I hope he doesn't find out that Harriet is crying herself sick over a rebel raider," he said low.

"Be careful," warned his mother, glancing over her shoulder. "Willie, you can carry some hot tea and toast up to Harriet. Hessie will get it ready. And Willie"— she seldom used that childish derivative except in times of stress, knowing how he hated it— "try to comfort her a little."

Harriet was lying on her bed in the dark when he blundered up the stairs carrying a tray and a lighted candle. She sat up quickly, all her hair falling around her shoulders.

"Go away!" she ordered. "I'm not dressed."

"Put on something then." He halted at the door. "I brought you some tea."

"I don't want it," she sobbed. "I just want to be let alone!"

"You'd better drink it," persisted the boy. "Hessie says if you don't drink it she'll come up here and hold your nose. She will too."

"I'm not a child! I won't be ordered around."

"Go downstairs and tell them that. I dare you! Put some clothes on. I'm coming in before I drop this tray and you'd better eat what's on it or Ma's feelings will be hurt. And one weepy female is enough in this house."

"Wait then." She slid off the bed, found a robe and twisted into it. "William," she said, when he had set the tray awkwardly on the bed, "did you ever feel like life just couldn't be endured any more?"

"Most every day." He perched on a chair, his long arms dangling between his knees, his sleeves sliding far up on his knobby wrists. "Usually when I get tired of being ordered around down at the bank. If you think things are tough here you should work for Pa. They say Lincoln is going to put an end to slavery but I don't reckon he can do anything for me!"

Harriet sipped the tea, looking at him over the edge of the cup. "Willie," she began, "are you going downtown?"

"Tonight? I don't know. I'd have to sneak out. Pa would raise some objection. He thinks I talk too much."

"Are you for the South, Willie?"

"Don't call me Willie! You know I hate it. I don't know what I am. I'm supposed to be in the Union army, anyway Pa paid some poor country boy to get killed in my place. I reckon I'm neutral like Kentucky."

"Kentucky's not neutral any more. You know it. Tom

40

said we should have kept all our own soldiers in the state and run out the Union troops and Confederates, both."

"Then they'd have run Tom out, first thing," William said.

"Then maybe he wouldn't have enlisted. William, if you can get downtown, see if you can hear anything. About John Morgan, about that battle over on Licking River," she pleaded.

"If I talk to people Pa may hear about it and raise Cain."

"You don't need to talk. Just listen. People will be talking. They're always talking about Morgan because he came from around here and so did a lot of his men. They took the wounded all down to Tennessee, Mrs. Findly sent word, and Tom could be dead by now. If he is dead his horrible old father likely wouldn't even have his body sent home. Tom said that when he did come back he doubted if his father would let him set foot on the place."

"Pa's got a mortgage on that farm, I reckon you know. They keep up the interest and payments on the principal, though, Mr. Merrill said. Why do you go on being sweet on Tom Findly when you know he'll likely end up with nothing?"

"When you fall in love you'll know why," his sister told him. "I'll love Tom till I die, no matter how poor he is. All I pray for is for him to get out of this miserable war alive."

William rubbed his knuckly thumbs over one another, his eyes on the rag rug his big feet had scuffed. He was in love but he couldn't admit it, not even to himself. He was in love with another man's wife, lush, lovely Denise Nesbitt, and even to think about it was shame, yet he couldn't stop being in love with her. She fevered his dreams at night and made hot tremors of wretchedness run over his body

41

now and then through the day, so that his tongue burned and his eyeballs hurt and he found his fingers twitching.

If Harriet loved like that—but she couldn't! Nobody could know the kind of aching anguish that tormented him, he was certain with the naïve egotism of the very young. Nobody at all! Not Tom Findly, with his drawling speech, his smile and indolent indifference to irritations that would goad William himself to fury.

If Harriet was really in love enough to challenge everything that was important to her, even to defy poverty and the violent opposition of their father, it must be a different kind of love. Or did love come in patterns, changing as the sky changed with dawns and storms and sunsets? Had there been a special kind of love arranged for each person when he was created? Definitely he could not picture his smug and selfish sister inflamed with the same sweet madness that consumed him.

At least Harriet had not been fool enough to let her heart run yearning for another heart that was not free. He gave her that much and a bit of sympathy, seeing now the quiver of her lips, the tears that brimmed in her eyes. He got up and patted her paternally on the head.

"I'll go, Sis. I'll slip out the back way and prowl around some. If Pa starts any fuss tell Mama to tell him I'm in bed. He can't do anything but jaw anyway. I'm too big to lick and he only pays me a dollar a week so he can't dock my pay enough to be profitable to him."

"Thank you, William," she said, and squeezed his hand. He gave her another awkward pat and a brotherly soft poke in the nose.

"Keep that lip stiff," he ordered. "Time enough to go to pieces if you get word that Tom's dead. He's tough, they can't kill him. I'm betting they can't kill John Morgan either."

42

"But Tom was shot in the back." She began to sob again.

"You mean, they were running?"

"I do not! Mrs. Findly wrote that he was swimming his horse across a river and the Yankees fired on them from the bank."

"All right, all right! Calm down and I'll see what I can hear downtown. Leave your door open so I can slip in quiet when I get back."

There was no lack of excited groups gathered up and down the main street. Men who conversed in mutters, with an ear cautiously cocked toward the provost's men or the despised Home Guard. Men who ranted their Union views loudly with fists banging and eyes wary to see if any of General Boyle's men heard and approved their shouted loyalties. William moved like a lean shadow from group to group. Only one man marked him, a sullen fellow who muttered, "Yonder's Hume Harper's bird dog. Get all our notes called in the morning."

The town seethed as Kentucky seethed, torn from river to river, to mountain ridge. Morgan had burned Cynthiana. Morgan ought to be hung! General Jere Boyle ought to be hung. Simon Bolivar Buckner was a dirty turncoat. Buckner was a hero. How many men had followed him down to Tennessee, when he turned his back in scorn upon the Union? Five hundred, some said. Men were heroes, they were traitors, but of Tom Findly, who had been one of their own, who had leaned against these same lampposts, not a word.

William went home at nine o'clock, let himself in the back door with Hessie's carelessly hidden key, tiptoed up the stairs. He put his head in at Harriet's door and hissed cautiously. She got quickly out of bed, pulled him inside and closed the door.

"Nothing," he said. "Plenty of gab about Morgan but

43

not a word about Tom. Don't reckon it has got around yet about him being shot. If he's alive you'll hear from him before long—might not, though," he remembered. "I heard them talking about that brother-in-law of Morgan's, named Duke—"

"Basil Duke."

"They said he captured two engines down on the railroad and sent them head on into each other in that long tunnel the road runs through. Won't be any trains coming through there for a while, they said."

"Well, thank you anyway, William," she sighed. "I'll just have to go on living and hoping, but it's going to be mighty hard!"

"Might as well. Not much anything else you can do!"

5

HENRI NESBITT WAS TWENTY-TWO YEARS OLD.

By the practical standards of his home town he had never been counted a promising youth. Too full of dreams and fancies, always reading books and drawing pictures that looked like what they were supposed to represent but had no monetary value whatsoever. Some of the money his mother, Amalie, had inherited, had been spent to send him east to college but after a year in Boston he had sickened of things academic and come drifting home again.

The North and East were too full of radicals and abolitionists, he reported, not a comfortable spot for a Southern man who believed in the sanctity of property and State Rights, no place for an introverted fellow who wanted nothing but to be left alone to draw and paint. His mother sympathized with his artistic aspirations, his father worried about his son's future but said little, being a grave old man who had been already well into middle age when Henri, his younger son, was born.

Because he loved the judge and hated to disappoint him Henri read law a few hours every day but his heart was not in it. Torts and mandamuses were to his mind mere stupid combinations of words by which men clothed their petty differences and quarrels with the rigid respectability of the law. He sat in courtrooms and heard his father preside over trials that appeared to Henri a silly waste of any man's time and intellectual energy.

Milo, his older brother, had already passed the bar examinations and had his nose canted toward the more profitable field of politics, when the festering carbuncle of rebellion came to a violent head and burst at Fort Sumter, sending a wave of sectional hatred foaming through the veins of men all over Kentucky.

Along with the current of confusion and consternation that swept over the state had come John Hunt Morgan from Lexington, trumpeting destiny like a proud stallion. A thunder of hoofs, a blaring bugle, glittering weapons, insolent banners, Morgan roared like a splendid whirlwind through the quiet Kentucky towns. To the young man he was Robin Hood, he was Tamerlane, he was David out to smite the Philistines. He was glory and adventure on horseback. Overnight Milo caught the fever of this magnificence and daring and was gone.

After Milo rode away Henri went back to the little room behind the kitchen where he had an easel and brushes and all the comfortable, unmolested mess of the work he really loved. There he tried to sketch a trooper on horseback, horse spurning the ground, mane and tail blowing, but his heart was not in it. Nor was it in Blackstone nor the Acts of Kentucky XXII to XXXIV. Unrest tormented him despite Beauregard's victory at Manassas, and the pronouncements of Jefferson Davis or Abraham Lincoln.

The first call for Union troops settled things in his uneasy mind. He knew that his father's loyalties were with the Confederacy, though Judge Horatio was a discreet and quiet man. Also he was rigidly honest and honor demanded that he proceed on his judicial duties without prejudice. Henri knew about the Confederate bonds that were brought home a few a time, always after dark, and locked away in his mother's little hair trunk. But he made no comment and asked no questions.

When for a short time in April Braxton Bragg's Confederate army held Frankfort, exhilaration sparked the tense and waiting atmosphere of the old Nesbitt house. Then the Confederate control was swept away and so were Fort Donelson and Fort Henry. The Union took over Kentucky and the legislature promptly passed what Judge Nesbitt called, with some bitterness, the Acts of Malice.

Any person enlisting in the Southern army, any one supporting the Confederate cause was liable to arrest, six months' imprisonment and a fine of one thousand dollars. Denise hid her Confederate flag when her father-in-law reminded her that she could be arrested for possessing it. That day Henri closed his lawbooks and cleaned and wiped his brushes.

"I'm going," he announced abruptly. "I'll slip down the river at night on some freight boat. The pious Union sympathizers don't mind turning an easy dollar selling pork and stuff to General Judah's Confederate commissary."

"I can't encourage you," said his father. "I can only assume that being of age you know what you are doing."

"I know what I'm doing," Henri assured him. "My one fear is that I might bring trouble on you, Father."

"Your brother has already gone. You can do no more than he has done. A man must follow his convictions. If trouble comes I shall meet it calmly," the judge declared.

So Henri rode away, but before he left the county he turned north on the road to Thad Briscoe's farm. Teresa came running to meet him.

"I'm going," he told her. "I hate the whole stupid business but then I hate the law too. I seem to hate all things that men do to other men. I'm a poor figure of a man, Little Tee, but whatever there is good in me belongs to you!"

"Oh, there *is* good in you, Henri!" she cried. "Only it's a beautiful kind of good and not anger or contention or greediness for power." She held tight to both his hands. "That little picture you painted for me—the willow tree and the girl in the pink dress—it's beautiful! I look at it every time I have a chance. The way you painted the sun coming through those branches—"

"The way I painted you!" he laughed, with the faintest edge of disappointment. "So badly that you didn't even recognize yourself. The girl in the pink dress!" he repeated, gathering her closer.

"But I did—I did!" she protested. "I hoped you meant it for me but I didn't want to be vain about it. Oh, Henri, you might be killed!" Tears filled her eyes.

"I could be," he admitted. "Or I might lose an arm so that I could never paint again. But at least, Little Tee, I shall have faced one issue in my life and gone through with it. I've never finished anything before. I've always compromised, read a little law, painted a little, everything half done, nothing ever completed. Now, I'll finish this war or

47

let it finish me! Will you wait for me? It may be a long time."

"You know I'll wait, Henri. Be careful, for my sake?"

All over a tortured land women sobbed those words, so useless, so wrung with anguish. How sweet she was with her great dark eyes bright with tears, her strong sweet mouth tremulous. He kissed her soberly and then with more fire and less restraint.

"I'm riding north," he said. "At the river I'll send the horse back and find a boat going south. I'll write if I can."

"I'll write too, Henri. Every day! Oh, my dear—" But he was gone. A wave of his hat, damp earth flying from the heels of the borrowed horse, and the shaded road hid him from her sight. That had been May and now it was August and the trouble that Henri had dreaded for his father had happened ruthlessly and with malice.

A boy from home brought the word south to where Henri Nesbitt waited with Kirby Smith's forces in the eastern ridges of Kentucky, poised to support General Braxton Bragg's planned invasion of the state. Henri lay on his side, head propped on an elbow, listening to the country lad in too-short linsey pants report that his father had been marched off to some Yankee jail.

"But we-uns'll git him aloose!" promised the boy. "Do we march up there and take Lexington, the hull state's bound to rise. We'll run them Yanks plumb back to Indianny. Up yonder in the bluegrass people ain't talkin' because them Home Guards have got spies everywhere but there ain't nobody there scarcely for the Union."

"You heard that?"

"I shore did. I walked all the way down here to the Gap and soon as folks knowed I was headin' south to fight they took me in and fed me and one man gave me a dollar. I got it yit." He tugged the big coin from his pocket earnestly.

48

"Are things bad up home?" Henri inquired, dreading the answer, almost certain what it would be.

"Plumb mean. Them Yanks figure they got us bottled in a jug and that General Boyle's sittin' on the cork. They been takin' mules and horses till a feller can't farm nor do nothin'. Hogs too, and cattle. Some they pay for with pieces of paper, but the one my pa got wasn't good for nothin'. Storekeeper only give him a little poke of flour for it, and it wrote to be worth more'n a hundred dollars."

"How does it happen they didn't get you in the Union army? We hear they're drafting men."

"Yeah, ole Abe, he's callin' for troops but the boys is hidin' out mostly or runnin' like me. I laid up two weeks while Pa fetched me some corn bread and meat. Then he come where I was hid. You git down to the Gap, boy, he says, and help our fellers run this here Boyle and his varmints out of Kentucky. And Pa said if I see Judge Nesbitt's son I was to tell you your pap got tuck. Where do I go to fight at?"

"You come along with me. I'll find an officer to sign you up." Henri got to his feet. A slow, great anger made all his muscles quiver and his blood seethe with avenging fire. He had an issue now with the enemy that was personal and bitter. This he would finish if it took the last ounce of his blood.

"Reckon I better figure on gittin' home, plowin' time," said the boy, "if Pa has a mule left to plow with. But I'll shore fight till then."

Never did an army face an opportunity so propitious and never did any Confederate force fail so miserably at pursuing an advantage.

In a hot, dry September Braxton Bragg's army moved to the westward from East Tennessee, while Kirby Smith's troops crossed the mountains into central Kentucky. At Richmond Smith completely annihilated the Federal forces and took possession of the rich heart of the state. Through all the bluegrass, just as the boy had predicted, the people welcomed the Southern soldiers. Confederate flags appeared in windows, were waved boldly in the streets. Women rushed out with fried chicken and apple pies, hot corn pones with fried ham inside, slabs of boiled beef in big buttermilk biscuits.

But the Union troops fought viciously, contesting every mile of ground. There were regulars, there were Home Guards and State Guards, armed with old guns but fiercely determined to hold Kentucky for Abraham Lincoln. Henri Nesbitt fought in a kind of bloodshot dream. Never before had he killed so much as a squirrel but now he shot men down and felt no qualm or quiver. He was an automaton, ramming a wad of cotton into a hot gun barrel, dragging it out blackened with the smoke of carnage.

He saw men's bodies jerk and fall grotesquely, and he kissed the hot barrel of his rifle, stepping over them as though they were so many fallen logs. More down, in vengeance for that proud old man, his father. More vermin exterminated who would never again contaminate his beloved Kentucky!

Kirby Smith's army was confident and elated. Before them lay the state, Lexington, Cincinnati, Louisville. But Bragg had elaborate and dilatory plans. He moved on to take Frankfort, to announce that Kentucky was now seceded, to set up a provisional government. He even appointed a governor, who held office for one brief afternoon.

Bragg's delay gave the Union commander, Don Carlos Buell, the advantage he needed. At Perryville, the Union army was poised and ready. The bloodiest battle ever to be fought on Kentucky soil roared into frightful fury, and within a week the Confederates were retreating, back into Tennessee, heartsick and discouraged.

All their fine hopes, all Bragg's promises and proclamations, his boasts that Kentucky would rise to a man and purge the Union radicals from her borders, had come to disaster. This was retreat and the word was bitter in men's mouths. They spat often in muttered anger and frustration.

There had been a few compensations. Kirby Smith had captured or destroyed millions of dollars' worth of stores. Arms enough for twenty thousand men. Now, fleeing Kentucky, the Confederate wagons were loaded with thousands of barrels of pork and enormous supplies of clothing. The wagon train was so long that it took two days to pass a given point.

Buell's army followed, harassing the rear, where Henri, on a stolen horse, rode along with Joe Wheeler's cavalrymen, unquestioned. Any man who could find a horse was welcomed to help stand off the Union pursuers, who kept up the chase far into the mountains. They did manage to repulse them, but this was not victory, this was not even battle or glory. It was flight, ignominious, degraded, and Henri was sick with disappointment because though the army had moved within a few miles of home he had had no opportunity to see his mother or Teresa. He had sent letters by runners on their way to contact Bragg's troops, but he had no assurance that these had ever been delivered and there were no answers.

It was futile for the officers to argue that all was not lost. Powerful and important Kentuckians had been recruited to the Confederate army. A son of Henry Clay was riding up front, and more than two thousand men had joined up. But these seemed inconsequential to Henri when his own shoes were worn thin, when Kentucky was lost again to the Confederacy and his father still a prisoner.

51

The ridges of Tennessee were touched already with early frost and in the hollows fog lay late in the mornings. Henri told himself that he should be grateful that he had not been wounded, that he had not been left behind buried in some trench in a Kentucky meadow, that he now, temporarily at least, had a horse to ride after marching so many weary miles.

Most of all he should be grateful that in all the violence and chaos of battle, he had not been afraid. That had been his inward dread since the day he had stowed away on the flatboat down the Ohio. When the crucial moment of conflict came he feared he might prove himself less a man, a craven, a coward.

There had been desertions in plenty. Men who sobbed and slobbered, cursing Jefferson Davis and General Bragg, then vanished into the woods at night or plunged into the rivers. But Henri had not been of their shabby company. This awareness stilled a doubt in himself that had been a festering unease all through the long summer. He had finally faced a situation and had not faltered or failed to finish what he had to do. Even on this retreat, this duty of skulking and hiding, striking at enemy cavalry, scattering small bands of attackers, he was carrying on. In scarecrow rags, his socks thrown away, his hat flopping from a bullet hole in the brim, he rode with a kind of pride, and a tinge of surprise at his own adequacy.

They would all be issued new outfits in Tennessee, the officers promised. They would again be well fed. Henri heard the rumbling of his empty belly and felt the autumn chill strike through his thin coat, ignoring these discomforts, supported by a stiffening satisfaction. For too long he had been content to take himself at the valuation other people had put upon him. Horatio Nesbitt's do-less son, the boy who would probably never amount to anything. A war,

52

he decided, that could make a man of a confused and bewildered failure such as he had known himself to be, could not be all bad.

Suddenly Henri wanted to tell Little Tee about it, to brag a little, walk tall before her. He could not tell her of the men he had killed, undismayed. Horror would darken her eyes, and it might be that she would recoil from him, brutality making him a stranger. That some of those men had been Kentuckians would make it even worse in her eyes. Whatever belonged to Kentucky belonged also in her heart to Little Tee. And she belonged to the green meadows, the quick foaming streams, the apple trees blooming, the lush extravagance of tobacco rows shaking out ragged gray polls of bloom.

His mother, he knew, was a woman of the city. She wanted only to look out upon a close and busy street. Spaces intimidated her. She was nervous even in her own garden because it had no enclosing wall.

Denise, his brother's wife, was meant for drawing rooms, with velvet carpets under her feet and curtains to shut in the shadows and repel the raw glare of day. She was akin to candles in brass sconces and flowers in bowls; no flowers growing wild on bushes with nature's untamed disorder would please her. Trailing skirts and wine in sparkling glasses were the right background for Denise. But Teresa belonged on a hilltop under a tree blown by the wind.

He carried that picture in his mind over the rivers and up the ragged ridges where the retreating army of Jefferson Davis's Confederacy plodded and rumbled, when finally they had shaken off their pursuers. He had painted her once like that, painted badly, but when this nightmare war was ended he would paint Little Tee again. And his hand would not be hampered by that old inner dread of never quite attaining.

53

He snatched off his ragged hat and whooped the rebel yell as he kicked his tired horse into a lope to catch up with the dust-clouded rear of Kirby Smith's command. For the first time since his voice had changed, Henri Nesbitt felt himself a man.

6

THE WAGON JOLTED OVER THE NARROW ROAD, RUTTED AND worn with chuckholes by the pounding passage of guns and military wagons, and every jar was pain to Tom Findly.

It was October but the sun was still hot and the fields and bushes were dry and dusty. The horse was slow and the Negro man who drove alternately dozed and roused himself to shout abuse at the animal and slap its lethargic rump with the reins.

They had been assured that now the Confederates held Kentucky. The word had come south and it had been decided that all the wounded men of Morgan's regiment would be sent home. The sad parade of carriages, carts, and wagons had been rattling and rolling north from the Gap for two days. Rain had fallen the night before but only briefly, enough to dampen fires and make the men's clothes and blankets soggy and cold, where they lay on a ragged slope of timber along a creek. Now the sun beat down again but in the coves the fog still lingered and Tom, huddled in the bed of the wagon with two legless men from Bourbon County, shivered against the chill.

At every bump the loose planks of the wagon bed lifted and fell and chaff drifted up from what straw remained. Part of it had already been fed to the gaunt horse and the rest had sifted down through the cracks. The hard boards had rubbed Tom's hipbones raw, so that he struggled up to a sitting position, groaning at the effort.

The two Bourbon County boys leaned against the seat, their bandaged stumps propped on their rolled blankets. They were shaking dice languidly, a pointless activity to Tom's mind since none of them had any cash money. They had been paid in Confederate scrip; "Benny money" they called it in Morgan's command since it was assumed to have been issued by Judah Benjamin, Jeff Davis's Secretary of War. But all along their slow journey no shopkeeper had been willing to accept it, not even for a scrap of tobacco.

"How come our money ain't no good, if we done took Kaintuck?" asked the narrow-faced lad with the hard mouth and shifty eyes, as he laid out two more shin plasters when the dice rolled against him.

"Ain't heard it down this way, I reckon," observed the other. "Reckon Kirby Smith has took Cincinnati by this time. Reckon they've run them Feds clear to Chicagy and maybe my paw has got his Negroes back. He better have 'em back. I ain't figurin' on workin' tobacco on one laig."

"I aim to have ole Cole Warner whittle me a wooden leg, paint it up red and put a brass collar on it. My girl likes red, if she ain't took up with some feller sittin' out this here war in his breeches," worried the thin boy. "Old Tom here, he's lucky. Totin' home the bullet that hit him so nobody can't say he wasn't in the fightin'."

"Totin' it home in his back! Some low-down cuss is bound to say he was runnin' when he got hit."

"I seen him hit right there in the middle of the river. Ain't nobody sayin' that where I can hear 'em. How come they didn't dig that ball out of you, Tom? You could have kept it to show your girl."

"Doctor said it was too dangerous to try to probe it out." Tom shifted his aching legs. "At least I've got two of 'em." He looked down at his emaciated legs, his ankle bones sticking out like knobs. "Doctor said the ball was too close to some big blood vessel. Reckon I'll carry it long as I live. Till it kills me anyway."

"Anyhow, we git to go home! And the pesky Unions will all be run out of Kaintuck. Look, white boy, you nigged on that throw! Put down another piece of Benny money. Might be I can spend it when I git up yonder where Bragg and Smith are at. I hope my maw has got a blackberry pie cooked up."

Home! They were going home. But where would he go? Tom was wondering. If his father still had the home gate padlocked against him? He had heard that heavy lock snap shut and the chain clank on the day he rode away to join Morgan.

"You've picked your road. Now travel it," the elder Findly had said grimly.

No farewell, no backward look. But from the kitchen porch he had seen his mother's apron flutter briefly. It was still painful for him to stand for long or to walk. The tortured muscles still cramped in agony when he tried to straighten his spine. He still had sickened days when cold sweat jumped out on his skin and he shivered for hours, racked with convulsive nausea. A kidney had been damaged, the doctor had told him. Luckily, said the doctor, he had two. It would be a long time before he would be able to work again, perhaps never again the hard, grueling work his father and the farm demanded. Sixteen hours in a hot, breathless cornfield swinging a hoe, pitching heavy gouts of hay or sheaves of wheat, slogging endless furrows behind a plow.

It could be that his father had fared like the other Kentucky farmers, his team and saddle horses requisitioned, by one army or the other. There were no Findly Negroes to come straggling back. Tom lay awake a long time that night wondering where he would go if his father remained adamant against him. Nobody would hire a man who had to limp and could lift nothing and went lurching about with a cane.

And there was Harriet. He would not have so much as a red-painted wooden leg to offer her. Only a maimed body and a handful of Confederate promises to pay.

Tom had lost his illusions about this war, given up his dreams of glory. Even if Kentucky did go into the Confederacy there was still Grant and the river forts left, there were still Sherman and Buell and McClellan and for this region of the South no outstanding leader had yet appeared. The men of Morgan's command had a poor opinion of General Bragg and that opinion had come all the way down from John Morgan himself. Now it was whispered that Nashville was lost.

It was on the road south of Lebanon that abruptly catastrophe rode into view. The Negro man urged the tired old horse suddenly off the road into a cornfield where the shocks stood in thin, ragged rows.

"Soldiers!" he shouted, pointing ahead.

"Good Lord—they're ours!" cried Tom, as the approaching dust revealed a marching army.

"Can't be," argued the narrow-faced boy. "Our boys is plumb to Louisville and Cincinnati by this time."

"That's Bragg's army," declared Tom in a hopeless voice.

"There's the flag—and the guidons. Something has gone wrong. They're retreating."

"Can't be," insisted the boy. "You heard the officers say down yonder that Bragg and Smith had took Kaintuck. Had 'em a governor, even."

Tom scrambled from the rear of the wagon and went hobbling toward the road where the approaching army was churning up a choking cloud of dust. A tattered and dejected army, men with bandaged heads, men slogging along wearily with no weapons, guns rattling, drawn by sweated, jaded animals, the gunners slumped half asleep on caisson and limber. Tom held up a hand as the line passed.

"What troops are these?" he shouted.

A dust-blackened, evil-looking man shambled out of the file, sank down beside the road and brushed dust from eyelashes and ragged beard.

"This here, son," he said soberly, "is the noble army of General Braxton Bragg. And trailing behind us is the magnificent aggregation of General Kirby Smith. Behind them is Joe Wheeler's cavalry, fighting off the army of Don Carlos Buell, to keep them from slaughtering or capturing all this here army before we get through the Gap. Licked, boy. Licked at Perryville. Licked by Buell, all to hell and gone because the noble General Bragg was fooling around up in Frankfort making speeches and got there too late. Buell was ready and they beat the whey out of us. God knows how many men we lost, killed and took prisoner. Some says ten thousand. I dunno. Now we've got our tails between our legs running back to Tennessee. Where you from, soldier?"

"Morgan's Lexington Rifles. I was wounded at Licking River and been in hospital down below Monterey since July. Heading home now—that is if I can get home. What's up there, soldier? Yanks got everything?"

"Nothing to stop 'em. Where's your home?"

"Bourbon County."

"We had that county. Could have taken Louisville too if Bragg had got moving. We had our own way, three or four weeks anyhow. Even set up a government. Had folks dancing in the streets, stars and bars everywhere. Then Buell hit us like a tornado. Bloodiest battle I ever saw. You'll never get there, soldier. They started arresting people before ever we got out of hearing. Women too. We've got some wagonloads of women back there, heading south through the lines. We picked up some plunder—Smith did—but things will be mean in old Kentuck' now, boy, plumb mean. You turn that wagon around and head back to Tennessee. That old Nigra you got, they'll catch him up and put him in their army."

"He's too old," Tom said. "He'd be no good in an army."

"I'm old too. Fifty-three. My feet give out on me but I got a few of the varmints before they run us off. Better turn that wagon around, and I'll ride with you. I've marched far enough for an old man. You'll get captured sure if you head north."

"There are more wounded men behind us, and two other boys in that wagon, each with a leg off. Our officers thought that Bragg held Kentucky, that's why they moved us out. I'll see what the other fellows have to say." Tom limped back and the dirty trooper followed him.

"Get these men back to Tennessee, black boy," he shouted, climbing uninvited into the wagon. "Bragg's licked and them blue-bellies up yonder have got squads out catching up all the Johnnies and Nigras as fast as they can round them up."

The old Negro rolled frightened eyeballs. "'Fore God, Mister, the gin'ral told me to git back to Lexington to Miss

59

Kitty. Them Unions up there, I shore got to git to Miss Kitty."

"He belongs to some of General Morgan's family," Tom explained. "Boys, the Confederate army is in retreat and Buell is following them. Do you want to go on, and take your chances on some Yank jail?"

The strange soldier did not wait for a decision, he snatched the reins out of the old man's hand. "Turn loose, black boy, or I'll throw you out and drive myself!" he snarled. "You get out and go on to your Miss Kitty. Me and these men are riding back to Tennessee."

"Now, wait a minute!" Tom stormed. "This is our wagon, detailed to us by the Confederate command. You get down and get back to your own outfit."

"Ha, figure to throw me out do you, limpy?" jeered the stranger. "What about you boys back there? You going back to nice safe Tennessee with me, or you hone to head for Kentucky and maybe get captured or shot by Buell's army? Maybe you got you a Miss Kitty up there too."

"We want to git home," pleaded the country boy. "We can take a back road and miss out on them Yanks. Anyway they ain't goin' to worry with no wounded men, likely they got enough of their own. Push him out, Mose. Git back in the wagon and let's git going."

"I'm driving this wagon back to the Gap," announced the dirty soldier. "Anybody don't want to go along, fall out."

The narrow-faced boy with the feral eyes and the slit of a mouth quietly rolled over on one hip, eased himself about and dragged his rifle from beneath him. Slowly and deliberately he lifted it, took aim and shot the intruding stranger through the back of the head.

"Roll him out, Mose," he ordered coolly. "Roll him out and drive us along. Hunt a little road nobody don't ever travel. Probably he was a guerrilla anyway. Could be a Yank deserter. Git aboard. Tom, we're bound for Bourbon County."

The Negro, teeth chattering, tugged at the bleeding body till it collapsed in a huddle on the ground between the wheels. The horse did not flick so much as an ear.

"He got two pistols and plenty ammunition," Mose said.

"Get 'em then. We may need 'em. And you keep us clear of Bragg's turntail army, and them Yanks that are after 'em."

Tom dragged himself back into the wagon, cold and sickened. If the shot had attracted the attention of the weary troops thronging the road they gave no sign. Even the officers rode oblivious, slumped in their saddles.

"You didn't have to kill him, boy," Tom protested. "Four of us, we could have thrown him out and got rid of him."

"And got shot—armed like he was! A mean-looking bugger if ever I seen one," flared the killer. "I'm goin' home and anybody tries to stop me gets the same treatment. Drive on, Mose."

Through the rutty little lanes and country roads that ambled and twisted around the hills the wagon lurched on northward. That night they camped on a slope of the South Fork after crossing the stream at a ford where the horse slipped on slimy rocks and lamed himself. They now had arms in plenty, and though no Union patrols appeared they took turns standing guard until dawn.

The little farms they passed the next day were quiet. Older men, women, and a few Negroes worked in the cornfields, dug yams or picked the last of thin, rain-stained cotton.

"Yanks ain't been along here," commented the country boy. "These folks have got plenty provender."

Beyond Lebanon he dropped off at a gate before a long unpainted house. Tom knocked at the door and three women came flying out, tearful and excited. Tom helped them load the boy into a wheelbarrow and trundle him into the house, accepting their hysterical gratitude and a jug of fresh buttermilk.

Ten miles from home Tom's throat began to cramp and his heart to pound. Today—tomorrow at least—he would see Harriet again. It might be that he could see his mother too. Would Harriet look at him and wince away from his emaciated and crippled body? Or would she see past the damage of war, see the love and devotion in his eyes? Would she recognize the hunger for her that had gnawed at him all these anguished months of riding, fighting and suffering?

Outside the town Mose halted the wagon. "I ain't goin' th'oo no town," he announced. "I ain't goin' th'oo no town till I gits to Miss Kitty. I ain't goin' be picked up and put in no army. You gittin' off here, Mist' Tom. You git home all right."

Tom dropped off, pulling his gun and battered haversack and blanket after him. The other boy was riding on to Lexington. Off the road Tom limped into a field and hid his gun and gear under a rough outcropping of rock. If he was stopped by Union forces he might talk his way out unarmed, but carrying Confederate weapons would be risky or even fatal.

For an hour he walked the road painfully. Then he dropped beside a rail fence and fell asleep. A mule snorting in his ear wakened him with a start and he sat up as a wet tongue slobbered across his face. A small colored boy astride the mule looked down, bug-eyed, staring at him.

"Gawd' sake, White Folks, I thought you was daid!" he gasped.

Tom struggled up, steadying his quivering legs by holding to the mule's shoulder.

"Whose boy are you? Where you riding?" he asked.

"Takin' this mule up to Mist' Cass Rooney's place."

"You Cass Rooney's boy?"

"No, sah. My mammy b'long to Missus Murphy, but Mammy say she done free. We ain't run off though, we ain't got no place to go. This Mist' Cass Rooney's mule, we done borried him to haul in our tobaccy. You been to the big war?"

"Yes, I've been to the war and got shot. Now I'm heading home, four miles out north of town. How about giving me a ride as far as Rooney's place?" Tom asked.

"You been to the rebel war, Mister? Mist' Cass Rooney, he Union. Dis yere a Union mule. Dunno would he tote a rebel."

"I'll give you a piece of money." Tom pulled out the slim bundle of Confederate scrip from his pocket. He had forgotten that he had been paid. Now he had to get rid of the money before some zealous Home Guard picked him up. "I'll give you all this money," he offered.

"That ain't no good money," scorned the boy. "That ole Jeff Davis money. Ole Jeff Davis money won't buy nothin'. Ole Jeff Davis ain't lettin' no Negroes go free and dis yere mule ain't lettin' no rebel ride, neither." He kicked the mule in the ribs and rode away.

Tom found a flat rock and hid the Benny money under it. The warming October sun was giving way to cooler airs drifting down from the mountains, as he started his slow way into the town. Dusk was already falling when he reached the main street. No one had halted or hailed him, the street was quiet, almost deserted. He saw no one he knew, no one who paid him the least attention. It was obvious that wounded, dislocated, shabby men were already commonplace.

At the corner before the bank he stopped for a minute to rest and suddenly the front door opened and a cloud of dust was flirted out into his face. He coughed and turned about angrily, looked into the startled face of William Harper.

"Tom!" exclaimed William, dropping the broom.

"Willie!" Tom clutched at him, his cane falling and rolling into the gutter. "Lord, am I thankful to see somebody I know! I thought the whole town was dead."

"Scared," said William, recovering the cane. "General Boyle has got plenty tough since the Union army chased Bragg out of Kentucky. A lot of people just packed up and left to keep from being arrested. You got shot, I heard?" William's voice dropped sympathetically. "We got the word and Harriet has been weeping and moping around ever since. I better hurry on home and tell her you're alive. Your folks coming for you, Tom?"

Tom shook his head. "They don't know I'm alive either. I wrote my mother but I doubt if she ever got the letter."

"She didn't, I reckon, or she'd have got word to Harriet some way. I wish I could drive you home, Tom, but Pa wouldn't let me have the buggy—not to carry one of Morgan's raiders, wounded or not. Not after Morgan robbed that bank at Mt. Sterling. Were you in on that?"

"No, I wasn't, and neither was Morgan. It's all right, Willie, I'll hobble along," Tom said. "But I don't know if my father will let me in or not. He was plenty mad when I enlisted."

William fidgeted uneasily. There was no telling what his father would do if he found his son standing here talking to a returned Confederate. William scratched his long head.

64

"Tom, I know. I'll take you over to Judge Nesbitt's place. Mrs. Nesbitt and Milo's wife are all alone now—"

"Milo was in my company. He picked me up when I was wounded. Is the old judge dead?"

"He's in some northern prison," William said. "Boyle had him arrested back in the summer. Mrs. Nesbitt takes in boys that are hiding out—Confederates, I mean. Boys that get separated from their outfits and have to hide out from the Yanks. You wait here till I lock up and we'll go. And tonight," he grinned, "might be I could slip Harriet out and fetch her over there."

"You're a true friend, Willie," declared Tom huskily.

"Thunderation, you're practically a member of our family. Only if you belong to our family you've got to stop calling me Willie."

"All right, William, I'll try to remember. You think Harriet will be glad to see me?" Tom asked anxiously.

"Man!" William laughed. "She'll eat you alive. Mama and me, we've had a time keeping Pa from finding out what she was moping and sniveling about. She wrote a letter every day but then she was scared to mail them for fear some sneaky person in the post office would tell Pa that she was writing to a Morgan raider. Anyway, the way the rebels have been tearing up the railroads you'd probably have never got 'em."

"Not likely. We were always on the move till I got hit."

"You wait—no, I'll tell you. You walk along slow over there, go around to the back and I'll meet you. We have to be careful because they're even arresting women. Nothing personal—no offense, Tom, but after all you are a Confederate soldier."

"I was a Confederate soldier," corrected Tom.

"And that," confided William, "is probably what I'd like to be, if I dared to, Tom—when I see the way these Yanks are persecuting good Kentucky people. Well, see you in a few minutes."

Tom limped away feeling strange. He was no returned hero in this his native town. He was jeopardy to whosoever would be kind to him. He was a liability, he might even find himself a fugitive. It gave him a sick, hollow feeling.

But there was one bit of brightness left. At least Harriet still loved him.

7

AMALIE NESBITT GATHERED TOM, ALL SODDEN AND sweated and dust-stained as he was, into motherly arms.

"Poor boy!" she crooned. "You do right to bring him here, William. Now he shall bathe and then he will eat, such as we have, our poor fare. But William—the buttons! He must not wear the Confederate buttons. He could be captured—shut up in prison. I shall find him one of my Henri's coats."

"His breeches are mighty worn too," William remarked, "but I reckon Henri's pants would be too long. Henri was a mighty tall fellow."

"I—me, I will cut them off," announced Denise. "Poor Maman, she has given away so many of their clothes that our men will be naked when they come home! But they will not be angry, not if their clothes keep warm our boys of the South."

66

Amalie came back with a black, long-tailed coat and instantly Denise gave a little shriek.

"Milo's wedding coat! Oh, Milo was handsome in that coat. No, you shall wear it, Tom Findly. You will be handsome too, *n'est-ce pas?* Ah, it is tight. You are bigger man than Milo but not so tall. But not braver—no, no one is more brave than my Milo. My sweet Milo, I love him and I hate him that he runs away from me to this General Morgan. Ah, *voilà,* Maman, is he not beautiful, this Tom in my Milo's wedding coat?"

Tom pulled a hand out of a pocket of the heavy broadcloth coat. "A flower." He looked at the dried scrap in his hand. "A little faded flower."

"From my wedding," choked Denise. "Give it to me, my little wedding flower!" She began to cry like a child. "All I have. All I have of my sweet Milo."

"Me—I have nothing!" Amalie flung out her arms in a desolate, dramatic gesture. "Gone—all gone! My husband. My sons."

"I saw Milo in Cynthiana," Tom told her. "He was fine then."

"You see my Milo?"

"We were there—I got wounded there, but that was in July of course."

"And since July always they ride," mourned Denise, "and always some are killed. Poor Maman, she has sorrow for Papa too and Henri. We weep together, Maman and me. Then comes some boy, some Tom Findly, and we do for him what we can, for Papa and Milo and Henri. Is it not so, Maman?"

"My Henri," sighed Amalie. "Only across the river was that army and my Henri could not come even such a small way to see his maman! Only a little river and I may not see him. Maybe I never see him again."

Tom was uncomfortable in the tight coat, watching the sorrowful faces of the two women. He cleared his throat roughly.

"We met them, Bragg's army and Kirby Smith, farther south. They were retreating."

"Henri? You see my Henri?"

"No, we had to turn off another way. I didn't see Henri."

"Poor Tom." Amalie recovered her composure quickly. "We do not give him anything to eat. We make him sad with our silly tears. Come, Tom. We have eggs and bread. But no coffee. Never any coffee now in the shops nor any sugar."

"My father says"—William had perched on the edge of a chair, a trifle embarrassed by so much female emotion—"that the storekeepers are afraid to stock goods for fear they'll be raided or have everything requisitioned by troops of one side or the other. And the people who haven't taken the oath can't buy stock anyhow."

"Dear William!" Denise gave him a little pat that made a crimson flush fly over his eager face. "Always he is the banker. So practical. With explanations. But he is dear, our William, and brave! *Voilà*, he comes here when we are all suspect, and the angry father too he dares because he loves us. You do love us, William?"

"Oh, sure—sure! But I'd better get home now. I'll be late for supper. I thought I'd bring Harriet over tonight, Mrs. Nesbitt, if I can manage it. I'll be careful, I won't let anybody see us. Much obliged for letting Tom stay here till he —till his folks know he's back."

William hurried out, remembering to keep to the dark places, avoid being seen. He had heard at the bank that the Nesbitt house was being watched, but they were clever about the boys they took in, hiding them so that no one had been caught as yet. The temper of the decent people of the

68

town was on their side. Everybody was still resentful and touchy about the way the old judge had been treated by the military. Nobody would inform on the judge's family except some scurvy Home Guard or somebody courting the favor of the Union provost. But if Tom was discovered in their house it could mean trouble for Mrs. Nesbitt and Denise.

William thought of the Nesbitt mortgage and the interest that was long overdue. Hume Harper considered the Nesbitt place a valuable piece of property. If Harper was letting the interest go by default and making no effort to collect it, William was certain that his father had some future action in mind. Undoubtedly he would welcome a definite sign of disloyalty on the part of the Nesbitt women, something so flagrant that Harper would feel justified in seeing them dispossessed and sent south through the lines with no money, nothing!

William had a fresh pang to gnaw at him, Denise kissing that silly old dried-up flower and crying over it because Milo Nesbitt had put it in the pocket of his wedding coat. He even let himself harbor the wicked idea that perhaps Milo was already dead. Everybody knew that Morgan was ruthless with his men, that he scorned danger and took reckless chances and if his men were shot out of their saddles Morgan shrugged and galloped on. But when William pictured Milo toppling dead on the frozen ground it gave him a guilty feeling of somehow having already murdered Milo in his heart.

He did let himself remember however that a hot hatred and dread of Morgan's raiders was building up in some sections. A ravaged countryside, a raided shop or looted bank made for bitter reprisals. Nobody could ever blame William Harper if Milo Nesbitt never came home. And it was certain that nobody could censure him for nursing his love for Denise, for that was his own preciously hoarded secret. Not even Denise suspected, though there were times when he felt a touch of panic, seeing the sparkle in her eyes, hearing her laugh at him indulgently. Dear, brave William indeed!

He ached to show her how brave he was but there was only one way that could prove his gallantry and courage in Denise's eyes. He would have to enlist in the Confederate army and William was resigned to the fact that he was not brave enough for that.

It was very late when he knocked again at the back door of the Nesbitt house. Behind him Harriet shivered, her head and shoulders concealed by a dark shawl, her face carefully hidden. She was trembling all over and when the door was opened a guarded two inches she grabbed at William and held tight to keep her knees from collapsing under her. Denise stood beyond the door, a candle in her hand.

"Who is there?" she whispered.

"Me," answered William. "I brought Harriet. Let us in, Denise."

Denise blew out the candle before she opened the door. She reached a hand to Harriet. "This way. We must be always afraid, always someone perhaps watches. We hide the Southerners, we go to jail. Two times they bang on the front door. Once they come so big and bold into the house, they search all our rooms—*voilà*—nothing! Maman and me, we laugh."

Harriet tiptoed after Denise, William stumbling behind. He crashed into a table in the darkness and heard crockery jingle but nothing broke and he was relieved when they were led into a room dimly lighted by a dying fire. Tom Findly was sitting before the fire in a deep chair. He wore the long-tailed coat and a pair of tight brown breeches, strapped under his ankles. The ragged beard was shaved

70

off and he looked thin, his jawbone sharp, as he slept with his blond head tipped back.

Harriet cried, "Tom! Darling!" and gave a little barking sob.

Denise's fingers dug into William's shoulder. "We go now. You will listen at the back door. Me, I watch the front. You hear something—you come quick!"

"Suppose somebody comes? 'Lish McBride or some of the provost's men?"

"We hide Tom. We hide them both," giggled Denise. "Maman has a place fixed. Behind the chimney in her room, a little cupboard with a little door, and over the door she hangs her nightrobe and her chemises. If any man looks, Maman she is so embarrassed! She covers her garments *intime* with a sheet, then she shows them—so embarrassed! She is an actress, that maman! Go watch, William, and if anything moves, you come *quick!*"

The kitchen was cold and dark and smelled of dead fires and neglected grease and mice. There was the cold wet smell of the cistern under the floor. William perched on a stool, a little stiff with apprehension, worrying for fear Ellen Harper might find both him and Harriet gone. He tried to convince himself that they could depend on their mother, that she would not rouse their father or make a fuss. He had wanted to tell her about Tom, but Harriet had argued that it was risky, that Harper might overhear or worm it out of his wife, and then immediately consider it his loyal Union duty to turn Tom over to be locked up as a Confederate prisoner or even as a spy.

Governor Magoffin had tried to establish amnesty for all returning Confederates but so far the military had prevailed against him. Since Bragg's invasion tension and suspicion had tightened ominously. There had been too many raids, too much property destroyed, and already guerrilla bands were roaming the country, bringing terror to the inhabitants. To Union men every guerrilla was a Confederate spy or a Copperhead, while sympathizers with the South damned them as Yankee hoodlums or deserters from both armies.

An hour passed and William's feet grew cold and his legs ached stiffly. Then Denise and Harriet came quietly back through the dark. Harriet was still shaking when she clutched at William's arm.

"Be still!" cautioned Denise. "Those Negroes back in the alley, they watch and listen. Be still like mouses. Do not worry, Miss Harper, we keep your soldier safe."

Like mouses, William was thinking as he hustled Harriet out by the back way, hurrying her from shadow to shadow, thankful that a chilly, thin rain was falling and the heavy, enveloping darkness hid his own face.

If Harriet had been able to see him she would likely have demanded in her blunt fashion what he was grinning about. She was even capable of picking out of him remorselessly some small pitiful fragments of his fatuous dreams of the deliciousness of Denise, the small, wise, lovely smile she had as she closed the door shutting in the lovers, all the little tricks and nuances of speech that had William walking almost drunkenly in a mixture of young misery and blind ecstasy of remembering.

"Mouses!" he said suddenly aloud, in tender oblivious abstraction.

"Shut up!" warned Harriet acidly. "Milo Nesbitt's wife is the silliest thing I ever knew. And she had better leave Tom alone!"

"Huh!" sniffed William, remembering Tom as he had looked earlier, limping and stumbling, foul and ragged with his unkempt beard and long dirty hair. Denise, he was certain, would want no part of Tom Findly. "You needn't worry," he said scornfully. "Nobody wants your Morgan raider. Nobody but you."

He had put the back door key outside on top of the cistern and now he turned it cautiously, pushed the door open and hurried Harriet in, locking it again. Silently they stole up the stairs. There were no sounds from the bedroom below and once inside Harriet's room they lit a candle and stood holding to each other, Harriet giggling nervously.

Suddenly she clutched William, whispered, "Thank you, William, you're a dear! Oh, it was so wonderful! William, you'll take me again tomorrow?"

"Maybe," he evaded, heading for his own room.

He was not going to do this every night, he determined. No matter how Harriet begged he was not going to take too many risks for themselves or for the Nesbitts and Tom Findly. Anyway Tom had a home and he appeared to be in pretty fair shape. He'd have to go to work or go back to the farm, do something anyway, if he had any idea of marrying an expensive girl like Harriet.

Hume Harper was a prudent man and a hard man toward his son but William knew that Harriet got almost anything she wanted. He had resented this partiality at first but had gradually became reconciled to it. Now he saw in it another element of danger. His father would not hesitate to denounce Tom or even the Nesbitt women if his suspicions were aroused. He would feel that he was protecting Harriet from her own folly and in that William was ready to concede that his father could be right.

Certainly, incapacitated and impoverished as he was, Tom Findly could never by any practical reasoning be considered a promising suitor for the hand of the banker's daughter. Harriet ought to see how hopeless it was. But there his own infatuation rose up to confound William. He could imagine what his father would have to say about a sprout of eighteen harboring dreams about a married woman years older than himself.

It was a long time before William Harper went to sleep.

8

THE BEARDED MEN WHO RODE INTO THE YARD OF THE BRIScoe house had a familiar look to Lennie. It was a foggy October morning and Thad was plowing a hill field with his one horse and a borrowed mule. Old Lum came stumbling and panting up the slope.

"White mens down yonder. Miss Lennie, she skeert, she say you come quick, Young Marse."

Thad tied the team to the fence, his face darkened and taut. "Watch them, Lum, don't let them tangle their feet in the trace chains. What the hell now?" he demanded wearily of the gray sky.

"Dunno, Miss Lennie say you come."

Thad stalked down to the yard, swung over a gate without bothering to open it. Four mounted men sat grimly in their saddles beside the mounting block. On the block stood little Wade, a toy gun Lum had whittled for him pointed boldly at the intruders. Two of the men Thad knew. They were country fellows enlisted in the obnoxious Home Guards. The others he had seen around. All four wore stiff, military scowls.

"What do you want, McBride?" Thad demanded.

'Lish McBride, a bully with a prison record, spat obliquely. "Got your young one trained good, ain't you, Briscoe? That brat yonder says he's fixing to shoot my head off."

"Can too!" declared Ward undaunted. "Bang through the eyes, you ole Yankee you!"

"Hush, Ward!" admonished his father. "So you boys are out making war on children now, eh?"

"Young ones says what they hear said," declared a red-bearded man. "We come here on official business, Briscoe. It's well known you ain't never took the oath. That rates you disloyal to the Union."

Thad looked over his shoulder to where Lennie's white face showed at the kitchen door, the girls huddled behind her.

"I'm loyal to the Constitution of the United States," he stated firmly. "That's more than Abraham Lincoln can say."

"Told you he was a traitor!" snarled 'Lish McBride.

"I'm no traitor. I've taken no side in this war," argued Thad. "All I'm doing is minding my own business and trying to make a living for my family with what little means the Union army has left to me. They took six good horses from me without any payment as yet and most of my other stock. What more do you want?"

"We take it from your own mouth, Briscoe," said the red-bearded one, "that you ain't nothing. You ain't took the loyalty oath to the Union and you ain't got the guts to own you're for the Confederacy. You ain't denying that your gal is fixing to marry one of old Judge Nesbitt's boys, and him enlisted in the rebel army?"

"Leave my daughter out of this!" snapped Thad, his eyes darkening dangerously. "If you've got business with me, state it plain and get off my place!"

"Don't talk so big, Briscoe," warned a third man, a black-

75

smith whom Thad knew to be a ranting abolitionist and a windy drunk. "You're so loyal to the Constitution, why ain't you took the oath?"

"It's a radical oath." Thad was stony cool now. "It binds me to support this Republican administration, and I go along with most of Kentucky in being in opposition to this administration, even if Lincoln was born in this state. How many votes did your man Lincoln poll in this state two years ago? Everybody knows. Out of a hundred and twenty thousand votes, Lincoln got a little over thirteen hundred. In Kentucky I stand with the majority. A Democrat would never have set a lot of helpless colored people free and loose with nobody caring a damn what happens to them. That's my stand. Now state your business if you expect me to stand here and listen."

The redbeard, who was obviously in command, swung a leg over his saddle. "As I see it, Briscoe, you talk all around and don't say nothing. You're on the black book as a Confederate sympathizer. There you stay wrote down till you take the oath. Could be you'd have to git pardoned by the president, that is if Lincoln could see fit to pardon you. We're tightening down on you Copperheads now, tightening down hard. Reckon you heard about the L. and N. depot being burned over yonder?"

"I heard that guerrillas burned it, tore up the rails too."

"Them guerrillas wouldn't be friends of yours, I reckon?"

"Friends?" demanded Thad. "I've laid out many a night with no arms but pitchforks, and no help but three old Nigras, waiting for them to come and burn me out. They've burned three barns and killed two men already down this road." Just in time he had remembered that he was not permitted to have arms. That order had been issued earlier, and he had cannily hidden all his guns.

"Them guerrillas was your Confederate friends, Briscoe,

and seeing as how they burned down the depot and nobody made any attempt to put out the fire, we're levying on all you Confederate sympathizers for money enough to build a new depot," stated the leader. "We want twenty dollars out of you. You got ten days to turn in the money."

"Those guerrillas were no more Confederate than you are," Thad said hotly. "They're scum and thieves, deserters from both armies, out to loot and burn and kill because there's no real law now in Kentucky. You tell your Union command to stop meddling with the courts and we'll get a few of those outlaws hung."

"Twenty dollars. Ten days," repeated redbeard. "You'd better pay up or the authorities will have to levy on your stock or other property."

"What authorities? Useless Grant or Jere Boyle? What stock? You've taken all my stock. I have to borrow animals to plow my land—and where would I get twenty dollars?"

"I dunno. That's your problem. Just come up with the money to the provost's office, that's all we got to say. All right, gentlemen, we'll ride!"

"Gentlemen!" Thad spat out the word with bitterness as the four wheeled their mounts and trotted off. Little Ward slid off the block and pulled at his father's trouser leg.

"You get me a real gun, Pa," he begged, "then I can shoot bad mens that scare Mama."

Clemmy came running. "Pa—the black horse! You saw it? It was Dasher. It was our black Dasher that those soldiers took. My very own horse! Who were they, Pa? Not Union army. Those soldiers said they were taking Dasher for the Union army."

"I saw him, Clemmy. It was Dasher all right. I've seen our big bay too, around town, ridden by some of these same fellows. They call themselves part of the army, maybe they take orders from the army. Anyway they've got Dasher."

77

Thad walked to the porch, holding the hands of his children. Lennie still waited anxiously at the door. "Don't worry," he told her, "I'm not arrested. I have to pay twenty dollars to help build back that depot the guerrillas burned the other night."

"Twenty dollars?" gasped Teresa. "Do they think you burned the depot, Pa?"

"My friends burned it. My Confederate friends."

"Bosh!" snorted Clemmy. "Those old guerrillas burned it and they know it."

"Where can we get twenty dollars?" worried Lennie. "We've hardly got enough corn to see us through the winter and nothing to sell—only those few chickens and two poor hogs! And they're likely to be stolen any night."

"I'll manage somehow." Thad could not bear the gray look of trouble that dimmed his wife's face so often now. "I've got to get back to plowing."

One thing worried him, leaving Lennie alone while he was out of earshot in the fields, with six children. The old slaves were faithful but they were slow and stubborn and Jericho was growing very deaf. Once he fell asleep it was almost impossible to wake him. They were mighty little protection. He wished that Ward were the eldest rather than Teresa. Ward had the makings of a fearless little firebrand already.

The child was like his own brother, Boone, Thad realized. Boone Briscoe had been a young brand too, swiftly kindled. He had fought a duel before he was twenty, choosing to ride south and fight it on the identical ground on the Tennessee line where Andrew Jackson had killed his man more than forty years ago. Boone had also slain a young adversary, then he had galloped away to enlist in the army under Winfield Scott to fight the Mexicans and had died on some arid hill in a far country. Now his spirit lived on in his brother's child.

At suppertime Lennie showed Thad a covered basket. "I was going to send Judge Nesbitt's wife some meal and eggs and a little piece of seasoning meat," she said. "Tee worries all the time for fear they may not have anything to eat. She's bound to marry that boy, Thad, if he comes home from the war, and I reckon there's nothing we can do about it. Now I guess you and the horse will both be too tired to make a trip to town."

"If you've got the stuff ready I'll walk," volunteered Thad. "I want to see a man anyhow. Only you've got to keep Lum and Ceph in the kitchen till I get back. I'll leave you a loaded gun and Tee can shoot as straight as I can."

"You mean—they might come back? Those men?"

"No, they won't come back likely, but I just want to feel safe about you. I wish I had another man on the place. A young man."

"I wish we could get Jigger back. He was such a trust-worthy boy. I was never afraid when Jigger was on the place," sighed Lennie.

"Jigger's probably in Canada by now. They scared him off when they started all that talk about enlisting Negroes in the army." Thad sat down at the table. "I'll eat now so I won't be late."

"You're so tired, Thad, and it's two miles to town! Thad" —a sharp note of apprehension came into her voice— "you're going to try to borrow money and we owe the bank already."

"I'm going to see Harper and try to talk him into dis-counting some of those warrants I got for the horses they took last year. They talked confiscation because I hadn't sworn the oath then but I made that young captain from Indiana sign the papers anyway. He was young and green and scared so he signed. They say I'll have to wait till the end of the war to collect but Harper can afford to wait better than I can. He said when he was out here a while back he might consider taking the warrants toward our interest. Maybe I can talk him into advancing some of it— twenty dollars anyway."

"Might be he'll think he'd rather wait and foreclose on us and take the place," worried Lennie.

"Well, there's a little matter of that drove of hogs I sold to Harper last year. Supposed to go to the army. I found out where the hogs went," Thad said slyly.

"That's dishonest, Thad, threatening Mr. Harper."

"No threats, Lennie. Threats wouldn't make any impression on Hume Harper. He's built himself a solid silver armor and he sticks behind it and money still talks, even if it has to whisper behind the door. Just a gentle reminder maybe will be all I'll need with Harper." Thad pushed his chair back. "Call the boys in, you lock the door then. And keep that gun hid unless you need it. They're taking arms away from people like us, anyway Ward would like to get hold of it. He's hankering to shoot somebody."

"Ward would too," put in small dark 'Ria, "if it was an ole Yankee."

"We'll let the Yanks and the Johnnies do their own fighting, you young ones stay close now and mind your mother." Thad picked up the basket and went out, shouting for Lum and Ceph. Two hours later, knocking on Amalie Nesbitt's front door, he was a little startled when Denise's voice called through the panels.

"Who's there?"

"It's Thad Briscoe, Mrs. Nesbitt. Lennie sent you some eggs."

The door opened quickly and Denise pulled him inside. "So wonderful—to see a friend!" she cried.

80

"What's wonderful about it?" asked Thad, bewildered. "Judge Nesbitt had more friends than anybody in this town. Here—here's a little mess of meal and stuff. Be careful with those eggs—they're breakable. Look here, Mrs. Nesbitt—" He looked sharply at her drained face and trembling hands. "What's wrong? Why are you so scared?"

"They came," she cried in a choking rush, "they were not friends. Beasts—horrible creatures!"

"Who came?" Thad caught the basket before she dropped it.

"Soldiers. They say they are soldiers. But I know them. They are white trash. Impossible! Look—" She pointed at a curtain pulled down, a cabinet overturned. "Upstairs—our beds, they fling all on the floor. Everywhere they search. They swear at us. They call us traitors. We are vile, they say, we are Confederate. But—" she added with a nervous giggle, "they do not find him!"

"Find who? Who's here? Milo home—or Henri?"

"Come." She took his arm. "Not here—these walls, they listen. Out there, the street—it listens!" She walked ahead of him with a wavering candle into the back room where a fire glowed thinly, the only light.

Amalie Nesbitt was slumped in a chair, a wet towel folded over her face.

"Maman fainted," Denise explained. "I screamed at them. I screamed and screamed. 'Now you have killed her! You beasts who make war on women.'"

"Who is it?" Amalie took the towel away. "Ah, it is the good Mr. Briscoe."

"Maybe you'd better sit still, ma'am," said Thad uneasily. "I'll just put the basket here."

"I am well," declared Amalie in a brisk voice. "I did not faint, but I pretend good, eh, Denise? It is you though, *ma petite,* who scared them away. Never did anyone scream so

81

loud, Mr. Briscoe. In the street I hear the people running. The evil ones—they go out quickly, and they did not find him. Poor Tom—you may come out now, Tom. It is only Mr. Briscoe, our good friend."

Some white garments hanging near the fireplace swayed and fluttered, a tiny door opened and a sooty, stooped figure draped in cobwebs appeared.

"Good Lord, Tom Findly!" Thad exclaimed.

Tom brushed off his clothes, slapped soot from his hair.

"Crawled up behind the chimney," he said, "but they might have got me anyway if these women hadn't been mighty brave and smart."

"When did you come home? I thought you rode off last year with General Morgan?"

"I did. I was wounded in July. They sent me home when Bragg invaded and these good women took me in. Now I have to go, Mrs. Nesbitt. I can't let things like this happen to you on my account."

"Why don't you go along home?" Thad asked. Then he remembered. "I reckon it's your father?"

"You know my father, Mr. Briscoe?"

"Everybody knows your father, Tom. Dead set for the Union. More so than anybody in this county, I guess. You think he won't let you come back?"

"He locked the gate and wouldn't let me tell my mother goodbye when I left," Tom said. "Now if he wants me back he'll have to unlock it again and invite me in."

"Bravo, he is proud, that boy!" applauded Denise. "But where can you go, Tom? He is still sick of his wound and lame and not strong."

"I'm not sick. Just now and then a little fever comes back but I can work at something," insisted Tom. "Sitting down anyway."

"You'd be picked up in two hours if you were seen in

town," said Thad, "and these women could get in bad trouble for harboring one of Morgan's men."

"I know. Maybe I can slip down the river. Or across into Missouri. I can still write and figure."

"Can you milk a cow? And keep a gun ready to protect a woman and a house full of children?" asked Thad.

Tom's face brightened. "I rode with Morgan. We did plenty of shooting and generally we hit what we shot at. But I had to bury my gun, I didn't dare come into town with it. I reckon I could still milk a cow."

"If you want to come home with me, I'll come for you with a rig tomorrow night. You'll get board and room but I can't pay you. We can go after dark and dig up your gun. I've got some hid in the hay too, and a couple of pistols in the house in a sack of beans. It will be a place for you to hide out till you get your strength back and it will be a favor to me too," Thad said. "I'm having to work my land myself. What field hands I've got left are all old and rheumatic. They can potter around and feed but that's about all, so I worry about leaving my wife and girls alone with so much lawlessness going on."

"It sounds mighty inviting, Mr. Briscoe, and I'm grateful but I reckon you realize I could be a danger to you. I heard those men who were here a little while ago tell Mrs. Nesbitt that it was a thousand dollars fine and jail for harboring somebody like me."

"We've got hiding places too. When my grandfather built that house this was still Indian country, and the house sits on a hill so you can see them a long way off," Thad reassured him. "I'll take the chance if you're willing."

"You've got yourself a man, Mr. Briscoe." Tom sighed with relief. "I've been feeling mighty guilty about jeopardizing these good women."

So it was settled. Tom Findly removed secretly and

without incident in the dark of the night. Thad forgot for a little his disappointment at getting no encouragement from Hume Harper in his relief at having somebody on the place to ease Lennie's nervous dread. Only Harriet was unhappy. She stormed and wept when William told her that Tom had found asylum at the Briscoe farm.

"I'll never see him! He won't dare to come to town and Pa would never let you drive me out there. Those Briscoe girls—he'll forget me in a week."

"The Briscoe girls are just young ones." William tried to be comforting. "All but Teresa and she's Henri Nesbitt's girl. Denise says Henri plans to marry Teresa when the war's over."

"How does it happen"—Harriet was acid—"that you call Milo Nesbitt's wife by her first name? I consider it very disrespectful. A woman who has been married for years and is so much older than you."

"She's not so much older and she's my friend. Anyway there are two Mrs. Nesbitts. What do you want me to call her—Mrs. Milo?"

"I think you should not go there at all! After all, the whole family is disloyal to the Union and you can imagine what Pa would have to say about it. He was Judge Nesbitt's friend but he disowned the judge when he found out how the judge stood toward the Union."

"I don't need to imagine what Pa would say about it. I know. I know what he'd have to say about you too, sneaking out to meet one of John Morgan's raiders," snapped William.

"Tom's out of that now. I'll change him. I'll make a loyal Union man out of him before I marry him."

"You'll stay an old maid a long time then," drawled her brother.

"I'm willing to wait. You'll see, Mr. Smarty!"

84

"You'd better be grateful that Mr. Briscoe took Tom in before somebody blabbed and Pa found out about you two. Pa'd have him up at Johnson's Island in a hurry, and they all die up there, they say downtown. And you'd better be glad too"—William was grim—"that the Nesbitts are my friends and can be trusted or you'd never have got to see Tom at all."

"I thanked them. I thanked them enough."

"You couldn't. Not for being in danger all the time of being arrested and maybe sent away south. Some women Mr. Merrill down at the bank knows got sent south through the lines because they baked pies for Kirby Smith's soldiers, and their folks got word one of them had to sleep out in the cold rain, so she got lung fever and died." William had the last word.

At least he wouldn't have to drag Harriet over to the Nesbitts' and he could slip in to see Denise any time he got a chance. He was young enough and naïve enough to believe that Denise was always glad to see him. Anyway she called him her dear and her sweet William. He rolled that comforting morsel around to warm his heart every night after he went to bed. It kept him from thinking too much about the way her eyelashes lay in soft tempting shadows on her cheeks. Not that he wanted to be kept from those thoughts, but already there was a certain unease attached to such dreams that troubled him.

His whiskers were growing briskly now. He wondered if Pa would ever buy him a razor, or would Denise like him with a nice brown beard.

9

$\mathcal{T}$OM FINDLY FACED A NEW APPROACH, A NEW ATTITUDE toward life those first days in the Briscoe house. These were people who were gentle, who loved each other and did not disdain to show it, who were considerate and gracious. To Tom all this was strange and new.

He had grown up in a house where the dominating atmosphere was one of dread, of endless evasion and placation, of his mother's desperate endeavors to please his father, baffled usually by the elder Findly's grim determination not to be pleased by anything, to please no one and to ease no burden, even upon himself. Tom Findly, Senior, drove himself fiercely and that stern drive had a relentless impact upon every person, every beast, even upon the land he tended. He would not own slaves, arguing that slavery was an offense against God, but his son had early decided that his father's prejudice against slavery had no basis of altruism.

Findly's arguments against the institution, to his son's mind, were as hypocritical as the long prayers he made on cold mornings while the biscuit chilled and the fat bacon congealed on the platter. Slaves had to be fed and clothed and they had naïve and shrewd ways of evading the brutality of hard work, the special kind of brutality which was Findly's religion.

Labor, in his book, must be hard and exhausting for labor's own sake. A growing boy might need sleep but because labor was sacred a boy must be routed out of bed in the icy darkness of a winter morning, even before the animals he was to tend had awakened.

Tom remembered napping in the haymow for many a bleak hour before dawn, only to be startled awake by a blow on the back with the handle of a pitchfork or a bucket of icy water dashed over his head.

As for his mother, Tom had been away from home now long enough to know what a long-drawn-out misery of frustrations and petty persecutions her married life had been. When he saw Thad Briscoe take a heavy bucket of water from his wife's hand with a grin and a reproaching pat, he thought of the times he had seen heavy wooden buckets thrust into his own mother's hand with a snarled complaint because the gourd dipper scraped the bottom. And Marcia Findly had been as gently raised as Lennie Briscoe. She had come, very young, trustingly, to her husband's home, bringing two slaves with her, only to have them sent back promptly to Mississippi and the onus of their slavery loaded upon her slender shoulders.

Lennie wondered that Tom's mother had not sought him out, had sent no word. "Haven't you written to her, Tom? Thad could take a letter and somebody we can trust would carry it to her."

"He wouldn't let her have it," Tom said resignedly, "and he wouldn't let her leave the place for fear she might find some way to see me. Once in a while he used to take her to church but her clothes were all old-style and he wouldn't buy her any new ones so long as they held together and covered her. So he goes to church alone but church doesn't do anything for my father. The only God on our place is the farm and the mortgage."

"We've got a mortgage too but it's a devil, not a god," said Lennie. "Thad's father borrowed a lot of money to buy more Negroes and horses and add to this big house, and then he died and left the mortgage for Thad to struggle with and a war coming on. We could just as well have lived on in the old house, the way it was. This kitchen and the dining room are part of the old house—but Thad's father had elegant notions. He wanted big parlors and a spiral stairway and pillars—so we've been carrying that burden for fifteen years now. In good years we could cut the mortgage down a little but now it's as much as we can do to keep the interest paid."

"My father could have been free of debt long ago," Tom said, "even though he came out here from Pennsylvania with mighty little money and had to borrow to buy his first hundred acres. But as soon as he paid that out he borrowed and bought more, and it's been going that way ever since. Now he owns nearly six hundred acres, and it's a millstone on his own back, he grinds himself with it and everybody else, even while he worships that land. To him it's a sign of how shrewd and thrifty he is."

"You talk well, Tom," Lennie told him. "You should be a lawyer or a preacher."

"Mother wanted something like that for me but after I'd learned to read and figure Pa said that was enough. He put me behind the plow before I was thirteen years old."

"I can rake hay and shuck corn and I'm only ten," announced Priscilla, lovingly dabbing buttermilk on her plump little arms where the summer sunburn faded. "But I sure don't like it much."

"I don't hate work," Tom insisted. "But work for work's sake does irk me. I've hoed a cornfield clean many a time and been sent back the next day to hoe it over for fear I might be tempted to go fishing."

"Corn," stated practical Clementine, "has shallow roots. Lum says you can hoe corn to death and get nothing but nubbins."

"Lum," said Lennie, "always has some very reasonable argument against any form of manual labor."

"It's nice being here with you, Mrs. Briscoe," Tom said, "but I worry about endangering you all, and not earning my keep."

"Would you like me to throw cold water in your bed when you don't wake up mornings?" teased Clementine. "Then you wouldn't have to eat cold hominy for breakfast."

"He's been sick a long time," interposed Lennie. "Tom has to get his strength back. Anyway, I feel safe with you in the house, even though Thad's out so much. That's worth what little you eat."

There was one rainy night of gloom when Thad came home with a bleak, discouraged face. "Harper won't touch those warrants," he said. "He says I've never taken the oath and he can't afford to have anything to do with any papers with my name on them."

"He'd collect them if he had them. Every penny." Lennie was bitter.

"He can afford to wait. I can't. Maybe I ought to go take that damn' oath, Lennie. Maybe I ought to swear to uphold something I don't believe in."

"You do as you think best, Thad, but it looks to me like it's too late now. They might not even let you swear, knowing you'd be swearing a lie."

"They've got a new general now. Named Rosecrans. Lincoln fired Buell for not following Bragg's army into the East Tennessee mountains. But we've still got Jere Boyle here in Kentucky."

"Thad, the twenty dollars!" fretted Lennie. "What will we do?"

"May have to sell the red hog. That is if I can find somebody with cash enough to buy a hog. It will leave us short of meat for the winter but if I don't pay they'll take the hog anyway, maybe take both of them and we need the sow." Thad punched savagely at the fire, faced them all. "What's the sense of this war, Tom? Here we are—neighbors, fighting and hating all over Kentucky. Property destroyed, men killed, whole families uprooted, white and black—and we're not even a seceded state! And for what?"

"I asked myself that question for a year," said Tom. "I never came up with an answer."

"This has been a good summer for the Confederacy"— Thad dropped wearily into a chair—"but too much has been thrown away. No reason at all why Bragg couldn't have taken Louisville, it was wide open, but he lost the chance fooling around over at Frankfort setting up his provisional government. And how long did that last? About two hours, they say. That Lieutenant Nelson, the same fellow who armed all these Home Guards Boyle has got on our necks, was all ready to give up Louisville and retreat into Indiana. Then Nelson got shot by another Union officer—name was Jefferson Davis by the way—shot him down right in the hall in the Galt Hotel. It's all here in the *Courier*." He pulled a folded newspaper from his pocket and tossed it in Tom's lap.

Tom unfolded the sheet, a small issue, blurred and not well printed. Everything was showing the effect of war, even the newspapers. Some had even been suspended by the Union command.

"They've been fighting in Maryland and Virginia," he read. "Bloody battle at a place called Sharpsburg. Drove the Yanks out of Harper's Ferry, it says here. This man

90

Lee that they put in command last spring seems to have put some guts into our army. He'll give McClellan and Pope a rough time up on the Potomac. We've got the advantage now, Mr. Briscoe. The question is, can we hold it?"

"Did you read that piece about the old lady up there in Maryland? When Stonewall Jackson's troops marched into Frederick, Lennie, this old lady rushed out into the street and threw her arms around some of the boys and hollered, 'God bless you ragged, dirty souls!' "

"Butternut, that's our army now," said Tom drearily. "Old faded jeans and home-dyed pants. Bragg's men looked like a lot of beggars when we met them on that retreat down south, though they had wagonloads of plunder. Some of our boys said that General Lee was still wearing his old Union uniform with Confederate buttons sewed on it. Where's the money going? I rode for a year with John Morgan and got paid seventy Confederate dollars. Then I had to bury the money out in a field. I was afraid to come to town with it on me."

"You could dig it up, Tom, and lend my daddy that twenty dollars," suggested Priscilla, artlessly.

"It was Confederate money, Prissy. It would do your father more harm than good."

"You all stop fighting this war and go to bed," ordered Lennie. "It's bad enough having it tear up Kentucky without fetching it into this kitchen to scare the children."

"I'm not scared," declared 'Ria. "No ole Yankee is going to scare me, ever."

"Ha!" snorted Rowena. "You'd dive under the bed mighty quick if anybody knocked on that door."

"I would not!"

"Me not neither," stated Ward grimly.

"That's enough. Out of here, all of you," ordered Thad. When the knock did sound on the door later, not one of the children wakened and Thad was glad of that. He pulled on his pants and picked up a pistol, went through the wide hall to the front door. Over his shoulder he saw Tom limping down the stairway.

"You'd better keep back," he warned, low. Loudly he called, "Who's there?"

"It's Ranse Ridley, Briscoe," answered a voice. "Open up."

Thad shot back the heavy bolts. "He's all right. Ridley," he told Tom. "Ranse Ridley."

"Lives next to us," said Tom.

The man at the door carried a dim lantern and was alone. "Hello, Thad," he said. "You got Tom Findly out here?"

"I'm here, Ranse." Tom stepped into the circle of light. "Who wants me?"

"It's trouble, Tom. Your folks."

"How did you know I was here?" asked Tom, sharply.

"Briscoe told me a few days ago. Asked me could I get word to your mother that you were all right, but I didn't have a chance till tonight. Now there's trouble out there—these night riders." Ridley used a bitter epithet. "Some say Morgan and some say guerrillas, anyway they burnt your pa's barn and run off some of his stock and your pa's shot. Dunno how bad. I stopped in town and sent Doc Warner out but you better come. Your mother's alone and needs you. I brought a wagon."

"Hurry, Tom," urged Thad. "And here—you take this rifle. Your father's Union—might get to keep it. Can't tell when you might need it."

"It wasn't Morgan," said Tom loyally, but without much conviction, for how could he be sure? How many barns had he seen fired and horses caught up and led off on those wild raids through Tennessee and Kentucky?

"Anyway they sure ruint your pa," Ridley said.

"Wish I could go along to help." Thad shook Tom's hand. "But I can't leave Lennie and the children alone."

"I saw the fire," Ranse Ridley was saying as he urged his mule into a trot along the road. "Got over there as fast as I could. They'd gone by that time, took two horses and some steers, your mother told me, and when your father shot at 'em they shot back and hit him. Then one of 'em knocked him down and rode over him. Horse trompled him. Fired the barn after that and rode off yelling."

"How bad off is he?" asked Tom.

"Couldn't tell. He was bleeding pretty bad. Looked like the ball went in his belly and come out his back. Right over his hip. Head cut up bad too where the shod horse trompled him. You know your pa, Tom, talks loud and bitter. Been saying Lincoln ought to send a black army down south to learn the rebs what war is. Preacher warned him on the street just the other day. There's folks feel strong against your pa, even good Union people. So it could have been night riders, could have been some of Morgan's men—but I doubt that. Wasn't many of 'em by the sign. Could have been just some rough county folks had a grudge against your father. He was a mighty hardheaded man."

"Yes, I know."

And now I'm going back, now he'll have to let me in, Tom was thinking. How he'll hate being dependent on me! He would not let himself think that his father might be already dead. There was a stony and unyielding fiber in Tom Findly, Senior, that to his son's mind would defy even death. At least he would see his mother again. He thought of her fondly, so slim, so slight, her shoulders a little stooped, an awful patience in her face that dimmed the little that remained youthful, reminiscent of the pretty girl she must have been. Her still-fair hair was dimmed too, fading now, brushed back into a plain hard knot.

Ranse Ridley was talking on. "Your mother is a real nice woman, Tom. We never knew her very well. When she first came a long time back people thought she was kind of proud and not very friendly, her folks being quality down in Mississippi, but it wasn't so."

"She was proud, but it wasn't true that she was unfriendly," defended Tom. "She would have loved friends —but she never had a chance."

"I know. Old man kept her close. Happens when a man along in years marries a real young woman, he gets jealous."

Tom tried to think about that idea—the idea that his father had ever loved his mother enough to be jealous of any other intimacy for her. It refused to crystallize.

"He wasn't jealous, Mr. Ridley. She was just something he owned, he showed more love for a horse than for her, she was about as important to him as a good sow!" Tom cried, angrily. "And I was about as important as a calf—less, a calf was worth money. I wasn't supposed to have any mind or feelings. All I was supposed to do was get strong enough to work. Like a mule! Mother too. He worked himself that way too. Mr. Ridley, maybe I'll burn in hell for it, but if my father's dead when we get there I won't shed a tear."

Ranse drove on another mile in silence. Then he cleared his throat.

"Reckon that's why you run off and joined Morgan. Your father was strong for the radicals, strong against the South."

"I know why he felt that way," Tom said. "It was because Ma came from down there. When he married her she owned slaves. He wouldn't have them on the place and he talked abolition worse than that crazy fellow, Garrison, or Harriet Beecher Stowe or anybody. It was just to humble Ma. So—I joined Morgan's Lexington Rifles to humble him! My uncle in Mississippi sent me the money to buy a horse and saddle. He sent the draft to Harper's bank and Pa tried to draw it but I'd come of age then and they wouldn't pay it to him. So after I signed up I rode out to tell Ma goodbye and he locked the gate and wouldn't let me in."

"Been locked ever since," Ranse said. "Them riders fixed that. They tore down the fence. He didn't aim for you to come back, I reckon, but now likely he'll be thankful to see you—if he ever sees anything again."

"He won't be glad, 'cause if he lives I won't stay. And I'll take my mother away somewhere just as soon as I can. I'll take her away from him before he works her to death. She's not an old woman. I'm twenty-two, she was nineteen when I was born."

The dull glow of the dying fire was visible now as they approached the Findly farm.

"Burned pretty hot awhile. Lighted up the whole country," Ranse said. "Barn was full of hay."

Other people had gathered, horses were tied to the fence, and against the lighted embers Tom could see men moving about. "Doc's here," Ranse said. "Yonder's his old white horse."

A man came up to the wagon before they got down. "Oh, it's you, Ranse. They sure ruint old Findly. Took his young team but there's an old horse left and the cows got loose. Some of the boys are rounding 'em up now, they can put 'em in the shed. It didn't catch. Who you got with you?"

"Young Findly—old man's boy."

"Heard you was off with Morgan, boy. Some of our boys figured Morgan done this, but I seen 'em. There wasn't more'n six. Met 'em on the road when I started over here after I seen the fire. They was leading the team and driving some steers ahead of 'em. I could have got a shot at 'em but

95

they would have knocked me off my horse, too many for me, so I ducked into the woods and let 'em ride past. I got seven young ones depending on me and you don't try to be a hero when you got that many to feed. Your old man's hurt pretty bad, boy. Dunno will he make it or not. Doc's with him now."

Tom said nothing. Beside Ranse he walked woodenly toward the house. There were lights upstairs and down. He had never seen the house lighted up before. Now he realized that it was a good house, a good brick house with all the trim white with new paint, every post and spindle standing straight, and smoke issuing from three chimneys. Never before could he recall any fires being kindled, except in the kitchen. All his memories of winter were of an icy bed and water freezing in the pitcher and slop jar. A strange woman was making coffee at the kitchen stove.

"You're Tom!" she exclaimed, as he entered, blinking. "We thought you'd run off to the war. My—your mama will be glad! Mrs. Findly!" She raised a voice trained to bugle up a husband or offspring over long distances. "Mrs. Findly—your boy's home!"

Marcia Findly came running. Tom was startled at her smallness, her thinness, and that there was still a trace of youth left in her face. Her mouth worked and tears poured down her cheeks as she came into his arms.

"Tom—Tom—you came! I couldn't believe it when Ranse told me he was going for you—all this time—"

"There," he said stupidly, yearningly, hugging her close, patting her back. "There! There!"

"All this time! And you were so near—and I didn't know."

"I was wounded," Tom said, his cheek against her hair. "I had to hide out. He said I couldn't ever come home."

"He's bad off, Tom, it's in his stomach." She stood back

96

and he saw the blood then, on her apron, on her sleeves. She followed his eyes, shocked and recoiling. "I tried to lift him. He was too heavy. Then Ranse Ridley came—and the Carpenters." She gave the watching woman a little grateful nod. "They've been so good. Other people too. Ranse sent the doctor. He's trying to stop the bleeding. They trampled him and cut his face and his head. You come see your father, Tom."

He stood stock-still, his face stiffening a little.

"No. No, Mama." He had not called her Mama since he was very small. She began to cry again.

"Tom, you go!" argued the Carpenter woman. "Could be he's dying and he's your father."

"No." He was obstinate. "He wouldn't want me. He'd hate to see me if he knew."

"There's forgiveness," insisted Mrs. Carpenter. "We got to forgive if we hope to get forgiven. Mrs. Findly, you go get those soiled clothes off and then I'm going to give you a good hot cup of coffee. Cream in it, too. We ain't had any coffee in a time. Ain't a pound to be had nowhere, Carpenter says."

"You come, Tom." His mother's eyes beseeched him. There were tears in them but he saw love there too, a relieved, almost incredulous love. He gathered her close again.

"Mama, I know he wouldn't want me. If he should rouse up it would make him worse to see me. You go clean up. I'll be here. I'll be around till he sends me off again."

"Were you badly hurt, Tom? You're so thin!"

"In my back. They couldn't get the bullet out. They ambushed us when we were crossing a river. Over by Cynthiana."

"You're going back?" she asked faintly.

"No, I can't ride any more. Not the way I'd have to ride

97

with Morgan. I told you I'd be around—unless they take me, the Yanks I mean." He was instantly sorry, seeing a look of fright come into her eyes. "I don't reckon they'll bother me as long as I'm here," he added quickly. "They know how strong Pa was for the Union."

"Morgan's been back. Tearing up things all over Kentucky," said Mrs. Carpenter. "Keeps the railroad tore up as fast as they build it back. Was you with him?"

"No, I got shot in July. I've been in a hospital down in Tennessee. They sent me back two weeks ago. I've still got the ball in my back."

"In your back?" repeated the woman.

Tom bridled a little, his face flushing. "I told you we were ambushed crossing a river. I reckon I'll hear all the rest of my life that cowards get shot in the back!"

"Calm down, son, I didn't mean anything," said the woman. "Sit down here and have some good hot coffee."

He was home again. It was the same and it would never be the same.

He had gone away a confused, angry, resenting boy. He had come back a man.

10

OCTOBER HAD BEEN A MONTH OF DROUTH WITH THE RIVERS low and the small streams dry. At Vicksburg the troops of Porter's expedition had labored frantically to cut a canal across a narrow point of land to turn the Mississippi River away from the forts of the town so that Union gunboats could pass without being under fire. But though four thousand men worked day and night the river fell faster than they could lower the bottom of the ditch. They were never able to turn the water in.

The fighting in Kentucky had been a fight for water, for the scanty pools of the fork of Salt River. For that water more than seven thousand men of the armies of Bragg and Kirby Smith had died before the Confederates were able to push the Union forces back from the river. But Bragg had not been able to hold in Kentucky and Buell's army had given up the pursuit into Tennessee, finding no subsistence for the troops in that wild, stripped mountain country.

At Harper's bank there was heated discussion of Lincoln's move in removing Buell and putting Rosecrans in his place.

"Lincoln wants to hold East Tennessee," declared Harper. "Those railroads down there are the lifeline of the Confederacy. Buell should have pushed on to Knoxville."

"An army can't march forever on empty bellies," defended Mr. Merrill, who now and then got up enough courage to speak out. "With Joe Wheeler's cavalry guarding Kirby Smith's rear Buell could have lost half his army up in those mountains. Anyway, it's coming on to rain."

It came on to rain. In the east the Rappahannock rose and the Pamunkey roared into flood. The armies of Robert E. Lee and Stonewall Jackson, of Longstreet and D. H. Hill marched and countermarched through the swamps and valleys of the Chickahominy, the Shenandoah, the Rapidan, and the Potomac, pursued and pursuing, flanking and bewildering the army of the Potomac under General George McClellan.

It came on to rain and November was cold and bleak, with freezing ground of nights and heavy fogs at dawn. Men died and women shuddered, thinking of roads deep in freezing mud and men marching with shoes worn too thin or no shoes at all, sleeping where they could on the frigid, hostile ground. Lying wounded perhaps in some lonely place, uncomforted, ignored.

It was not known in Atlanta that November of 1862, not believed in Richmond or Alabama or arrogant South Carolina that the summer tide of the Confederacy had reached its highest point. Through the dreary days of sour clouds, brief sunlight and icy air the ebb was slow but it was relentless. Except for stubborn Vicksburg the Mississippi was lost to the South, and along the eastern and southern shores the grim blockade tightened. In Kentucky the iron hand of Union control closed ruthlessly and so far as freedom or commerce was concerned the state might as well have been in the Confederacy. Louisville was the only point south of the Ohio where trade could enter without a permit. Goods shipped without clearance were subject to confiscation.

Only the staunchest Union men got permits and there were no delusions in the state about the intent of these regulations. Drive the Southern sympathizers out of business, close their shops and little industries, suppress their newspapers; and if personal grudges and tyranny crept into enforcement, this was war and let the protesters come forward and swear the oath of allegiance and in case of doubt bring along six known loyal Union men to vouch for them.

Each morning at the bank every move of the war was fought over and William lingered about, listening and keeping an eye on the glass of the front door. Sometimes Tom Findly appeared out there briefly, looking in and jerking a thumb, and then William had to invent an errand to slip out and find Tom and learn what message was to be carried to Harriet.

Tom came boldly into town now, riding his father's remaining horse or driving it hitched to a buggy. It was rumored that word had been passed to the Home Guard and provost's men by some colonel, that Tom was to be left alone. No one knew exactly who had arranged this temporary amnesty for Tom, but William had heard gossip that his father was mixed up in it some way, some kind of business deal in which this Colonel Bisbee and Tom's father were involved. Now it was important that old Tom Findly be brought back to health and cared for, even if it meant overlooking temporarily the rebel activities of old Tom's son.

William wondered how long Hume Harper's forbearance would endure if he ever found out about the notes William carried home at night and slipped into Harriet's pocket or tucked under her pillow. Certainly his father did not hear the quiet closing of the back door or the footsteps tiptoeing up the stairs much later; if he had, the explosion would have rivaled any blast an army of sappers could engineer. If his mother knew that Harriet was slipping out again of nights she gave no sign. At home she wore her usual calm, repressed demeanor but William himself was growing a little weary of being continually dragged in as a messenger. Inevitably there was going to be a row and inevitably he would be involved in it and William was certain that he had troubles enough already.

Over in Missouri across the river Hindman was reorganizing an army to take the state back for the Confederacy. Missouri was too close and there were too many nests of rebels on the Mississippi down Kentucky's western shore. Another call for Union troops had gone out and people were beginning to look hard at young William Harper.

One woman had given him her scowling attention already and remarked with no subtlety at all that William was a husky young man to be out of uniform and that certainly Grant and Sherman needed every man. Whenever his father heard any of these remarks he would come strutting out pompously to inform all and sundry that his son was already in uniform by a substitute, that he had arranged this at Lincoln's first call. But that only made William feel worse and when the cashier, Mr. Bolt, muttered "bounty boy" at him William flared into fury.

"I don't see you enlisting. You're not so old," he snapped.

Bolt's answer to that was only a dry grin. "I served my hitch in Mexico, bounty boy. Got three different kinds of dysentery down there."

It was beginning to snow a little on the raw morning when he caught Tom's signal outside the door. Reluctantly he got his overcoat and cap and signaled Bolt to let him out the rear door of the bank that was always kept carefully barred.

"You'll have to come back in at the front," grumbled Bolt, who spoke so seldom that his speech always had a kind of desiccated rasp, as though all his words had been kept away from fresh air too long. "I'm not coming away back here again. What do I tell him this time?"

"Tell him nothing," barked William.

Bolt gave him a dry, pitying look. "You tell her to stay away from that cemetery," he said, as he pushed the door shut behind the boy and shot the bolts.

Perturbed, William faced Tom Findly in the room behind a feed store that had a convenient door on an alley.

"You've got to be careful," William fumed. "Bolt—or somebody—saw you in the cemetery. If Bolt knows, it's just a question of time till Pa finds out and then all hell will break loose."

"Well, slip her the word that I can't come tonight," Tom said. "The doctor wants to bring some army surgeon down to see Pa. Some man from Boston. They think there's a bone pressing on Pa's brain and Doctor Warner says he may never come to himself unless it's removed. He thinks this army man might have some ideas about it."

"Your father's not paralyzed, is he?"

"He moves his hands a little and his eyelids twitch, but he doesn't seem to know we're there and he's so weak from that wound in his belly that sometimes we think his next breath will be his last," Tom told him.

"If he dies they might send you to Libby or Johnson's Island," William reminded him. "Your mother couldn't save you. She's a sympathizer too."

"Maybe not," said Tom amiably. "Maybe I'll walk into your house one of these days and ask your father for his daughter."

"You'd never dare!" scorned William. "And you'd never get her. Pa would send her off somewhere, east or someplace, before he'd let her marry a Confederate."

Tom smiled his slow, amiable smile. "When you grow up and fall in love, Willie, you'll learn how brave a man in love can be."

"You think I'm about ten years old, don't you? You and Harriet. You think I'm not dry behind the ears yet. Well, I'm tired of being your go-between. Get somebody else to carry your notes. I'm sick of it and I won't be mixed up in it any more."

Tom gave him a gentle poke with his fist. "Easy, boy. Don't go off half primed. I like you, but I don't like some things I've been hearing. There's a place you ought to stay away from, Willie. Morgan's regiment is heading back to Kentucky."

William felt the hated crimson flood back into his face. "I don't know what you're talking about!" he grumbled. "I reckon Morgan will lay for our bank again and Pa will make us lie down there all night in the dark and cold."

"Don't worry, Willie. I'm not talking. She's a good-looking gal but too old for you. Give Harriet the word, will you?"

"You'd better be a little careful yourself instead of handing out so much unsolicited advice," said William with young truculence. "You'd better worry about your own affairs and leave mine alone."

"I rode with Milo Nesbitt for over a year," Tom remarked, at the door. "Milo shoots mighty straight—and fast."

Harriet was out when William went home, so he scribbled a note and hid it under her pillow. She always looked there immediately he came home, and tonight when she came down to supper he knew she had found the note, for her face was like a thundercloud. As soon as Harper had settled himself by the sitting-room fire with the newspapers she shoved William into the kitchen and, passing Hessie's curious eyes, maneuvered him out to the back porch. It was cold out there with a bleak wind blowing, and William in his shirt sleeves shivered resentfully.

"What you want?" he growled.

She clutched his elbow, her nails cutting through his thin sleeve. "Did you see him? What did he say?"

"Just what I wrote down. He can't come."

"I'd like to know why? He promised. I haven't seen him in a week."

"Four days," corrected William. "I'm going in. Hessie's curious, next thing she'll blat out something. It's his father," he added in irritation. "Some army doctor's coming out to see him."

"That horrible old man—why doesn't he die?" stormed Harriet.

"Lemme go!" William pulled away and hurried back into the kitchen.

Hessie looked up from her dishpan. "She slippin' out to-night?" she asked blandly.

"Shut up! You don't know anything," flared the boy.

"I knows plenty and no good come from any of it. Your ma know too. Just trouble. Bad trouble."

"Watch yourself!" William warned in a whisper later when he passed Harriet on the stairs. "Hessie's on to you."

She gave him a furious look and ran into her room. Her door slammed and she did not come out again. William spent a dreary hour over the Louisville and Cincinnati papers, not even aware of what he was reading. His father dropped into a doze with his head tilted sideways, his round mouth pursed gently, breath issuing from it in jerky gusts. Pa looks like a catfish, William thought as he tiptoed past his mother's chair.

"I'm going downtown. Be back in a little," he said low.

Ellen put up a gentle hand, caught at his wrist. Her face took on a sharpened, anxious look. "William, don't do anything impulsive and foolish!"

"Like what?" He twisted his hand and pressed her fingers, keeping a wary eye on his father, but Harper did not stir.

"You know—the army. I know how you feel."

He let her hand fall, flicked his fingers. "Don't worry, Mama. If the army wants any more of me than they've got, they'll have to catch me."

He wanted no part of the Union army, he was certain. Not that bullying force that was treating good Kentucky people like criminals. Interfering with the elections too. He had heard that at the bank.

"There's another army," Ellen said softly. Her eyes were big and dark and tender with a kind of sorrow lost in them as dying flower petals were lost in the depths of a pool. What she mourned her son could only guess, but looking at his father, paunchy, swelled up with petty authority, his hands looking as always somehow cruel as they clasped his round stomach, William's imagination took a wild run and wound up hard against a blank wall.

Had his mother ever loved this strutting little man whose cold, too prominent eyes were veiled now by thick pale eyelids that had a vaguely reptilian look? Had there been tenderness ever, passion ever, ennobled, free of lust? That was the wall against which William's naïve spirit was brought up with a jolt. Imagination could not go further. Beyond lay something sick that he had to put out of his mind.

Here was he, and upstairs was Harriet, and he knew how children were begotten. He hadn't lived eighteen years in an adult world and grown to this thinly bearded length of body deaf and stone-blind. The thought was abruptly revolting, shaming his lady mother. He could not endure it. He gave her hand a comforting pat and tore out, closing the front door carefully, without sound.

Outside whirls of snow spinning in the thin orb of the lanterns set high on the four corners of the square made a pale pattern against a black sky. Back in the trees stood the courthouse where occasionally he was sent to deliver papers, a place he hated because there were always sly-eyed loafers about and the military being too officious and swaggering, pulling up their pistoled belts. Hated it too because there were so many spittoons in it. He had had a nightmare once of being made to clean all the spittoons in that courthouse and the place had repelled him ever since.

On opposite corners stood the bank and the Nesbitt house. The house was dark and shuttered and though his feet tingled toward it, William set them resolutely in the opposite direction. The alley back there by that rear gate was suddenly a menace. Those low, mean cabins where little fires burned and candles and tallow dips made sultry circles of light in which white eyeballs moved and dark ears listened. In the weltering muck of life on that alley lust lived and violence. Greed too and slyness. How did Tom Findly know that John Morgan's legion was returning to Kentucky?

A legion of hellhounds, men fumed on the streets. John Morgan the worst of the lot. Evading orders, riding roughshod over authority, where was he when Bragg needed him? Huns, thieves, murderers, those were Hume Harper's words for Morgan's raiders. Murderers who shot very straight and very fast. William walked fast across the street away from the Nesbitt house and did not look back.

A few men were congregated in front of a saloon and William slowed down for a moment to listen to their angry arguing. But it was all slavery again. He heard loud voices issuing from a saloon and smelled the warm, vinous odor drifting out from it, wondered how it would feel to walk in there and spend a quarter of his week's pay for a drink of whiskey? Somebody would be sure to tell his father, his mother would smell his breath and be grieved, so he put that piece of defiance out of his mind. Reluctantly he turned toward home. He might as well go to bed. There nobody, not Hume Harper nor anybody, could censor his imaginings and his dreams. They were fleshly dreams, troubled and breathless, even a little frightening, but they were his own, secret and intimate.

He passed Harriet's door on his way to his room and immediately she whispered to him out of the darkness, "William! Come in here!"

He stood uneasily at the door, not entering.

"I can't stand it, Willie. I can't stand it away from Tom. What shall I do?"

William had no chance to answer before his mother hurried up the steps.

"What is it?" Ellen was breathless. "Is she sick? I heard her moaning." She followed William to his room.

"Lovesick!" snapped the boy. "She makes me sick too."

"I'm so worried," Ellen whispered. "I want her to be happy. I don't know what to do."

"Leave her alone," growled the boy. "People have to live their own lives."

"Tom is a good enough boy—but your father—"

"Leave her alone, I say," flared William. "She's spoiled. Spoiled rotten. She wouldn't listen to anything you'd say anyway."

"But I'm her mother!" Ellen began to whimper too and William threw his coat across the room and flung himself down on the bed.

"Women!" he yelled, smothering it into his pillow. "They make me sick!"

His mother tiptoed out. He heard her tapping softly at the other door. There was no answer. After a little she went slowly down the stairs.

11

THERE HAD BEEN ONE BRIEF HOUR AT MURFREESBORO when brother met brother.

Henri Nesbitt, geared, alerted, and resigned to a long march to the west, looked up on a frozen woods lane to see his elder brother, Milo, sliding out of the saddle.

"Good Lord—Milo!" Henri dropped his canteen and blanket roll and flew to pump his brother's hand. They pawed each other affectionately and beat each other on the back, tears running unembarrassed down their cheeks. Henri scrubbed his eyes with a frayed, grimy cuff.

"Half an hour and you would have missed me!" he exclaimed. "How are you, Milo?"

"Still alive. We ride too fast for 'em. Yank bullets can't catch us." Milo thumped a hard fist on Henri's shoulder. "God, you're thin, boy! Don't they feed you in this army?"

"Now and then." Henri laughed and stood straighter. All their lives this tall elder brother had been a bit overpowering. Admiration mixed with awe and a tinge of envy had always been Henri's portion but he had never known resentment. That, he knew, was because he was so darned humble, always tearing himself down in his own estimation. "We don't break into grocery stores and rob warehouses the way you bullies do." He kept his tone light. "We have to be satisfied with robbing the Yank army."

"You did pretty well for yourselves when you got out of Kentucky, we heard," Milo remarked. "Now I hear you're off to clean up Arkansas."

"The new Department of Trans-Mississippi," Henri said. "The West is too far from Richmond and from Johnston's headquarters in Chattanooga, so they're setting up this new department across the river with Shreveport as headquarters. Kirby Smith has been made a full general and put in command and our brigade is marching west this afternoon."

"Now it's going to be mighty important not to let the Yanks take Vicksburg," Milo said thoughtfully. "They could cut us in two. Arkansas is a nasty spot, maybe you've heard?"

"We've had warning." Henri twisted the sorrel mane of

Milo's horse. "No civil government left out there much, bushwackers and thieves defying the military government on both sides. Grant's trying to hit Vicksburg from the south but he's pretty well mired up in the swamps and Porter hasn't been able to get his gunboats past the forts, so anything could happen. Only one thing is sure, none of it will be good. Are you riding out now, Milo?"

"North again." Milo pulled a twig from his mount's tail, broke it in small pieces in his fingers. "We take infantry along this time, which doesn't make the boys happy. They don't mind getting down off their horses to tear up a railroad or burn Union stores, but they hate waiting for a lot of foot soldiers to catch up."

"Our brigade is always griping about the cavalry. Goes with a war, I reckon. Kentucky!" Henri looked off, his face working a little. "Any chance you'll get home?"

"I'll try. Might manage one day. Depends on how tough the Yanks are up there. We may have to fight our way every mile. Anyway right now we're crossing the Cumberland to clean the garrison out of Hartsville."

"If you should get home and have time, ride out to Briscoe's, will you?"

Milo looked uncertain. "Look, boy, the Union is holding that country as grimly as though they had it in a bear trap. I'm going to have to sneak in after dark if I get home at all. Unless Morgan decides to take that town. He might do it and he could do it. If he does, there are a few scoundrels I'm nominating to be hung."

" 'Lish McBride for one," Henri said. "You knew that they've got Father in one of their damned prisons?"

"I got word through General Morgan. He has good informers up there. No letters in a long time."

"You've been too busy tearing up the railroads."

"They can't defeat Father no matter what they do nor

how they treat him," Milo said. "They may oppress Kentucky, Henri, they may trample on her rights, but they can never conquer what's inside a Kentuckian. They have to kill him and then two more stout fellows will spring up where his bones are planted. What's out at Briscoe's place? A girl?"

"My girl," Henri said.

"Something new! You mean little Teresa? Is she out of pigtails?"

"She's going on eighteen. You might be able to get a letter to her anyway, Milo."

"Listen, Henri, no matter how innocent a letter is it can be a dangerous thing. Maybe you know. If they took me it could involve Thad Briscoe's whole family."

"I won't mention any names. I won't even sign it. If I've got time—let me see if I can find any paper and something to write with—" Henri hurried off, returned in a moment with an old Nashville newspaper. He tore off the margin, sharpened a charred stick from a dead fire to a point for a writing implement. Only a few words but they were enough.

I love you. I think of you under the willow tree. All is well.

Milo rode away after a farewell embrace with the soiled little fragment folded inside his jacket.

December had brought snow and freezing weather and then a thaw and the road from Lebanon to the Cumberland River was a trail of pure misery. The general's plan was for the cavalry to ride ahead five miles, dismount, tie the horses and march on foot. Trailing behind through the deep cold mud churned up by the horses, the infantry would come up to the tethered mounts, mount and ride till it was again the turn of the cavalry to take back their horses. All fair enough, except that the infantry, soaked and muddy to the knees, soon found their feet freezing in the unaccustomed stirrups. They were glad enough to turn the horses back to the cavalry, but those troopers, now wet too, soon had the same wretchedness, their wet clothes freezing to their legs.

Milo lost his accustomed horse, got it back from the man who had pre-empted it only after a wrangle that came finally to blows. All down the lines there were fights, cursing, the cavalry swearing at the infantry, and the miserable men on foot waving fists and shouting abuse.

"If Morgan gets this outfit across the river," Milo remarked to a Texan as they came up to the Cumberland, "he'll end up on the other side with mighty little infantry. Those fellows are so waterlogged they'll hit the bottom like rocks if they lose their footing in that ford."

They waited at the ford for the men on foot to catch up again and Milo took Henri's little missive out and looked at it. All the charcoal writing had smeared until only the last three words were visible. Milo folded the rest of the scrap over them as carefully as he could. Small hope that little Teresa Briscoe would ever read Henri's desperately contrived message. Milo was dubious that he himself would ever have an opportunity to put it in her hand. Old Henri and a girl! It was an intriguing surprise. Milo had never considered his young brother had spirit enough for even so gentle an enterprise as falling in love.

"River's rising," grumbled the man from Texas. "What's this Hartsville that it's worth all this trouble to take it?"

"Two thousand Union men garrisoned there. We cross tonight and hit them at daylight."

"A river's bad enough but a river in the dark is pure hell!" complained Texas. "Why they got to have so many rivers, so much water and mud in this country beats me. Out where I come from if a frog wanted to travel to the next county he'd have to carry his drinking water along with him. I've drove cattle sixty miles to a water hole many a time."

"Maybe we'd better persuade Old Abe and Jeff Davis to move this war out to Texas," suggested Milo, "but when cavalry ride they've got to have water."

"Well, here we go! Horse, you keep your legs under you, you hear me? I'm a Texas boy and I don't aim to be dumped in no river. Water never did agree with my stummick."

"Eee-eeyi—yi!" the rebel yell shattered the wintry air at daylight on the north shore of the Cumberland. Wet, weary, unfed, hollow-eyed for want of sleep, John Hunt Morgan's troops swept upon the town of Hartsville like a thundering avalanche of wild men and wild horses. Whooping, firing, galloping, contemptuous of danger, fired by the impetuous recklessness of their commander, it was small wonder that the Union commander believed he was attacked by a much larger force. Within an hour he had surrendered two thousand men.

Then the dismaying order came down the ranks. Back to Tennessee! Back across that icy river, deeper now, with two thousand prisoners to guard at the crossing and a Union force from Castalian Springs marching down upon them, three times as great as Morgan's whole command.

"Thought we was headin' for Kentucky," grumbled the Texan as he kicked his tired and reluctant mount back into the frigid shallows of the river. "Thought, man, there'd be vittles up there and down this-a-way there ain't nothing but the same durned stinking mud we stirred up yesterday."

The rear-guard fighting was hot and remorseless, men slipped, ran, fell into the river and were swept away, horses went down screaming and unhorsed troopers grabbed wildly at the stirrups of mounted men. Milo got his mount safely over, the reins twisted around his knee, both hands busy with the rifle he fired back at the Union pursuers. Not even noon on this dour December day and Morgan's men had marched forty-five miles, crossed a river twice and fought a fierce battle.

Not today, Denise, Milo was thinking bitterly. And not tomorrow. Deliberately he took Henri's pathetic little note from his pocket and tossed it to the winter wind. It whirled and fell and the feet of the horses behind pounded it into the mud.

Murfreesboro again, and Milo dried out his uniform, wrapping himself in a sodden blanket while his trousers and jacket steamed, suspended on a stake over a low fire. Those pants were getting mighty thin. He could see the fire shine through the frayed fabric of the seat. Beside him the Texan was draping his own sorry apparel on a sprangly piece of brush.

"Felt a draft in the rear coming down," he grumbled, poking a finger through a hole in the cloth. "Had me some good leather breeches out home, sure wish I had 'em. When they going to issue some clothes? There was plenty good breeches on them wagons we fetched back in October."

"Blue," Milo reminded him. "Ride out in new blue breeches and our own boys would take a shot at us."

"Wouldn't stay blue long. Mud-color, that's the color of an army, Yank or Johnny. What'd we capture 'em for, anyway? Just to keep the Yanks from wearin' 'em? Let 'em ride with a cold rump on a cold saddle, same as us."

"Some of the boys drew some of those pants," Milo said. "They were made out of shoddy. Poor stuff. The Yanks up north are making money out of this war too, I reckon, for all the noble speeches they make."

"Like that rotten beef they sent up here from Mobile. Maggots had 'em a whole town built in it—courthouse

114

even. Only get one war in a lifetime, generally," gloomed Texas. "Wars cost money and somebody's got to get a hunk of it. What's all the excitement down at headquarters?"

"Things happening." Milo brushed mud from a dangling sleeve with a whisk contrived of dry grass. "Morgan's been promoted to a Brigadier-General and day after tomorrow he's getting married."

"Thought he was married?"

"Wife died—or maybe she left him. Not sure which. Anyway he's marrying a Miss Ready. General Bragg's coming to the wedding with all his staff and Lieutenant-General-Bishop Polk is performing the ceremony. The girl's mighty pretty, the boys say. Need a currycomb on this job!" He dug with angry thumbnail at the mud encrusting his pants legs.

"What good is a wife when you're in the army? You've got a wife. How long since you've seen her?"

"One year and five months," answered Milo, grimly.

"Ain't right. Ain't healthy. Risky too. Woman gets lonesome. They got feelings same as us. Along comes some feller, he ain't off fighting, in the mud, lousy and dirty, hair too long, whiskers all over him. Can't blame 'em."

"Not my wife."

"You hope. We going to see the general married?"

"We are not. We ride out of here in the morning, heading north again. A Christmas raid. General will catch up with us a few days later."

"Let that mud dry and it will come off easy," advised Texas. "Question in my mind is, do we get to Kentucky on this raid or do we turn around and ford some dum river back again? Trouble with this here army they can't make up their mind where they're going. Morgan knows he's going where the next notion takes him. Orders don't mean a thing to Morgan. Everybody's speculatin' who's going to head up the Confederate cavalry, Morgan or old man Forrest or that boy out of West Point, Joe Wheeler. It's a safe bet it won't be Morgan. He's too independent to suit them fellers over at Richmond or General Bragg."

"He licks the Yanks," remarked Milo. "Joe Wheeler's a good cavalryman."

"Yeah. You take General Bragg now, he don't know for sure where he's going either. March the pants off an army, fight a little battle, march 'em back a thousand miles to this place. Know why Bragg keeps coming back here to this part of Tennessee? There ain't no vittles left here but he always comes back because the water is good for his kidney complaint."

"He has a sick wife here, that could be a reason."

"Reckon when Morgan gets him a new wife he'll be dragging us back here every other Sunday. Just one thing I've got to say, my pants won't take it. I wish I could find me a good piece of leather. I'd put a patch on them that would turn weather, but there ain't any leather either or this regiment wouldn't be tramping around barefoot half the time! Well, Kentucky, here we come again." The Texan shook out his damp clothing, thrust his legs into his worn trousers. "Anybody up there has got a rooster or a jug of homemade liquor, I'll invite myself to Christmas dinner."

Christmas, and General Braxton Bragg had visions of spending it with his beloved wife and some friends. But out of Nashville, forty thousand strong, came General Rosecrans, lately put in command of the Union Army of Tennessee, to precipitate the bloody slaughter at Stone's River. There on the second day of the New Year Breckenridge's Fourth Kentucky, the "Orphan Brigade," lost almost half its men within an hour. Twenty-three thousand men died in that battle, and after three days of fighting no one knew who had won. Bragg settled the matter during the night by withdrawing to the south, taking up winter quarters at

116

Tullahoma, blocking Rosecrans out of Chattanooga, but there was deep mourning in Kentucky for eighteen hundred boys lying dead in that river-bottom meadow of Tennessee.

Milo Nesbitt heard it everywhere as he rode through the wintry country; heard it and felt it, the resenting, the stony withdrawal that moved into women's eyes, and made men's faces turn bitter when they saw the uniform—any uniform. War was the enemy that winter in Kentucky.

"The Unions is bad but Morgan is worse," snapped a blacksmith whom Milo had known for years and had finally persuaded to shoe his horse. "Did I do right, Milo Nesbitt, I'd turn you in to Burbridge or Boyle. Don't you know you got no business riding up here alone? How come you ain't been shot yet? All the raiding and destruction Morgan's done up this way, even his own kin have turned against him."

"I'm heading home. Furlough," Milo told him. "The general got married and it made him softhearted. So he gave me three days to go see my wife and mother. I ride at night, but this is a job that needed daylight, so I had to risk it."

"Knew your father well," stated the smith between clanging blows of his hammer. "Judge was a fair man. Always shod his horses for him and set the tires of his buggy."

"I know. That's why I dared stop here. But I'll lie hid till dark before I head into town."

"You do that. And let me hide your horse too. I've got three turned out down in my swamp timber. Morgan comes through, everybody hides their horses. Reckon I ain't very smart to tell you where I've got stock hid, forgot for a minute that you was one of Morgan's raiders."

"Your horses are safe and if I can manage it I'll see they

stay safe," Milo promised. "Now how am I going to pay you? I've got nothing but Confederate money."

"Can't use it, not even to paper the backhouse. Don't want it on my place. You pay me when the war's over. Reckon you'll get back to practicing law then and if there's as many mean folks left around as there are now I'm likely to kill somebody and need defending. War can't last forever. Grant takes Vicksburg, I say that will end it. Hadn't ought to have started it, no way. South Carolina! Loud noise and big brags and now what do they do? Won't send their men out of the state to fight, say they got to keep 'em to defend Charleston. My grandson gets killed down there in Tennessee and he wasn't but seventeen. That'll be four bits you'll owe me, Milo. Anything you need, get it out of your gear and I'll hide the saddle in my corncrib."

Thin snow was whitening the ground and coating the roofs with silver when Milo leaped the back fence and crept through the garden to tap on the kitchen door of the Nesbitt house. In the darkness of the back hall Amalie and Denise hurled themselves, weeping, into his arms.

Back in the shadow someone brought a candle and Milo, over the top of Denise's head, glared.

"Who are you, fellow?" he demanded.

"Why, my love, my angel, this is William!" Denise cried. "Our dear William who has been such a friend, such a comfort."

"William Harper, Milo. You know me—Henri's friend," William said.

"But you were just a little boy when I went away," exclaimed Milo, putting out of his mind a bit slowly the memory of the Texas trooper's observations about lonely wives. "You were just a gangly brat."

"You've been gone quite a long time," remarked William, putting the candle on the table. "I'll go now, Mrs.

Nesbitt. I just wanted to be sure you were all right. But would you mind telling me, Milo—is Morgan likely to raid our bank tonight? I've lain down there two nights already and I'm getting mighty sleepy."

"I can't tell you where the general is, but he won't raid your bank tonight," laughed Milo, pulling Denise close to him again. "But—if he did, William, it would take more than you to stop him!"

"Oh, sure, I know that. The trouble is my father doesn't."

"Well, get out of here now, William, and give me a chance to kiss my wife. I haven't had a kiss in more than a year."

They were locked again in a passionate embrace before William closed the back door and slid out unhappily, making his accustomed way through the bushes to the alley.

He felt a little sick. He glared at the sullen cabins, their blank, dark windows, and thought of the people sleeping inside, and that made him sicker. Back there, Denise's bright head nuzzled into the collar of that uniform coat! He made himself stop thinking because thinking was suddenly horrible.

He marched home and found his father in a fury with his overcoat buttoned tight, his hat sitting on his round head.

"About time, young man!" he snarled. "Get that pistol and look to the priming and follow me down to the bank."

"You should get some sleep!" worried Ellen, very pale. "Both of you—exhausted. You should sleep."

"And let that scalawag loot the people's money from the bank? As he did at Mt. Sterling?" shouted Harper. "Get moving, William!"

"There's no need to go, Pa," said William smugly. "There won't be any raid on the bank tonight. I know."

"So you know? All at once you know! And how do you

know, young man?" Harper was popeyed, his jowls crimson.

"I know, Pa. Morgan's miles away from here. Busting up a railroad someplace," William improvised desperately. "Anyway, if he wanted to come and loot our bank, we couldn't stop him. I know—" he added, head high, his eyes impudent. "Now and then I know something—and it's so!"

12

THE CHURCH SMELLED DUSTY AND REMINISCENT OF ALL THE people who had prayed there, grieved there and coughed and breathed there. Motes danced in the slanting gilt and ruby beams that sifted through a high, colored window. There were signs on the pew where Hume Harper proposed to sit that a mouse had been there. A paper fan had a corner chewed to bits and Harper brushed the litter off impatiently before he sat down beside Ellen.

Ellen wore a gray veil that made her skin sallow and murky and behind it her eyes were drained and swollen. A pity, Harper was thinking, for his opinion was that Ellen's eyes were her only claim to beauty, now that her hair was fading and little folds of flesh sagged under her chin.

Standing on the pulpit steps, his long-tailed coat catching the sun so that the green slickness of it was dismally apparent, the minister droned on and the young couple standing so white-faced and nervous before him began to be tremulous. From where he sat Harper could see Harriet's hands shaking.

Some kind of a homily about the responsibilities of matrimony, all stupid and superfluous in Hume Harper's mind. Holy Matrimony! And what was holy about a sickening business like this? Get it over. Get it behind them. At least it was some consolation that he wasn't sitting here in the Presbyterian church where he was the leading deacon, holding a shotgun. At least Harriet had saved him that final humiliation. He would not concede that Tom Findly had been man enough to come up to scratch without coercion. He would concede that fellow nothing.

The nuptial pair were kneeling now and Ellen bowed her head over her clasped hands. A sick little sob shook her and Harper reached a hand and laid it reprovingly on her wrist. Beside his mother William cleared his throat and raked the floor, shifting his big feet. A hymnbook fell with a thud and the minister blinked and lost a breath in the middle of the blessing.

Then it was over and Harriet turned and was almost running down the aisle, clutching at Tom Findly's arm. They looked straight ahead, ignoring Marcia Findly, huddled uneasily across the aisle in her faded country clothes, ignoring the Harper family. The minister came down the steps and began shaking hands, murmuring congratulatory remarks that got brief uneasy answers from these witnesses to the marriage. Hume Harper saw Marcia Findly rummaging in a shabby purse.

"I'll take care of this," he said loftily, laying a crumpled greenback in the minister's hand. He did not wait for Marcia's thanks but hurried Ellen quickly out of the church. Outside the sudden sun of May beat down on the quiet street where a few people went indifferently about their own affairs. A half block away waited the Findly buggy with Tom and Harriet already seated in it. They waited for Marcia to catch up with them, then drove rapidly away.

Hume Harper watched the buggy swing around a corner and an animal snarl of pure rage welled up in his throat.

"Well, there she goes!" he snapped, his grip on his wife's arm so suddenly taut with fury that she gave a little strangled cry. "There goes your daughter!" Harper would not have admitted that he was fighting an agony in his own throat, a pain that pressed upward making his chin harden, jowls congested with blood under his tight collar. "There goes the fine wedding you've been planning on for years! Let's get home."

William was already untying the Harper mare, hitched to a chestnut tree beside the church. He unsnapped the tie strap from the bit, looped it over his hand, walked around the carriage and got in, turning it, cutting so short that the wheels rasped on the cramp iron. He drove out to the street, stopped and waited, his shoulders slumped forward, shoulder blades riding out high like wings through his coat.

Harper helped Ellen in, squeezed in beside her, his plump buttocks pressing painfully against the wrought-iron supports of the leather top.

Ellen spoke for the first time in hours. "Do you want William to drive you back to the bank, Mr. Harper?"

"No," said Harper, "I'll go home."

"I put her clothes in his buggy," William said. "I reckon they'll go straight out to Findly's place."

"Of course," said Ellen quietly, "they couldn't leave that poor old man alone for long."

"Fine honeymoon!" snorted his father. "I took your mother to New York and Canada and Niagara Falls."

"There was no war then, Mr. Harper," his wife reminded him.

"Niagara Falls is still there," he grumped back.

"Costs money," remarked William. "Sure you don't want to go to the bank, Pa?"

"I said I wanted to go home," testily. "You heard me."

"Yes, sir." William flirted a fly off the mare's rump with the whip. "I thought more people would come to see Harriet married."

"They spared us that, at least," remarked Harper. "You must have managed to keep your mouth shut."

"My Lord, I didn't know it myself till Mama told me this morning!" protested the boy. "I knew they were mighty sweet on each other but I didn't know they were in such a tearing hurry to get married."

Hume Harper felt the dig of his wife's elbow in his ribs. This is an innocent, said the jabbed reminder, he doesn't know. Keep quiet. So Harper said no more, gnawing on his anger and pain, letting it choke and blind him.

This was his town. These somnolent streets, eddying warmth under the widespread trees. Around that corner was his bank with the new wide window and safe vault, the iron safe that had had to come all the way from Pittsburg by water and mule-drawn wagons. There were his two copper-barred grilles and in the safe were mortgages on most of the good farms in the county. Old Tom Findly's place for one. Interest paid up, however. He had looked that up last night and felt foiled in a ruthless desire for vengeance, only to be halted and baffled by Ellen's eyes. Eyes that had challenged him for the first time since he could remember, dared him to make trouble for the Findlys.

This was his town, he was the most important person in it, he could tell himself without egotism. Down there by the North Fork of Licking River was a turning mill where hickory and dogwood were lathed out for spindles and shuttles and items like chair legs, potato mashers and rolling pins. Now the mill had a good contract for wagon spokes for the army. A profitable contract. Making the right friends in the commissary department had been another piece of his own shrewdness.

The mare trotted through the square and the dirty greenish windows of the courthouse caught the afternoon sun and winked with a beer-bottle glint. On one corner of the square was the bank and on the corner opposite the Nesbitt house. Judge Nesbitt was still in that Union prison. It was said the two women stayed on there alone. Needed paint, Harper observed, needed new shingles and bricks to top the jagged mouths of four chimneys.

The yard was a bit slatternly too, boxwoods unpruned, vines swarming up the peeling pillars. Harper studied the house speculatively. Two Nesbitt sons in the Confederate army, nothing heard from them since the first of the year. Killed like enough, both of them. If the judge lives through his imprisonment he'll return an old, broken wreck of a man, Harper was thinking. All his fortune sunk in this unstable Confederacy. That was a good business site. That trunkful of Confederate bonds the judge's wife was rumored to have wouldn't help her any if he, Hume Harper, suddenly decided to foreclose the neglected mortgage.

That elegant French wife of the judge had been aloof and proud, swishing her silk skirts to Mass in the mornings, nodding coolly to passersby. Harper wondered if Amalie Nesbitt had holes in her shoes now. If she had, she could patch them with some of those heavy green papers bearing the red seal of the Treasurer of the Confederate States of America. A brick block would look good on that corner. Harper ran his tongue over his lips and could fairly smell the raw mortar that would lay up those bricks. The Harper building.

His own house pleased him. It was a smug-looking house with a prim veranda, new white paint and bright green blinds kept closed across the front so that the summer sun would not rot the long lace curtains. The narrow lawn was raked and clipped and every shrub pruned to a stolid roundness. William turned the mare in at the drive and she stopped from habit squarely beside the mounting block.

Ellen looked up at the house as she got down, her chin quivering a little. "It's going to be so empty now!" she choked, dabbing at her eyes, tangling her handkerchief in her veil.

"Nonsense," clipped her husband. "You still have a husband and a son."

He unlocked the side door with a heavy brass key, let Ellen pass him, and turned back to give his son orders.

"Water her and give her a quart of oats. Hang that harness up properly, then you go back to the bank. They'll be closing in an hour, and you have all your work to do."

"Yes, sir," said William woodenly. If Pa didn't notice that he still had his good suit on, why should he remind him?

Harper entered the dining room where a polished oak table was centered with a silver caster and crossed the narrow hall to the big bedroom at the back of the house. Ellen was already brushing the dust off her bonnet, putting it back in the bandbox. The huge bed with looming black walnut headboard had stiffly starched shams over the pillows, embroidered with grapes and leaves. The counterpane was fluffy and white and Ellen's gray gloves lay upon it, looking somehow small and helpless, like limp imploring hands.

She began getting out of her gray dress. It had been made wide for hoops but she could not bring herself to bother with hoops today, so it hung lankly about her feet. She pulled it over her head and, turning, looked at her husband. He had taken off his heavy cutaway churchgoing coat and was removing his wallet from the inner pocket before he hung the coat carefully in the wardrobe. His high, cramping collar came off next and he went to the washstand, poured water into the bowl and scrubbed the sweat from his neck, rubbing the red crease hard where his chin was chafed.

"Well, out with it!" he ordered abruptly, tossing the towel at the rack. "When is this disgrace going to overtake us? Just how soon are we going to see sly grins on people's faces and hear them snickering behind our backs?"

Ellen hung her dress in the wardrobe, buttoned on a long challis wrapper, went about putting her gloves away.

"I don't know what you're talking about, Mr. Harper," she said nervously.

He glared at her. "I still say I should have shot the scoundrel."

"What good would that have done?" she cried, her eyes desperate.

"You knew it all the time. You knew she was seeing him. You must have known it. Even if he never set foot inside this house. He knew better. He knew I'd boot him into the street."

"Tom's not a bad boy, Mr. Harper. He's not really bad at all. He is taking care of their place and his old father and he's not strong from that wound."

"Shot in the back. Ha!"

"Crossing a river. They were ambushed. The Union soldiers were behind them."

Harper opened his collar box with a snap, got out a clean rigid collar and slapped it with a throttling movement around his neck. Abraham Lincoln had made flying-wing collars and puffy cravats fashionable but Abraham Lincoln was president of the United States. He could wear what he pleased. Home-washed shirts, some people said. Hume Harper disdained to ape any politician. He liked his collars high and hard and bullied their one servant, Hessie, into starching his shirts like iron. His pink jaws rode the linen ridge arrogantly and if the pressure made him look a bit popeyed and congested at least he felt adequate and dignified.

Ellen drooped enough for a whole family. No matter how much whalebone and crinoline stiffened a garment, Ellen softened it, molded it to her own gentleness. Her hair was always curling softly away from pins, chignons or combs. Even when she wore hoops they could not hide the fact that she had practically no hips at all. As for a bust, it was nonexistent. She wore ruffles over her chemise hopefully but even these softened eventually. No fiber in Ellen, Harper was thinking. No steel, no framework of decision in her mind. If there were they might not now be faced with the dismal certainty of a scandal. Since the beginning of time there had been sly watchers, male and female, remembering dates, counting on their fingers.

"I was figuring that eventually I would have to take over that Findly farm. When the old man dies, anyway," he said now. "Old Tom has always kept his payments up, but with that slack young no-good running the place now they'll never be able to meet the interest let alone cut down the principal. It's a good bluegrass farm and any man with gimp in him could make it pay. Old Tom built it up from that first little forty-acre piece to a substantial plantation, but I've always included the whole place in a lien to protect the bank. Now it will go to destruction likely, land grown to sprouts and fences tumbling down."

"Why do you want more land, Mr. Harper? You've taken over two farms already."

"Land lasts. It won't die like cattle or collapse like stocks. There's only so much of it. There'll never be any more." He flirted his cravat into a snug knot.

127

"But you couldn't take the Findlys' place away from them now and put your own daughter out of a home. Think how people would judge you!"

"He thought of that, likely—that young scoundrel."

"But you're an important person, and a respected deacon in the church. You can't afford to do something unworthy of you."

She could always appeal to his vanity. It was her only weapon. She had never had any other, not love, no pleas for consideration, no reminder of duty. She had early worn these blunt against the sublime armor of his conceit, been frustrated and baffled by the failure of every appeal to reason, so that she had come to depend on flattery to soften his hardnesses. She knew that he was aware of her tactics and that her success with them made him hate her a little, but also hate himself more because her system worked. She had seen him brace himself against it, determined to provoke her to some outrageous outburst, something that would justify him in shouting a refusal, but always in the end his spirit failed.

"My own daughter concerned herself very little about me." He glared at his reflection in the mirror. "Or about you—her mother. Or about decency or the speech of the people. How the devil could she—"

"I don't know!" Ellen sighed, sinking on the edge of the bed, her face in her hands. "She didn't tell me anything, only that she was going to marry Tom Findly and marry him right away—and when I argued with her she looked at me —pityingly, I thought—and told me it was no use to raise objections because she *had* to marry Tom. She did say that she was sorry she was disappointing us, but that love was enough for her and that nothing any of us could say would make the least difference."

"Love!" The word was a snort.

There was a picture of small Harriet in his mind, the little girl he had been proud of in his remote and inhibited fashion. Soft fluff of brown hair, not really reddish like her mother's but a fruity autumn color with purple high lights in the wave of it like the oaks in late October. Her rounded face had been shaped like his own and her expressions were like his, and he liked to think that she had inherited his strength of character too. But that strength had obviously sharpened into defiance.

She had faced him coldly at the last when his wrath had exploded so furiously that it had dismayed even himself.

"There's no use talking, Pa." Behind a frigid and excluding wall she had withdrawn herself from the impact of his anger. "It's done and I ought to be sorry and ashamed but I'm not. I'm marrying Tom and I'm not going to let you talk to him or go near him because you'd be abusive and after all the fault is mine. You can be thankful that Tom is willing to marry me at all."

"Thankful!" Harper had feared for an instant that he would burst a blood vessel. "Keep him away from me! Keep him far away before I wring his rotten, cowardly neck! Anyway you needn't be uneasy, he hasn't got the guts to speak to me."

There was another matter that fed the blaze of Harper's rage. Old Tom Findly out there, unable to move, muttering only incoherencies, people said—and what had become of the bonds old Tom was to buy and hold for Hume Harper and Colonel Bisbee? Harper had fended the military away from young Tom, even arranged for Tom to have a pass in the hope that the old man would be kept alive and come to his senses, but now there was still uncertainty—and on top of all that irritation this disgusting impromptu wedding! He took his silk hat out of its box, dusted it on his sleeve, clapped it on his head.

"May as well go out and face it," he told his wife.

"No one knows—yet," Ellen said hopefully.

"They will. By tomorrow. A scrambled-up, makeshift wedding. How keep a thing like that quiet in this town? They're probably talking already."

"Even William doesn't know," said Ellen.

"Ha!" snapped Hume Harper.

He stalked out and marched through the front door, closing it firmly. An impatient, bumptious little man with his head high.

Ellen Harper looked after him, her lips drawing straight and gray. Hume Harper of the bank, of the Harper mill, the Harper farms, the bonds and mortgages. Of gold in steel boxes, the gain of torturing war, and he did not know that his wife stood now beside her bed, hating him.

It came to her abruptly, standing there, that she had hated him for a long time. And it also came to her with a sick, sinking certainty that if he did know it would not greatly matter to him.

He had collected antagonisms for a long time, gloated over them, over the power they gave him. The armor of his vanity was scaly-hard against shafts of resentment and hatred. Ellen could almost see the projection of her own bitter detestation breaking off short against that metal aloofness as weakly as a thrown feather.

13

*M*AY WAS A WANTON, MAY WAS DELIRIOUS WITH BLOOM and growth over all the country.

Even in the wilderness tangles along the Rappahannock and the Rapidan where Robert E. Lee's sixty thousand Confederate troops faced twice their number; the proud, seasoned, boasted Army of the Potomac under General Joe Hooker. Even there little flowers pushed up through the undergrowth to die crushed beneath the pounding feet of Stonewall Jackson's tirelessly marching brigades.

May was hope and May was tragedy. For Hooker confusion and frustration, his great army divided and mauled, retreating baffled across the fords to "cover Washington." With the Southern cavalry under gay impudent J. E. B. Stuart circling their camp, the banjo player Sweeney thumping out an accompaniment to the cavalry's taunting song: *"Old Joe Hooker, Won't You Come Out of the Wilderness?"*

And for Lee there was tragic anguish. At Chancellorsville Stonewall Jackson died in lingering agony, after being mistakenly shot by a North Carolina brigade that had come late into battle.

May was a time of desperate struggle for Grant and Sherman, searching for a dry place on which to stand an army, a solid bit of ground to station artillery to conquer the insolent forces of Pemberton and silence Pemberton's forts at Vicksburg.

And on Pea Ridge, in Arkansas, Henri Nesbitt, promoted to sergeant, stood by helplessly and watched commissary officers condemn a wagonload of pork and beef, desperately needed rations for a regiment, because one barrel spouted fermenting brine when a hatchet was slashed into it.

"Ain't all them rations bad," grumbled a trooper standing by. "They got them spoiled barrels picked so they can knock open the right one. Plenty of food there, good food too, but will we get it? No! Them commissary robbers will hold it out for themselves and get rich sellin' our grub. You want to get rich in this here Jeff Davis's army you got to get into the commissary."

On the Findly farm, May was green peas showing above the dark soil, little chickens running frightened by the approach of the buggy, and looming behind tall maple trees the square, uncompromising Findly house.

It was a Yankee-looking house, Harriet was thinking as the buggy jigged up the lane approaching it on this her wedding day. But it was essentially a good house, the chimneys narrow and tall, not vast and extravagant needing loads of logs to feed them. The porch was narrow too and uninviting, implying that no idle woman wasted time rocking in the sun when there was work to do on old Tom Findly's farm. Harriet got down from the buggy a bit numbly, walked on nerveless feet to the back door following this complete stranger, her mother-in-law. Tom drove away toward the sheds without a backward look. He was, Harriet suspected, nervous and a little frightened too.

Marcia held the door open, her eyes holding an eager, welcoming look.

"I've always thought about the day I'd open the door for

Tom to fetch in a new wife," she said, cheerfully. "Now I want you to know you're welcome and I'll do the best I can to make you feel at home. I came here young to this house myself and everything was mighty strange—and hard too. I was plantation-raised and I'd never done for myself much, my folks owning a right smart lot of Nigras."

"Thank you," said Harriet, trying to be gracious. "I'm awfully ignorant too. We had Hessie and she would never let me into her kitchen. I'll try not to be too much of an exasperation, Mrs. Findly."

"Now nobody can do more than their best," agreed Marcia, briskly, "and you mustn't let Mr. Findly upset you. He had a bad time after those night riders shot and injured him and he's just coming to himself, mighty slow. He's contrary, he can't talk right yet and I have to wait on him hand and foot, so it's agreeable to me to have you here for company and encouragement. Tom does his best but he won't ever be able to work real hard again."

"I know," said Harriet, still standing at the door and looking back to where Tom had disappeared into the shed.

"His father held it against him because he went with Morgan," went on her mother-in-law. "Mr. Findly held it against me too that I was for secession, but I still say we had the right, and they haven't beaten us yet." She took off her old-fashioned bonnet and gently smoothed the faded ribbons. "Now, you come along with me and I'll show you your room. Tom will fetch in your things when he gets the horse turned out. We've had to manage poorly since they burned our barn and hay and oats. I don't know when Mr. Findly will be able to take hold and build the barn back."

Harriet walked into the kitchen, where the iron stove still was warm, with a heavy iron kettle simmering upon it. She braced herself rigidly and her face was very white.

133

"Do you hate me, Mrs. Findly?" she asked abruptly. "Do you hate me for marrying Tom—the way we did?"

Marcia flicked dust from her bonnet. "Why no," she said slowly, "I couldn't hate you. It could have been done differently, is all I see. A girl raised the way you were raised—of course men are men and nobody knows that better than a woman who's married one. It's just kind of hard to reconcile in a person's mind. But now it's done and I'm thankful my son was honorable enough to accept his responsibility and do what he knew he ought to do. It was the war that changed all you young people, I reckon. Violence changes people. Maybe they feel they have to snatch at anything they want right quick before war destroys it. You come along now and quit worrying. We'll get along fine."

The stairs were narrow and steep, uncarpeted, the walls of gray plaster that had never been papered or painted. Above were two rooms and Marcia opened the door of the south chamber where two narrow windows looked out across a meadow and a sprouting field of corn. In here the walls were gray and cold-looking too and the bare floor, painted gray, had one small rag rug before a heavy oak bed with a calico quilt spread on it.

There was a pine wardrobe in one corner, a washstand of pine with an ironstone pitcher and bowl, a round-topped trunk, one hickory chair with a seat of splints, and nothing else.

"You brought your trunk, didn't you?" asked Marcia patting up the pillows. "You ought to have a looking glass in here. And a chest for your pretties. I declare, it's been so long since I've seen any young-looking clothes! Mr. Findly is a good honorable man, but he was raised by a German grandmother up east and they're mighty thrifty, hard-working people up where he came from. Maybe I can manage a looking glass out of the egg money. We've just got used to handling money, Tom and me, since Mr. Findly was stricken. When you haven't had a penny in your hands for years it's slow getting the habit of spending again. But of course when Mr. Findly comes to himself he'll manage everything. He always has."

And then we will leave, Harriet was thinking. Tom said he would never stay with his father running the place again. She heard Tom on the stairs now, stumbling up slowly, under the weight of her small trunk. She hurried to help him but Marcia put out a restraining hand.

"You'd better not," she advised. "You'll have to remember not to lift or strain or reach your arms high. Wait, Tom, I'll help you."

The two of them were alone in the room after a little and Tom stood off, looking fondly at his bride, uncertain whether to take her in his arms or respect her withdrawn attitude, oddly mingled of a judicial look of weighing him in her mind and a dutiful kind of affection.

"Well, we're here," he said awkwardly, reaching a hand to give her a brief caress. "You're married, Mrs. Findly. And somehow"—his face tightened a little and the lines that pain had cut at either side of his young mouth deepened—"you look like you didn't like it very much."

"Oh, I do!" insisted Harriet hurriedly. "It's just—it's all strange. Give me time, Tom."

"We've got a lifetime." Tom grinned. "You wouldn't want to give your husband a kiss, I reckon?"

She stood on tiptoe to kiss his cheek. He pulled her close and kissed her hard, so that she struggled to free herself, stood back trying to smile and not doing too well at it. "I'm sorry," she stammered. "I guess I just wasn't ready—"

He could have said many things then, she realized with a flare of panic. He could have reminded her that she had

135

been ready enough at other times, but there was nothing of remembering in his face, only a tinge of anxiety.

"I love you, baby," he told her brusquely. "Just you keep on remembering that."

"I will. And I love you too, Tom." She had taken off her little chip bonnet with the bobbing rose at the back and was looking about for a place to put it. "Tom—do we have to see him? Right now?"

He hunched a shoulder. "Might as well get it over. He probably won't know who you are or why you're here. He tries to say words but most times they don't make any sense, then he gets mad and yells but you don't have to mind. Just remember he's a sick old man with not much hope of being any better. I'm the one you married—not Pa or Ma, but me —little Tommy. Find room to put your things?"

"I guess I'll just have to leave everything in the trunk. Your mother said we ought to have a chest and a mirror, but it won't be for always, will it, Tom? When he's all right we can have our own home, can't we?"

"We'll think about that when the time comes. You come on down. I've got to feed and milk and pretty soon Ma will be fixing supper. You can see Pa after supper. Don't let him scare you. He can't move and he doesn't know what he's saying usually."

He went out and she heard him limping down the stairs and turned mechanically to putting her dress and petticoats away in the narrow wardrobe. The flaring crinolines had to be pressed out of shape so the door would shut. Like Harriet Harper Findly, being shoved into a bleak place where she seemed not to fit at all, she thought with a troubling touch of bitterness.

When she had put on a plain cotton dress she went downstairs. Marcia Findly was stirring something in a pot on the stove.

"I don't reckon you know how to make biscuits?" she asked, casually, her calm tone implying that she would not be dismayed by a negative answer.

"I never did," Harriet replied. "You could show me. I guess I ought to know, I ought to know everything."

"Now with all the Nigras getting free everybody's got to learn to do for themselves," remarked Marcia. "Over there's an apron. The bread bowl's in that flour bin. The sifter too. You'll have to fetch lard from the wellhouse. That's through the door there and the lard in a crock with a cloth on top. Put the cloth back tight. Take those two cups, those old ones. I keep them on purpose. Get some buttermilk too out of the churn. Half a cup of lard and a cupful of buttermilk. One thing"—she smiled—"anything you cook in your fix will turn out good."

Harriet had never heard that country superstition but her ignorance of all the aspects of pregnancy was complete, reared as she had been in the inhibited atmosphere of her class. Nice girls did not know such things, Ellen had always said. Not till they were married. Before that they were to assume that babies arrived in a doctor's black bag or were found under cabbages. Of the treacherous fire that could flare in her own blood, stirring her to madness of which she had never dreamed, she had had no warning at all. Afterward she had been stunned and incredulous, loath to believe that such a thing could happen to her.

In secret she admitted that for a brief time it had been thrilling and somehow right and lovely to love Tom so much that she could forget everything that belonged to being a lady and her mother's daughter. But now the thrill was gone and how had it died so soon? Now there was only this inner flinching that made her draw away from Tom's caress and dread to look at that very clean bed. And this was marriage and it would go on forever. This was being a mother and it was a frightening, sickening business.

Smells revolted her. In the cool wellhouse she had to fight nausea as she dug into the crock of lard. The buttermilk helped a little. She drank a cupful and calmed her turbulent stomach. She was flat still and slim-waisted and her breasts were small and round and virginal but she had had a shock when this morning before her wedding her mother had folded a wide-girthed wrapper and laid it in Harriet's trunk.

"You'll need this before winter," Ellen had said.

"That big thing?"

"A child is growing in your body. You haven't told me but I know. There has to be room." Ellen was crimson with embarrassment. "You were both big babies. William weighed ten pounds. Then when he was seven he got sickly and never did get fat again."

"You didn't tell me," reproached Harriet, faintly. "You didn't tell me anything. I had to find out the best way I could."

Ellen tears had glistened again. "They'll blame me," she choked. "They'll say I'm not a good mother."

"Oh, you were! You mustn't blame yourself, Mama. I reckon I was just born bad. Anyway I'll be married."

Folding the nauseating grease into the flour at Marcia's direction, Harriet nursed the slim comfort that if her own mother had failed her, Tom's mother had failed too. This was not something she had done alone. Never need any of them imply by word or look that all the shame had been hers!

"Mr. Findly won't like me," she said to Marcia, abruptly, as she struggled with the damp, soggy dough. "What do I do with this now? It's all sticking to my fingers."

"Put some flour on it and press it out flat. Then you roll

it and cut the biscuits with that baking-powder can that's in the bin. Make them thick, Tom likes thick biscuits." Marcia flipped over some fat pork in the frying pan. "Mr. Findly could be a changed man when he gets over this," she went on. "He hated Tom for taking up with the South. They had some real hot arguments about it. But I took the stand that Tom was grown a man and every man had a right to his own belief. Then after Tom was wounded his father said it served him right but I told him it wasn't justice. How old are you, Harriet? I'm going to call you Harriet and you might as well call me Ma—Tom does."

"I will be twenty in September."

"I figured you for twenty. You've got a quiet look in your eyes, not like a real young girl."

"I grew up in a quiet home. I had a martinet for a father, Mrs. Findly."

"I know. I know your father—that's why, well I was a little surprised when Tom told me your trouble. But might be that a stern father breeds rebellion in his children. Tom's father has always been a mighty severe man. Now my father spoiled us all rotten, but those were easy times before the war tore up everything."

Living was a bit grim in the Findly house and though Marcia was fair and kind and Tom anxiously devoted, Harriet wondered if she would ever feel at home. Her one visit to the shrunken, dreadful old man who lay so flat in the bed in that lower room was an ordeal that made her shudder to remember. His body seemed so small and dry under the sheet that was his only cover. One eye was made grotesque by an angry scar that ran from the brow down to his cheek and both eyes were sunken but they blazed at her with impatient fury that he struggled to make audible.

"This is your new daughter, Pa, and she's a radical Yankee like you," Tom had volunteered in placation. But the old man had not responded, only the blaze of anger in his reptilian eyes.

"He knows what he wants to say," said Harriet. "That he can't say it makes him mad." And if he could get the words out they would be horrible, she was thinking. She stood calmly, with terrific effort, but her legs shivered so they would hardly hold her up and her tightened hands turned to ice. Back in their room she gave way to a nervous fit of crying, burrowing her head into the pillow and ignoring all Tom's anxious efforts to comfort her.

"I have to tend Pa and he hates it," Tom was trying to explain. "There's a clot on his brain or something. He doesn't mean a thing when he yells at you."

But later when he went downstairs Harriet heard Tom's mother explaining that it was Harriet's "condition" that made her so upset. Then panic gripped her as Marcia's voice ran on. "Don't take her in there again. He frightened her and she might mark her baby."

Like a blow it came to her that this child, who was hardly a reality to her as yet, would be a Findly. It could be a calm, serene person like Tom's mother, or it could be—almost she screamed aloud, clapping her hand over her mouth to keep down a cry of protest.

I'd smother it, she told herself fiercely, I'd smother a baby that looked like him!

The heat grew as the grass grew and the room under the roof was stifling hot of afternoons, after the southerly sun had beat on the wall all day. Marcia insisted that Harriet must rest after the heavy noon meal and she tried to relax, lying on the warm bed that smelled of the straw in the tick and the oil in the feathers of the pillows. Everything smelled! Odd that she had never noticed before the redolence of even the most innocent things. Tom quickly learned to change his shoes before he came into the house and leave the fragrant bucket of warm milk outside on the porch till it was strained and taken to the wellhouse to cool.

"I don't know what makes me so silly," apologized Harriet. "I never did anything like this before."

"Well, you never had a baby before," remarked Marcia. "Every woman has something she just can't stand. With me before Tom was born it was chickens. I had to tend them, the little ones, and they were so squirmy and nasty and the corn-meal mash I had to cook for them made me sick till I almost gagged myself to death. I was dead sure Tom would be born with pinfeathers all over him. It goes away about the sixth month usually."

The baby would have to have clothes, Marcia reminded her.

"And I don't know how to sew," wailed Harriet. "I don't know anything."

"I've got some things put away in a trunk up attic. They'd be old-fashioned now. Used to be, a baby's dresses had to sweep the floor when you held it up in front of you, but the few times I've been to church I've noticed the babies only had dresses about a yard long. I could cut those old ones off for you if I could get any time to sit still."

"You won't get the time," said Harriet. "Mr. Findly always starts shouting the minute you sit down."

"I know. I try not to get aggravated. It's a sin to begrudge doing things for him but he can't make me understand and that only makes him worse. I just have to ask over and over and finally I can tell by his eyes when I hit the right thing. I could show you how to make over those baby clothes. We'll have to make do, I reckon. About all the cash we'll make on the place this season will have to go to the bank, but I guess you know about that!"

"No, I didn't know."

"There's a mortgage. Mr. Findly borrowed when he

bought that last meadow, that lower hundred acres. But the mortgage is a lien on everything, crops and all. Mr. Findly means to pay it off when the government pays him for all the stock that was requisitioned from this place, but it could be years after the war is over before they get around to pay all the claims of all the people."

Harriet had only a vague idea of what a mortgage was. She knew only that mortgages gave her father power over many people and her mother had hinted that some people resented this hold upon them. She wondered now if she would be a kind of hostage, an implement used against Hume Harper to lift the pressure off the Findly mortgage. Her child would be a hostage too, for as Marcia had reminded her, her child would be grandchild to her father and to Ellen.

What gentling power could a child have upon those two grandfathers? On that grim, sadistic old man in there on the bed; on Hume Harper who had showed so little gentleness or affection toward his own children?

Tom came in then, his face worn and flushed with the heat.

"Worms in the tobacco," he said wearily. "We'll have to buy lime, Ma, or Paris green. I'd better go to town in the morning, then I can dust in the afternoon."

"You go with him, Harriet," urged her mother-in-law. "Do you good to get out of the house. You could see your mother."

Harriet ran her hands over her body. The little bulge, already she could shape it with her hands. Were they talking in town, gossip buzzing, avid tongues whispering the scandal of Harriet Harper?

"I—I think I'd rather stay here with you," she faltered. "I'll stay here—and sew."

14

*J*UNE WAS HOT AND STORMY. IT RAINED OFTEN AND HARD, wild winds swept out of the west to lay the corn over so that Thad Briscoe and his elderly Negroes tramped the field to set the stalks upright and trample the roots into the damp soil. Small Ward marched along too, row by row, dancing on the uptorn hills with his hard, bare little feet.

"I trompled more corn than anybody, Mama," he boasted at night as Lennie scrubbed his blackened legs in the kitchen.

"You'll be a man before I am," teased his mother.

"Huh, you can't ever be a man," jeered the little boy. "You're a lady."

"I don't look much like a lady," sighed his mother, "but if I'm not a man then I won't have to go and fight in the army."

"You can cook," he suggested. "Pa says they have cooks in the army. Pa said they took our cows and the army would cook and eat them."

"Mama could go to Vicksburg and cook rats and dogs," Thad said, dunking his muddy feet in a bucket. "Down there the poor people are living in caves and eating all sorts of varmints. It's in the Louisville paper."

"Ugh!" Teresa shuddered. "I hope they have more than that to eat in Arkansas."

"Over there they may be able to live off the country. Have to do it with Porter's fleet of armored turtles hammering everything up and down the Mississippi," said her father. "Not much can get across the river."

"It looks bad for us, doesn't it, Thad?" worried Lennie.

"If they'd accept Longstreet's plan"—Thad reached for a towel—"they'd reinforce Bragg all along the line from Tullahoma to the railroad and clear up to Cincinnati. Then they'd move some men out of that Virginia army to reinforce Johnston down in Jackson, in Mississippi, hit Grant in the rear so he'd have to give up Vicksburg. That's Longstreet's plan—a solid line from Tennessee to the Ohio. Smash Rosecrans, take back Nashville and Tennessee, then move on Grant and cut his communications. But General Lee wants to invade the north and it looks like the people over in Richmond are all for his idea. Anyway they move we'll still have Burbridge and Boyle here in Kentucky to tell us when we can move and how often we can breathe."

"But if General Lee goes north, Pa, that will take most of our army far away and how will they get food and ammunition away up there?" argued Teresa.

"It will be a long haul with the Yanks attacking the wagon trains every mile, likely. I'd feel better in Kentucky if they'd listen to Longstreet. Keep the army where the people can support it, I say. Not send it marching off into enemy country. But the paper sort of throws off on Longstreet. Says he thinks he ought to lead General Lee by the hand instead of obeying orders. Oh, yes, I heard some more news. Ira Bacon rode by this afternoon and told me that Tom got married. He married Hume Harper's daughter two or three weeks ago."

"Our Tom?" exclaimed Clementine. "You mean our Tom married Harriet Harper?"

"So Ira said. Mighty quiet. Family never told anybody. Some folks are just finding it out."

"Harriet was a mighty proud girl," remarked Teresa. "She was never friendly with the other girls after her family sent her to that expensive school in Lexington. All they learn there is music and French and how to enter a drawing room, the girls used to say."

"I don't know what good French will do her out on that farm," Clementine sniffed. "They say Tom's daddy is a mighty mean man. You know he must be, for Tom was scared to go home."

"One thing sure, they haven't got any drawing room," said Lennie. "So that part of Harriet's education will be wasted. Tom told me his mother scarcely ever went out, not even to church."

"It must be love," sighed Teresa. "I reckon people will say you all are crazy if you let me marry Henri but I'd live with him in a log cabin with a mud floor and never care a whit."

"What if he comes home with a leg off?" asked Priscilla.

"If he came home with both legs off Tee would wheel him around in the wheelbarrow," Clementine said. "Mama, Marshy never worked the buttermilk out of this butter at all. It's messy as everything."

"Her hands are so crippled and stiff, she does the best she can," said Lennie. "I'll work it down in the morning. At least, Tee, you do know enough to stir up a batch of corn bread. I doubt if Hume Harper's daughter ever set foot in a kitchen. I know I never did till I was married and then it goes mighty hard when you have to learn it right up from the bricks. Let your breeches down, Ward, and for pity's sake keep those feet clean till you go to bed! I washed thirteen sheets this week and with no grease it's hard to make enough soap."

Teresa hurried with the dishwashing when supper was over. She had a letter. Somehow it had crossed the Mississippi through that Yankee flotilla, somehow been brought to the post office where her father had collected it, on his last trip to town. She kept it hidden from her sisters' prying eyes, folded inside her one good chemise at the bottom of her trunk. She shared a room with Rowena and Maria, but being very young they were not too curious and she could lie on her bed while they undressed and read the letter, over and over.

Things are mean out here, Henri wrote. *Too much drinking in the company, too many low characters slipping in from the backwoods with jugs of the vile stuff they distill back in the coves. I'm a sergeant and supposed to maintain discipline in the ranks but knocking their heads together is about the only treatment that is any good. You'd be startled at how quick I've gotten with my fists. They all carry knives and keep them honed razor-sharp and two or three get cut in fights every night.*

Oh, Henri—Henri! You wanted to paint beautiful pictures. Willow trees and sunlight through the leaves, all gold and misty lime—no, she must remember the color with the odd name, zinober! And chrome yellow. She had a little book Henri had given her with all the colors properly named. Never say pink, pink was madder—and tan was sepia. She would study that book and know all that Henri knew when he came home. Then they would go somewhere where it was quiet and beautiful and peaceful and have a little house and Henri would paint all day long. Someday he was to be as famous as those artists he talked so much about, Rembrandt, Rubens, and the rest.

But as always at this part of her dreaming the practical reared its ugly head. Where could they go—and what would they live on? Even famous artists must eat and what if nobody bought the pictures Henri painted? Teresa had learned the starkness of reality these last years and she knew what lack was, what poverty could be. At fifteen she had had pretty dresses, horses to ride, there had been beaux and dainty bonnets, dances and barbecues and picnics. Riding out to make long visits in the carriage with Jericho sitting proudly up front wearing his tall silk hat. Then abruptly everything swept away. The servants disappearing. The horses taken by two armies, all her dresses outgrown and no way to replace them. Priscilla and Rowena wore them now, cut down, turned and made over. And Jericho tottered around the place collecting eggs in his high silk hat.

Pa would build them a little house somewhere on the place—but there a sharper worry cut in to gnaw at her with relentless teeth. What if Pa lost the place? Every time Mr. Harper drove out in his buggy Thad's mouth set tighter and Lennie's shoulders stooped a little more and the gray look of worry came over her face and dimmed her pretty eyes.

Pa had had an idea one day of selling the west hundred that lay across the pike road, lifting the load of indebtedness a little, but that hope was swiftly blasted. The whole property was involved, Mr. Harper had said, and no part of it could be sold till it was all clear.

"Your father is one of the thousands they want to destroy," Mama had said bitterly. "Maybe he should have taken their oath but he said he couldn't honorably swear to support a government that was a tyranny and was destroying the freedom of all the people in Kentucky."

War was so stupid, so useless, so futile! Where was Jigger now, the bright houseboy who was Marshy's grandson, almost a member of the family? And Lizzie, his mother who had kept all their frilly frocks and petticoats ironed so beautifully? Maybe Lizzie was even hungry now, existing in one of those miserable shack towns that had sprung up on the outskirts of every city, every army camp. Lizzie's cabin was empty and forlorn; the little girls played in it, cooking mud messes on the hearth, putting their dolls to bed in Lizzie's abandoned cot. The old battered dolls that Teresa and Clementine had loved and played with.

Poor Clemmy! Who would there be for Clemmy to marry? Willie Harper hadn't gone to war but Willie was about the only boy left in town and Teresa dismissed him from her mind with pity. With a father like Mr. Harper how could Willie ever amount to anything? The Briscoes had given up going to church since Union rule had arrayed people in silent hostility, one side against the other, but even with such scanty social contacts as they had now Teresa had begun to sense among the young people the beginnings of contempt for Willie Harper. Henri might return from the war with a crippled body but at least he would not be maimed in spirit by the condescending pity of the people he had grown up with.

"If Willie wasn't a coward he would run away," she had flared at Clemmy once. "It's all a dream of yours anyway. You've never spoken fifty words to Willie Harper."

"I have too," defended Clementine, "and when I went to church he always smiled at me."

Even a dream could be important now when a girl had so little left. So Teresa said, "I'm sorry, Clemmy. Probably Willie wants to go for the South and then he'd be like Tom, he wouldn't dare go home."

"I wish somebody would shoot Mr. Harper," Clementine said. "Then Mama wouldn't be so sick with worry every time he comes out here."

"Mr. Harper wants money and there's no way to get any. You were too young, but I can remember when Grandpa was alive and people thought the Briscoes were rich. Mama had dresses ordered out of New York and when the tobacco and stuff was sold Grandpa Briscoe always bought everybody a present and gave all the Negroes a pair of new shoes."

"Jericho needs new shoes now. The soles of his shoes are all holes and he ties them on with string."

"Well, we're not much better off. Priss has hers tied on with two old hair ribbons."

"*C'est la guerre!*" chirped Clementine. "That means it's the war. French—Mrs. Nesbitt told me."

"So you've been saying it and that's where Ward got it. The other day when he tore his shirt and Mama scolded him he grinned and said '*C'est la guerre.*'"

"Ward's too smart for his own good. He'll come to some rascally end, you watch. Pa spoils him rotten."

"I'll be too busy to watch Ward. I'll be raising my own children."

"Nesbitts." Clementine shrugged. "All full of loony notions!"

Teresa could forgive her sister even that now, lying in this delicious daze reading her letter.

Cotton speculation is the shameful business down here. Henri's beautiful and precise script was as artistic as his little sketches. *Men fighting for trading permits to sell cotton belonging to widows and orphans and slipping in hundreds of bales with the connivance of corrupt officials, last year's cotton that they'll sell at a dollar a pound, and make fortunes for themselves. What a pity we haven't got a few thousand bales to sell on this inflated market, Little Tee, then we'd be rich and never have to work again.*

At the end was the bit that made Teresa's heart cramp with anxiety. The letter had been long on the way. What might not have happened since the date in April when it was written?

Why doesn't Johnston march to attack Grant from the

rear and make him lift the seige of Vicksburg? Why doesn't Bragg reinforce him? We hear that on every hand and we hear too that we may be sent down to Port Hudson to help hold the river for the South. Four months now and this idle company hasn't smelled powder. I made a little picture for you. It shows my gallant boys at their customary occupations.

The picture was drawn with a pencil on a soiled sheet of paper. It showed half a dozen bearded and bleary-eyed men in limp clothes and flat-topped caps. Three knelt beside a blanket spread on the ground, shaking dice, one hung an indefinite garment on a bush and two cooked over a tiny fire, one with a bit of meat suspended on a pointed stick. At the bottom Henri had written, *Any one of these could be Sergeant Henri Nesbitt, Esquire.*

Rowena crawled up into the bed. "What's that picture?"

"Soldiers. Henri drew it."

"They're all mighty ugly," observed the little girl. "Will you marry Henri if he has old whiskers all over him like that? Why do men wear nasty scratchy whiskers anyway? Pa looks like the lion that ate Daniel in my Bible book."

"The lion didn't eat Daniel. The Lord shut up their mouths so the lions couldn't eat him."

"If Daniel had a lot of whiskers I'll bet the lions wouldn't want to eat him," said 'Ria. "Whiskers would choke them and tickle."

"Worse than the pinfeathers Marshy always leaves on the drumsticks," put in Rowena. "Let me sleep in your bed, Tee? 'Ria snores so, she keeps me awake."

"And you kick like a frog," hooted 'Ria. "Old froggy Ro! Her legs go just like my frog did before I lost him. He was a nice frog but Ward was bound to throw him back into the creek. He got away when I chased Ward with a tobacco stick."

"Ward said you were mean to that frog," said Rowena.

"I wasn't mean. It was Ward that wanted to drop a rock on him. Ward's plenty mean himself."

"Tee, if you'll let me sleep here I won't kick any," begged Rowena.

"The answer is no. You've got the wide bed and this is narrow. I need all the room in it."

"Let me sleep here then and you sleep over there with 'Ria."

"I still say no. I don't like to sleep with anybody."

"How are you going to get married then?" demanded Rowena. "Mama sleeps in bed with Pa, and she said all married people slept in the same bed. I'll bet old Henri Nesbitt snores. Sometimes when I wake up at night I can hear Pa snoring away up here."

"Pa is tired. Both of you go to sleep now or I'll blow out the candle," Teresa threatened. "Back in your bed, Ro, and no more out of either of you."

"Ole meanie!" grumbled Rowena, throwing thin brown legs in the air as she dived into bed. "I hope when you do get married your husband beats you."

Relenting, Teresa kissed the two hot, flushed little faces, pushed back Ro's tangled yellow hair. Ro's face was so pretty, her eyes bright with mischief. She would be a beauty and what lay ahead for them? No war then, please God! No strain and sorrow of parting. No savage men riding through the land to burn, kill and destroy. None of the children were allowed out of sight of the house now and the guns Thad had kept hidden were brought out and kept primed and ready. Lennie worked in the kitchen with a rifle standing by the door and from some illegal source Thad had obtained two pistols. One he wore belted under his shirt and Teresa had been taught where to lay a quick hand on the other.

How would it feel to shoot a man, she wondered, as she went down the stairs. Henri must know, he had been through those battles with Kirby Smith in Kentucky and down in Tennessee. Had he winced at pulling the trigger, been sickened when he saw a man crumple and die? Henri, who had been so gentle she had once seen him free a struggling lightning bug tangled in a flower.

Thad and Lennie were sitting in the dusk of the front porch, the other girls perched below on the steps. Ward lay asleep on his mother's lap when Teresa burst abruptly out the door.

"Pa, did you ever kill a man?" she asked boldly.

"My Heavens, Tee, you made me jump!" protested Lennie. "We were just sitting here getting cool. It's too hot to go to bed."

"Did you ever kill anybody, Pa?" persisted Teresa.

Thad cleared his throat. "No, I never killed anybody. I beat a man once, but he was trying to kill my brother. I stunned him but he didn't die."

"Boone killed him, afterward," Lennie reminded him.

"Our Uncle Boone? That daguerrotype in the parlor?" asked Clementine.

"It was a duel. Men fought duels in those days. Before you were born."

"Now they just get up a war when they want to kill people," complained Priscilla, "so we can't even go out and pick the peaches for fear some old scalawag will come along and hurt us."

"I'll send Ceph and Lum to gather the peaches tomorrow. You girls stay close to your mother," Thad ordered.

"I'll have to dry them," Lennie said. "No sugar to can with and we couldn't afford it at a dollar a pound anyway."

"Speculators!" said Thad angrily. "They grease the right

palm, fetch it up here from Louisiana through the lines and make a pile of money."

"Cotton too. They're speculating in cotton, it's in the letter I got from Henri. A dollar a pound for cotton, he said. I wish we could grow cotton, Pa."

"Frost comes too early. No help any more. You want to go out and pick cotton?"

"I would. For a dollar a pound. Then maybe I'd have a new dress," sighed Teresa.

"And new shoes for me!" exclaimed Priscilla. "Almost I'd give up any hope of being an angel, if only I could have a pair of new shoes!"

Thad Briscoe groaned inwardly. Out here the summer night was still save for the shrilling of the frogs down at the creek and a low singing that came from the Negro cabins, but in Thad's heart was no stillness, no peace.

He rose abruptly, took the sleeping child from Lennie's arms and strode into the bedroom where he laid the boy in his trundle bed. When Lennie came in she found her husband striding up and down the dark room beating a fist into his palm.

"My word, Thad!" Lennie put the candle down on the chest. "Don't get so worked up just because you can't raise cotton at a dollar a pound."

He turned on her a drained, set face. His voice shook harshly.

"Lennie, I'm going!"

She gasped. "Going where?"

"To the army. To Braxton Bragg. I've got to enlist. Lennie, I've got to go."

"And leave us here alone? Thad, you can't?"

He beat his half-open fists hard on his temples. "Don't you see—I've got to go! You'll have three colored men and they'll stay faithful. Corn's laid by. The hay is all in. All that you'll need. I've got to go till spring anyway, Lennie—we've got to get this war over! Living's no good till we get it over. The South has got to win. It can't win without every man."

"You've been so fearful for us—and now you'd go and leave us!" she cried incredulously. "You're too old, Thad. You're past forty."

"They're taking them older. Forty—fifty—boys no older than Tee and Clemmy. General Lee's not a young man. Can't you see, Lennie, the only thing now is to get it over?" His voice rose to hysteria. "Get it over! I'm going, Lennie, I've got to and help get it over!"

"What if those night riders come while you're away?" she asked with a touch of bitterness.

"They could come while I'm here—come and shoot me. It's a chance we have to take. Everybody is taking the same chance, everybody in the whole South. Ira's boy is going back early in the morning. I'll go with him. I'll take the rifle."

He left before dawn. If anyone inquired, he told her, she was to say that he had gone to Lexington to try and trade for some mules.

They did not waken the children.

"Tell them," he said to Lennie, too frozen with grief and consternation to weep, "that I've gone to help the South end the war—so Prissy can have some new shoes."

15

WILLIAM HARPER WAS A MYSTERY AND A BAFFLEMENT, even to himself. Growing up sickly and lanky with no meat on his bones, a droop to his spine and a wistful, lost expression at times, he had nevertheless known strange inward angers and longings that were peculiarly his own.

Everything he had ever had, all the life he had lived in his father's smug house, smothered by his mother's too solicitous affection, all this he had disliked. He had always felt alien, withdrawn, different, judging his family but troubled by that judicial irritation. These were his own people but there was nothing, he believed, of him in them and little, so far as he could discover, of them in him. Not a thought, not a belief, not an action was in sympathy.

Guardedly but perversely he had for the last two years set himself inwardly in opposition to everything his father stood for. His father he considered the only galvanic unit in the Harper family. Ellen was a shadow, timid, obedient, placating. Harriet was little more than an echo of resented voices. Never till now had he even considered his sister as more than a nuisance to be endured and little considered. Now she had upset all his ideas.

How had Harriet, molded as he had always believed in a prim prison of nicety, ever gotten enough spirit and independence to get herself into such a mess? In William's secret and slightly lurid imaginings he tried to picture his smug sister in such a situation but it was a vision that would not come clear. Not Harriet with her prissy aloofness, her arrogant pride, her dainty ways of dressing and carrying herself.

His parents believed that Harriet's marriage had been achieved so quietly and expertly that there might conceivably be no repercussions of gossip in town. For that William pitied them a little. He had been around enough to know how many curtains swayed when his father strutted by, buttoned into his tight black coat, his hard hat cutting a ridge in his bulging forehead.

At the bank neither of the two employees so much as looked at each other when Harper was around but with William they were less discreet. While he swept and dusted and was set occasionally to add up some rows of unimportant figures, Bolt and Merrill talked behind his back, taking little trouble to keep their voices down. Not only did they talk but they snickered. William knew their reaction. In their minds the mighty were laid by the heels and that was the time for the humble to be exultant and superior.

William had no delusions about his own importance in that bank. He was practically one of the fixtures, less of consequence than the safe, only a little more to be considered than the cuspidors. He held to his remoteness, not willing to let Bolt or Merrill know that anything they muttered could hurt or touch him.

A wall had been breeched that had heretofore set the Harpers apart as superior beings. The foxes of sensationalism had leaped through the opening and slavered at the taste of such elegant meat. No Harper, so the attitude of his father's employees implied, was to be dreaded any more, and only very reluctantly respected.

To William none of it mattered too much. He had never

been a part of any group. In school, when his mother had allowed him to attend, he had been good at his books because there was nothing else for him to do and nothing that interested him. Schoolyard sports and fights he had avoided, knowing that he stood no chance with tougher boys though he liked to fancy that he would have made a good Indian fighter. He could make himself practically invisible, Indian fashion, and approach any group so silently that he overheard a great many things not intended for his ears.

When he had been smaller and could slip away he had liked to go into the woods. Lying very still there in some thicket, he let his vivid imagination go back to Blue Licks or Harrodsburg, to the stockaded stands along the trails where lonely men had scouted and had died, standing off old Pluggy or the Mingo or the Shawnee. Building Kentucky. Years had gone by since Daniel Boone and Ben Logan had fought red men with British guns, to hold along the Elkhorn or the Kentucky River, but to William those days came alive whenever a rare opportunity came for him to be alone in a quiet place.

Because often he found arrowheads or shards of broken clay vessels on these wanderings, young boys had sometimes trailed after him. He had suffered their company, not caring much one way or another and happily never knowing that these same lads were afterwards questioned sharply by their parents, who distrusted the odd Harper boy. Now Harriet's behavior would sharpen the old suspicions of the Harpers, but William did not know that either. He merely catalogued Harriet as female and therefore incomprehensible in her madnesses.

There were times, however, when William wondered about his father. He had long been reconciled to the knowledge that Hume Harper was both greedy and unscrupulous but until this scandal had sharpened its beak against the family the boy had never thought of his father as male. Where his family were concerned sex had only lately entered his awareness. Now unhappy speculations began to boil up in his mind. Waywardness was inherited, he had heard Mr Merrill say. Impossible for William to believe that Harriet had any taint of it from their mother, but that left an unanswered question and William let his troubled mind run wild in pursuit of it.

Maybe his father had a woman somewhere. He had heard no sly whispers or any innuendoes, only mutterings that Harper was a hard man, arrogant and often ridiculous with his pompous airs and his exaggerated self-importance.

As he walked down the hot, sun-drenched street on a July day, his body bent forward, his big hands flopping at his sides, William pictured all the women in the town, even some out on the questionable outskirts, but found no candidate for any secret surmise about Hume Harper. There was only one woman in town whom Mr. Bolt and Mr. Merrill thought a trifle too gay, and that was Denise, and whenever William heard her name whispered he burned with wild prickles of defending fury. Denise was no light woman. With Milo off to fight with Morgan she tried for happiness but if her laughter bubbled it came only from the bright spring of joyousness that was essentially a part of her, and no moldy bank clerk or anybody else had the right to mutter dry asides.

Not that he had ever risen to the defense of Denise, knowing such rashness would only add fuel to the murky fires in the minds of Bolt and Merril. The knowledge that he, William, hoarded secret dreams about her would have stirred them to vicious and unholy glee, had they so much as suspected it. Not even his mother would have believed that the Nesbitt house was the only place where her son felt relaxed and at home. Lately, since the affair of Harriet and

Tom, he had avoided the place, but today, answering a sudden urge, he turned into the alley, slipped through the rear gate and tapped on the back door.

It was opened by Denise, clad in some very thin garment, and she gave a little yelp on seeing him and thrust her feet quickly into a shabby pair of slippers, twisting the robe tightly to hide her white legs.

"You beast, Willie!" she exclaimed, letting him in. "Why do you desert us so long? Come in—come in! Maman, here is our bad boy, William. Months, he never comes to see us and now he knocks on our back door like he should sell the vegetables, eh?"

Amalie Nesbitt looked very gaunt and raddled to William's eyes. She greeted him a bit nervously, patting his hand with her own thin fingers, and said, "It is not wise that you come here, William. You know that they watch us by day and night. Now that Milo rides back to Kentucky they watch us more fiercely."

"So Milo's back." William remembered that New Year's Day when he had hated the thought of Milo in that house.

"Morgan. They ride again. We hear things—by the little birds," remarked Denise. "To the Ohio—and who knows then? Maybe they ride east to join General Lee who will take Pennsylvania—and New York, it could be! So the wicked ones out there they keep a sharp eye on this house. Maybe they even think they will take Morgan in Amalie Nesbitt's house!"

Amalie gave William a gentle push. "You go, boy. Your father will be much displeased if you are seen coming here. We love you the same always but for your good I tell you, go!"

"Not till he has a glass of homemade wine, Maman," insisted Denise. "Me, I pick the berries and Maman makes wine for that day when there will be no more fighting and

159

hiding. When Papa comes home and we all sing and shout and are silly and happy and no more afraid. So, my sweet William, you shall have one taste before Maman makes you go out the door."

"Maybe I'd better not. They might smell it on my breath," worried William.

"Ah, such a simple little wine!" Denise rushed to the big oak sideboard and tilted a decanter over a small glass. "I know! On our back porch are Maman's onions, where they dry. You shall chew on one as you go and nobody will smell our poor little wine, no? Here—drink."

The yellow robe twisted about her slim hips and William felt his pulse pounding, but when he gulped desperately at the wine it strangled him so that he had to be pounded on the back.

"My wine is so bad, no?" teased Amalie, her big dark eyes laughing at him as she thumped between his shoulders. "It will not go down but maybe sideways?"

"It's just—I'm not used to it," panted the boy, gasping for breath.

"He has been so piously reared, our lad," laughed Denise. "Maybe it is that he should not associate with such bad characters as me and Maman. Maybe we should get him very drunk so he can go out and beat all the wicked people who persecute us. Would you fight somebody if they say we are spies and traitors, William?"

"Nobody says that. Anyway they better not where I can hear it," bragged William, straightening his shoulders.

"Ah le pauvre petit!" sighed Amalie. "All by himself he would defend us. But we will not let you come to harm on our account, William. Already they make the martial law in all Kentucky. It will be bad then for anyone who is a friend to the poor Nesbitts. No pass to walk abroad. No one to sell them anything in the shops. Will you be sad, my boy, if they

160

send us south through the lines? We cannot live even in New Orleans, for there also is the Yankee, the dreadful General Butler. It is a bad time for us, William, so you go now and do not come any more."

"I will not," squawked William defiantly, his voice betraying him treacherously as it still did in times of stress. "First give me some more of that wine."

"No, no—you must not!" protested Amalie but Denise tilted the decanter again, laughing delightedly.

"It is a frolic for William if he is made a little drunk," she said. "It is that he is briefly free. Free from the stern papa and the maman who will lead him by the hand."

"And the spittoons!" bleated William, swallowing the wine in one gulp. "The stinking spittoons."

He did not choke this time or on the third glass though Amalie watched him worriedly. Then she put her hands on his shoulders and shoved him deliberately toward the door.

"This I will not permit," she said sternly. "This is not to be in my house. Eat the onion now, I command you, and do not talk or it will be too loud and shameful. That bad Denise! Always mischievous, always making a joke. Out now, *mon fils,* and God go with you!"

She thrust the onion into his hand but before he reached the gate he hurled it wrathfully across the alley. It fell on the doorstep of a cabin and two small Negroes raced for it and fought over it. William heard their furious yells as he went down the alley. He was not drunk, he told himself firmly. Nobody could get drunk on a little homemade wine. It hadn't been very good wine actually, light and dry and not sweet as he had expected good wine to be. Maybe that kind of stuff was all right in New Orleans and those places in Louisiana where Denise and Amalie had been raised but he would bet that Henri would laugh at such a sissy drink.

His only sensation as he went lightfooted to the bank was

161

a pleased kind of exhilaration and a sudden and very pleasant desire to kick every cuspidor in the place across the building. He even lifted a foot and took aim, then halted the gesture in mid-air as he saw his father scowling from behind his desk.

"Where have you been? Dinner was over an hour ago," snapped Harper.

"Oh, around," returned William blithely.

"Come here, sir!" ordered Harper.

William lost some of his simulated bravado and shambled up to the desk. "Yes, sir."

"You've been drinking!" stated Harper, with what was intended for blasting scorn. "Own it, sir. You've been drinking!"

William straightened his spine. He threw back his head and jutted his chin and for the first time in his eighteen years looked Hume Harper boldly in the eye. Wild rebellion was boiling up in him, almost choking him as words fought to force themselves through his tightening throat. They came out in a gusty yell.

"Yes!" he shouted. "Yes—what of it? The family is disgraced anyway! What the devil does it matter what I do?"

Harper's face swelled to a bulk of crimson, his eyes looked ready to fly from their sockets. From behind their copper grilles Merrill and Bolt stood stunned, staring incredulously.

Then before Harper could explode all the wrath that was seething within him, setting his eyes on fire, there was a wild commotion at the door.

Two men burst in waving flimsy bits of paper and yelling at the tops of their voices.

"War's over! Grant's took Vicksburg! Meade smashed Lee up in Pennsylvania! Place called Gettysburg!"

One was dancing a wild jig. "War's over!" he kept shouting, beating his heels hard on the floor. "War's over!"

Harper marched out and took the yellow dispatch from the hand that held it. The other man kept on dancing, whooping, "Hooray! Hooray! The rebels are licked. Grant's took Vicksburg!"

Harper frowned over the news flimsy. "This is a great victory," he said crisply, "but it hasn't ended the war."

"Why not?" yelped the dancer. "Lee's licked! Who else have they got that can fight?"

"They have Johnston and Bragg and Hood. They have John Morgan and Forrest and Joe Wheeler. This is victory—but it certainly is not the end. When Robert Lee surrenders then the war will be ended."

"We've got the Confederacy cut in two," argued the first man. "What can they do with Farragut and Porter and them others holding the Mississippi?"

"They can fight on, which they will do," declared Harper. "Has anybody taken Richmond? What about Atlanta and Chattanooga? Lee's army wasn't captured, it says here. It wasn't destroyed. Lee has retreated across the Potomac. Longstreet and Early with him." Harper flipped the paper indifferently and handed it back. "We can rejoice over this good news but it's no time to let our defenses down, no time at all."

"Hump!" snorted the dancing man. "You take it mighty cool, Harper."

"We need cool heads now—now more than ever," argued Harper. "Especially with Morgan raiding again in Kentucky."

He stalked back to his desk and sat down, jerking a pile of papers into order before him. The two messengers who had entered so jubilantly shrugged their shoulders and tramped out, muttering between themselves. William went into the back room and lurked there, pretending to hunt for a duster. At least the diversion had taken his father's attention from him but he knew that a reckoning would come. His jaunty and defiant attitude was wilting a little under the pressure of a new worry.

Morgan was at Burkesville, in Kentucky, his legion two thousand five hundred strong, William had heard only the day before. Maybe he would be smart to run away and join Morgan. Trouble was, he had never been on a horse in his life. He would make a sorry picture with all those brash hell-riders. He hoped Pa wouldn't make them stay in the bank all night waiting for a raid. All foolishness anyway, against a mob of armed desperate men. All Pa could do was get them all shot, as Mama had pointed out time and again.

William made slow work of his cleaning and a dilatory business of walking home to supper. His father had already finished eating and was buried in the Cincinnati paper. He recognized William's presence only by a grunt. Nothing was said about keeping watch at the bank and when William had a chance to glimpse the paper he read that Morgan had left Lebanon and Bardstown and headed west toward the Ohio.

Their march was spreading terror over the country, the paper reported, and somebody had already written a song about it:

Morgan, Morgan, the raider and Morgan's terrible men,
With bowie knives and pistols are galloping up the glen!

Fascinated, for days William watched the reports of Morgan's smashing raids, of bridges burned and the pleasant country of southern Indiana given a bitter touch of the reality of war. Of Morgan's march to and from Cincinnati, the maddest expedition ever undertaken by so many men, taking along their wagons, their wounded, halting to fight, marching ninety-five miles in thirty-two hours, feinting to the north to draw off the troops blocking their way, passing through the very suburbs of the city.

Then came calamity. At Buffington's Bar on the Ohio Morgan tried to cross back into Kentucky to find his way blocked everywhere. A few men escaped into Kentucky but Morgan led the remnant of his command north again trying to evade pursuit. Toward the end of July at Beaver Creek, the jaunty general and three hundred and sixty-four of his men surrendered and the papers reported that Morgan and seventy of his men were in the state penitentiary at Columbus, Ohio.

That was the day that General Burnside declared martial law in the whole state of Kentucky. Alarmed, William hurried at his noon hour to the Nesbitt house. But when he came through the garden he found the house silent, the doors locked, and there was no answer to his knock.

A Negro woman standing on the stoop of a shanty across the alley yelled at him.

"Ain't nobody home, White Boy. Miz' Nesbitt and her gal done gone."

"Gone where?" demanded William.

"How I know?" the black woman snickered. "Sloped out in the night and they done gone. No use you hangin' round no mo', White Boy."

"You go to blazes!" stormed William. The angry cry was half a sob.

16

SUMMER DRIFTED BY AND THERE WAS QUIET ON THE
Rapidan but in Kentucky anger simmered to a white heat.
Martial law was sporadically declared, sporadically lifted,
but every citizen held to his pass for fear of being hauled
before the provost. An election for governor impended, the
Peace Democrats nominating Charles Wickliffe, the Union
Democrats Thomas Bramlette. Very promptly the Union
army took control of the elections. In many counties Wickliffe's name was stricken from the ballot and thousands of
voters were declared disenfranchised.

On the 25th of July General Boyle issued an order confiscating all rebel property, and shortly after, a declaration
that a vote for Wickliffe would be taken as proof that the
voter was a Confederate sympathizer, a rebel and a traitor.

Hume Harper was jubilant. "We'll elect Bramlette by
fifty thousand majority," he gloated at home. "He'll support
the war and the Federal Government and with their property confiscated we'll be rid of these verminous rebels. Spies,
every one of them!"

William felt a little sick. He knew what his father meant.
The Nesbitt house. That fine corner that would be an ex-
cellent site for a business block when the war ended. Every
day William walked on that side of the square to look up at
the blank shuttered windows, dreading the day when he

would see a red placard nailed on the door. But then he learned that his father had already taken steps to insure possession of the property. He had filed foreclosure proceedings and also a claim with the Union authorities to protect his interest.

"You carried the papers to the courthouse yourself," Bolt told William.

"If I had known I was carrying them I'd have thrown them into the gutter!" declared the boy, hotly.

"That would be stupid. They'll lose the property anyway." Bolt had become more loquacious with William of late. William knew that Bolt had signed that paper entitled "An Address To The People and The Congress Of The United States," a document setting forth the outrages perpetrated by the Union military and intended for the eyes of Congress and President Lincoln. William had not given Bolt away though Mr. Merrill had hinted that there could be grim reprisals.

Newspapers from as far away as Indiana ran outspoken articles calling the Kentucky election a farce and an indignity thrust upon a free people and William read them all avidly, rescuing the pages his father crumpled and threw angrily away. Bramlette was elected.

At Chickamauga the rivers ran red with the blood of thirty thousand men and at Knoxville Longstreet and Burnside battled for possession of a vital railroad center. The Union forces threw dead horses and mules into the Tennessee River to drift down on the Confederate camp and the Confederates hauled the animals ashore to salvage the precious metal shoes with which they were shod. Then Longstreet was retreating slowly through Tennessee and William followed that anguished winter march, his imagination picturing the frozen mud, the stripped and hungry country. His interest turned to sharp unease when an order went out from Secretary Stanton to draft three hundred thousand men in Kentucky.

"Join up with an old regiment, boy," Merrill bantered, "and you get three hundred dollars bounty. Sign up with a new regiment and you only get a hundred dollars, but wait around and let the draft catch you and you get nothing."

"I'm already legally in the army," William reminded him. "Pa keeps my records straight, he's continually reminding me of it."

"Ten thousand men will stay in Kentucky to protect the state," Merrill persisted. "Go with them and you won't have to go far from your ma. Won't be much danger defending the state now they got Morgan in jail and Bragg run clear away from Chattanooga. They've got a few rebel gunners' nests to clear out along the Mississippi and then that river will be under Union control and no more contraband cotton coming north. Too bad. That was a nice profitable business while it lasted. For them that had the capital to finance it. Be hard on the Johnnies down there too. No more percussion caps or barrels of pork going down to be unloaded at New Madrid or Baton Rouge."

William prickled helplessly, knowing what Merrill hinted at. Those whiskery river boatmen who slunk into the bank sometimes at closing time. On those days Harper always sent William home early, whether he had finished mopping the floor or not. On those days his father did not stage his usual three-thirty ceremony of locking the safe. William knew that Harper carried a pistol now, a short deadly little blue-barreled gun in a holster under his long-tailed coat. The coat was always kept buttoned even on the hottest days.

Came colder weather and Kentucky rocked with counter-waves of discreet laughter and of renewed dread. John Hunt Morgan had escaped from the Ohio penitentiary. He was reported to be in Lexington, he was reported to be

168

hiding in the town. Captain Tom Hines, who was rated a desperado and an outlaw by the Union Command, was said to be on his way to burn New York City.

William stood by apprehensively while half a dozen soldiers broke the lock on the door of the Nesbitt house and tramped in, searching every nook and corner, with armed men watching at the rear. A rumor had spread that Milo Nesbitt and General Morgan were hiding in that house. Harper sent William back at night to repair the lock, and the boy wandered desolately through the rooms where the orange-blossom fragrance of Denise's perfume still lingered. It was obvious that the two women had taken all their clothes with them but William found a bit of yellow ribbon and tucked it in an inside pocket. The prowling soldiers had drunk all Amalie's wine and left the bottles rolling on the floor, leaving sticky trails of lees on the carpet.

All the silver had been hidden long ago. William himself had helped Henri scramble up the wide dining-room chimney, both of them half naked. High up there was a ledge that had once been a fireplace opening into an upper room. The fireplace had been bricked up years since but in the niche they stowed the tow sacks padded with straw that held the ornate teapots, goblets, pitchers, ladles, spoons and forks that had come from Louisiana.

Balancing there, Henri had hauled up the buckets of wet clay that William tied to the end of a rope, and had plastered over the sacks thickly. William stooped now and peered far up the wide flue but no fresh soot had rained down and he decided that the Nesbitt treasure was still safe. There would be a problem recovering it, though, if eventually his father had the house torn down.

Heavy footsteps jarred the floor and two Home Guards came tramping in. "What you doing here, boy?" they demanded.

"My father sent me to close up this house," William said stoutly, though there was a hard, cold knot in his stomach.

"Who's your father? Judge Nesbitt?"

"Naw, that's Hume Harper's boy."

"My father has foreclosed on this property," announced William. "The Nesbitts let their mortgage go by default so he is foreclosing. And he isn't going to like the way your troops tore up this house."

"Yah, just ask your pappy what he's goin' to do about it!" sneered one. "Drunk all the old lady's wine, the dirty rats! You get on out of here, boy, and stay out. This house is due to be took over by the Union command."

"Well, it won't be because it will belong to my father and he's a staunch Union man and a personal friend of the colonel."

"Yeh, him and the colonel both mighty staunch. Made more money out of this here war than anybody," snarled the other. "You get goin', boy. General Burbridge figures to quarter officers in this house."

"My father will see about that!" threatened William. He went out, glaring back at the soldiers, who slammed the door behind him.

There was one comforting thought. If his father did take over the Nesbitt house there would inevitably come a day when he himself would inherit it. Then, no matter what manner of structure had been erected on the lot, he would give it back to the Nesbitts. He imagined the scene, squaring his shoulders a little and putting on a magnanimous and humble mien, the benefactor, the friend who would see that justice was done.

He took out the scrap of ribbon and smoothed it gently between his fingers. Where was she now, Denise? Was she hungry and miserable and afraid? If they had gone south through the lines, of course she was hungry and miserable.

The papers were full of the plight of the South. All South-erners, declared the Northern press, were hungry, homeless, bereft, their men killed in battle or away in the armies.

"I didn't lock the door," he reported to Harper. "There were some soldiers there and they said the army was taking over the house for officers' quarters."

"I'll see about that! I'll see Colonel Bisbee right away." Harper jumped up and went for his coat and hat. "And early in the morning, William, you harness the mare. You're going with me on a business trip to the country."

"Before breakfast?"

"Your mother will see that we have breakfast. I have bus-iness to attend to before the bank opens. So you'd better get to bed. I'll call you at five o'clock."

It was very raw, with a threat of snow, and dawn came late and grudgingly as they drove north on the Cynthiana road. The mare's breath fogged smokily on the icy air and Hume Harper drove with his collar turned up, his face fiery red. William huddled in the corner of the seat with the buf-falo robe pulled up to his chin. After a mile he surmised where they were going and suspected his father's errand. It made him a bit resentful that he had been brought along on such a dubious enterprise. He was not surprised when they turned in at the lane gate that led up a gentle slope to Thad Briscoe's house.

"Why did you want me along, Pa?" he asked. "There's nobody but women and children here."

"I did not bring you to defend me, sir." Harper was stiff. "I am about to make Lennie Briscoe a very generous offer and I want you to hear my proposition and be a witness to what she has to say. I am tired of being criticized by my own family."

"I've never criticized you, Pa." William forbore to add that he had never been brave enough to voice the many criticisms that had boiled up in his mind. "Nor Mama either."

"Unspoken criticism can wound as deeply as words," Harper said. "I am not a monster and I dislike being considered monstrous even if no one has the temerity to accuse me verbally."

His conscience is hurting him, decided the boy, a slightly startling thought and quite new, for never before had he believed that his father had any conscience. That Harper had feelings that could be hurt was new too; always he had seemed as insensate, as invulnerable as though his inner consciousness was armored with marble. There had always been that repelling arrogance, that aloof superiority that fended off any reproach. William felt a slight confusion but no feeling of being drawn any closer to this stiffly erect man beside him. It was the same old unease that had troubled him all his life, having a tinge of guilt in it but no desire to overcome it. He was silent as he haltered the mare at Briscoe's mounting block and followed his father up the front steps.

There was a long wait after Harper rang the old-fashioned doorbell, then the door swung inward a little way and Teresa's big dark eyes lost their look of dread as she saw them. William caught the quick gesture with which she hid a heavy pistol under her apron.

"Oh, Mr. Harper!" she exclaimed nervously. "Come in. It's mighty cold out this morning. Good morning, Willie. If you want to see Mama, Mr. Harper, you'll have to come out to the kitchen. It's warm there and we haven't made fires in the other rooms yet."

"Very well." Harper laid his hat on a table and William stuffed his cap in his pocket. "Come along, William."

Teresa said, "You've grown awfully tall lately, Willie."

William mumbled something indefinite as he followed

172

her down the frigid hall. The furniture was elegant but neglected, he noted, the carpet of dark red velvet had not been swept lately and little fluffs of dust lay under the chairs and tables. A tall clock showed some bygone hour with paralyzed hands and in a copper urn raddled peacock feathers drooped sadly.

They went through the chilly dining room where obviously no meal had been eaten in a long time. The kitchen seemed very hot after the bleak atmosphere of the other rooms, and it looked full of children. So full of dark, guarded eyes staring at them inquiringly that William drew back a little from the impact of that challenging gaze.

Lennie Briscoe was ladling porridge into bowls and when she saw Hume Harper she started and dropped the ladle on the stove and the spattered mush smoked and sputtered. Clementine jumped to retrieve the ladle, laying a quick, steadying hand on her mother's arm.

Harper said, a bit lamely, "Good morning, Lennie, you will pardon this early visit."

"I was just feeding them," stammered Lennie. "Will you take a chair, Mr. Harper? You too, Willie. Bring some more chairs, Teresa."

William helped Teresa fetch two more chairs from the dining room. The seats were icy cold and he noted that his father sat down gingerly, removing his overcoat and folding it in his lap.

"Please go on with your children's breakfast," Harper said. "I came early because there is little time. What we have to do must be done quickly. Lennie, it's known of course that Thad is down south with the Confederate army."

"Thad's with General Hardee. Somewhere around Chattanooga the last I heard," Lennie said faintly. "I had one letter. A neighbor that got sent home brought it—"

"You're not supposed to tell, Mama," warned Priscilla soberly.

"Mr. Harper is no informer," Lennie said. "A wounded man can do no more hurt to anybody."

"You're referring to Ira Bacon's boy, I suppose?" said Harper. "I understand he was shot in the lung and hasn't much chance to regain his health. Lennie, you may not have heard of General Boyle's last order. They're proposing to confiscate the property of all known Confederates. Of course they rate a man fighting against the Union as definitely an enemy and in rebellion against the United States. I mean to protect this property. You know, of course, that I hold the mortgage? It's in bad shape, Lennie, mighty bad shape—in fact in such bad shape that I couldn't ask the bank to carry it any longer. I had to take it over personally. There has been no interest paid and nothing on the principal, of course, for a year and seven months. All together it amounts to something over eight thousand dollars."

Lennie's face was drained and chalky. Clementine pushed her mother gently into a chair, giving the Harpers a condemning look.

"So—you're going to put my children out of their home, Mr. Harper?" Lennie's voice was a sick croak.

Harper squared his plump shoulders, pulled in his stomach and his chin. "I have not said that, have I? If the Union takes this place away from you—and they may do that with justification according to their rules, Thad being listed as a traitor to the Union—"

"My father is no traitor!" put in Teresa hotly.

"The Union government would disagree with you, young lady. They count any man a traitor who takes up arms against it. Hear me out," Harper said firmly, "before you judge me, please? It is possible, Lennie, that I can keep this place from confiscation, from being put up for sale at some government land office to any Northern investor who comes down here to take advantage of the misfortunes of Southern sympathizers in Kentucky. And they will come! Don't believe that they won't come. This is a fine bluegrass farm and it was at one time a very rich property. Now—if I can foreclose my mortgage promptly, a very proper and legal procedure, after certain legal formalities the title to this property will pass to me."

"What difference would that make?" cried Lennie. "My children would still be out in the big road with nowhere to lay their heads! Where could we go? In winter? You know all my own people are dead except my brothers, and they're in Johnston's army and their wives hard put to take care of their own families." She sprang up, tilting a bowl off the table. Rowena jumped to rescue it. "If you can do such a heartless thing, Hume Harper—"

William was writhing in sympathetic misery, suffering under the leveled scorn of six pairs of dark eyes. He could not bear to look at his father and the sudden change in Harper's voice made him start.

Harper was saying, very gently, "I have no intention of putting any children out into the cold winter, Lennie. There is a law of redemption. It is true that after process of law the property would be vested in me. I hold the trust deed made by Thad's father. You will continue to occupy the place as my tenants. Later, if Thad survives the war, he will have an opportunity to redeem the land, but"—his voice rose a little—"if this place is confiscated, there will be no chance of redemption. Then your children will be out in the big road, maybe even sent south through the lines. Already some women in town have been sent because their sons or husbands were fighting for this so-called Confederacy."

"Mrs. Nesbitt and Milo's wife," put in William.

"I had not heard where they have been sent," corrected his father. "I did hear that they were being taken to some women's prison in Indiana, for harboring rebel spies and Morgan's raiders. But perhaps you are better informed than I, William?"

"I don't know. I just know they've gone somewhere."

"It is wise to avoid rash statements." Harper was bland. "Now, Lennie, do you understand what I have been trying to explain to you?"

"I understand, Mr. Harper," Teresa said. "I understand that whatever happens we lose this place. If you take it it happens a little more slowly, that is all."

"You wrong me, my dear. If I take title to this property you will have every opportunity to recover it. Realize that your father does owe me several thousand dollars, an honorable debt which he has always acknowledged and promised to pay."

"Thad couldn't help himself," defended Lennie. "He inherited that debt and we did pay off some of it before the war came. Then they took our stock and never paid for it and our Negroes ran away, those that were able to work. We were just helpless, Mr. Harper. These little girls have been working like hands in the fields." She began to cry thinly and Rowena started crying too, flinging herself upon her mother, wailing desolately.

"I admire your courage, young ladies." Harper's approving look around the room evoked a cool and withdrawn silence. Teresa's lips were drawn straight and judicial, Clementine's eyes smoldered, but little Ward stiffened himself in the middle of the floor, his fists clenched.

"You get outa here, you ole Yankee!" he piped out fiercely. "My daddy tole me to be a man around here. You get outa here and don't you make my mama cry!"

"Hush, Ward!" Lennie pulled him toward her and

smoothed his ruffled hair. "You mustn't talk that way to Mr. Harper. He didn't make the war and all our trouble. There's nothing I can do, is there, Mr. Harper? No use for me to say anything at all."

"You can do this, Lennie, in all fairness. You can understand that the proceedings I shall institute against Thad immediately I get back to town are for your protection as well as my own. You will still have a roof over your head. You will still live here, undisturbed—"

"Paying rent, of course?" put in Teresa.

"We will arrange those matters come planting time. Now I must hurry back to town to forestall any action General Boyle's agents may have in mind against Confederate property in this county. Please try to feel as kindly toward me as you can, Lennie, you and your daughters. Come along, William."

Harper buttoned his overcoat. Teresa led them through the cold hall, slipped two bolts and a chain and opened the front door.

"Good day, sir," she said primly, closing it after them.

Henri Nesbitt, his friend, meant to marry Tee Briscoe, William was thinking as he unknotted the hitching strap, stiff with cold. There must be some sweetness and warmth in Tee, else how could Henri have fallen in love with her? Certainly her eyes had not glinted like amber ice in the millpond at leaf-falling time when she looked at Henri.

"Remember, William, what you have heard this morning," Harper ordered as he picked up the reins, settled the robe over his fat knees. "Remember if ever you hear your father called a heartless man."

"Maybe the Union wouldn't ever get around to confiscating that farm at all," William demurred. "Mr. Merrill says there's twice as much Confederate property in this county as there is Union. He says they couldn't seize it all and sell off a whole county. He says Kentucky would secede if they tried it."

"Mr. Merrill is not a well-informed man," Harper said. "If he were as clever as he thinks he is he would be president of the bank and I would be posting accounts for him. Kentucky will never leave the Union and the Briscoes owe me a great deal of money which for some time they have made no effort at all to pay. Now, we will return to our work. You will keep entirely silent about this morning's events, you hear? I can let my actions speak for themselves. They will be their own defense."

That Clemmy—she had grown tall and pretty, William had noticed. In school the boys had teased him about Clemmy Briscoe and he had dismissed their banter with embarrassed impatience. Clemmy had been thick and childish then, and sometimes she had given him an adoring look that had made him painfully uncomfortable. This morning she had looked at him as though she hated him.

Were the animosities his father collected and seemed to be very complacent about, going to spread like spilled poison to embitter William's own life and make him a junior monster in people's eyes?

I reckon I'll have to get clear away, he was thinking, his cap pulled low over his eyes. I'll have to get far away if I want ever to be me—and not Hume Harper's bird dog!

17

OMETHING DROVE HIM, SOMETHING IN HIMSELF, SOME-
thing that had been growing there a long time but now
burgeoned up like a sudden-blooming plant, yesterday
nothing, today a leaf, a bud, a flower, a fragrance. He had to
go. He had to free himself of the reproach of all those dark
eyes.

Anybody he talked to, anybody at all, would tell him it
was a fool idea. His father would order him sternly to mind
his own business, to stay out of affairs that did not concern
him. His mother would never understand because loyalty
to Hume Harper was a duty in her mind, she had formed
her own life by it and tried to mold the lives of her children
to the same pattern.

In his heart William owned that he was going because he
had to go, because suddenly the approval of Lennie Briscoe and her daughters was necessary to his peace of mind,
their contempt and resentment unbearable.

It was like the pain of Denise's leaving without saying
goodbye. A gnawing thing that preyed on some tenderness
within him which no one had ever suspected or would have
believed that he owned. When people looked at William
Harper they saw only a not-yet-coordinated length of leg
and arm, feet and hands too big for the sparseness of his
body, shoulders stooped already because all at once too

many doors were built too low. They saw clothes that never quite fitted because they were so soon outgrown they must be bought too large and then thriftily worn out, till they drew tight across chest and thighs.

They heard a voice slowly settling into a decent baritone but still prone to betray him with startling tenor squawks. They never saw what lay in his eyes, deep and vulnerable, nor the flinching gentleness of his mouth, a mouth that hated all cruel things. His father's cruel-looking hands, for one. Just now William was realizing that in all his years he had avoided as often as he could looking at his father's hands.

He would have to go on Sunday and he would have to walk. Somebody would see him on the road inevitably but that was a risk he would have to take. If tales were carried he could always own bashfully that he had gone courting at Briscoe's, but even that excuse would not appease Hume Harper. Harper would order him to do his courting in a loyal Union household and remind him that his sister's folly was enough political embarrassment for one important citizen to live down. After all, Tom Findly's father was a staunch Union man, but the Briscoes were all outright rebels. Even that one who had stood square on his stubby little feet and shouted at Harper, calling him an old Yankee.

There would be a row but William knew as he waited for Sunday that he would have to risk it. From the south the news of the war was disheartening for the Confederacy. Braxton Bragg and Hardee were being pushed south through the Gap at Ringgold, Georgia, with heavy losses. William debated saving a Louisville paper to carry out to Briscoe's, but decided against that idea as no kindness. If the Briscoes did not know how Bragg had divided and weakened his army, how General Grant had abruptly taken

180

over to speed up the Confederate disaster at Chattanooga, they would not have a fresh and sharp worry to draw them in upon themselves, barring sympathizers out.

He went to church dutifully, and sat through an hour-long sermon, his feet numb with cold. Now and then some elder got up and heaved a chunk of wood into the iron stove with a great clanking and poking but the preacher's breath fumed white about the pulpit before at last he came to an ending and William noted that his father's nose was slowly reddening and that his mother had her hands tucked inside her little muff. None of the Briscoes were in church. There were many empty pews though some soldiers in blue occupied former worshiping seats of families gone over to the Confederacy.

Judge Nesbitt's old, well-used Bible still lay on the bench just below the pulpit and a sergeant of the Union infantry looked at it curiously before he pushed it gently aside and sat down. But there was no flowered bonnet with bright hair under it, no soft rustle of wide skirts, no merry glint of eye as the congregation filed out, to catch William's sidelong glance and answer it with a little private smile that meant that they two, he and Denise, knew that the minister was a windy old bore.

William observed with some dismay that except for a couple of stodgy-looking girls in unfashionable bonnets, he was the only young person in church. The woman who had demanded last summer why William wasn't in uniform was there, and as always when he met her she gave him a contemptuous look that moved over to include his father.

Sunday dinner was always ceremonious in the Harper house. It was the only meal of the week when Harper took time to say a long, unctuous grace, thanking the Lord for Hume Harper and the success of all his enterprises, and asking the Almighty's forgiveness for all the sins committed by the family, and especially for that sheep strayed so far from Thy Righteousness and Grace.

Hessie brought in the steaming dumplings and on this day she bumped the dish down so that Ellen looked up with anxiety in her eyes. When Hessie flounced she was always mad about something.

Harper had informed them firmly that emancipation would shortly be an accomplished fact in Kentucky and William knew that his mother was pondering the necessity of soon having to pay Hessie wages and wondering if it would be possible to get enough money from her husband to keep Hessie content in the kitchen.

There was a dried apple pie, not sweet enough, and William ate it reluctantly, hating the stuff but wanting no sharp order from the head of the table to finish what was on his plate. Today he tried to be as inconspicuous as possible. When his father had settled himself with the *Lexington Observer and Reporter* William got his overcoat and cap.

"Going out to walk some," he told his mother as he went through the dining room.

She was at her daily task of washing the china cups and saucers in a pan of soapsuds and she looked up anxiously.

"Son, you wouldn't be walking—out there, would you?" she whispered wistfully.

He frowned. "You—mean, out there?" There was one name that was not spoken in that house. That name was Findly.

"I'm getting worried," his mother sighed. "It would be a relief to have some news."

"It's a long way—and he'd hear about it," William evaded.

It was two miles to Lennie Briscoe's too and there would undoubtedly be some snooper to tattle, but William had to go today where unease drove him. He would not admit, even to himself, that he had been seeing Clemmy Briscoe's eyes upon him all week, flashing anger, or that it had mattered to him.

"If I don't have some news soon I'll go myself," declared Ellen, swishing a cup furiously through the suds. "I'll go if I have to walk."

"He wouldn't let you. Anyway he wouldn't let you walk."

"Of course, William, if you aren't concerned about your own sister—"

William buttoned his coat. "Was she concerned about you? About her own mother, about any of us?"

"Very well. Don't hang around please—the wrong places. Those soldiers, they do gamble and drink and use bad language."

"I've got nothing to do with soldiers," flared William. "I hate their guts!"

"You needn't be vulgar—and don't be late. We won't have supper till after church. I have to let Hessie go to their meeting. I gave her my old blue bonnet. It's too young for me now anyway. I have to keep Hessie happy."

"Why don't they let the Negroes alone?" demanded William. "Keeping them stirred up all the time!"

"It's that worthless son of hers. She's afraid he'll go into the army but Secretary Stanton has promised the governor not to keep any Negro troops in Kentucky. Some agent has been around offering them bounties and Hessie's afraid the boy will be sent across the Ohio."

"Mr. Merrill told me about that bounty business. The government pays the bounty and with the colored soldiers the agent keeps most of it and slips the poor Negro a few dollars. I've got to go, Mama. I'll be back before dark."

He hurried out through the kitchen where Hessie sat picking meat off a chicken back with her spatulate, lavender fingers. He said, "Hello, Hessie," but got no answer save a slow, disdaining look from muddy eyes.

Be tough on his mother if Hessie didn't show up some morning, if a knock on the door of the cabin by the back gate brought no response. Ellen could cook a little, make preserves and stuff, but she had never done any real work around the house outside of making her bed and maybe polishing a silver piece or a mirror.

Hessie did the washing on the back porch in big wooden tubs, no matter how cold the weather was, heating water on the kitchen stove and lugging it out in buckets. She even made the soap in the big iron pot hung under the mountain ash tree. Some days she ironed all day, banging heavy irons down on the stove lids, sweat rolling down her face in hot weather. It occurred to William that colored people had it tough and what would it be like to know that you didn't even own your own body, that if his father chose he could sell Hessie as he would sell the mare?

He debated this matter and came up with no answer as he trudged out of town and over the freezing ruts of the Cynthiana road. The sun had come out thinly, turning the frosted leaves of the oaks to bronze as they still clung to the branches. Oaks were mighty independent trees, they scorned to follow the passing seasons. They held onto their leaves when all the gums and hickorys had shed theirs, in spattering golden showers. The dogwood let their scarlet foliage go early and the sumac dropped great crimson hands with multiple fingers but the oaks were hoarders, like old people who had lived a long time and despised change. They put out new leaves in the spring when they got good and ready but likely they knew and were vain about knowing that no farmer ever planted corn till oak leaves were as big as a squirrel's ear.

Even in winter, Kentucky was pretty, he was thinking.

Peaceful and rolling, the grass holding some green still under the thin snow. At the Briscoe gate William saw an old Negro man in shapeless clothes leaning on the fence, dribbling salt through his fingers to be nuzzled by one lone horse. He looked at William and grinned, his blue gums showing.

"Lettin' her out, pick 'round a little," he said. "Got to stay here and watch or Miss wouldn't have no hoss. Lock the stable, Boss, lock it day and night. Bad times. Bad times."

"Sure are, uncle," agreed William. "Bad for everybody."

"Name's Jericho," went on the old man. "Can't work no more but Miss depend on me to tend this hoss. Be a hundred year old do I live fo' mo' years. Come yere fum Virginny with Ole Marster. Injuns here then and man got to tote him a gun do he plow corn. Old Marster built him a log house. 'Jericho, you heave up them logs,' Ole Marster say. Hi yi! Stout buck them days. Jericho lif' a big hickory log like it was a hoe handle, yas suh!"

"Folks at home, Jericho?"

"Reckon they is. Don't dast set foot out no mo' skeercely. Bad times!" mourned Jericho, rubbing his pale palms together to rid them of the salt. William left him licking his fingers and mumbling to himself.

This time he did not ring the front doorbell, but walked around to the back and knocked on the door there. Priscilla opened it, warily, let him in to a cold back entry where washtubs sat on stools and a churn stood with wooden dasher and lid upturned.

"My goodness, Willie Harper!" exclaimed the little girl. "Why did you come to the back like a Negro?"

He took off his cap. "Just thought I'd come out for a little visit," he said. "Which Briscoe are you?"

"I'm Priss. And don't you call me Baby—everybody does

185

and I hate it. Mama's in the kitchen popping corn for the children, Tee's upstairs writing a letter. Come along in."

The kitchen was warm and the same battery of eyes assailed William as he followed Priscilla in. Lennie was shaking a skillet at the stove and she stared at him, not hiding her astonishment.

"Why, Willie Harper! Is your father here?"

"No, ma'am. I came alone. I walked. I thought I'd come out and see you all."

"Well, that's friendly of you, Willie." Lennie was obviously relieved that he had come alone. "Clemmy, get Willie a chair. We could sit in the other room but the children make such a mess with popcorn." She tilted the skillet over a pan and a few grains popped out and flew high to be chased by Ward and 'Ria, squealing happily.

Clementine pulled out a chair and said, "Have a seat, Willie. You'd better take off your coat. You'll freeze when you go out."

"I never did see it turn so bitter so early." Lennie shook salt over the pan. "Now, you children use your own bowls and don't grab and fight and spill it. Is your mother well, Willie?"

"Yes'm, she's fine." William folded his overcoat and laid it beside him, looking bashfully at Clemmy. There was no hostility in her eyes today and she blushed a little as she said, "I'll put your cap over here."

"Don't bother, I'll just put it in my pocket." Someday he would have a real hat. A tall hat like gentlemen wore.

"'You don't go to school any more, Willie?" Clementine inquired politely. "I thought you'd go off east to college."

"I might, if the war hadn't started. I might be called up to active duty any day now." He expanded his chest a little. "That is, if the Confederates don't give up and let this war come to an end." Too late he realized the tactlessness of this remark but only the little children bristled.

"My pa won't ever surrender," declared Rowena. "Not if they shoot at him and stab him with swords and everything."

"My pa will kill all those ole Yankees dead and dead!" orated Ward, waving his arms and scattering popcorn.

"You think we can't win, do you, Willie?" asked Clementine, seeing his embarrassment.

"Nobody ever wins a war," he said. "Look at all the country, torn up and full of hate and destruction. Thousands of men killed and people homeless, black people and white people. And what have they won? Ruin, that's all. Even here in Kentucky look at all the ruin already."

"My horse gone!" sighed Clementine. "The Yankees took him and some old Home Guard rides him now, not brushed or curried or anything."

"It was the Confederates took our cows," put in Priscilla. "Mama said she hoped Pa would get a pair of shoes out of their hides when he went south to fight."

"Let's not talk war," urged Lennie. "Have some popcorn, Willie?"

"No, thanks, Mrs. Briscoe. I just had dinner."

"We all have to stay in now, on account of so many rough men all over the country," complained Clementine. "I've read every old *Harper's Magazine* and *Godey's Book* in our attic, and all Grandma's old novels. We pieced quilts till we ran out of thread and there wasn't any at the store when we sent Jericho."

"Jericho's the only one we dare let go," Priscilla added. "Mama's afraid to let Ceph or Lum off the place for fear the army will catch them up and put them to building roads or something."

"Jericho's so old they wouldn't have him," Lennie said. "Old and silly in the head."

"I saw him." Willie was looking at Clementine's chin. A round, pretty little chin, firm and decisive, and her throat was round and pretty too. "He told me he was almost a hundred years old."

"He could be. Great-grandpa brought him to Kentucky from Virginia right after the war, the British war when they burned Washington."

"1812," William aired his knowledge. "That was fifty-one years ago."

"Grandpa Briscoe was a grown man then but he wasn't married. Got married in the stockade down at Harrodsburg and came up here and built a cabin for his bride. Lum and Marshy live in it now. Grandpa built the old part of this house before Pa was born. Jericho helped build it. He says he pegged on every shingle. Great-grandpa was pretty old then and he sat out under the mulberry tree and whittled out thousands of hickory pegs, so he used to tell us." She sighed. "Our family has been on this land ever since there was a Kentucky."

William ached to say something reassuring or sympathetic but he had been well warned not to discuss his father's business.

"Clemmy, you and Willie go sit in the front room," Lennie said. "I want to sweep up here, then I'll go with the children and see if the hens have laid today."

Clementine said, "Come along, Willie," and led him across the hall to a big room where logs burned low in a fireplace and there was a high bed, puffy and white under a tester, and some rocking chairs with faded velvet cushions. A vast walnut wardrobe filled one corner of the room with bandboxes piled on top. Clementine indicated a chair by

188

the fire, said, "Excuse me a minute, I forgot," and ran out, coming back with a pistol that she laid handy.

"Whoever stays in the house alone keeps this gun handy," she explained. "Pa's orders—on account of the guerrillas. They haven't bothered us yet, I reckon they know we haven't got much left worth plundering. We keep everything locked up, even the henhouse, but Tee says locks wouldn't help much if they set the buildings on fire."

"The Findlys, my sister's in-laws, had their barn burned and they shot old Mr. Findly." William was feeling a comfortable glow of complacency. He was, obviously, assumed to be calling on Clemmy and she was, for a wonder, being very friendly and sociable. He was a little vague about the technique of courting a girl. His hands and feet felt enormous and his Adam's apple had spasms in his throat so that his voice wobbled dangerously at times but he managed to keep a casual flow of small talk going and Clementine listened politely. Nobody had ever listened to him before, not for long anyway, and certainly nobody had ever implied by their attention that he had anything of consequence to say.

He was doing very well when the door opened and Teresa came in. She looked slightly tousled, her hair all fluffed around her face so that to his eyes she was prettier than ever. She regarded him with surprise.

"My goodness, Willie, I didn't know you were here. Ugh, I'm cold! It's freezing upstairs."

"Sit here and get warm." William leaped up gallantly, offering his chair. "I must be going anyway. It's a long walk back to town."

"You walked all the way, in this cold wind? Oh, then if you're going back to town will you mail this letter for me?" Teresa asked. "I wrote it in bed with the cover pulled up to my chin so the address is sort of wobbly."

"Yes, I'll mail it in the morning when the post office opens."

"I've got a quarter here." Teresa untied a knot in her apron string. "It's my last quarter so Henri won't get any more letters."

"Mama said he wouldn't even get this one," Clementine told her. "She said the Yankees are stopping every boat that tries to cross over to Arkansas."

"I'm not sending it to Arkansas. I'm sending it to the War Department in Richmond. Mama sent a letter to our father there and he got it."

"After six weeks," said Clementine. "Anyway," she hedged warily, "we heard he did."

"Maybe I'll write to old Henri. I always liked old Henri." Willam tucked the letter into his pocket.

Teresa sighed. "It was nice in the old days, wasn't it? Before everything got hateful and horrible, when we were all young and silly. We didn't know then the old people were going to set the world on fire and leave us to put out the blaze. Remember the barbecue out at Bacon's grove, Willie, when you and Henri knocked that hornets' nest out of the pecan tree?"

"We had to run faster than anybody," laughed William.

"Clemmy couldn't run fast, she was so fat, and she got stung," Teresa added with an enchanting giggle.

"In three places," grumbled Clementine. "It was bad enough being stung but you all laughed at me, and that made me mad."

"It made you madder when Mrs. Bacon put mud on your face," William remembered. So good to laugh again, so good to see a young girl smile, to feel her hand in yours, bidding goodbye. So good to feel like a man, walking home high-headed, whistling a little in the purple December twilight.

Maybe he wouldn't have to leave for a while, but before long he was going to have to get away, clear away, to some-place where he could earn some money. Real money.

One thing was certain. A man couldn't get married on a dollar a week!

18

HUME HARPER HAD ALWAYS DISDAINED TO ROAR. HIS throat swelled and his too-prominent eyes bulged till they looked, as Harriet had once impudently remarked, like hard-boiled eggs, but what issued from his mouth was a mixture of bark and bleat. He supplemented the inade-quacy of his voice by beating his flat hand on the table till the vinegar cruet jumped in the caster and Ellen looked ap-prehensively at the kitchen door where Hessie was un-doubtedly lurking and listening.

"Please, Mr. Harper," she begged, her face white and twitching though her mouth and chin were set as neither her husband nor her son had ever seen them before.

"I say," repeated Harper, dragging his voice down to a rasp, "that you are not going! We have to bear this disgrace. We do not have to countenance it and we will not!"

"I will," announced Ellen so firmly that her husband blinked and shook his head, unwilling to believe his ears. "I'm going. She is my child and I've already packed some things. As soon as Tom Findly finds the doctor and comes for me, I shall go and I shall stay as long as Harriet needs me. You and William will be all right here with Hessie to do for you. My mind is made up and there's no use saying anything, Mr. Harper, no use at all!"

"So you don't care what people say?" Harper sputtered, seeking some firm ground for his toppling authority.

Ellen folded her napkin, laid it precisely in the silver ring.

"I do care what people say. That's why I'm going."

William went to the window, pulled the curtain aside. "Going to snow," he remarked, keeping his back to the pair who were glaring at each other on opposite sides of the table. He always felt itchy and unhappy when there was a family scene, never feeling free to take one side or the other in any argument. If he did put in a word it would be ignored, reminding him of how inconsequential he was in this house, or else his father would yap out an order for him to mind his own business.

Harper jerked his chair back with a snort, slamming it against the wall. "You've been seeing her, I suppose? You've been letting her come here for the whole town to see and snicker at?"

"I have not seen her. Not since May," Ellen retorted coldly. "I respected your order even when I considered it preposterous and unjust. But I shall see Harriet today," she went on grimly, "and after that as often as I choose."

"She's not coming here! Not to this house. I made that very clear to her before she married that fellow," he yelped.

"I doubt," said Ellen as she turned away, "that she would wish to come here."

She walked deliberately across the hall to the bedroom and closed the door. William let the curtain fall.

"Bad weather coming," he said lamely.

Harper shrugged, pushed down his vest, ran a finger

around his rigid collar. "It's always bad weather in December. You go and harness the mare and drive your mother out there. If she is determined to go I won't be beholden to Tom Findly. She'll go in her own carriage."

"But he's coming here." William knew the protest to be futile before he voiced it. "She told him she'd be ready."

"You heard me!" barked his father. "You come straight back too, and finish your work at the bank when you return."

William put on a sheepskin-lined jacket and knitted cap and slogged out to the stable, wincing as the frigid wind nipped at his face. Every day since that visit to the Briscoe farm rebellion had been brewing in William's soul, tamped down but burning and gnawing. He knew he could never make his discontent vocal. His father would blast him with those edged words that always worked a kind of paralysis in William and his mother would probably cry.

To win any freedom at all he was convinced he would have to run away and how could he do that with no money at all? On a wage of a dollar a week?

"You are fed, you are clothed, you are housed, what more do you need?" was his father's impatient argument.

He and Harriet had often complained to each other at being financially cramped and restricted but grumbling was their only relief, as they knew well—so much protesting into the wind. William had considered joining the army, but it would have to be the Confederate army to escape his father's continued control, and from Tom's reports those men weren't being paid either. And according to the news lately about all they were doing was to stand, or retreat and die by thousands.

As he warmed the frigid bit in his hands before bridling the mare, William's mind kept racing like a rat in a trap beating impotently against metal bars. Never in his life had he faced up to any situation with decision. Soon he would be old enough to vote and even then he supposed his mind would be made up for him, his work laid out for him, and he would be bullied into it. There could be no change in his situation without a battle and he knew it would have to be a furious battle to penetrate the icy shell of his father's self-esteem. His mother, William was convinced, was as helpless as he, though she had shown a startling bit of spirit today.

He knew that Ellen had inherited some money and never seen any of it, seldom handled a dollar of her own. Even her clothes were chosen by her husband who selected the material, haggled with the sewing woman over the price of dressmaking, chose the style and pattern and the bonnet to go with it. Harriet had won a trifle more indulgence but she had done it by flattery and cajolery—both weapons that William scorned. Now likely Harriet never laid eyes on a dime. He wondered as he backed the mare into the shafts if Harriet right now was ruing her impulsive folly and wishing herself back home again.

Ellen was waiting on the steps when he backed the buggy around. She wore her cloak and shawl with a knitted scarf tied over her head. She carried two large bundles besides her carpetbag and umbrella.

"I've had these things ready for a month," she said as he stowed the parcels under the seat. "Old sheets and flannel and little things I've made over. I hated to deceive your father but as Hessie says, what a man doesn't know will never give him a headache. I feel a little shaky now facing Mr. Harper down as I did, it's the first time in twenty years that I've deliberately gone against him. He's a good man but he's terribly stubborn. So in this affair I just had to be stubborn too."

"Pa's got a heart like a grindstone!" William growled.

194

"And you know it. I'm glad you had the guts to stand up to him. Every time he bugs those cold eyes at me I sort of wilt and I hate it. Sometime I'm going to blow up and cuss him to his face."

"No—no, son," she protested. "It's just his way. Your father loves both his children very much."

"He shows it," snapped William, "turning Harriet out of the house just because he didn't pick out the man for her to marry—the way he picked out her hats!"

"You don't understand, William. You mustn't blame your father."

"I do blame him," he went on recklessly, "for being selfish and mule-headed and calling it pride and independence. He's not proud. Not too proud to do a lot of mean things. Things I wouldn't do, like taking people's homes away from them and making money out of the misery of this war! You know it's all true, Mama, how can you justify him?" It was a long speech for William and he was a little breathless. He slapped the reins on the mare's rump. "Get along, you! You want to jog here forever in one spot and freeze to death?"

"Too bad to make you take this long drive in the cold," said his mother. "I could very well have gone with Tom Findly."

"No, you couldn't. That wouldn't have been doing things Pa's way."

"Why didn't I think to put a couple of bricks in the oven so we could have put our feet on them?" Ellen ignored the boy's outbursts. "I suppose Tom will stop at our house. I should have left a note, but anyway Hessie knew where we were going, so he won't wait. He said he thought it would be today. You know your sister is having a baby, don't you, William?"

"Sure I know. I guess everybody knows."

"It's coming too soon. Of course there are seven-months babies who live but it's hardly seven months and that's hard on your father. He has always held his head so high in this town and now—his only daughter—" Ellen seemed to be talking to herself. "Maybe we did wrong about the wedding. We should have had a nice wedding at home, if it *was* wartime, but of course with Tom just out of the rebel army that complicated things. It would have been dreadful to have the bridegroom arrested in the middle of the ceremony. Anyway Harriet wouldn't have a real wedding. She just wanted it over with and when she sets her head she can be as obstinate as her father. You're more like me, son."

"I hope so!" he exclaimed bitterly, then with an effort as though he dragged up words from some deep place within himself, a painful effort as though each word had jagged edges, he hurled at her, "Mama, I want to get away from here."

She did not start or register surprise. She did not answer till the silence had stretched for at least a mile. Then she said quietly, "Where, son?"

"I don't know." As though a dam had been loosened words tumbled out of him in urgency and confusion. "I don't know. Anywhere! Away from that darned bank. I hate it. I hate the way people look at Pa, as though they half envied him and half despised him. And the way they look at me. As though I wasn't even there. The boss's son. Can't even add six figures and get the right answer but he has to be kept on because he's Harper's son. Oh, Lord, Mama, I hate it!" He was almost sobbing. He slashed at the mare with the whip in his agitation and she gave an angry snort and a disgusted caper, then broke into a ragged lope, bouncing the buggy over the frozen ruts.

"You know your father controls all my money, William," his mother reminded him. "He never tells me much about it but he did say he had invested it well and that if anything happened to him I and my children would be secure."

"Nothing is going to happen to him," declared William, dejectedly. "You'll die and I'll die and Pa will go right on foreclosing on all the good farms in the county. He has filed papers on the Nesbitt place and Thad Briscoe's farm already."

"Oh, no! Not poor Lennie Briscoe! With all those children. How could he—with her husband off to war?" protested Ellen.

"That was the reason, he told Mrs. Briscoe. With Thad in the Confederate army the Union might confiscate the property. He told her that if he held it they might be able to redeem it. It was true, I was there. He took me along for a witness—of how generous he was, he said."

"Perhaps he did mean well, William. We have to believe it. We can't let ourselves believe that he is so stony-hearted as he appears to you. And you must remember that he has great responsibility to the depositors and people who trust him with their money."

"I know. I hear that every day. But it wasn't bank money that was loaned to Thad Briscoe. Pa held that paper himself. He told Mrs. Briscoe he did it to protect the bank."

"Oh, dear, I hope it wasn't my money he used," sighed Ellen. "I would hate to think I had any part, no matter how innocently, in taking land away from people whose family have owned it for generations."

"Have you any idea how much money you had, Mama?"

"Oh, my child, women are never told anything! We're supposed not to have any brains. I was already married when my father died, and the lawyers and the bank and Mr. Harper managed everything. I do know there was some property sold and I had to sign the papers, and I know it brought twelve thousand dollars but how much more there was I was never told. I had to trust your father."

"Twelve thousand dollars!" William's voice cracked a little. "They get eight and ten per cent at the bank—in ten years it would almost have doubled itself. Why don't you make Pa tell you? Why don't you ask him straight out how your account stands and what he's done with it? Other women do. I hear them in the bank, they make Pa bring out all the papers and show them the figures and everything. Maybe he bought cotton with it," suggested the boy, stiff with excitement. "That contraband trade made thousands and thousands of dollars profit."

"Not contraband, William. Surely your father wouldn't deal in contraband?"

"Ha!" shrugged William. "Where do you think all that money comes from he brings home and hides, that never goes into the bank vault?"

"I can't see Mr. Harper taking a risk like that. But there is a lot of money."

"In that steel box in your wardrobe. Of course I'm not supposed to know about it."

"It has worried me," said Ellen, "having it in the house with so many lawless men around. They would kill and burn for gold now with most of the paper money practically worthless."

"Down south they just print it. Anybody with a printing press down there can run off a lot of money. It shows up at the bank all the time. Notes on banks in Mobile and Baton Rouge, even from down in Texas. Pa and Mr. Bolt always refuse it. Even regular issue Confederate money isn't worth anything any more. No gold or specie behind it." William enjoyed airing his knowledge of the banking business, without being warned sternly to shut up. "Pa certainly couldn't refuse to tell you how your account stands, Mama."

198

"I tried once," she said. "When I wanted you to go to college."

"He said I was naturally stupid, didn't he? That the money would be wasted. I remember." Bitterness was back in the boy's voice again. "Oh, Lord, it's snowing!"

"There comes Tom. He's overtaken us." Ellen was a bit relieved to put an end to her son's financial dissertation. Not that she was not sympathetic with William. With a beard showing and his voice deepening he wanted to be counted a man, he needed respect, not continued bullying and hectoring. "I'll ride on with Tom now." She began collecting her bundles. "You go straight home before this storm gets any worse. Oh, Tom, we should have waited for you but Mr. Harper was impatient."

"I'm a little impatient myself." Tom helped her out after pulling his own rig over to the side of the road. "This all your stuff, Mrs. Harper? Wait, I'll help you in. It's going to be a bad night, I'm afraid."

"It always happens." Ellen laughed nervously. "Hurry now, William. Tom will bring me when I'm ready to go home."

William waited till the Findly buggy had disappeared in the white swirl of increasing snow, then backed and turned, trying to keep away from puddles and freezing mud. If he got the buggy dirty he would be ordered to wash it, a miserable job in bitter weather. All the way back to town his mind churned away on one idea. Figure it anyway at all, his mother must have at least twenty thousand dollars.

He knew his father's shrewdness. Even sardonic Mr. Bolt agreed that Hume Harper never turned a dollar to anything that did not show a profit. There was plenty of money in the bank, he knew. He had had to carry those heavy sacks of gold outside times enough, to be buried in the iron chest in the back yard whenever Morgan's men came back to

Kentucky. Usually at night it was all locked up in that stout new safe and only his father had the combination.

He rolled the buggy back into the stable, knocking the mud off the rims of the wheels with the pitchfork, drying the mare's fetlocks with a tow sack. He tossed down some hay, locked the barn door and tramped back to the bank, bending against the stinging wind and cold lash of the snow.

At three o'clock Mr. Bolt slammed the shutter down behind his grated window and began counting the checks and cash in his till. William officially closed the front door, pulled down the shade on which was painted CLOSED. Half an hour later Bolt and Merrill carried all the cash and papers into the vault and Hume Harper marched behind them, making a ceremony of seeing everything stowed in the safe, then importantly slamming the door, turning the lock and spinning the heavy dials.

Then Harper left the bank but the others stayed on, figuring in ledgers and grumbling.

William polished the door of the safe, studying those nickel dials with their cryptic black numbers.

"Suppose my father dropped dead tonight, how could the bank open tomorrow?" he asked Mr. Merrill. "Nobody knows how to open that safe."

The old clerk lifted a bony shoulder. "The bank wouldn't open. It would stay shut three or four days with a big bow of crepe on the door. Then if you could get that blue card with the combination written on it out of your father's wallet, we could open the bank again and be in business."

"The stockholders would take over and elect a new president," said Mr. Bolt. "Sonny here would probably inherit his father's stock, eventually, but he's not of legal age even to sit in a meeting. The court would have to appoint somebody guardian for him."

"Who are the stockholders?" William inquired.

"Your family hold most of it," Mr. Merrill said. "A few outsiders, enough to make it legal for the institution to be chartered by the state."

Twelve thousand dollars, at least, of that hoard behind those dials was his mother's money. And in due course of time half of that would be his inheritance.

It was after midnight when he crept barefooted down the stairs at home. Warily, remembering that deadly little pistol Harper carried and kept ready under his pillow at night, William tiptoed into the big dark bedroom. He knew where his father carried his wallet. In the inside pocket of his long-tailed coat, and at night the coat was always draped precisely on the back of a certain walnut chair. The snow outside made a little light and it was obvious that his father was sound asleep. His breath rasped and blurted and occasionally he ground his teeth. William dropped on all fours and crept cautiously toward the chair.

The wallet came out easily and he grasped it tightly in both hands for fear something metallic might drop out of it and clink, as he inched his way back to the hall. There he got to his feet and went quickly and stealthily to the kitchen where he closed the door, lit a candle and found the blue card exactly where Mr. Merrill had said it would be.

On a paper he had brought down with him he carefully copied the figures, the "Right" and "Left" directions, replaced the card precisely where it had been, blew out the candle and made a silent trip back to the bedroom and the coat on the back of the chair. A button tapped softly on the chair post as he replaced the wallet and William held his breath as Harper stirred a little, gave a strangling cough and then resumed his rhythmic snoring.

In his own room again, William locked the door and made a better copy of the combination, tearing up the first hasty draft, burning the scraps in the candle flame bit by bit and flicking the ashes out an open window into the snow. Then from a place where he had hidden it he brought out a blank draft, the kind they were always handling at the bank. Very carefully with pen and ink he filled in the face of the draft.

DEBIT THE ACCOUNT OF MRS. ELLEN HARPER, ONE THOU-SAND DOLLARS.

The draft and the safe code he put in an envelope, sealed it and pinned it inside his coat.

The room was cold and his feet were lumps of ice when he crept into bed but his breath blew hot in his nostrils and his heart was racing like a wild steam engine.

19

ELLEN HARPER APPROACHED THE FINDLY HOUSE A BIT fearfully. She had seen Marcia Findly in church a few times and noted that Mr. Findly was usually in attendance whether his wife came or not, but she could not remember ever having spoken to either of them except those few nervous words to Tom's mother at the wedding.

A year had passed since she had seen old Tom Findly and the sight of him as young Tom led her into the kitchen gave her a start. The old man was huddled in a deep rocking chair padded with calico cushions, his thin legs resting on a pillowed stool. His eyes were deep-sunken and one of them was a little twisted by a dark scar that gave his face a weird, sinister look, but both eyes blazed at her as she approached hesitantly and his lips struggled to form a word.

"Begone!" was what finally came out, and Ellen turned back to Tom, putting out a groping hand as though to steady herself from a blow.

"Don't mind Pa, Mrs. Harper." Tom was loaded with her baggage. He set it down, opened a door and called up the stairs, "Here's Mrs. Harper, Ma."

There were quick light steps on the stairs, flying down, and Marcia Findly hurried in, fluttering both hands eagerly. She reached for Ellen, helping her off with her scarf and coat.

"My, am I thankful to see you!" she exclaimed. "Harriet kept saying Mama won't come, but I said now you wait. I know mothers. She said her father wouldn't let you come but I told her you'd be here and to stop fretting. You get warm now. I've got the kettles all hot and I'll make you a hot cup of tea. Everything is all right upstairs for a little bit. You go up, Tom, and tell her her mama's here. Warm your hands first, and hang that coat up to dry. Surely did turn winter all of a sudden, didn't it?"

She bustled about answering Ellen's anxious questions, pouring boiling water into a teapot, getting cream and sugar and some thin cookies from a safe.

"I'm fixing some for you too, Mr. Findly," she placated as she set out the cups. "This is Harriet's mother and she'll be here for a little while."

She shoved the rocker nearer the table and put a cup of tea, much diluted with milk, in reach of her husband's clawing hands. "He can feed himself now," she ran on. "It surely is a help. But something is still all wrong in his head so don't be upset by anything he says." She went to the chair and laid a gentle hand on Findly's thinning hair. "You're going to be a grandpa, Mr. Findly, you know that? We're going to have a nice baby in this house." She breathed deeply and Ellen saw how fagged she was, her eyes reddened as though she had not slept for days. "I can hardly wait!" she sighed. "Tom was such a lovely baby. I surely did feel bereft when he started to grow up. You want to go up now, you just go along. I'll have to tend Mr. Findly till he finishes his tea."

"There's no hope?" Ellen began uncertainly, watching the old man wistfully spoon up his tea and dip a cookie into it like a child.

"It's been a year now. There's some improvement, he's out of bed anyway, but he's got no use of his legs and his mind is still foggy. I told Tom to put your things in the north room upstairs. He made a fire. I'll be up directly but I'd better wait down here till the doctor comes."

So bare, so bare, thought Ellen as she entered that upper room where Harriet lay, turning and sweating, her hair flung out damply on the pillow.

"My dear!" Ellen murmured, bending to kiss the flushed, wet forehead. Tom had been holding Harriet's hand but she loosed it and reached up to clutch at her mother.

"Mama, you came!" she cried. "Oh, Mama, you didn't tell me it would be like this!"

Tom looked worried, gnawing his lip. "The doctor ought to be here pretty soon. Don't they give them something, Mrs. Harper? Opium or something?"

"It will be over soon and then she'll forget it." Ellen put all the confidence she could summon into her voice. "You go down, Tom. You'll need to be there to take care of the doctor's horse. Harriet and I will be all right."

There was so little that she knew about birth. Only her own two and she had been the tended one then, paying little heed to what went on around her. She straightened the cover and Harriet's nightgown, wiped her face with a damp towel, patted it dry and mended the fire in the small iron grate.

"I was sure Pa wouldn't let you come," said Harriet. "I told Tom it was just no use to go but he said he'd try anyway. Does he still hate me, Mama?"

"No—no! You mustn't think that. Your father would never hate you. He misses you I know—"

"He hates Tom. Did you know he came out here—last summer? In August it was. He didn't mention my name and I kept out of sight. It was something about some sort of cotton deal he had with old Mr. Findly before Mr. Findly got hurt. Pa kept asking Mr. Findly questions and of course he couldn't answer. He just got excited and beat his hands on the table till he skinned his knuckles. Pa was mad and he began barking—you know how he does—so finally Tom interfered and told him it was impossible for Mr. Findly to tell him anything and he might as well let him alone. So then Pa turned on Tom and demanded to know where the bonds were?"

"What bonds?" asked Ellen.

"We don't know. Nobody knows but Mr. Findly and he can't tell. Pa threatened to send the sheriff out but nobody ever came. You don't know anything about it, Mama?"

"Goodness, how would I know? Your father never discusses business with me."

"I think it's some kind of shady business like those river deals Pa was mixed up in. Oh, I know, Mama, and you do too—so you needn't put on that dutiful face and try to defend him. Oh, Mama—the pain!"

"Hold my hands, dear. Pull hard!"

"I can't bear it! I can't bear it!"

It was getting dark when the doctor arrived. The snow

was five inches deep, he reported, be sleighing weather by morning.

"Now let's get this young one born, young lady," he ordered briskly. "Get it over by Christmas anyway. Looks like the war might be over by Christmas too. Both sides plumb worn out the way I see it, even the Union enlisting little boys and middle-aged men. They're just sort of standing still and slapping at each other now. Few battles down in Tennessee and a little skirmishing around in Texas, but no big campaigns on. Got to rest up the armies and shoe up some horses—run some more ammunition too. Hold that lamp closer, Mrs. Harper. No, Tom, you'd drop it. You stay out of this woman business. Go downstairs and get drunk. That's my advice to all fathers."

The baby, born at midnight, was very small with Tom's long eyelashes and very little hair.

"My Lord!" muttered Tom, bending over his mother as she bathed the child and wrapped a voluminous flannel band around the little bandaged middle. "She looks just like a little monkey!"

"She looks just as you looked when you were a half hour old," retorted his mother. "She's got a nice mouth and a chin like Mrs. Harper's. What are you going to call her?"

Tom looked uncertain. "I don't know. We planned on a boy and I was going to name him Robert E. Lee."

"Tom, you couldn't! Not on this place. Not a boy with two grandfathers red-hot and radical for the Union."

Tom's mouth set a little. "I'd have named my son whatever Harriet and I agreed upon no matter how many grandfathers he had. But a girl—I reckon it's for Harriet to say."

"Well, don't name her after me," said his mother. "You'd mean it for an honor but it wouldn't be, not for me or the baby either. All over Amite County where I was born down in Mississippi there were slave girls called by my name and every one of them called Marshy, just as I was."

Ellen came down then, looking worn and tremulous from the day and night of unaccustomed strain. Birth was so much more dreadful to witness than to endure, especially if the moaning, writhing sufferer was your own child.

"She has dropped off to sleep," she said with a tired sigh.

From the table where he was eating fried eggs and sausage, the doctor looked up, wiped his mouth and grinned.

"They do that. Wear out a whole houseful of people and then go off to sleep as though nothing had happened."

"Tom and I were just wondering what to call the little girl." Marcia eased the small, squirming arms into the tiny sleeves of a flannel wrapper that still smelled of lavender and camphor. "You wouldn't believe it but I wore this gown." She folded the skirt over the baby's feet. "They wove goods to last in those days. I've already given orders to Tom not to name the baby after me, Mrs. Harper."

"Nor after me. Mine's an old-fashioned name," Ellen said. "She could be named Harriet Mary for her mother."

"My mother's name was Mary," said Marcia. "So was Mr. Findly's mother's. She was Mary Fiegelbaum, back in Pennsylvania. He never told me but I found it on some papers they sent back here from Lancaster when the old people died."

"Harriet Mary." Tom nodded. "We'll call her Hattie— tell them apart." He took the small red creature from his mother, grinned at the smacking mouth, the reaching claw-like hands. "Hello, Hattie! You make gestures like your Grandpa Findly. Golly, I didn't know they were so little and so soft."

"Six pounds she weighed on the chicken scales," said Marcia. "You leaving now, Doctor? Tom, give me the baby and you get the doctor some money—out of that tin box on my bureau. I put the last of the tobacco money in there."

"Three dollars," said the doctor. "Come higher when they get you out at night."

"Now, Mrs. Harper, you look ready to keel over so you go straight up to that spare room and get some sleep," ordered Marcia. "The room may have cooled off some but there's wood handy. Tom and I carried up plenty yesterday and there's extra blankets in that big trunk in the hall. All right, Miss Hattie. I'm putting you in this clothesbasket here by the fire till your mother wakes up. You go rest now, Mrs. Harper."

"I'll be all right," insisted Ellen. "I want to help. If I could have some hot tea—"

"Better than that. I made a pot of coffee for the doctor and there's plenty left. We're luckier than most people. Mr. Findly always was a good provider and when the war first began he laid in a lot of bags of green coffee. I roast it along as we need it and grind it fresh every morning. You sit right here and I'll cook you some eggs too. I've got a few hens left but we have to keep them locked up, with all these poor hungry colored people wandering around."

With the strong coffee reviving her Ellen sat and looked at this young son-in-law whom she hardly knew. He had said, "Mind if I have a cup of that too?" and dropped down beside her. "What we both need," he smiled, "is a stiff toddy but Pa would never allow any liquor on the place."

"I've rarely had any—only a little wine at parties when I was younger. Never anything since I was married to a deacon. But in my father's house there was always a decanter on the sideboard and kegs of wine in the cellar too. Are you disappointed, Tom, that the baby is a girl?"

"At first I was. But now—with the war and so much

trouble maybe a little girl will have a chance at a better life than a boy. I hope she'll grow up pretty like her mother."

"She hasn't much hair now but when it comes in I'm sure she'll be fair-haired like you, Tom. Your mother says you had a German grandmother. You have that coloring. And her eyes will be blue, I'm certain." Ellen was thinking that she had never considered Harriet a really pretty girl. Harriet had nice skin and eyes but her mouth was like Harper's and a deliberate mouth and stubborn chin were no asset to a woman. "You do love Harriet, Tom?" she asked abruptly.

He looked at the floor and a flick of pain tightened his brows for an instant.

"Maybe more than she loves me, Mrs. Harper." He was thinking of that moment last night when Harriet had cried and he had hurried to the bed and taken her hands. She had crushed his fingers in a spasm of travail, then as it relented had flung his hands away. "Leave me alone," she had gasped. "Haven't you done enough to me already?"

Now he stirred his cup round and round. "I never had a chance to tell you, Mrs. Harper. It was my fault—Harriet and me."

"Don't tell me now, Tom." Ellen held up a detaining hand. "It's over now. It's between you two. No one else."

"It was my fault," he persisted. "I was so crazy in love with her and I thought she was with me too and it isn't just between us two, Mrs. Harper, it's between Harriet and me and—Hattie."

"Perhaps not, Tom. Children aren't curious. About dates and what is past history. Do you know the date of your mother's marriage?"

He looked startled. "Why, no—I never asked her. Sometime in eighteen forty I think but I don't know the month or the day. But I still say it was all my fault, Mrs. Harper."

"Perhaps," she said gravely, "it was my fault. A girl properly reared would not have yielded."

She rose then and carried both cups to the table where the water bucket stood and a dishpan hung on a nail. Pouring hot water into the pan, she washed all the dishes and dried them on a bleached-out sack that hung over a wooden bar. Marcia Findly was busy caring for her husband so Ellen gathered her skirts and went back upstairs.

Such a meager house for all its prosperous-looking exterior! Nowhere within it were more than the bare essentials of living. True there was a parlor, she had glimpsed it, but it was a cold room, kept closed, no fire laid in the fireplace that was stopped with a fan of newspapers. There were four wooden chairs in the room, a round marble-topped table on which were a Bible and a hymnbook, a lamp kept shining-clean and filled but obviously never lighted. The white curtains were stiffly starched, the green shades drawn low.

She had never entered the room occupied by the elder Findlys but from glimpses through the open door she knew there was nothing ornamental or dedicated to comfort in that chamber either. There was no dining room. In Pennsylvania, Marcia had explained, the Findly family had always eaten in the kitchen.

"Of course at home the kitchen wasn't even a part of the house, but we had people—slaves to fetch and carry," Marcia said. "But Mr. Findly thinks wanting things easy is a mortal sin. He thinks life ought to be hard on us for the good of our souls. I've tried to make things as easy for Harriet as I can, Mrs. Harper," Marcia said, "but I can't call this a happy house for young people and that's the sad truth."

"I own a black woman, Hessie, but I suppose they'll all

be free now, though Kentucky has never accepted that proclamation."

"The black women may be free but the white women won't be," said Marcia with a touch of bitterness.

In Harriet's room the fire had been renewed and blazed brightly, and Harriet lay very flat in the bed, staring into the blaze.

"All his life, Tom said, he'd never had a fire up here before," she mused. "His father said it was a waste of wood. We'll have a fire this winter and there's nothing he can do about it." She was crisp. "Mama, I don't want my baby called Hattie. All the tacky girls I know have names like Hettie or Lizzie or Minnie."

"You can call her Mary then."

"After his old mother—Mary Finkelbaum or something? I wouldn't please him that much!"

"My mother was named Mary. That's where you got the name. Your father's mother was named Harriet. Your husband wanted to name her after you and I think you should be pleased. I never had any chance to give you a name. As soon as you were born your father announced that your name would be Harriet. I stuck the Mary in myself, when you were christened," Ellen said.

"The thing to do," said Harriet dryly, "is to be effusively grateful for every little scrap of kindness—or even of fairness or justice, isn't it? That's being married. I should have known, watching you all my life. Never getting your own way, accepting what you're given and making the best of it. Oh, I know what the Bible says about wives being submissive. St. Paul, the sour old wretch! Mrs. Findly says Mr. Findly thinks he patterns his life after St. Paul. Whenever he can put four words together and make any sense it's always something out of the Epistles. Mama, you must get some sleep. Go lie down this minute and pay no more attention to me. I have to storm around once in a while or explode. The trouble is Tom and his mother are both so beastly patient!"

"It's a blessing to be born with patience and not have to learn it the hard way. Though I suspect Marcia wasn't always a weak character. She strikes me as a person who would rise to an emergency if it occurred."

"He crushed her spirit, that awful old man. Tom told me. And there's a picture of her when she was sixteen, in a ball dress. She was lovely and stylish. She keeps the picture hid for fear he'd burn it. Vanity, he says." Harriet was sarcastic.

Before she went to bed Ellen admitted to herself that she could be almost as bitter as her daughter in her feeling toward the elder Tom Findly.

After her short nap she had dressed the baby in a long white dress and ruffled cap and carried the child down to the warm kitchen where the old man sat in his rocking chair, staring out at the snowy countryside.

Out there the farm lay, glazed with a glittering icing of white, every fence post capped and jaunty. On a trampled place before the shed a few hens picked corn and in the lot beyond Tom was forking hay from the top of a stack for two cows, a horse and a calf.

All peaceful, the restful peace of a winter's afternoon, but in the malevolent eyes of Tom Findly there was no peace. As he turned them upon Ellen an angry fire burned there and he glared at the sleeping child in her arms.

"Our grandbaby," Ellen said. "Our little granddaughter, Mr. Findly. Isn't she sweet?"

That he heard and understood, she was certain. A kind of contempt made leering lines in his tallowy face, his lips drew down hard, fighting to drag up a sound. When it came, wrenched from some evil place deep within him, it seemed to crack on the air like a shot, and it was as if he tasted it, poisonous and horrid, savoring its malice. It was a dry, weedy cackle of awful laughter.

20

THERE WAS NOTHING IMPULSIVE ABOUT WILLIAM'S DEcision.

He had lain awake late for two nights mulling it over, making plans. Sometime he was going to do it, but there was no definite date in his mind. There was his mother to consider and William dreaded the idea of hurting her though she couldn't expect him to stay around forever. Even birds heaved their young unfeelingly out of the nest after allowing a reasonable period for maturity. Anyway Ellen would now have a grandchild and that would be a new interest, grandparents being assumed always to be doting, absorbed, and indifferent to previous attachments.

The third day after Ellen's departure it became apparent that Hume Harper had no intention of being classed with the indulgent or the forgiving. Tom Findly appeared outside the bank and, catching William's eye, made his familiar summoning gesture. This time William resorted to no subterfuge but went boldly out the front door and took

Tom's message, standing bareheaded in the street. When he returned he went directly to his father's desk.

"Well, Grandpa," he remarked coolly, "you have a new granddaughter born the day before yesterday. She weighed six pounds, her name is Harriet Mary, and Mama says to tell you she won't be home for a week."

For an instant Harper gave alarming indications of an inner explosion that would send his eyeballs flying like blazing missiles from his head. His throat swelled, his face purpled and every button on his coat strained dangerously, but William did not flinch or flee. Giving his father an amused and slightly impudent look, he said again, "Grandpa!" and walked away.

"Grandpa," he told Merrill and Bolt. "He isn't happy about it."

"Better not congratulate him then." Merrill looked toward the front desk. "Girl or boy?"

"Girl."

"Can't name her after him then. Eases the pain of age slightly when they name them after you. Grandfathers aren't important anyway. It's grandmothers who make all the fuss. I know, I'm married to one."

William had never thought of old Merrill as a home man with a family. Now he had difficulty separating Merrill in his mind from the dusty routine of black and red ink, imagining him going home to a house with people in it, being different, relaxed, grandfatherly. Mr. Bolt, he knew, was not married. William had the impression that Bolt liked the women, especially if they were slightly tangy, but that he shied away from being married to one of them.

It was at suppertime that William discovered how deep and wild and bitter was the hurt fury in his father's breast. Harper marched into the kitchen wearing a stony face and a belligerent air.

"My daughter has borne a child," he announced grimly. "The child of disgrace, the child of a blackguard, a rebel and a traitor! That child will not be spoken of in this house, do you understand?"

William, who had taken to hanging around the kitchen during his mother's absence, muttered some vague uneasy acquiescence but Hessie, who had recoiled at the blast of wrath, turned a slaty gray and her eyes rolled in her head.

"'Fo God!" she exclaimed to Harper's retreating back. "We got us a baby chile and the Boss mad about it? What kine of man he, anyhow?"

"Stone," said William levelly. "Ice and conceit."

"Miss feel bad she can't see her baby chile," mourned Hessie. "Ain't right. Ain't natural."

"Hessie"—William's voice was amazingly firm and baritone—"someday, and it won't be too long either, I'm going to take my mother away from this place. I'm going to make a lot of money and take her clear away where she can be free to do as she pleases."

Hessie nodded approval. "Yeh. You take me too, Marse Willie?"

"Sure I'll take you if you want to go. But don't you tell, Hessie, don't you talk about it, not to Mama or anybody."

"When you git rich I tell, huh? Reckon I mought be daid then."

"You won't be dead. And you'll be taken care of, all your life. But don't you let any old Yankee talk you into going off someplace where I can't find you, you hear?" He squared his shoulders and stiffened his spine, marching into the dining room where supper steamed in dishes, neglected, where his father sat at the head of the table, glowering.

Nothing he says is going to matter one darn' bit, decided the boy. It will be just words, just a noise coming out of that pursy mouth of his and I don't even have to hear it. I don't have to care. Now he knew his decision was made. His plan was all worked out, fortunately, and it was very simple.

He ate his meal mechanically, waiting for the tirade to begin. Yell loud, Pa, his coolly deliberate look advised. Yell and slap the table. Lay down the law. This is your last chance.

What sins were heaped on his head in the next thirty minutes he did not even hear. Amazing how easy it was to be deaf and impervious when he put his mind to it, enclosed as it was in a shell of contempt that let his thoughts go on spinning in a sheltered place, where accusations, reproaches and even threats cracked around his head as harmlessly as summer lightning.

It was all there, he got from briefly assimilated smatterings. He was lazy, he associated with low characters (That's you, Henri!), he deliberately and disobediently embarrassed his father by visiting notorious Confederates (The Nesbitts, the Briscoes. So somebody had blabbed. Never mind, Clemmy, I'll be back!). As a further indignity, so ran Harper's angry complaint, he had been taunted by his only son who made sport of his father to his employees behind his back.

"Oh, I know! I know what goes on back there. I'd discharge both those disloyal men tomorrow if I knew where I could replace them."

One fellow you'll replace tomorrow, William was thinking, will be your spittoon jockey! It gave him a calm and superior feeling to realize how little he cared, how slight would be the wrench when he walked out of this house, out of that damned bank perhaps forever! Only one thing remained yet to be arranged. He had to write a letter to his mother.

"You will not go out tonight, sir," ordered Harper,

when Hessie came in to gather up the dishes. "Get to your room and go to bed early, you hear?"

"Yes, sir," said William, thinking as he went up the stairs that those two words ought to be illuminated on parchment and framed in gilt. Last words ever spoken to his father by William Hume Harper. Forget the Hume. He would never use it, never acknowledge it. Not even the initial. When he was of age he would go to court and have it eliminated legally.

It was past midnight when he finished his letter and sealed it. He would mail it perhaps from some town miles away so he would be long gone when Ellen received it. She wouldn't be back for a week. Then it occurred to him that when he was discovered missing in the morning his father would likely go charging out there and compel her to return. That could happen, so maybe it would be better to mail the letter here in town.

Dear Mama, he wrote. *When you get this I will be gone away. I am a man now and Pa thinks I am some runny-nosed brat to be ordered around and abused and cussed at. I can't stand it any longer. I am going to make my own way and be somebody and maybe when I am rich then he will have some respect for me. Mama, I have borrowed some money from you and that is not stealing, even if he says it is, which he probably will. I am going to pay you back every cent and 8 per cent interest, not compounded though. You will get every penny back and if Pa makes it out a crime he can just do it, and who cares? I will let you hear from me later, so don't you worry. Your loving son, William. P.S. Mama, don't bring that baby to our house. No telling what he would do.*

While he had been escorting Harriet on her nighttime visits to the Nesbitt house he had perfected the technique of getting out unheard. He had his good shirts and underwear in a tight bundle tied around with his mackintosh. He filled his overcoat pockets with small articles and a contrivance on which he had labored several nights when he was supposed to be sleeping.

It was a money belt cut from the soft leather of an old jacket that he had outgrown. A double row of pockets had been laboriously stitched on it with thread borrowed from his mother's workbasket and waxed on the bottom of the candle. There were twenty-five pockets in each row and each pocket would hold a twenty-dollar gold piece. Then it had occurred to him that he would need money to travel on, so he had filled one pocket with the medal he had won at school for reciting "Webster's Reply to Hayne." The medal was exactly the size of a double eagle and he had used it to measure by.

The streets were very dark until he reached the square and no prowling patrol or provost's guard appeared to challenge him. The wind was rough and cold, blowing south from the Ohio River, and there was a coating of ice on the sidewalk. By the thin flicker of the street lantern in front of the bank William found his key and unlocked the front door. If anyone appeared to question him he had his story ready. His father had got word that Morgan was headed south again, and had sent him down to guard the bank. That this had happened before made the story entirely plausible.

Also William had a pistol. He had stolen it out of a drawer in Merrill's desk and that gun was the only thing that was not honestly his by right. He had even thought of leaving some money to pay for the gun and a note made out to his mother, but he remembered enough about banking to know that a note signed by a minor was worthless so he had abandoned both ideas.

Inside the bank he unlocked the vault, grateful that his

duties required him to be entrusted with a key. Then, shielding a lighted match under the tent of his overcoat, he studied the paper on which he had written the combination to the safe. The match burned his thumb and he lit another, as he maneuvered the dials with the fingers of his free hand. They turned smoothly and he carefully followed the code. Left eighteen, right fifty-nine. The year the safe was bought. Then the month, the date, and finally Hume Harper's age, left forty-eight. He heard the tumblers fall, cautiously turned the ratchet of the lock. It creaked a little, then snapped sharply as the heavy bolts disengaged. A tug, and the thick door was open.

Another match lighted the interior. The heavy bags of gold, the stacks of currency. He knew how to force the seal on the bags, he had seen Bolt do it sometimes when the count was wrong. Move the wire, press back, count out fifty of the milled gold pieces, slip them swiftly into the pockets of the money belt, all but one. That went into his pocket. He loosened his clothes to buckle on the belt. It felt heavy and cold but he knew that it would not clink. Then, taking the draft drawn to his mother's account from the envelope, he propped it up in the front of the safe, where it would be seen immediately the safe was opened.

As he had watched his father do so many times he closed the safe door, shoved the ratchet over hard, spun the dials. Moving his fingers cautiously over the floor he picked up all the burned matches, dropped them into his pocket. Locking the vault again, he picked up his bundle and slipped out the door.

In the street he had an impulse to throw away the bank keys, then thought better of that and returned them to his pocket. He smiled to himself as he tramped down the street toward the railroad. Merrill and Bolt would get a shock in the morning when they found no humble flunky in the bank, no fire built, no books and ledgers brought out ready on their desks. But it would be Hume Harper, banker, who would get the most acute shock when he opened the safe and saw that document confronting him and one sack of gold lighter by a thousand dollars.

Of course Harper would probably already be upset at not finding William in his bed, or at the bank. Hessie would be called and Hessie would discover that both the boy and his clothes were gone. William wondered as he tramped down the cold streets what his father would do next. Rush out and harness the mare and go pelting out to Findly's expecting to find William with his mother?

Then, having alarmed and upset his wife, would he be doubly furious when the opened safe presented him with the evidence of William's financial manipulations, rush out maybe for the sheriff, the Home Guard and the provost, or would pride prevail and both the men in the bank be sworn to secrecy concerning his son's defalcation?

It was too bad not to be able to stick around carefully concealed, to listen and watch and see the effect of his disappearance. Except that his mother would probably cry and that was something he did not like to think about. He remembered the letter to her, then, and circled a block to the post office, slipping it through the slot in the door.

He passed the depot, locked and dark, and knew because he had made inquiry that no train would go west or north until morning. However, he had no intention of boarding a train here in the town where he was known. The next station was seven miles up the track, a long walk on a cold winter's night, but it was a march to freedom and William tramped along doggedly, stumbling a little on the icy cross ties, thinking with young regret of the hot supper he had barely tasted.

It occurred to him that it would have been smart to get a

little change out of the petty cash drawer in the safe. To have nothing but gold with which to pay a fare or buy food might attract unfavorable attention. He might have to go hungry till a bank opened and he had a chance to change the gold into greenbacks.

His bundle grew heavy and he slung it on his back, holding it by the sleeves of the mackintosh till his hands grew chilled and numb. Then he stowed it under his arm again to warm his fingers in his pockets. About four miles along the roadbed he heard the distant hoot and rumble of a southbound train. He leaped off the track and crept behind a snowy bank to avoid the glare of the kerosene headlight, crouching there while a long line of freight cars clanked by. The wide-mouthed stack of the engine spewed out sparks as it chuffed and panted past.

On one flatcar William saw the shrouded shapes of cannon. Going south, to Grant and Sherman, going down to where men were killing each other, where Thad Briscoe was and Henri, Tee's sweetheart and William's friend. The desolation of war seemed to roar past with those guns and to become part of the desolate gloom of the night. A heartache and a heaviness big enough to weigh down a world!

The train vanished and he brushed himself off and slogged on. He had no way of knowing what time it was but after a while there was a feel of morning in the air, thin, cold currents stirring, and far off a rooster crowed to be answered by a howling dog from over a distant hill. Then after what seemed like an endless misery of putting one tired foot before the other William walked into a circle of reddish light from an overhead lantern signal. Dimly ahead outlined against the sky was the darker bulk of a building.

As he came near to it a flaring light showed through a dirty window and a man came out carrying a lighted lantern. He was gathering up an armful of wood as William came up and he looked up from under a greasy cap.

"Ain't no more trains due till ten o'clock," he said, as the boy followed him into the cold, odorous station. While William stood by silently shivering the man piled wood and kindling into a stove, doused it with coal oil from a jug. The fire roared, shaking the flimsy iron pipe, and smoke curled from every crack in the iron.

"Where can I get something to eat?" asked William.

"Wouldn't know, this time of morning." The man wiped dirt off his hands onto his breeches. "Ain't nobody up yet 'less they got to git up, like me."

"What times does the bank open?" A thin heat had begun to temper the bleak air around the stove and William spread his hands to it, flexing his aching fingers.

"What bank?" asked the man, shaking the grate vigorously so that a pale drift of ashes grayed his greasy apparel. "Ain't been no bank in this town since the army took over and old man Trylord had to refugee south. Where you headin' anyhow, boy?"

"Louisville, I reckon." It was an indefinite statement. He had thought of St. Louis. St. Louis was a city but it was across the Mississippi and getting across now he knew was complicated by all these Union regulations. He still had his pass but it had his name and his father's name on it and he did not want to show it unless he had to.

"Train to Louisville, due at ten o'clock. That don't mean nothin' though, could be four or five hours late, way things are runnin' now. Might not come at all if the rebs have tore up the track again. I got to go home and milk. You figure to wait around, throw in another chunk tereckly."

William sat down on one of the benches when the man had gone. The place was still cold and he wrapped his overcoat around his aching legs. Beyond, the smeared window showed a lime-green streak on the horizon. Day was beginning. Presently a sickly gray light seeped in, illuminating all the ugliness about. In a cuddy behind a slatted grill, a telegraph key stuttered briefly then was silent, and a mouse gnawed with a brief crackling spurt of energy. A boy in a faded Union uniform, too large for him, stuck a head in the door and asked, "Moody here?" and went his way again, lugging a tin dinner bucket.

William took his gold piece from his pocket and turned it in his fingers thoughtfully, but in that shining circle all he saw was food. Had Hessie cooked some fat little sausages this morning and waited for him to come down and spear a fork into their hot, luscious, oozing bellies? Maybe popovers bursting open, showing delicate golden lace inside their lacquered crusts?

There was poverty and lack all over Kentucky but till now there had always been meat and plenty on Hume Harper's table. The brick smokehouse hung with hams and flitches coated with red pepper to discourage mice and skippers, the cellar was well filled with potatoes and apples and jars and crocks filled with the products of his mother's and Hessie's canning and preserving. There was beef brined down in kegs and slabs of salted meat, and no requisitioning commissary foragers had ever appeared to deplete the Harper store. It had given William a queer, guilty feeling when he had seen the Briscoe children being fed on mush.

Now his empty belly gave a hurting grumble, just from thinking about food. He got up to look for water, found a bucket on a shelf with a little in it, a film of ashes on top, but he tilted it and drank, quieting briefly the gnawing in his insides. Somehow he had to hold out till the Louisville train came and then there would be the problem of persuading whoever was running that train to change his money.

There was one worn cliché his father had flung at him, time after time. That he had everything, food, comfort, clothes, whatever he required handed to him, that it was Hume Harper who had earned it, not he, William. Slumped on the bench, hungry, sleepy, and cold, the boy reluctantly gave his father his due. Harper had been a good provider, of everything but love and understanding.

Then, after an interminable stretch of time, during which people came and went, tramping in and out with muddy feet, staring at him curiously, a whistle hooted and the Louisville train clanked in, breathing steam and hissing.

William forgot his nostalgic musings and was on his way. To adventure. To life, he told himself.

Anyway, to someplace!

21

THE CAR HE ENTERED HAD HARD WOODEN SEATS AND was crowded with soldiers going home for Christmas furloughs. Their clothes were rank and odorous in the hot air, overheated by an iron stove in the middle of the car that a brakeman stoked and poked repeatedly. William put his gold piece deep in his pocket, stuffed his gloves in on top of it, dropping off to sleep. The conductor had to shake him hard to wake him and then grumbled at the twenty-dollar coin.

"I can't change that. Where you going? Why didn't you buy a ticket?"

"They couldn't change it either," fibbed William, "so I had to pay on the train."

"I'll see if I can rustle some change. Any of you fellows got change for twenty dollars?"

A loud chorus of hoots and guffaws was his answer.

"Got a hatful of Confederate money," yelled a whiskery corporal.

"How about some of these Louisiana bank notes, awful purty? Says on 'em they're issued by the bank of New Orleans."

"When was payday in old Joe Hooker's army? I forget. Last spring sometime," remarked another. "Anyway my old woman got all my money."

"Sell you a diamond ring, boy," volunteered another, jumping up. "Found it in one of them caves where they holed up in Vicksburg. Some woman stuffed it in a crack and run off and forgot it. How about it? Wanna buy a genuine diamond?"

"Genuine glass!" scoffed his seatmate. "Had it tied to a string, I'll bet. Pull the string and blow that cave down on top of you. They done that up in Shenandoah. Six buddies of mine got killed and buried when a smokehouse blowed up, was trapped that way. Found a silver spoon, gave it a yank and touched off a fuse was wired to it. Reckon they're buried there yet."

"Does this train stop for dinner?" William asked the conductor. "It won't do me any good though if I can't change my money."

"Yeh, stops at Frankfort. Here—here's a dollar. You eat on that till I get you some change."

"I might not see you in Frankfort."

"You got my dollar, ain't you? I ain't got your twenty. I'll see you in Frankfort," promised the official.

William was dirty and starved and the whole expedition was beginning to wear a dismal aspect when he trudged down the track in Frankfort to a little eating house identified by a Negro man in a white apron who stood in front of it vigorously ringing a bell. But within, the place was clean and redolent of roasting meat and a fresh-faced, middle-aged woman showed him to a table, welcoming him briskly.

"You've been to the army, I can tell." She set a huge bowl of soup in front of him. "They sure do wear you boys down to skin and bone. Anyway you'll get home to your folks for Christmas. Now I got beef and pork and potatoes but that's about all. Used to get collards and stuff like that but now we're lucky to get meat. I can fill you up though for a dollar, six bits."

"A dollar is all I've got," William said, "till that railroad man brings me some change."

"Tall feller, run that train? That's Carney. He'll fetch it. Eats here. Sleeps here too. You eat that now, and just say beef or pork and I'll fill you so full you'll forget all that salt mule and hardtack."

William decided on the beef as being more filling, applied himself to the soup. It was thick and rich and he felt much better when the plate was clean. Then the outer door opened and Carney came in.

"Got that money yet?" He came to the table. "Here's your nineteen dollars—less three eighty for your fare. Had to take greenbacks but they got Washington back of 'em, not a lot of wind like some money. And you ain't going to Louisville today. Army took over the whole train. You got to wait till tomorrow."

"He's army," said the woman, putting a filled plate before William.

"In them pants and coat?" demanded the conductor.

"I'm army, but not in the army right now," said William. "My enlistment's up. Where can I get a room if I have to wait here all night?"

"Why, right here!" said the woman. "You can sleep in with Herman for a dollar and breakfast throwed in."

"Well—thanks, but I guess I'll walk uptown a little. I've never been in Frankfort," William hedged.

"Supper's at six, and you can leave your bundle right here. What did you say your name was?"

"Williams." He felt lucky that no one asked to see his pass. Maybe controls weren't so rigid over in this part of the state. He was going to be Williams till he was challenged. Then he could explain that that was his first name, that he'd given it absent-mindedly. He took his bundle with him. He had no intention of sleeping with Herman, not with over nine hundred dollars in gold strapped around his middle. The belt sagged heavily on his hipbones now, he kept looking down nervously to see if it showed through his clothes, but fortunately his father had had this suit made a size too large, so he could grow into it, and it bagged in the right places.

He found a decent-looking hotel and paid six dollars in advance for a room. It was late afternoon now and the quick winter dusk was descending, clothing all the town's shabbiness, glamorizing roof and chimney top with purple haze. From the window he could see the river below high bluffs, and an old man shuffling along with a short ladder, who mounted to light the square lanterns set at every corner.

A hansom cab rattled by and three cavalry officers with sabers trotted their horses down the street. Somewhere an engine voiced a lonely mooing. William cleaned himself up, brushed his clothes and shoes and splashed cold water on his face, scrubbing hard with a rough towel to drive away the bleak homesickness that was beginning to weigh him down like a pain. He had been thinking about his mother and Harriet. What if his sister had died? Women did die sometimes, even when their newborn children were days old. If Harriet died he wondered if his father would let her be buried in the family plot. He would never know, of course. That was a grim thought. Nobody would know where to find him though home was only a few hours away.

Anyway he couldn't go back. Even with nine hundred and eighty dollars left of his borrowed money he could never face his father again. Likely all the cash in the safe had been counted by this time and in Harper's mind his son was already branded a common thief.

Then another thought brought a sudden surge of panic. What if his father was so violently enraged that he ordered William searched for and arrested? William was vague about the methods used in the pursuit of wanted men but he knew they were brought back from far places, even runaway slaves. It came to him that he had better get out of the state as fast as he could before some officer came knocking at the door to take him into custody for bank robbery.

Hastily he took two more gold pieces out of the belt, repacked his belongings into a neater bundle. Maybe if he went out right now he could find a shop open and buy a carpetbag. At the desk below he approached the clerk.

"I have to get to St. Louis right away. They told me the army had taken over the train. Would there be a stage or anything going to Louisville tonight?"

"No stage that I know about," said the man. "Might be a freighter hauling over that way, you could inquire around. You'll have trouble getting over to St. Louis anyway, even after you get to the Ohio River. Army's got control of all the boats, nobody rides without a special pass. If you were a free Negro you could buy a pass for a dollar, they say, but white travelers get mighty few favors. You paid for your room, might as well use it, might be a train in the morning."

"I have to go tonight. I only used one towel—"

"Sorry, no money refunded. Come again, Mr. Williams, when you're not in such a hurry." William thought he caught a note of suspicion in the man's voice and he hurried out to the street, lugging his belongings.

Louisville, he had learned, was only fifty miles away but beyond the river lay a long, strange distance; he did not know if there was even a railroad over there. He did know that most of the traffic went by water. South to Paducah, north up the Mississippi to the Missouri city that had grown to such tremendous importance during this war.

Out in the street he found a dingy little shop just closing and bought a shabby carpetbag for a dollar, and with the weight of it dragging down his arm he tramped back to the station. There were no passenger trains till next day, they told him. A freight was panting on a siding headed west and attached to it was a single dilapidated passenger car, full of noisy men who were drinking and whooping.

"Where's that car going?" he asked a quiet fellow who sat smoking on the step of the car.

"St. Louis. Work gang going down the river to work on those ironsided gunboats the Union Navy's building down by Cairo. They're all drunk in there, lot of roughs and gamblers and cutthroats, scum gathered up back east to work on those contracts for Eads. Rob you as quick as look at you. You looking for a job, boy? Stay away from that crowd in there. They're poison. I signed up but I got me a private car picked out up ahead. Full of blankets going down to the army in Arkansas. I figure to hide out in it till we get to the river. They haven't locked it yet."

"Reckon I could hide out with you? I can pay," said William eagerly. "I've got to get over to St. Louis right away."

"Might arrange it. How much have you got?"

"I'll give you five dollars. Any danger any officers might come snooping and searching that car?" William inquired.

"Not after they lock it, likely. Give me the five—and maybe a little more to buy us some grub, if you've got it. It's a long way to St. Louis. Could be locked in there two or three days the way these trains run."

William handed the stranger seven dollars, said, "I'll wait here." Maybe he had been a fool. Maybe the fellow would simply disappear with the money. But in less than half an hour the man was back carrying two big bundles.

"Come on. Down here," he ordered.

The car stood in darkness, close under a dripping water tank. The door was still unlocked and the stranger pushed it open cautiously and they climbed in, dragging it shut after them.

The blankets were baled like cotton and of the bales they built a sort of room at one end of the car, invisible when the door was opened. The stranger, who said that his name was Titus, hacked open a bale and pulled out four blankets.

"Might as well be comfortable," he said. "These will most likely be stolen anyway before they get where they're going. Stolen by speculators and sold south to Texas or someplace where the rebs will pay a high price for 'em. This is a thieves' war, boy, you know that? Army that wins this war will be the army that has got the smartest thieves on their side. What outfit you running away from?"

"I'm no deserter," stated William crisply. "I've got a man fighting in my place. Paid him—paid him plenty."

"Bounty man, they don't fight worth a damn because a man you can buy to fight wasn't worth a cuss in the first place. I'm from Baltimore. Fought since 'sixty-one with Pope's army, got a ball in my foot at Fredericksburg and they gave me a discharge, unfit for duty. I looked this war over and decided nobody but speculators were going to get anything out of it but you've got to have a stake to get into that game, so I signed up with that contractor to get passage out to where they say the pickings are richest. But I couldn't stomach that crew back yonder. All right, we're home. Let's eat."

They had two loaves of bread, a hunk of cheese, and some salty dried beef. They had one canteen of water and four bottles of beer. Titus had a knife and with it he portioned out the food scrupulously, warning William to go slow on the meat as it would make him thirsty and what liquid they had would have to last till they got to the junction.

"Suppose they never unlock this car till it gets to some place down in Arkansas?" William suggested.

"Don't be uneasy. I already fixed that," Titus reassured him. "See that trap door up yonder? It's supposed to be bolted on the outside but it ain't. I fixed the bolt so it looks all right if the brakeman walks over it, but when this car stops all we have to do is climb up on a bale and shove and we're out."

Titus had dice, but the car was dark and to William's relief he put them away, grumbling that it was too dark to see the spots. When the long night ended and day began to sift faintly through the cracks William was still fighting to keep awake. He hated to be suspicious of this stranger who had seemed honest enough but the gold around his waist was an anxiety and he forced himself to lie buried in the blankets, only dozing fitfully, while Titus slept heavily in his corner.

The rattle and jolt of the car was deafening and bone-jarring and when occasionally it stopped with a grinding of brakes all the bales tilted and threatened to topple, so that they had to jump up and brace the walls of their hiding place to keep from being buried alive.

A wind came up and whistled through the cracks in the walls and the floor was so drafty that blankets spread over their legs heaved in little billows. The wool was dusty and made William's nose itch and about the second night the boy was so on edge and weary with the confinement and lack of sleep that he kept grimly quiet, not wanting to show irritation and provoke some unpleasantness. At last when it seemed he could endure no more the car stood still for an hour or more. Titus climbed up on the bales and gave an upward heave to the trap door, lifting it a few inches. Chill air rushed in and through the small opening William could see the stars. Titus jumped on down.

"Come on," he said. "This is the junction. We'd better get out before they start switching. You go first and I'll hand up your stuff. Climb down on the dark side and don't start running. Just move away quietly."

"Well, goodbye." William held out a hand when they were outside in the cindery yard in the sour dark before dawn. "Much obliged and good luck."

"Reckon I'll just go your way," said Titus. "I did sign up to build those darned Union turtles but lucky I didn't sign my right name."

William had no wish for company but he could not refuse the man who had helped him out thus far. He said, "Let's find a place to eat and I'll buy your breakfast."

"Guess not." Titus drew back. "If you want to help me

out just lend me some money and I'll be on my way. Man can get lost easy in St. Louis, I guess."

William handed over four dollars, said goodbye again, and Titus disappeared into the darkness. After all, the boy was thinking, Titus could have been a deserter from Pope's army.

It was noon when William reached the river, having paid a free Negro for a slow ride in a mule-drawn wagon over a road hub-deep in churned-up mud. The wagon was loaded with the carcasses of four dead hogs. The hogs had died on him, the Negro confided, but them commissaries would pay for any kind of meat just so it didn't stink. At the river the Negro directed him to a venal officer who took ten dollars from William for a pass to cross the Mississippi on a freight boat. After dark, chilled and famished, he arrived at a river-front hotel where a woman with hair dyed a startling red took twenty dollars from him for a room he could occupy for one week.

It was not an elegant room but the bed was clean and an amiable Negro woman agreed to brush and press his clothes for two bits. Restored to something like respectability, he set out to find a place to eat, not fancying the slatternly look of the dining room in the hotel, where the tables were bare wood and the men ate with their hats on.

The streets were full of people, soldiers and Negroes, bold overdressed women who looked him over impudently, rough workmen with muddy boots and loud voices, even an occasional Indian whose black plait of hair hung from beneath a wide-brimmed black hat. All doors looked mysterious and some even sinister, but through the small glass panes of one William saw tables and women and dim lights. So he opened it venturously and went in.

There was a huge, dim room with a bar at one end and a piano being played softly by a young man who had a pair of

233

crutches propped beside him. The small tables were mostly occupied by officers in blue and men in civilian clothes accompanied by stylishly dressed women. William angled among the tables seeking a single place and very near the bar he saw her.

She was sitting at a small table with a major of artillery, by his stripes and epaulettes. She had on a flowered bonnet with a blue bow under her chin and an elaborate gown of blue silk cut low in the neck. Her long lashes were fluttering as she smiled at the major and William got a breath of the old familiar orange-blossom perfume.

His heart gave a sick downward plunge and then flew up to choke him. For an instant he struggled with the urge to crash across the space between them and throttle that debonair, dissipated major with his bare hands. Before he had control of himself he had cried out her name.

"Denise!"

22

DENISE TURNED SWIFTLY, TURNED WHITE, TURNED RED, UPset her wineglass as she jumped up.

"Willie!" she shrilled, with the same little upward shriek of joy that had always twisted his heart and made his pulses pound. She rushed to meet him, clutched at his arms with winged hands. "Willie! My sweet William!" She pulled him over to the table where the major had gotten to his feet, looking hostile and annoyed. "It is our William from home, Major. Our dear little friend."

Her eyes were dancing, she was squeezing the boy's arms till they ached, but she did not kiss him, to William's great relief. The major looked dour.

"How do you do, sir?" he grumped.

"This is Major Crawford, William," Denise explained in a rush. "And this is William Harper, our dear Willie. What do you do in St. Louis, William? Sit down—sit down—a chair, *garçon!*"

William squirmed into a chair, uncomfortable and bewildered. "What are you doing in St. Louis, Denise?"

Her laughter rippled. "I ran away! I will not be in their wretched bastille, I swear. I will not be sent south to starve. What do I care for their silly war? Me—I am not mad at anybody. So—the major helped me to run away."

"Very good of you, sir," William said, suddenly hating this brown-faced officer, his smug air, his jaunty mustache, his bold eyes.

"Simply arranged," said the major. "However, the old lady did complicate things somewhat."

"Mrs. Nesbitt—she's here too?" William inquired.

"But *naturellement*," exclaimed Denise. "Poor Maman, she resisted. Milo is in the prison, where we do not know, but we compelled Maman to run away. The major comes to St. Louis, so we make preten' we are his family. But you —how are you here, William?"

"I just decided it was time to strike out on my own," said William with more assurance than he was feeling. "I didn't know Milo was in prison. They've been watching your house, expecting him to show up there, and Morgan too."

"That slippery scoundrel!" growled the major. "We'll take him yet and all the traitors who helped him escape."

He snapped a finger for the waiter. "What will you drink, Mr. Harper?"

"He has only wine," Denise said quickly. "He is so ver' young for all his legs are so long. William, listen, no more I am Confederate. Not here in St. Louis. Poor Maman, she is still Confederate but we do not tell, eh, Major? William," she explained, "is a Yankee. His papa, he is ver' fierce Yankee, more fierce than you, Major."

"But you're not in the army!" drawled the major, meaningly.

"I have paid a substitute since 'sixty-one." William was beginning to loathe this lame explanation. "My father's orders, sir. But I got sick of that arrangement, which is why I left home."

"Phil Sheridan needs men in Texas," said the major. "Being from Kentucky I suppose you ride?"

"No, sir, I never had the opportunity. My father is a banker. We have always lived in town."

"I remember your father." Crawford gave the order for a glass of wine for William. "A great friend of Colonel Bisbee, as I recall. The service can be tough if a man has to march into battle. The artillery is not quite so bad. I'm taking an outfit south in a few days."

"I saw some guns going south on the train," William remarked.

He was itching to get away. It was all wrong somehow, all distorted and cheap. A kind of revulsion made him a little sick. Once he had known a tremor of delight whenever he was permitted to be near Denise, now suddenly she looked old, older and coarser, too wise, even a littly sly with her painted mouth, her small smirks and cadences of laughter that sounded artificial.

"I'd like to see Mrs. Nesbitt before I—leave," he said, purposely leaving the future dangling in air.

"They have a room farther uptown," said the major.

Denise pushed aside her glass. "William, we go now!" She gathered up her bag and handkerchief. "We go now to see Maman. But not you, *chéri!*" She gave the major a smile and a little tap. "For you from me, *au revoir!*"

She had William by the elbow and twitched out of his chair before he could gather his wits together or take a real drink from his glass.

"Good night, Major," he managed to stammer. "Thanks for taking care of my good friends."

The major said, "Hmmph!" and they left him summoning the waiter again with impatiently snapped fingers.

Outside in the icy night Denise stood still, pulling her wrap up about her throat.

"Do not look at me like that!" she cried. "You shall not look at me like that!"

"But—I was surprised," fumbled William. "They said you had gone south. Then we heard you'd been sent to some women's prison. Colonel Bisbee has quartered troops in your house."

"You do not look at me surprised." Denise pouted. "You look at me like I am bad woman!"

"Well, are you?" he shouted at her.

She flung up a hand and slapped him lightly across the mouth.

"I hate you!" she cried low, hot, her eyes smoldering. "I hate you—that you come here. That you see me! No—no, I love you, my Willie! You are angry because you are jealous, no?"

"Jealous!" he stormed. "No, I'm not jealous. If I hate seeing you with a man like that, fawning at him, it's not because I'm jealous. You're like—my own sister, Denise. You are the sister of my best friend. I can't bear to see you making yourself—common!" He had started to say "cheap" but caught back the word in time.

She turned her face up to the wan light of a street lantern and he saw tears behind the overworked drama of her painted lashes.

"It is true, my Willie! I am common—but for what? To save Maman from what is too horrible. Those Yankees, if they send her away, she will die! She is an old woman."

"She's not so old. She can't be more than fifty," argued the boy.

"Sorrow and trouble, it makes people old. You—you are young. To you—all this passes. All will be past, says William Harper, he will be a man. But old people, there is not much time for them any more. They die. Your papa, your maman, will all die. Still, be William Harper, owning the whole world!"

He was silent for a spell, rebuked but not appeased. Then he blurted reluctantly, "You didn't have to sell yourself!"

"Ha!" She pulled away from him. "And what do I sell, *mon petit*? The Nesbitt silver? Better I sell Maman's poor heart. Anyway, how shall I climb that high chimney? For Henri, even, it is most difficult."

"They'll get it anyway," he said. "Pa will take the house when the army moves out. He'll take it on the mortgage and tear it down and where will your precious silver be then?"

"No, no—Maman will be killed! And poor Papa, when he comes from the prison and there is no more home!" she cried.

"He could have paid his interest and the principal," stated William severely, "but instead he put all his money in Confederate bonds. If Pa doesn't take the house the Union will confiscate it."

"But the bonds, they are worth much money, no?"

"If the Confederacy should win the war they might be —sometime. But look, Denise, the Confederacy can't win! Look at all the defeats they've had this past year. Gettysburg, Vicksburg, Chattanooga, all lost. New Orleans taken, all they hold now of any consequence is Atlanta and Richmond. Charleston's under siege all the time." William's voice held a tone of desperation. "Right now Mrs. Nesbitt couldn't redeem those bonds, even in Richmond. At the bank we knew about things like that. Where are the bonds? Still in the house?"

"No—no, in Maman's trunk. She would not leave without the trunk. The major was much annoyed. He told them he is taking us to some prison, instead he slipped us aboard a boat with soldiers and too many guns. He was most clever. We owe the major too much. You must not say bad things of him, *chéri!*" She pulled him to a halt again. "Here—in this house, we live. William," her voice sank pleadingly, "you will not tell Maman they take away her home? Poor Maman, she will die!"

"All right, but she'll have to know sometime."

"Maybe it is not true. Maybe the South will win the silly war and our men come home and then they fix everything." Denise's naïve optimism, which could never be long quenched, bubbled up again.

William viewed the pleasant room where Amalie Nesbitt sat, doing embroidery by the fire, with a sick, distasteful sinking of the heart. Somebody was paying for all this, that new silk dress Denise wore, rustling it so entrancingly as she flew about making tea, for this well-furnished room, even for the tea and little cakes. He was young, he had seen little of the world, but he knew that men did not spend money thus lavishly expecting no return. Not cool-eyed, sensuous-looking men like Major Crawford.

He wondered how Denise had met the man. For more

239

than a year he knew the Nesbitts had been under Union surveillance; likely the major had been in command of a detail ordered to remove Amalie and Denise and he had taken the opportunity to work out his own plans.

Amalie was effusively glad to see him. Her eyes looked a bit sunken, with deep purple shadows lying under them, and her mouth was drawn straight, with a controlled look of patience, but she smiled at William and kissed him maternally. At home they had called Amalie Nesbitt an aloof and haughty woman. How could she condone this ménage, this situation that even to a protected and ignorant woman should be obvious?

They took tea with him and William ate because he was hungry, having been poorly fed since leaving home. Then he went back to his hotel room and flung himself unhappily across the bed. He was almost nineteen years old, an idol had been shattered, and he ached with an irreparable sense of loss. Then presently he let himself think about Clemmy Briscoe, her gallant spirit, her indomitable little chin, her eyes and hair. Clemmy would never surrender, he told himself. If all was lost Clemmy would face it, head high, eyes full of defiance, proud spirit unconquered.

Clemmy would walk into a Union prison with no yielding in her eyes, no shrinking, no bartering what was precious for military favors. She was only sixteen years old but he was confident that not even to save her mother would Clemmy cheapen herself.

Not Clemmy or Little Tee, or even young Priscilla. Not Lennie Briscoe either. They might be dreamers who pinned their faith on false hopes of victory but they would never forget that they were ladies of the proud bluegrass land of Kentucky.

He stumbled up presently and decided he would write a letter to Clemmy. Tomorrow, when he could get hold of some paper and ink. She might never get it, but at least he would do what he could to let her know he had not forgotten her. He'd have to warn her to burn the letter, though, so no one would know where he was until he was ready to report to his mother.

Abruptly he faced himself in the mildewed mirror and asked himself what he was doing here anyway? Where was he going and for what? Here he stood, judging Denise, and how much better was he himself, only another runaway?

The trouble was that he knew what he ran from. Grimly he faced himself and made the tall, lean figure he saw in that glass own the truth. He was not running from his father, or from the bank. That was a half-truth he had concocted to ease his own conscience.

He was running away from that woman who had looked at him with scorn in her eyes demanding to know why he was not in uniform. He was running from the amused, half-contemptuous condescension in the faces of Mr. Merrill and Mr. Bolt. He was even running away from Major Crawford.

He, William Harper, was running away from the army.

Now that the stark truth was out and flung down like a challenge, which way to turn? Where could he go, with nine hundred dollars in gold? He pressed the belt hard into his skinny stomach, feeling pain and glad of it. It came to him when he had begun to think calmly that there must be banks in St. Louis. And recruiting officers.

Rid of the responsibility of the money, he would find means to make himself a man in his own estimation. He would get back his self-respect—but not in the artillery! That brassy-eyed major had damned the artillery forever in his mind. Not that the infantry was all made up of gallant and honorable gentlemen either. There was Colonel Bisbee, who had not scrupled against being involved in Hume Harper's money-making schemes.

Henri Nesbitt was infantry, even if he was deluded enough to be part of the Confederate infantry. Henri was willing to march and starve and sleep in the cold and mud for what he believed in. William faced that question. What exactly did he, William Harper, believe in? Abraham Lincoln? Mighty few people in Kentucky believed in Lincoln any more.

All I believe in is the integrity of William Harper, the boy told the figure in the mirror. And maybe the Union. Anyway if I fight I'd have to fight for the Union.

One thing he would do before he left St. Louis. He would see to it that Amalie Nesbitt had some money, something that was hers, that would protect her if that major went off south without making any arrangements to take care of her. Denise, he was sure, would take care of herself, but Mrs. Nesbitt stood only a little lower in the boy's estimation than his own mother. She was a sad victim of circumstance and he could do nothing about his own future till he knew she was secure.

Before he went to bed he counted out ten of the gold pieces, wrapped them in a clean handkerchief, and put them under his pillow. It was uncomfortable, trying to sleep in a bed with the money belt prodding his spine, but he had seen enough of the rough element of St. Louis already not to take any needless risks.

Immediately after breakfast, he put the handkerchief roll in his overcoat pocket, stuffed a scarf in over it, and set out to find again that house to which Denise had taken him. He walked several blocks out of his way before he located it, remembering the high front steps and the colored glass set in around the square window in the front door.

He knocked on the wrong door upstairs, but was directed

to the right room by a hard-faced young woman, who looked him up and down too boldly so that he was grateful when Amalie opened her door to him herself and hurried him in.

"The people in this house I do not like, William," she said low. "You come early, dear boy. You shall have coffee with me."

One cup was set out on a small table before a low fire, and Amalie brought another from a shelf.

"Denise—is she—" William began, awkwardly.

"She sleeps still," said Amalie, with a sigh. "She thinks I do not hear when she comes in so late, but I hear!"

"I can't stay, Mrs. Nesbitt," he said, seeing that her hands trembled as she poured the coffee. "I—I hope you'll understand, Mrs. Nesbitt, but I—brought you this!" He took out the roll and thrust it at her. "It's money," he went on, seeing her startled eyes. "I want you to have it, so you can go home—or New Orleans or someplace—"

"You give me money?" she asked, almost dropping the coffeepot. "But why is this, William?"

"Because—I've got to go. To the army or someplace. And I couldn't go with any peace of mind if I thought you were in need—or had to depend on—him!" His voice rushed in a kind of desperation. "I—I've got plenty—from my mother, and she'd want me to see that you were safe, I know. My mother is a good woman—and you're a good woman too, Mrs. Nesbitt."

He pushed the roll of gold pieces into her hands, and turned back to the door. Tears were running down her face; she stood very still and did not speak. She turned the roll in her grasp and one piece fell and rolled across the carpet. William recovered it, pressed it into her palm.

"You keep this—keep it hid," he ordered hoarsely. "It's a secret—between you and me. On account of you're my friend and Henri is my friend—and you keep it for yourself, Mrs. Nesbitt."

She choked, trying to find words. "You are a good boy, Willie," she got out then with difficulty. "I keep our secret."

He hurried out, closing the door softly, pelting down the stairs. Doors opened above and he felt watching eyes, but he was outside swiftly, in the clean cold air, relieved to be gone from that place, feeling no nobility, only a grateful sense of having done what he had to do.

By an unforeseen trick of fate he found himself, two days later, enlisted in the Navy of the United States.

He had gone to a bank to deposit his remaining gold. The bank business had been routine. He had even signed his own name, having been obliged to produce his pass.

"Just want to leave this money here till I get back from the war," he had told the teller.

A debonair young officer who had been standing near accosted him. "What service are you going into, young fellow?" he asked.

"Why—I hadn't decided," stammered William.

"We can use a man like you in the Navy. We're sending some boats down river Monday. Listen, boy, the Navy's the place to fight a war. You've always got a place to sleep and eat, no lying out in the cold, no sleeping in the mud or on frozen ground. No eating hardtack and parched corn or marching hundreds of miles with no bottoms in your shoes."

"Those boats blow up and sink though," argued William.

"Mighty little danger any more. We've got the rebs practically swept off the water now. They never had any real fighting craft anyway, just some old converted tubs with engines tinkered up out of rusty junk."

"I read about one ship, the *Alabama*."

"One ship! And we've got hundreds." The officer tilted

244

back his cap and pushed out his chest. "We've bottled them up in Charleston and New Orleans and all the big rivers. From now on any Navy man in this western department can lie in his hammock all day and sleep. You want an easy piece of this war, you come along with me."

At Cairo William sent a letter to his mother and one to Clemmy Briscoe. He was in the war, he could brag a little. Even his father would have to approve this action, if he could overlook the missing gold. Not that it would be easy for Hume Harper to condone even so little as a ten-cent error on the bank's books but at least he would know that his son was not wasting his substance with harlots.

Anyway, all the officers and men on this ironclad stern-wheeler, the *Seward,* insisted that the war would be over by spring.

"By spring we'll have Atlanta, and Richmond by the fourth of July."

Christmas was just another day and New Year's slipped by ignored. The chow was mostly beans and he ate from a tin plate, he was cold half the time but the man-feeling inside him was warming and good. It even reached down into the hollow place where sometimes homesickness gnawed till he thrust it down and bade it hush and not come whimpering out to torment him at night.

It was at Memphis that the oiler slipped ashore and came swimming back at midnight, clambering up the side of the *Seward* holding high and dry over his head the bottle he had brought, wrapped in a copy of the *Tri-weekly Commonwealth,* almost a month old.

The sailors tossed the paper aside but before it blew overboard William rescued it and folded it inside his shirt. By the wan light in the forehold, he read it eagerly. It was news from Kentucky, it was a word from home.

There was an ominous note of warning printed in it,

from General Burbridge; henceforth, ran the order, all returned Confederates and prisoners would be held responsible for the violence, murder, and depredation of guerrilla bands.

"The old—" William muttered a prime Navy epithet, of which he had accumulated a salty variety. "He can't do that!"

But it was a short item on the back page of the scanty wartime newspaper that brought him up with a shock.

TALLANT CITY BANK ROBBED, was the headline. MISSING CASHIER SUSPECTED OF THEFT OF ONE HUNDRED THOUSAND DOLLARS.

Icy currents of panic ran over William's body, freezing him where he stood.

"Bolt!" he cried aloud.

Desperately he tried to remember. Had he ever, since he left the bank, seen again that scrap of paper on which he had written the combination of the safe?

Had he dropped it there, unaware, and had Bolt, arriving early, found it?

Had he, William Harper, been the bungling cause of the looting of his father's bank?

With cramping fingers he crumpled the paper and dropped it over the side into the black murk of the Mississippi River. Now he could never go home! Never, never go home!

23

THE WORD WAS BROUGHT TO THE FINDLY FARM BY MR.
Merrill driving Hume Harper's mare and Harper's buggy.
He came dashing into the yard where the snow had melted
to a slush in a midwinter thaw. The mare was steaming and
Merrill's face was a mask of panic and consternation as he
knocked quick and hard on the kitchen door. When Marcia
opened it he pushed past her, out of breath.

"Mrs. Harper—is she here?"

"Yes, sir, she's upstairs tending the baby. Will you have a
chair? I'll call her." Marcia shoved a dish out of reach of her
husband's grasping hands and went to the foot of the stairs.
"Mrs. Harper? A man here to see you!"

Ellen came down quickly, eyes anxious, paling as she saw
Merrill.

"Mr. Merrill! Is something wrong?"

Merrill ignored the proffered seat and held to the edge of
the table with taut fingers. He swallowed twice before he
answered.

"Bank's been robbed, Mrs. Harper. We think it could
have been Mr. Bolt. He hasn't been seen today. And *he's*
had some kind of a stroke."

"Mr. Harper?" Ellen gasped. "Is he—is he—"

"He's not dead. Just fell over and hasn't come to yet. I

247

got a doctor and they carried him home but you better come back with me, Mrs. Harper."

"Yes—yes, I'll get my things. I have to tell my daughter —" She turned and ran back up the stairs.

Tom came in then, looked at Merrill and his mother questioningly. "What's happened? That's Harper's rig out there. Did Harper send you after his wife?" he asked sharply. "Well, she's not going till she wants to go."

Marcia put out a hand. "Wait, Tom. Tell him, Mr. Merrill."

"We got robbed last night," Merrill said. "Somebody opened the safe and took about all the cash. Harper has had a bad spell. I came for his wife."

"Where is she? Upstairs?" Tom went pounding up the stairway.

Marcia poured a cup of coffee. "Wouldn't you like to drink this, Mr. Merrill? You've had a cold ride. It will take her a few minutes to pack her things. Yes, Mr. Findly"—she restrained her husband's reaching hands—"I'll fix a cup for you too."

"What's wrong with him?" Merrill asked, seeing the old man struggle for speech.

"Guerrillas attacked him." Marcia put a cup in reach of old Tom, who had begun making weird sounds at Merrill and pointing at the angry scar on his face. "He's trying to tell you that they rode him down and injured his head so he can't talk."

"I remember hearing something about that." Merrill watched the old man clutch at the cup and Marcia move to steady it in his grasp. "Shot him too, didn't they?"

"He recovered from that wound. It's the injury to his head that he can't seem to get over. Some damage to the brain, the doctor said."

Ellen came down then with Tom behind her carrying her

carpetbag. From above Harriet's voice came shrilly, calling questions, and the baby's unheeded crying.

"You go up, Ma," Tom said. "She's all to pieces."

"I'll go." Marcia pushed the dishes out of her husband's reach. "Goodbye, Mrs. Harper. I'm so sorry—and we're grateful you could come. I hope your husband will be all right."

Ellen got into the buggy numbly, numbly noted that the mare had been sweated, numbly let the thought that Mr. Harper would disapprove creep out of the stunned chaos of her mind. She put on her gloves when Merrill advised it, nodding at him in a childish fashion.

"Thank you, Mr. Merrill. And you can tell me now. Is it very bad?"

He cleared his throat harshly, clucked the mare into a trot, mud flying wildly from the wheels.

"The bank business is bad, Mrs. Harper. Cleaned us out of cash practically. Bolt—if it was Bolt, took most of the gold and some packs of greenbacks, altogether almost a hundred thousand. That's as near as we could learn in a hurry. Some of the stockholders came in and helped me count it—came to ninety-eight thousand and some odd, best we could figure."

"It could have been Morgan's raiders," suggested Ellen.

"No, ma'am, it wasn't. Whoever opened the safe had the combination. Locked it again after it was looted, locked the vault too. That isn't the worst, Mrs. Harper—your boy's gone too!"

"William?" It was a cry.

"Yes, ma'am. He wasn't home last night. Never slept in his bed. Mr. Harper came down all upset. Said the boy ran off last night. Then he opened the safe and there was this draft—drawn to your account, ma'am, for a thousand dollars. That got Mr. Harper mighty disturbed, as you can understand—then we discovered the safe had been cleaned out, as you might say."

"But—he wouldn't—William wouldn't rob his father's bank!" Ellen cried. "That's utterly ridiculous."

"Well, when Mr. Bolt never showed up either it had us sort of confused. That draft certainly made it look like young William had been into the safe and when the sheriff came he seemed to think the boy was mixed up in the robbery. That's when Mr. Harper took this bad spell. He turned purple and started gasping for breath and then he just slumped down and hasn't come to yet—at least not when I left the house."

"They took him home?"

"Yes, ma'am, and called the doctor. We got some men to put him in a hack and when we got him home we put him on his bed—then I thought I'd better come for you."

She seemed to be talking to herself. "William—he told me—"

"He didn't tell you he was planning to rob the bank, I hope?"

"No—Oh, no! He just said he had to get away—from his father, from the bank. He felt cheated, Mr. Merrill. He felt shamed by the way his father had managed to keep him out of the army. But I would never have believed he would leave without telling me."

"He picked a bad time, I'll say that." Merrill spoke bluntly, then quickly relented. "I wouldn't worry, ma'am. May find him right there when we get there. Boy his age, they slip out nights—have a girl maybe."

"Oh no, not William. He was so shy. It worried me. And of course his father was—rather firm."

"I know," Merrill agreed. "He was kind of hard on the boy. Meant it for his good of course. Couldn't realize the boy was growing up. Is your daughter all right?"

"Yes—she'll be up and about in a few days. And a lovely baby, so good and sweet." Ellen relaxed a little, ceased to worry the folds of the robe and her bonnet strings.

"Doesn't look like old Tom, I hope." Merrill strove for a touch of lightness. "Poor old fellow looks like he'd been dead and buried a long time."

"He is very pitiful." Ellen was thinking that Mr. Findly was pathetic and his condition deplorable, but thinking too how much worse the situation would be in that house if the angry old man should suddenly regain all his faculties. Worse for patient Marcia, worse for Tom and Harriet, even for little Hattie. "What is happening at the bank?" she inquired.

"Sheriff took over. Army got into it too. There was some payroll money in that safe. Came in day before yesterday. That's what makes me think Bolt did the robbery. He'd been talking about those payroll robberies they've had— stage held up out west, trains robbed, all for the payroll of the Union army. Kept going back to it all day. For a man who scarcely ever said anything he talked a lot, all about the time Morgan stole the payroll down at Cave Springs. Made me sort of uneasy the way he harped on about it. Then this morning I walked into the bank—nobody there, no fire—I got a funny feeling."

"You said there were stockholders, Mr. Merrill. Just who are they?" Ellen was regaining her composure, her voice was cool and steady.

"Well, you're one, ma'am. And Mr. Harper. Between the two of you you owned the majority of the bank stock. But there had to be others, in order to charter the bank under state law, and those people might think Mr. Harper was mighty careless letting somebody get hold of the combination to the safe. The depositors aren't going to be easy to handle either. They were milling around outside the door, when I left. Rumor got started the bank was closed for good, so the sheriff went out and told them it would open again as soon as possible. I surely do hope your boy wasn't in with Bolt in this business, ma'am."

"He couldn't be! Why, William isn't—he isn't brave enough, Mr. Merrill. He has always been so shy and timid."

"Well, he stood up and sassed Mr. Harper back, few days ago. Cussed too. Showed he had a little spirit."

"William? I can't believe it!"

"I was kind of glad to see the boy had a little gimp in his gizzard. Well, we're here. I'll come in as soon as I put this horse up. I'll fetch your stuff."

Her house! It looked unchanged, the same door, the same lace curtains at the shining windows. She turned the knob and entered an unchanged dining room. No, there was change. Hessie's broom leaned against the sideboard with a dustcloth draped on the handle and Hessie herself was huddled in the hall, a black, shuddering bulk of fright. A neighbor woman that Ellen barely knew came tiptoeing.

"Oh, my dear Mrs. Harper! It's so dreadful!" she whispered gustily. "I came over the minute I saw them carrying him in. It's a blood vessel, the doctor thinks. He may rally. Let me take your things."

There were other people about but Ellen was hardly aware of them, though they came to press her hand and murmur sympathy. All she was aware of was that supine figure looking somehow so small in the white vastness of the bed. They had taken off his shoes and his coat but he still wore his trousers, and his suspenders looked absurd for some reason she could not have explained. Desperately her eyes searched. William was not there.

She approached the bed and the doctor, who sat on the edge holding Harper's wrist, made a little warning gesture.

"Please, Mrs. Harper—no hysteria! Give her some of that stuff in the bottle, somebody. Sit down, Mrs. Harper."

A woman scurried to obey, speaking sharply to Hessie.

"Get a glass of water for your mistress and make her a cup of hot tea." Hessie shuffled off, whimpering.

"I'm really quite all right," protested Ellen. "Doctor, is he—"

"Can't tell yet. Now, all you good people, please go out and give him air. Do sit down, ma'am. It's bad, but the heart is steadying a little. Maybe you'd better go upstairs and lie down."

Ellen's face was drained, but calm. A cold woman, the doctor's eyes seemed to judge her. "I'd like to stay if I may," she said. "I'll be very quiet."

"He can't hear anything anyway. Too plethoric. Too much blood. I'd give him strychnine but he can't swallow. We tried whiskey but he strangled on that," said the doctor. "A man of his humor can burst a blood vessel mighty easy. Your boy showed up yet?"

"I haven't seen him but he'll come, Doctor. I know he'll come," Ellen insisted.

"I hope so. Be bad if this took a bad turn and you couldn't find him." The doctor turned back to his patient.

Harper's breathing was stertorous and slow. His chest rose and fell more and more slowly, it seemed to Ellen. She caught herself holding her own breath till the faint exhalation came, and her head grew dizzy with the effort.

Merrill tiptoed in, stood watching for a few minutes, came and took her hand. "I'll get back to the bank," he whispered. "I'll be back—let you know."

The morning moved on. There was a smell of cooking in the house and Hessie came, balancing on the balls of her feet ponderously, to whisper that dinner was on the table and would the doctor come and eat?

"You go, Doctor," Ellen urged. "I'll stay here till you finish."

The neighbors had all gone now. She saw a little group talking together in front of the house and two women crossed the yard, shawls over their heads. What were they talking out there? That her son had helped to rob his father's bank, and then run away? That her daughter had just had a child months too soon for respectability? That the Harpers, who had always been so proud, were now humbled, the untouchables become part of the herd, the arrogant reduced to public scorn?

They didn't know, her twisting heart moaned, how much I longed to be just another woman, not the banker's wife! How I would have loved to run into another woman's back door with a plate of rolls or a glass of jelly. How I would have enjoyed pausing to gossip on the steps of the church, but for that stern hand on my elbow. So stern that all I could do was bow briefly and be remotely polite while Mr. Harper grudgingly touched his high hat. How I returned again and again to this house, untouched by friendship!

It was difficult now to relax, to meet halfway and graciously the people who knocked and were admitted to the chilly parlor by Hessie, recovered from her fright, now that her mistress was in command, and quite rigid with importance. Late in the afternoon there was still no perceptible change in Hume Harper's condition. Mr. Merrill came and helped the doctor undress his employer, and ease him gently into a clean nightshirt. Then Merrill took over the watch, leaving the doctor free to make his pressing calls. Ellen slipped away to sit by the dining room window where she could see down the street, unobserved.

William, William, my boy, where are you? How could he go like this and leave her alone in her trouble? Never could they make her believe that he had had any part in the robbery. Not even when the woman came who flounced in angrily and wailed that every penny they owned had been in that bank and now what would they do? And one thing was certain—her husband would never rest till whoever had done it was brought to justice, no matter who they were, high or low or whatever!

Then, after a little, Tom Findly came and Ellen was pathetically glad to see him. She clung to him and cried while he patted her back and murmured comforting words. Then he sat beside her and told her all he had learned in town.

The sheriff had padlocked the bank. Some people had milled around and there had been some threats and hard words but the sheriff had told them that the attorney general was coming from Frankfort and he reckoned the bank would open again and be sound as ever as soon as they got things straightened out. The bank had been in fine shape, so Merrill claimed. They had been paying 4 per cent on the stock in spite of a government order that every bank in this congressional district must make substantial loans to the people in order to get any government business.

"And they still blame Mr. Harper?" Ellen asked faintly.

"Well, you know how people are." Tom tried to be casual. "They have to have a scapegoat. They've already put out an alarm and got detectives out to catch this fellow, Bolt. If the bank opened tomorrow of course there would be a run on it right away, all the scared people trying to draw out their money, and no cash to pay off with. So that would only make things worse. When the attorney general gets here they'll make some arrangement to get back in business."

Ellen sat up suddenly. "Tom, there is money! A lot of money. I'm sure it belonged to Mr. Harper. He'd want to save the bank. The bank has been his life." She hurried to the bedroom and with Merrill watching curiously she searched through her husband's discarded clothes for his bunch of keys.

"Come here, Tom—you too, Mr. Merrill," she ordered as she unlocked the wardrobe. "It has always been up there at the back of the shelf. Yes, there it is—you'll have to lift it down. One of these keys must open it."

Almost she expected the man on the bed to sit up and shout at her as she turned the key and lifted the lid of the steel box but there was only continued heavy breathing. Merrill leaned over her and Tom's eyes widened as she opened the box. Stack beside stack, the shining gold pieces lay, padded around with sheaves of paper money. Good government issue, Merrill declared, examining it.

"Would this save the bank?" Ellen asked.

Merrill looked thoughtful. "We'd have to be mighty clever about it, Mrs. Harper. The sheriff and the attorney general would have to know about it, or somebody would start a story that Mr. Harper had robbed the bank himself and hid the money out."

"But it was his own money. From outside business ventures. It had nothing to do with the bank," argued Ellen.

"In that case," remarked Merrill sagely, "the first reaction of almost anybody would be—did Mr. Harper hide his own money at home because he was dubious about the bank? Somebody would be bound to find it out. You can't keep a secret in this town. You may need this money yourself, Mrs. Harper. If it should be decided that your husband was criminally negligent in not protecting the depositors' money, you and the other stockholders might have to make up the shortage. You'd better leave things as they are till the law takes over."

"I'd give it all gladly if it would save the bank," she said. "I must have lost a great deal myself. I had money in that bank."

Mr. Merrill put on a sober face. "Mrs. Harper," he said slowly, "I keep the books down at the bank. I happen to know that for some time, ever since the war began as a matter of fact, Mr. Harper has been systematically drawing the money out of what was your account. I knew when he put your money into the bank. I've been there, as you know, for many years, ever since before Mr. Harper was named president by the board of directors. Of course, Mr. Harper did not explain the withdrawals to me. There was no reason why he should. I merely knew that they were all written on that one account."

"You mean—that all this could actually be my money, Mr. Merrill?" she asked, evenly.

"It could be money that was earned by your money, Mrs. Harper—by various—enterprises," Merrill hedged.

"If you are talking about deals in contraband, Mr. Merrill"—she gave him a direct look, her head high—"speak plainly. I have heard that word before."

"I'd rather not be too explicit—having so little real information," evaded the old man.

She locked the box reluctantly, replaced it in the wardrobe. Perhaps she had done wrong to touch it at all. She hoped no one would mention it to her husband when he recovered from this attack. She went back to her post by the window and Tom Findly came to sit beside her, laying a hand on hers.

"You're a comfort to me, Tom." She sighed. "I may have need of a man now."

He pressed her hand gently. "I wish I was more of a man, Mrs. Harper. I'm mighty little use to anybody. Maybe I did Harriet a great wrong when I married her. There's the place—I can't work it as it needs to be worked. And there's Pa. He may live a long time and never be himself again. Mr.

Harper holds our mortgage, but I reckon you know that?"

"I don't know anything, Tom. No woman should be as ignorant and helpless as I am. You'll have to help me." Ellen sighed.

"I'll do what I can, but I was a Confederate soldier. That's against me. I reckon I owe it to Mr. Harper that I'm not a prisoner right now." Tom pulled his hands free and pressed his fingers hard into the flesh of his thigh. "There was some kind of a deal. You wouldn't know about it. Pa was in on it and Mr. Harper and a Colonel Bisbee. A deal to trade cotton for bonds, and from what Mr. Harper said when he came out to the place last summer, my father holds the bonds. Mr. Harper demanded them, but of course Pa couldn't talk or understand. I guess that's why they let me stay around—to look after Pa and keep him alive."

"You think it was something illegal, Tom?" she asked.

"I wouldn't know. Of course the officials wink at contraband trade if it benefits their side. Mr. Harper was pretty solidly in favor with the Union officers. But he and the colonel must have been sort of uncertain about this bond deal or they wouldn't have gotten Pa in on it. My father is known as a hard man, Mrs. Harper, but a man who can keep his mouth shut. Now everything is complicated by the fact that he may never get his mind back." He reached in his pocket. "By the way—I stopped for the mail. There was a letter for you."

She studied the grimy envelope. "From William!" she cried.

Tom laid a restraining hand on her wrist. "Don't open it here. It might be that you would want to burn it."

"Oh, no!" She got his meaning, turned pale, rose quickly. "Come," she ordered, leading him to the kitchen. There her hands shook so that Tom took the letter away from her and broke the seal with his knife. He ran his eyes swiftly over the single sheet.

"It's all right," he told her. "Willie didn't rob the bank. He says in this that he borrowed a thousand dollars from you and that he intends paying it back, with interest, when he makes his fortune." He laughed a little as he handed her the letter.

"Oh, thank God—thank God!" She read the scrawled page rapidly, tears running down her face.

"It might be a good thing to show that letter to the sheriff," Tom advised. "I'll take it to him if you say so. It might clear up some doubts in his mind."

"Yes—yes, he must see it! Oh, thank you, Tom. You are so good to me!"

"It's time," he said gravely, "that somebody started being good to you."

She put her arms around him impulsively. "I have a son!" she whispered. "Now in my time of need God has sent me a son!"

As night fell and the hours dragged on the doctor came back and paced impatiently up and down the big bedroom, his hands clasped under his coattails.

"Can't understand it," he muttered. "He should have rallied long ago. Must have been a blood vessel. It has to be a blood vessel."

Down in the square in front of the bank angry men still stood about, growling, and someone tossed a rock through the bank window. Shouting boys stuffed an old coat with straw and, hanging it to a tree, set fire to it. The Home Guards hung around, there were a few desultory shots, then later the crowd grew quiet, slunk home.

Everything was very still when at four o'clock in the morning Hume Harper abruptly ceased to breathe.

The doctor, spreading the sheet up over the dead, upturned face, looked across the room at Ellen Harper, sitting motionless and pallid as marble in her chair, and wondered briefly who would grieve for that man lying dead on the bed.

24

W HEN ALL WAS OVER ELLEN HARPER RETURNED GRATE-fully to her rocking chair by the window.

She was tired and her nerves felt like red-hot wires, but she was content. Surely Mr. Harper would have been satisfied with the elegance of his funeral; even the fact that neither of his children was there to see his broadcloth-covered coffin lowered into the grave might not have distressed him. Governor Bramlette was there, important in high silk hat and crepe-banded sleeve, and with him a half dozen officials from Frankfort, including the firebrand United States senator, Garrett Davis.

Colonel Bisbee had collected a military band and the procession moved from the chilly church through the streets to a slow dirge, so slow that even the black-tasseled horses pulling the hearse danced with cold and fretted. In a closed carriage Mr. Merrill had secured, Ellen rode with the governor and Lennie Briscoe. Lennie had walked all the way to town, not daring to risk her one horse now that horses were being taken from loaded farm wagons and milk carts by the army, by order of Secretary Stanton.

Ellen was pleased to have Lennie with her, and distressed that Lennie had had sad news of Thad, in Georgia. Thad, so Lennie told her, had died back in September.

"It was typhoid." Lennie was dry-eyed and flat-voiced. "Somewhere down there below Chattanooga. A neighbor boy brought me the word, the first I'd had in a long time. The boy didn't dare stay since General Burbridge is putting all the Confederates in jail, but he stopped to leave me Thad's watch and his father's Masonic ring. The girls cried, but I can't cry. I'd cried over Thad since July, I told Tee, and it seems as though my heart is just dried up."

"It was good of you to come," Ellen said. "To be—forgiving. William told me about—what happened. About your place and Mr. Harper."

"I'd thought about that, and the more I thought the more I decided that after all Mr. Harper did mean well by me and the children. So, both of us being widows, I thought the decent thing was for me to come—and maybe tell you how I felt," Lennie said with some difficulty.

"Mr. Harper was a man not always understood," Ellen agreed, wondering meanwhile if she herself had ever understood him. Had there been a hunger in him, inarticulate, lost, prisoned through his life within that chilled shell, a form he had created and accepted as embodying the manner of a man a banker ought to be? Had all his angers been frustrations, because never had he been able to act outside that grim shell of duty, of routine, of obligation?

In the black coffin now he rode in pomp and he would have approved that, and the mounted officers making their horses sidle and toss their heads as they paced beside it. The wheels turned to the rhythm of a thudding drum and frozen earth and slush dribbled sadly from the polished wheels. Just behind Ellen's carriage rolled another filled with important men and somewhere behind was the Harper buggy being decorously driven by Mr. Merrill with Tom Findly beside him. Tom had ridden the Findly horse into town but had hidden it in Harper's barn at Merrill's advice.

"Wouldn't surprise me to see a cavalry detail ride up and unhook the horses off the hearse before it got back to town," Merrill grumbled. "General Boyle ordered them to stop seizing people's stock but Stanton, up in Washington, condones anything will outfit an army and of course there are always tricksters around will pay a high price for anything with four legs under it. Grant is bound to mount his troops, even if the farmers have to hitch their wives to the plow. How they expect to feed a couple of million troops another year if no crops get put in the ground is a question I reckon even they can't answer."

At last they reached the wind-swept bleakness of the cemetery. The minister wore thick black gloves, a faded drape of crepe around his hat and a heavy gray knit tippet. As he stood across the open grave from Ellen the wind kept catching the fringe end of the tippet and flipping it over his mouth so that his words came muffled and jerky. She was grateful that Harriet was not there. Harriet always had difficulty suppressing a giggle when she watched the minister, even a funeral would not subdue her, and William would have shuffled and scuffed his big feet.

Ellen looked down at the raw clay that edged the grave and could almost see a pair of huge shoes there, scrubbing patterns in the mud. She reached for Lennie's hand and held it tight and felt Lennie shiver and a harsh, small sob jerked her body. Lennie, she knew, was seeing another grave, hasty, raw, ugly, unconsidered and abandoned.

"Come back to the house with me," she urged in a whisper, when they were back in the carriage. "I'll have Hessie make us some hot tea so we won't take a chill."

Lennie nodded, as the governor shouldered in beside

them. The Negro driver whipped up the horses and they broke gratefully into a warming trot. The governor made a kind of formal bow, sitting down beside her.

"You and the State of Kentucky have suffered a grievous loss today, dear Madam," he said.

Ellen murmured something polite through her black veils, but all she was thinking was that a great proud state like Kentucky should never elect a man for governor who had such a bad breath. What was the matter with her? Why did her mind run on such absurd thoughts when she should be grief-stricken and sunk in sorrow?

Bramlette got out at the courthouse, making his official farewell, and several other men came to the carriage to shake her hand and say things she scarcely heard. "Drive the ladies wherever they wish to go," the undertaker ordered the driver.

"We'll go home. I want to get all this stuff off my head," said Ellen as the carriage door closed. "I suppose I'll have to wear this gruesome veil every time I go out, but I could mourn Mr. Harper just as well without it."

"Tee wanted to get her grandmother's veil out of the trunk for me," Lennie said, "but I said no, I'd just wear this little one I'd worn when my children died. All my mourning I have to do inside, Ellen. They don't come and shake your hand when your husband dies in the Confederate army, not with things getting ugly as they are now in Kentucky."

"I hadn't heard. Are things worse?" Ellen asked.

"You wouldn't know. Your friends are in power. You've got nobody on the other side," Lennie said.

"My son-in-law," Ellen reminded her—and her son, where was he? Surely William wouldn't have aligned himself with the South, but how did she know? Torment tore at her for a little as the carriage racketed through the square and pulled up at the house where all the shutters had been closed for proper mourning. Then she was back in her rocking chair and presently Mr. Merrill drove in and she went to the door and called to him and Tom to come in and get warm.

And that, it came to her, was something she would never have dared do before, call out the door like some country-woman! My own door, she said it over with some satisfaction. My own house! Perhaps tomorrow the bank would own the house but tonight she was going to enjoy this stimulating freedom that had not been hers for more than twenty years.

"Get down the Christmas fruit cake, Hessie," she ordered. "This year Christmas will be just one more day."

"At my house too," said Lennie, "except for my old Nigras. They never forget and it's 'Christmas gift, Miss'— and not one thing to give them!"

Ellen had an impulse to say that there was fat meat in plenty in her smokehouse, but she remembered that one did not offer charity to people like Lennie Briscoe, whose family had known what it was to be wealthy and proud.

"But you're lucky to have a family with you!" she said. "You could be utterly alone, like me!"

"Yes, but how am I going to feed and clothe them? I don't even know if we have a roof over our heads. Mr. Harper said he was foreclosing, but that has to go to court and I haven't heard one word."

"There will be lawyers who will tell us what to do," Ellen said, moving her chair a little and directing Hessie to put a small table alongside and get down cups and saucers. "But I promise you your children will not be homeless if I can prevent it, Lennie."

"I reckon you think that's why I came today," worried Lennie, "but it wasn't even in my mind."

"I think that you came in friendship for me. Did it ever occur to you that I am practically a friendless woman, Lennie Briscoe?" Ellen demanded, a sharpness in her voice that troubled her a little.

"No, I guess I was always a little envious of you because you were a rich woman—with no troubles," Lennie answered.

Merrill and Tom came in and Ellen cut the cake, with Hessie worriedly holding plates.

"Git crumbs all over the carpet," she fretted.

Ellen tossed her head. "It's my carpet! I'll drop crumbs on it if I please. I—I might even throw it out. I always did hate it."

Lennie looked a little startled. "It's a good sturdy carpet, though I never did care much for brown," she agreed.

"It's horrible," cried Ellen, tingling with the stimulation of this strange rebellion within her. "Mr. Harper bought it in Louisville. He said it would last as long as we lived. Imagine, having to live all your life with a lot of brown snails with black streaks crawling on the floor!"

"One thing about Thad's father—" Lennie sugared her tea. (And where did they get sugar, these times? she wondered.) "He was extravagant and he left us in debt but everything he bought for that house was handsome and elegant. And elegant things need servants to care for them. I've tried to teach the girls but lately it seems to take all the strength I have just to keep them fed, and to wait for the war to end. Now—it won't matter if the war never ends!" she cried desolately.

The men looked embarrassed, but Ellen reached a comforting hand to Lennie. Widows, Lennie had said. And she too should be sorrowful, and instead she was filled with this troubling, restless resentment for everything Hume Harper had left behind. Suddenly she was hating this house and everything in it, everything that was so proper, so substantial, so smug and so utterly drab. I'll buy a flowered carpet, she determined, the biggest, brightest flowers I can find.

Tom was uneasy and anxious to hurry home, telling them that his mother would try to do the outside work if he was late, and that when his father was left alone he shouted and pushed furniture around and that upset Harriet.

"I offered to carry her downstairs before I left," he said, "but she dreads going down. She says Pa resents the baby and she's even got an idea he might try to hurt little Hattie."

There flashed through Ellen Harper's mind that postscript on William's letter: *Don't bring that baby into the house, Mama. No telling what he would do.*

What threats had Hume Harper made to move his son to pen such a warning? Ellen felt herself tingling with a wicked and disturbing satisfaction. You are dead now, Hume Harper! You turned my child out of her home, you hated your granddaughter, you drove my son away from me, but now you are dead, dead, dead! You are lying out there in the cold and you can never come back to rage at us again because in the end your fury and your rage killed you. So there is no grief in me, no tears in me, no sorrow that you are dead. I will buy a flowered carpet and my granddaughter shall dance on it, and you will not be here to sulk and be offended, Hume Harper.

I'm going mad! Almost she said the words aloud, almost she caught herself laughing shrilly. She drew long breaths to get control, holding them, gasping out, "Hessie—more tea!"

Merrill drove Lennie home then, and later in the evening he came back again.

"I'll bring the lawyer out tomorrow, Mrs. Harper," he told Ellen. "There may be papers here you can locate that he will want to see. So far we haven't found any new will."

"But surely Mr. Harper would have made a will. He was the world's most methodical person," Ellen insisted.

"I may as well tell you," said the old man unhappily. "I found his old will—torn to pieces and thrown into the trash the day William told him Miss Harriet's baby was born. The lawyer says he was never called to draft a new will, and nothing was said to me about witnessing his signature, like I'd always done before. The one he tore up was dated 'fifty-eight. It left everything to you for your lifetime, then it was to be divided between the children."

"It could be," said Ellen crisply, so that Merrill looked at her with a perplexed question in his eyes, "that most of the money was mine anyway. Certainly the money William took from the bank was mine and there's to be no fuss made about that, you understand, Mr. Merrill?"

"I understand, but the bank examiners might not, Mrs. Harper. Maybe you'd better give me a draft on your account to cover it, so the cash will come out even, William being a minor. Just to keep the record straight, you understand?" Merrill was flustered. This was a woman he had never known, this level-eyed Ellen Harper with decision in her eyes and voice. "Of course, if Mr. Harper did die intestate, the court will have to settle everything according to the inheritance laws of Kentucky. As for that money you've got there in that dispatch box—I wouldn't know to advise you about that. Maybe the best thing would be for you to claim it was your money all along."

"If I as a stockholder in the bank must reimburse the depositors for their losses by this robbery, likely I shall need that money," stated Ellen. "Has anything been heard yet as to what became of Mr. Bolt?"

"No ma'am, not yet. Country is so unsettled now, with

this war, a man can get lost mighty easy. If they do catch him, though, they might get some of the money back."

When he was gone Ellen went into the big bedroom and looked about her with distaste almost approaching revulsion. Here, for more than twenty years, she had slept and there on the back of that chair for all those years had hung Hume Harper's black coat. His hard hats still rested on the wardrobe shelf. The room smelled of him, of the pomade with which he had anxiously nursed his thinning hair, of his shaving soap and boot polish. She threw a window high and let the winter air rush in but somehow the wind smelled of that cemetery and of the raw clay where she had stood as that coffin went down.

"I won't sleep here," she said aloud. "Not ever again."

The spare room upstairs would be cold. She gathered an armful of lightwood and kindling and climbed the stairs to build a fire. The room, at the front of the house, was well furnished and had a good bed which had rarely been slept in. She jerked off the counterpane and pillow shams and made the bed with aired sheets and blankets from the chest in the hall, new blankets never before used. Now she would use everything. All the best, that had been saved so long. The wedding-ring quilt that her own mother had made, bright with gold and blue and daintily sewed with tiny quilting stitches in a fern pattern.

She had the room warm and the bed ready and was pulling her black dress over her head when there was a sudden hard pounding on the door below. She heard a woman's voice calling.

"Mrs. Harper! Mrs. Harper!"

She looked down through the curtains and in the wan light from the sky she saw a buggy in the drive. Fumbling into her frock, she picked up the lamp and hurried down the stairs. The open door brought in a cold gust that made the lamp flame leap and flicker, but its light showed her the stark face and enormous eyes of Marcia Findly.

"It's Tom!" Marcia cried, clutching at Ellen so that the lamp chimney jingled and she burned her hand righting it. "They arrested Tom! The Union—they came and took him away!"

Ellen pulled her in and closed the door. "But—why?" she demanded. "How could they arrest him? Tom hasn't been in the army for more than a year."

"They did. They came—even before he got back from Mr. Harper's funeral. They were waiting, standing around in my kitchen when he came home. They didn't give him time even to speak to his wife before they took him away," moaned Marcia, leaning weakly against Ellen.

Ellen felt herself growing icily calm. "Now," she said, putting Marcia into a chair, "tell me again, and slowly. Get your breath."

Marcia began to cry then, shaking all over, and Ellen went to the bedroom for a bottle of camphor. She held it under the other woman's nose till she sneezed and coughed, pushing it away.

"They came, six of them—and that Colonel Bisbee. I didn't know him but all at once Mr. Findly spoke out his name sharp and plain. 'Bisbee!' he said, and the colonel sort of sneered and said, 'Yes, it's Bisbee, as you know very well, you old robber! Still pretending to be out of your mind so you can rob and cheat people who trusted you!' Then Mr. Findly started screeching and beating on the table the way he does, and just then Tom walked in. So they told him he was under arrest. For treasonably taking up arms against the United States, they said."

"They waited more than a year and then suddenly discovered Tom had fought with the Confederacy?" Ellen asked bitterly. But in her heart she knew why Tom had been

269

unmolested until now. Hume Harper had managed it and now Hume Harper was dead. And because of some mysterious business deal or other Colonel Bisbee had turned vindictive.

"Tom asked them to let him go up and get some clothes and say goodbye to his wife," Marcia sobbed on, "but they said no—the rebs were too damn' slippery—those were their very words, Mrs. Harper. So I went and got his clothes, with Harriet screaming in hysterics and downstairs Mr. Findly still yelling. Then they hustled Tom off without even a goodbye to me, his own mother—but thank the Lord, they didn't take our horse! So I went out and hitched up and came for you. Maybe you can quiet Harriet. I've stood so much now I don't know if I can bear much more!"

"I'll get some clothes. You wait here," ordered Ellen.

She dragged her carpetbag out of the wardrobe and hastily stuffed garments into it, rolling dresses into shapeless wads, piling shoes on top of them. Then, standing on a chair, she reached far back and, pulling out the steel box, staggered with it to the bed.

"Marcia," she called. "Marcia Findly—come help me. We're taking this." She pointed to the box. "It's too heavy for me to carry alone. Help me put it in your buggy. It's money," she explained, as they hefted the metal container between them. "I wouldn't dare leave it in the house. Anyway—we may need it, and if we do," she stated firmly, "if we do, Marcia Findly, I shall use it!"

25

$\mathcal{A}$LL THAT BITTER YEAR OF 1864 KENTUCKY SANG ONE song and the song was a lament of dread, fury, and hate.

Around Richmond the armies of Grant, Meade and Pope beat and battered at the seemingly invincible army of Robert E. Lee. Entrenched in shattered Petersburg, the Confederate troops held on, undaunted even when Sheridan and Hunter ravaged the rich Shenandoah Valley and Atlanta fell.

After Atlanta Sherman moved through the South, a torch, a bludgeon, desolation with banners, ripping at the soft, helpless belly of a stricken country, the smoke and stench and whooping terror of that march to the sea a horror over the whole country. And over Kentucky slunk and thundered the frightful violence of guerrilla warfare.

Stirred by the outrages of lawless hordes of mounted men, both the state and the Union military moved blindly and furiously in retaliation to put down the menace, acting without much sense or justice or reason. Governor Bramlette issued a proclamation, seconding the Union army's already savage blood-and-iron policy. Revenge was the keynote. Revenge upon all Confederate sympathizers for the ravages of the guerrillas. Inevitably this unconsidered and vengeful attitude led to extravagant and vicious orgies of retribution.

Innocent people were arrested and executed for purportedly aiding and condoning guerrilla depredations, though often no definite connection could have been proven in a court of law. Any person aiding a Confederate soldier or harboring a returned or wounded man was liable to a heavy fine and imprisonment, and as the fury mounted even persons overheard whispering sympathy for any Confederate were by General Burbridge's ruthless order to be rated as traitors and spies and if convicted, so ran the order, "will suffer death."

This vindictive state and military pressure against all Southern sympathizers filled the country with the tautness of terror and dread. No man trusted another. Houses were searched, even for letters from soldiers already killed in battle.

On a hill behind the Briscoe barn Teresa and Clementine held a dim lantern while old Lum dug a deep hole. In it they would bury the two letters that had come from their father, wrapped in a little silk Confederate flag.

"What if they dig here?" worried Priscilla. "That flag would ruin us."

"Ain't gonna dig. I pile manure on top," declared Lum.

"No, you can't!" protested Clementine. "It seeps. It would ruin everything."

"Cornstalks, Lum," suggested Teresa. "They're clean. Throw them down and let the cows trample them."

"Cows are messy too," argued Priscilla.

Teresa had hidden the one letter she had had from Henri in a tobacco can, wrapped it in white silk, and buried it in the middle of Grandmother Briscoe's flower garden.

"But don't put up a tombstone for heaven's sake," begged Clementine.

"When they come you can show them that letter you had from Willie Harper," retorted Teresa. "The one where he said he was on one of Admiral Porter's gunboats heading for the James River. That will make them believe we are all Yankees."

"I won't be an old Yankee!" fumed Priscilla. "I'll let them cut my head off first."

"If they cut it off, your tongue would still be wagging," sighed Lennie. "We should burn everything, I suppose. Though everybody who is anybody knows that your father was in Bragg's army."

"Nobody who is anybody will come out here snooping. It will be Yankee strangers and white trash," declared Teresa. "They've already gone through all the Bacons' things. Delia said they found one songbook that had 'Maryland, My Maryland' in it, so they made all sorts of threats and tore up the book and burned it in the middle of the parlor floor. Their carpet has a big black hole in the middle of it."

Somehow Lennie had kept them together, somehow kept them fed. Whether she still had any right on the place she did not know, but no lawyer or deputy sheriff had ever appeared with a fateful paper. She had heard that Hume Harper's estate was still in court for settlement, but the bank had reopened with an Indiana man sitting behind Harper's desk. Ellen Harper, so the Bacons reported, had taken her mare and buggy and all her things and moved out to the Findly farm after the Yankee officers put young Tom in jail.

Ceph, with a one-horse plow, had managed to scratch a little ground, enough to plant a garden and a patch of corn. The one old sow, given the society of a borrowed male, had brought forth a litter of pigs in a secret shelter hidden under an old straw stack. Four of the pigs had been sold by practical Clementine for enough to buy two barrels of flour. Sometimes Lennie wept quietly into her pillow at night but daylight found her up again, chin firm, eyes sponged with cold water, doggedly attacking the task of survival for one more day.

Clementine, full of schemes as always, had begged a few tobacco plants from a neighbor and set out a little patch, and every morning she was out with Jericho, hoeing or whacking off worms into a tin bucket, barefooted, sun-darkened, her hair stuffed into an old sunbonnet. She was, so Teresa declared, a disgrace to the Briscoes, but Clemmy had a defiant answer.

"When Jericho and I get our tobacco cut and cured it will sell for enough to buy new shoes for all you fine ladies. Then you can parade around and restore the prestige of the Briscoes."

"But you're too big to go slopping around looking like a Negro," Lennie objected. "Even Marshy puts the back of the almanac in her old shoes to stop the holes."

"And blacks 'em with soot," Rowena added, "but I like going barefooted except when Lum cuts the grass and leaves it full of stickers."

"The back of the Bible wouldn't stop the holes in my soles," argued Clementine. "It takes money to be a lady but my tobacco will earn it."

"If they'll let you sell it. They'll say you're Confederate and likely take it all away from you," worried Lennie.

"They won't because Jericho and I will hide it and when Mr. Harris down the road hauls his crop to town he'll put mine in with it, and he's got trading permits and has already sworn the oath."

"She could be right," Teresa told her mother. "Clemmy makes you mad, she's so arbitrary and outspoken, but so many times she's right."

"I just can't bear to have you all get used to rough living," Lennie said. "These are cruel times and so much that used to be important has been lost, but the bad times can't last forever. We have to hold to what we had or be lost too."

"Maybe we won't go on forever, not if Mrs. Harper takes the place away from us."

"I can't see Ellen Harper doing that, but of course if the court comes into it anything could happen. I suppose nothing will be really settled till Willie is of age," Lennie said.

"Willie's no older than I am. Not much anyway."

"The war will make him seem older. It's making us all older. I feel every night as though I'd never been young in all my life."

"You're still young and beautiful to us, Mama," Teresa declared loyally. "When I was little I thought you were the most beautiful woman in the world. I wanted to look like you."

"I'm glad you look like your father, Tee. All of you got his dark eyes and when I look around at you all, I seem to see him, over and over. It's a comfort," Lennie said.

"It was all a foolish waste, wasn't it, Mama? Pa's going off to that war. He was too old and he wasn't strong because he'd never been raised to work hard and his dying didn't help the South any. Even if he was there to fight at Chickamauga, we were defeated anyway."

"In that letter he said nobody won at Chickamauga."

"But the Yankees stayed and we had to retreat," Teresa reminded her.

"Don't talk about it, Tee. I can't bear it. I have to make myself stop thinking about that retreat. Thad Briscoe, who always had a fine horse to ride and Negroes to groom and feed it, tramping over those hills, maybe with nothing to eat, no chance to rest, and for what, Tee—for what?" Lennie's voice broke.

"For honor," said Teresa. "Because he couldn't have lived with himself if he hadn't gone."

"Yes, yes, you're right." Lennie went back to her ironing.

275

Everything they owned now was so old and frail that it had to be ironed with painful care. Lennie had ransacked old trunks up attic for yellowed old petticoats, chemises, even tablecloths, anything that would hold together to be made over.

"Nothing for it," she sighed. "All of you will have to marry rich!"

"Only Yankees are rich," declared Priscilla.

"Speculators are rich. Henri told me there were plenty of speculators down South getting rich from the war," Teresa said.

"It takes money to speculate and nobody has any any more," Lennie said.

"That man who robbed the bank has plenty and they've never caught him."

"He probably went to Canada." Teresa jabbed her finger with a needle, and sucked at the blood. She was trying to mend one of 'Ria's old dresses so that it would hold together a little longer. "Willie Harper will have plenty of money. Clemmy won't have to worry if she marries Willie."

"I still say he looks like a shidepoke." Priscilla shrugged.

"He does not. He never did," flared Clementine.

Lennie looked up from her ironing board. "Stop your fussing," she ordered. "Tee, make another light. There's some grease in the pantry in a can. You can fix a new wick." There were no candles now in the one shop in which they were permitted to buy anything. Lennie frowned at the smoky arrangment of grease and a rag that sent a sickly light over the kitchen and made smoke eddy under the ceiling. Then she stiffened suddenly. "Be quiet! I hear something."

"It's probably Ceph at the woodpile."

"It's not Ceph. He'd call out. He's always afraid Clemmy will shoot if she hears a noise."

"I would, too." Clementine got the pistol from the

drawer in the safe. The others sat up alertly. They had been peeling the late peaches to be dried next day, and they held their knives in air.

"The back door," Lennie whispered.

"It's bolted."

They all heard it then, the soft cautious tapping. The entry between the kitchen and the door was dark and Clementine tiptoed in, holding the gun ready.

"Who's there?" she demanded. "Answer or I'll fire!"

Ward was at her heels, armed with his wooden gun. His shrill voice repeated, "Answer or I fire!"

"Tee?" called a hoarse voice beyond the door. "Tee!"

In a flash Teresa pushed past her sister, tore at the bolts, dragging them back, breaking her nails, ignoring her mother's sharp warning. "Tee! Wait!"

"It's Henri!" Teresa cried. "Henri!" She jerked open the door and dragged a scarecrow figure inside. "Mama—it's Henri!"

Lennie came quickly, closing the door, bolting it fast. Clementine stood, the useless weapon in her hand.

"Henri—you shouldn't have come here!" she exclaimed.

Henri put Teresa out of his arms, moved into the kitchen smiling at them all through a bramble of dirty beard.

"Nobody saw me, Mrs. Briscoe. I slipped across the fields and came in from the back road." His uniform was a shapeless and faded jacket, with few buttons, a limp pair of filthy, colorless cotton pants. He had no shoes and no hat.

"Stay back here in the dark till I pull all the shades." Lennie pushed him into the shadows. "If you should be taken, Henri, you'd be shot—and we," she added bitterly, "might be shot too."

Henri loosened Teresa's clinging arms.

"I'm not staying," he said, "but I had to see you, Little

Tee. I've been walking for a week, hiding all day and walking by night all the way from Owensboro."

Lennie's panic lifted a little when she had shaded all the windows. This could be her Thad walking home, she was thinking. Skulking home, walking in fear in his own country, hiding from people who had been his friends and neighbors.

Sing one song, Kentucky. A song of hate! But the day will come when it will be a jeremiad of shame.

"I'll get you something to eat, Henri," Teresa said. "Such as we have."

He had thirty days' furlough, he told them, before his command was to be sent south to Texas. He sat, sagged wearily in a chair, while Lennie fried mush for him and two precious eggs and Teresa ransacked the pantry for syrup and some butter. Clementine still stood watch near the door with the pistol.

Henri ate as though he had not eaten for days, wiping up every bit of grease with a crust of corn bread, not missing a crumb. Lennie's heart ached intolerably at the sight of him. Had Thad been hungry too?

"Know what I ate yesterday?" Henri asked Ward, who hung about close to him watching with eager eyes. "Nice fat white grubs! I found them under a rotten log. First fat I'd had in a long time."

"Did they wiggle?" inquired Ward.

"They didn't have a chance to wiggle. I gobbled them down too fast."

"Ugh!" Priscilla gagged.

"I ate raw corn the day before and some raw potatoes I dug. No salt. That's what we miss now—salt. Some used to come up from Texas but now the Yanks are down there and hold the mines."

"Here," said Ward, shaking salt over Henri's grimy palm. "Lick that up."

Henri licked at it, eagerly grinning at the boy, and Teresa gave a little gulping sob as she leaned against Henri's shoulder. It was his hands that hurt her most, those long hands that had been so graceful and deft with a brush, so quick and clean. Now they were dark and knotty, the nails broken and black. Henri looked down at them, following her eyes.

"Know what I'd like to do, Mrs. Briscoe?" he asked. "Wash! I got to Owensboro in the hold of a Negro's hog boat. The Negro hid me and fed me when he could. He let me slip aboard at Helena, because even dirty as I was, he recognized me. It was that slave boy of Cass Rooney's, the boy they wanted to lynch when Cass's old father was shot at. My father insisted the boy was innocent and he saved him and my mother hid him till Father could send him south. He was one of the reasons why Cass Rooney and those others hated my father. The Negro paid me back by helping me get home, but those hogs and the boat were mighty filthy."

"They're all gone, Henri, your mother and Denise," Lennie told him. "Willie Harper saw your mother and Milo's wife in St. Louis. He wrote Clemmy about seeing them there. He said Denise told him Milo was still in prison and they had had to run away to keep from being sent south. Union officers are living in your house. Prissy, poke up the fire and heat a lot of water. You can wash in the entry, Henri. And Tee, you go up and see if you can find some of your father's clothes. A shirt and pants, anyway. And a razor. We've still got a little soap. You knew Thad had died, Henri? He was with Bragg at Chickamauga and died on that retreat."

"No, I didn't know. I'm mighty sorry, Mrs. Briscoe."

Bathed, his ragged beard shaved off, his matted hair

279

washed and trimmed by Lennie, Henri's thinness, the bones that rode high in his gaunt face made Teresa's heart hurt unbearably. The agony was that he had to go back. Starting tonight, he insisted. The Negro would be going back down the river in five days for another load of Arkansas hogs, and Owensboro was nearly a hundred miles away. Henri could not risk traveling by daylight. Kentucky, they told him, was now a place where vengeful evil could lurk in any shadow.

They clothed him in a decent shirt, Tee working busily to rip the ruffles off the front, and some nankeen pants a trifle too big. But they could not supply him with shoes. All Thad's old shoes had been worn out through the winter by the old Negro men.

"We may get shoes before we're sent to Texas." Henri was cheerful, seeing the misery in Teresa's eyes. "In summer we get along fine. Shoes don't last long in swampy country anyway."

"I haven't worn shoes since April," Clementine told him.

"Me either," Priscilla sighed, "and now my feet are so big I don't reckon my old shoes will even go on."

Lennie put her head down abruptly on the table and began to cry. Everything came back too poignantly: Thad marching off to fight to end a war so that his little daughters could have new shoes! That memory like iron fingers at her throat, she sobbed hoarsely, the little girls pressing close and crying too. Clementine dabbed a tear from her own brown cheek and struck the table a hard blow with the butt of the pistol.

"Damn war!" she cried.

"Clemmy!" protested her mother, recovering quickly. But Henri slid an arm around the girl's shoulders.

"Clemmy's right. Damn war! We say it every day—like a prayer."

"I will too," Ward piped. "Damn war!"

"No, you mustn't," insisted Lennie. "Pray God to end war and bring the soldiers home."

"But our pa won't come home, ever!" Rowena wailed. "He always threw me up high on the hay and tickled my feet. I want my pa back!"

"I want my pa too," put in 'Ria. "Pa always saved me wild strawberries."

"Pa would surely be ashamed to see so many crybabies," Clementine said. "Tee, there's a cold pone in the safe and a little fried meat. You fix a snack for Henri to carry. Put some of these peaches in your pocket too, Henri. Then you won't have to hunt grubs for a day or two."

They brushed and sponged off his draggled Confederate jacket. Wearing it he would be a prisoner of war, he explained, if he were captured. Without it he could be shot at without explanation, for a deserter or a spy. They carefully avoided telling him that in Kentucky now any Confederate was likely to be shot at.

"Not that they'll take me." He tried for optimism, seeing Teresa's desolate face. "I found people all along, friends of my father's, who hid me, and they'll hide me on the way back. I found out something else, too, that no Union general, not even Lincoln himself has a friend in Kentucky. I heard more bitter oaths and more vengeance sworn than I heard in two years' fighting in the Trans-Mississippi District. We didn't hate the Yanks down yonder. We killed them when we had to, then there were times when we traded tobacco to them for newspapers and coffee. At Pea Ridge there were some boys who used to slip into our camp at night and play cards with us. They were from a New Hampshire regiment and they hated the war as much as we did. We were lucky, we won all their pay and hard money was scarce in Smith's command."

"It's these foul guerrillas," Lennie told him. "We hate

them as much as the military do, but the Confederates are blamed for every crime they commit. Southern sympathizers have had to pay huge damages, and innocent old people have been arrested and ordered out of the state, merely because they had boys killed in those first battles over near Columbus. There have been some awful reprisals too, Confederate prisoners dragged out and hanged. That only makes more hatred for the Union army, but the more they're hated the more savage their rule. So don't be caught, Henri."

Tactfully Lennie took her children to bed, leaving Henri and Teresa in the dim kitchen alone. The smoke from the oily light drifted under the ceiling and a few sleepy flies came out of the corners to sail aimlessly over the covered pans of fruit.

Teresa apologized for the sickly light. "There's no oil and some of the stores are afraid to sell to us because Pa was in the Confederate army. Anyway there's no money and nobody connected with the Confederacy has any credit any more. How long will it go on, Henri?"

He parted a lock of her fair hair and twisted it around his finger.

"Lee's holding them," he insisted. "They can't move him though they have three times as many men. They'll never take Richmond."

"But can we take Washington? How can it end, ever? The Yankees are worn out too. They're tired and desperate or they wouldn't turn on us so cruelly and senselessly here in Kentucky. They're treating us now worse than if we were a seceded state."

Close-clasped, they clung together. I'll remember, I'll remember, Teresa told herself. His breath on her cheek. His lips hot and eager on her own. Was her mother remembering things like that? Remembering with bitter pain. Oh, God—no! Bring him back, God, bring him back!

"How can I let you go?" she choked. "How can I ever let you go?" She held his face tight between her icy hands.

He did not answer. He kissed her deeply, solemnly, reverently. He held her face between his palms and looked at it for a long minute, then his eyes fell, he dropped his hands, blew out the light and picked up the little parcel of food.

A gust of fresh air into the warm smoky room told her when the outer door was opened. Then it closed softly and there were no more sounds, though she listened intently. No sudden fierce challenge. No shots.

He was gone. And summer was gone and the war was not over. Never, never, the girl's sick heart cried, would it be over! Never, till all youth and all love and every beautiful thing was dead and rotted under this pressing burden of hate!

She waited a little, standing taut with the pistol in her hand. Then slowly she lighted the light, bolted the door again and went slowly up the stairs.

26

LITTLE HATTIE FINDLY HAD CHOSEN A BITTER TIME IN which to be born. But oblivious of the turmoil that seethed through the land she grew fatter and fairer, a lovable yellow-haired cherub with dimples in her elbows and a gay curl over her forehead. She had begun to crawl about and pull up to things, and her two adoring grandmothers were convinced that Hattie was the most beautiful child ever born.

They kept her in the Findly parlor in the daytime, with a bar nailed across the door so Old Tom could not hitch his rocker through when the women were busy.

"He'd hurt her, some way," Harriet insisted. "He could push a chair over on her or throw something at her. He just foams with jealousy whenever he sees her."

Ellen, after that first desperate flurry of consternation when Tom was arrested, had debated taking Harriet and the baby back to her house in town. It had seemed the logical thing to do, especially when it became obvious that she could not have Hessie at the Findly farm. Old Tom went into such screaming tantrums of fury the first time Hessie walked into the kitchen that she walked out again instantly and stubbornly refused to return. So there was nothing to do but take Hessie back to her cabin in town.

"You come too, Miss," Hessie begged. "You fetch Miss Harriet and that baby chile and us all live good in our own place."

It had been a temptation, but there was Marcia. Marcia had made no plea but her eyes were bereft and imploring.

"We can't leave her alone, Harriet," Ellen argued. "It would be an inhuman thing to do."

"She has had a rotten life," Harriet admitted. "Her family practically sold her to that old man, Tom told me. They were horribly in debt and their plantation going to rack, and when Mr. Findly went down there to buy cotton they thought he was rich. She was just a young girl then."

"She's a young woman still. She can't be more than forty —which may seem old to you. I'm not an old woman either, though you have made me a grandmother."

"If only he would die!" mourned Harriet for the hundredth time. "What can she do with this place, with Tom gone?"

"I can do something with it," Ellen said. "I have money that is mine and I can do with it as I please."

"I don't know you any more, Mama." Harriet sighed. "You've changed into a different person since Pa died."

"I haven't changed, Harriet. Say I have emerged. Strength and common sense that I always knew I had has been allowed to emerge. After being pressed down and frustrated for twenty years, it is still as vigorous as ever, and it gives me a fine feeling of competence now to do things without being criticized or prevented."

"Well, however much money you have it's a shame to waste it on this old place! When the war's over and Tom gets home we'll never stay here. I've already made Tom promise me that."

They were in Harriet's room, the low fire the only light. Ellen sat brushing her long hair.

"And where will you go?" she asked.

"Anywhere—anywhere away from here! There's plenty of room at home. Tom could work, and you're so foolish about the baby—"

"No," said Ellen. "No, Harriet. I am fond of your baby, much more fond than you, I regret to say. And I'm fond of Tom too, but if he would desert his parents in their desperate extremity, there would be no room for him under my roof!"

Harriet stared, stunned. "How can you be so heartless, Mama? Anyway," she went on smugly, "half of what Pa left is mine. You can't take that away from me. And when Willie and Tom come home there is going to be a settlement, I can promise you that!"

"When Willie and Tom come home there may be a settlement of your father's estate—but not of mine, Harriet. Not till I'm dead. So we'll talk no more about it. Meanwhile, if you would rather go back home and stay with Hessie, I have no objection, but Marcia and I will certainly miss little Hattie."

"You mean, stay there alone?" demanded Harriet.

"I've told you that I shall not desert Marcia. And certainly there is no way she could abandon a helpless husband."

"But you know I can't take care of the baby alone. When she cries or throws up it scares me to death. Sometimes I think she doesn't even like me. If you or Ma Findly comes near she simply fights to get away from me," said Harriet.

"A baby needs love." Ellen washed her face in the crockery bowl. "Next time you go home, remember to bring back some more towels. And I'll send everything in for Hessie to wash. Marcia shouldn't bend over those tubs, frail and tired as she is."

"Oh, for heaven's sake! If you're determined to be a martyr—" Harriet threw herself across the bed. "I don't suppose anybody can stop you."

"No, no one can. Not any more," said Ellen complacently. "Tomorrow I'm going out and hire some free Negroes to work this land. I'll try to find a mule too—maybe two mules." But Harriet's head was buried in the pillow.

Many times during that summer, Ellen looked over the top of her granddaughter's bright head at the sullen face of her own child. All Harper, she thought sadly. That selfish, willful mouth, those judging, demanding eyes. I gave her her father, I cannot condemn her if she is like him.

If only little Hattie would inherit Marcia's gentle forgiving heart, if only she would grow up kind and patient like Tom. A great fondness for her absent son-in-law had been growing in Ellen lately. Maybe she had spoken too harshly

286

to Harriet, declaring she would not have Tom under her roof, but if Tom Findly was ever encouraged to stand on his own feet it would be his mother-in-law who would achieve that transformation, not his drained, weary, too-indulgent mother or his inturning, self-centered wife.

"And you, my pet, must have a father you can be proud of," Ellen told the baby.

Summer moved into autumn, coloring the hills and lanes with glory. Ellen's free Negroes worked well because she paid them well. The tobacco was hung, cured and stripped, and Marcia Findly put money in her tin box and the lines of worry softened in her face. The corn came in, golden and rich, and Marcia pushed old Tom's chair near the window so that he could watch the harvest being stored, but his sunken face showed little interest now and no animation.

He sat for hours, chin sunk, eyes closed, his hands limp on the blanket that covered his useless legs. Marcia devotedly read aloud to him all the political news in the Louisville and Cincinnati papers that Harriet brought out from town but there was seldom a response in his bleary eyes.

"Last spring he would have been excited if he thought that McClelland was going to beat Lincoln in this election," Marcia said. "But now he doesn't seem to care or understand."

"It will be war, on and on, however the election goes." Ellen was resigned. "Some people had hopes of that Peace Party but McClelland's letter accepting the nomination made it clear that he would stop at nothing to win the war."

"Does it matter who wins? So it ends?" asked Marcia. "You were disappointed at Burnside's failure at Petersburg. I was heartsick when General Lew Wallace turned back Early at Washington. Couldn't it be the same everywhere—the victory each side hopes for, the one that will end the war? All

I ask is for my boy to come home. You and I will be friends whoever surrenders first, Ellen."

"It's because we are reasonable people," Ellen declared. "We know that no one will really win the war. One army will be defeated, but both have lost. Fortunately, my boy doesn't seem to be in any serious danger. From his last letter William seems to be enjoying the Navy, but I too want to see Tom come home. Hattie hardly knows she ever had a father."

"They'll be strangers," Marcia sighed.

"Not for long."

More and more the need to comfort Marcia pressed upon Ellen Harper. It was because she herself now needed to be outgiving, and Harriet had so little need. Harriet was so self-sufficient. Where other women knew sorrow and the ache of loss, Harriet's reaction was always one of irritation and resentment. She even gave way to impatience with Tom at times when she was alone with her mother.

"He could just as well have taken that oath!" she fretted. "Even if he took it with his tongue in his cheek, he could have protected himself and us."

"No," said Ellen. "No, he could not have done it with honor. He could not have sworn a lie, to defend and uphold what he did not believe in. I doubt if they would have accepted his oath, when they knew he had fought with John Morgan. He would have had to ask for a pardon and likely that would have been refused too."

"Morgan!" snapped Harriet. "That god! That hero! Well, they killed his fine Morgan, shot him down like a mad dog, and I'm glad, you hear—I'm glad! There have been times when I'd gladly have shot him myself. Now I suppose I'll never get his ghost out of Tom's mind, his robbing, murdering ghost!"

Harriet did all the errands now, driving the mare into

town, taking her time returning. Now as the days shortened it worried Ellen when Harriet was late and Marcia wandered from window to window, voicing no anxiety but with a tautness of waiting about her.

When Ellen complained, Marcia was always quick to defend Harriet. "It's lonely out here. She's young. This is a dreary house for young people. I was young when I came into it and I shed some tears of loneliness then."

"She has a little girl to care for." Ellen was maternally critical.

"Well, I'll go milk, then I'll feed Miss Hattie with a spoon. She'll be drinking out of a cup pretty soon."

From Hessie Ellen had learned how Harriet spent some of her long hours in town. "Sometime she just curl up in you' bed and sleep, Miss," Hessie said, "and sometime she make fire and fetch young gals out here. They beaux too. She say tomorrow, Hessie, you bake a cake. Where I git aigs, I say, she say I fetch 'em. Then sometime she try on all her pretty clothes and cry because they too tight now."

It was true that Harriet was growing plump. She had a little double chin now and her frocks were tight on her round body. But she was still a young woman and with dusk deepening on the short November days, the roads could be unsafe for a girl, and especially for a good mare. Ellen was pacing the room when finally the carriage rolled in at the drive. She had angry, worried reproaches ready when Harriet came, head high and cheeks bright with cold, into the kitchen.

"Well, Lincoln's elected!" she announced, before Ellen could say a word. "He got mighty few votes in Kentucky but they elected him anyway. Here's your yarn, Mama, and the stuff Ma Findly wanted—I had to get brown sugar. They told me there hadn't been any white sugar in weeks. What's the matter, Mama?"

"You know very well that you have no business on the road so late, Harriet. And that the baby has to be fed."

"Oh, she's too fat already. She won't starve. I'll have to change my dress first. She slobbers all over me. Oh, yes—they had quite a little ruckus down the road last night. Some guerrillas attacked a place down there and the troops went out, and that Colonel Bisbee was shot and killed."

Marcia, who had come in with the bucket of milk, looked stunned. "That colonel who came out here, who arrested Tom? He was a mighty cruel man. I tried to kiss Tom good-bye, Ellen, and he pushed me right against the stove."

"Well, he's dead and gone now, Ma Findly," said Harriet smugly.

She was still, Ellen noted, aquiver with some suppressed excitement. She was impatient with the baby, who cried when she was bathed and undressed, and as soon as she could she hurried her mother upstairs and carefully closed the door of her room.

"Mama, I want to show you!" she whispered excitedly. "Put her down there. I'll give her this teething ring. I can't stand her yelling tonight. Listen, Miss Findly, you behave yourself now, you hear?"

Ellen felt a ragged hurt twitch in her breast. "You sounded exactly like your father, Harriet. Always when he gave an order he ended it by saying, 'You hear?' "

"Well, anyway Pa got what he wanted, you have to admit that. He turned everything his way generally. I hope I can be like him to that extent," Harriet said.

"But don't be hard, my dear. There are gentle ways of getting things done," admonished her mother.

"You do manage now and then, though I used to think you were as spineless as Willie, Mama, I really did. Look, sit over here. I have to drag out my trunk. It's under the bed." She dropped to the floor and began pulling out her low trunk, moving it slowly and cautiously. "I don't want them to hear it scraping downstairs. She might come up here. There's no lock on the door. Anyway she d think it was odd if we locked it. Now"—she breathed gustily as the trunk came free—"I'll get the keys. They're in my purse."

"What is this, Harriet?"

"You'll see." She lifted the lid and laid aside some folded garments. "They're down deep. I hid them. Tom didn't want me to do it but I did, right after Pa died. The day before his funeral I hid them here. There!" She stooped into the trunk and lifted out several bundles of green-printed papers, tied about with red tape. "Know what these are, Mama?"

"Obviously documents of some sort."

"My love, these are bonds! United States bonds. Fifty thousand dollars' worth of lovely United States bonds, and now that that old Colonel Bisbee is dead they're ours—all ours!"

"I don't understand, Harriet," Ellen said. "What did the colonel have to do with these bonds and how do they happen to be yours?"

"Mama, it was a deal. Tom heard enough from Pa and the colonel both to know that. When Pa came out here last summer and raised that row he let the cat out of the bag. He ordered Tom's father to give the bonds back then but of course the old man couldn't understand, or he pretended he didn't, and nobody else knew where the bonds were. Tom didn't, not then, nor Ma Findly. Finally they made Pa believe that and he went away."

"Tom told me a little about it, the day your father died," Ellen said. "He was worried about it then."

"Oh, Tom and his silly conscience! Look—" Harriet spread one of the bonds open. "Tom's father's name on every one! The way Tom understood it, it was a deal to buy contraband cotton and ship it up to Louisville, and Tom thinks Pa put up most of the money. Then the gunboats began stopping all the contraband shipments and seizing the cotton, so Pa got the colonel in on it, so they could bribe the right people to get the cotton up the river. Then they began arresting people for illegally trading in cotton and Pa and the colonel were both afraid of being involved, so they talked old Mr. Findly into factoring the cotton for them and putting the money into bonds. In his own name—and he was taking all the risk, but he was too greedy to care about that."

"You make it all sound very sordid, Harriet."

She shrugged. "But it turned out well, for us anyway. Nobody was arrested, and then the day after Pa died, Tom found the bonds. They were hid in some old saddlebags deep down in the oat bin. Tom thought he ought to take them to the bank, but I made him give them to me and I brought them up here and hid them. That night the colonel came out here and arrested Tom, I was scared to death for fear Tom would tell him where the bonds were, but he didn't. Tom said you could buy these bonds with greenbacks but that they pay interest in gold, and that anybody who held them long enough could double his money. Tom's father never intended to give them up, Mama. I'm sure he didn't. There couldn't be anything written down, no agreement or anything, because it was all illegal, they'd have been in jail if they were found out. But who cares about that? Who cares about breaking their silly laws, if it makes us all rich?" Harriet did a little dance step.

Ellen sat very still. Her face was stony gray and her lips moved a little as though she prayed. Even the baby was still, lying staring up at her, big blue eyes wide. Harriet ended her pirouette and frowned at her mother.

"Mama," she cried when the silence had stretched a little, "say something! Don't just sit there!"

"What shall I say?" cried Ellen. "What use to say anything?" She rose and stood, vibrant and tall. "That there is such a thing as honor? That the colonel had his rights and that he may have a family? You wouldn't understand, Harriet. You would never understand about honor."

"Would you?" her daughter flamed back at her. "What about that money in the steel box, the money you used to pay back the bank and run this stupid farm? Was that honest money? You know it wasn't! Pa made every penny of that on contraband, and you know it!"

"At least it was my own money that earned it," Ellen said. "The court agreed upon that when the books were examined. And it has been put to honorable purposes, no one has been cheated."

"You make me sick!" snapped Harriet. "You and Tom with your silly scruples. I'm going to keep these bonds, you hear? I'm going to keep them till that crazy old man dies and then Tom and I will take the money and when we do we'll go far, far from here! And"—she choked—"when we do we'll never come back! Never, never!"

It was the sounds from below that halted her furious tirade.

They both heard them. The wild sudden screaming. The hysterical sounds of laughter.

Hattie Findly began screaming too. But she was ignored as Harriet and Ellen both went running down the stairs.

27

*I*T WAS THE BLOOD THAT ELLEN SAW FIRST.

Blood on the floor and on the body, Tom's body lying bloody and inert where obviously the two soldiers who stood awkwardly just inside the door had laid it down. Blood on Tom's body and on Marcia's dress as she lay across her lifeless son, screaming wildly.

Harriet began screaming too. She rushed at the soldiers and began pummeling them with her fists.

"What have you done to him?" she shrieked. "What have you done?"

They shifted their feet and the rifles they carried. They put the girl off gently, holding her wrists, looking worried, their good country faces appalled.

"Lady, it wasn't us!" The taller one shifted his rifle. "It was a firing squad. We just brought him home because we knowed him. We didn't want old Tom buried in that trench out yonder, so we brought him home."

Ellen was trying to lift Marcia, who had gone abruptly limp.

"Help me," she pleaded with the others. "Help me."

One leaned his gun against the wall and came to lift Marcia, her hands dangling loosely, her face drained and ghastly, her eyes closed.

"Fainted dead away," he said. "Better lay her flat and put cold water on her face."

Ellen ran for the gourd dipper, wet a towel and began sponging Marcia's face. "Tell us what happened," she ordered the anxiously watching man. "Who did this to Tom?"

The other man was still holding Harriet's wildly beating hands and saying, uneasily, "Now, lady! Now, lady!"

"They took them out, six of them out of that prison camp," said the man holding the gourd. "Burnbridge's orders. If a Union man gets killed by guerrillas we got to shoot or hang two Confederate prisoners. But this time it was a Union officer that got killed, so we got orders to shoot six prisoners. We was on guard but they didn't put us on the firing squad and Ed and me was both glad when we seen that Old Tom was one of them they brought out. So— we brought him home. That's all. We're sorry, but that don't do no good, I reckon."

"No, no good at all. Will you carry her in for me, and lay her on that bed? Harriet—do be quiet, my dear! These men are not to blame for what has happened. They did us a kindness by bringing Tom home."

The soldier lifted Marcia easily, almost tenderly, laid her on the bed in the bedroom. "That lady—she his wife?" he asked.

"Yes, she is his wife. Tom's wife. And this is his mother."

"This here is a mighty rotten kind of war!" he sighed.

Harriet had ceased screaming. She was bending over Tom now, pushing the bloodstained yellow hair back from his white face.

"They killed you, Tom!" she kept repeating in a strange croaking moan. "They killed you!"

"Wasn't our fault, lady," defended the man she had mauled. "We didn't want no part of it. We just brought him home."

Sing one song, Kentucky! A song of frightful vengeance,

a song of hate. The song of a tortured land, of brotherhood lost and honor forsaken, of suspicion and terror and the agony of women. A sad song, Kentucky!

The men picked up their rifles again, uncertainly looked about them, heading toward the door. And it was then that old Tom Findly, dumb so long, prisoned so long in a gargling, horrible dumbness, dragged a blast of cackling laughter from his throat, rocking his body from side to side.

The soldiers halted, stared shocked as the laughter rose to an idiotic hoot.

"Crazy, is he?" one of them asked.

Ellen was trying to comfort Harriet but the girl put her off, fought her off, knelt keening over the dead boy on the floor, patting his face, calling to him. Suddenly that dumb old man, silent and inarticulate so long, dragged speech up from some dark depth within him, speech mixed with awful, vindictive laughter.

"Killed him!" he chortled. "Killed the rebel dog, by God!"

Harriet sprang up, glaring wildly at him for an instant. Then in a desperate rush she crossed the room and snatched the rifle from the hands of the startled soldier.

"You devil!" she cried, low and viciously. "You vile, horrible old devil!"

The gun went off with a crash before either of the three who had rushed at her could disarm her. She began to laugh herself then and tore away from Ellen's detaining hands, dropped the weapon with a clang and throwing her arms in the air, dashed out the door.

"Stop her!" cried Ellen, running out into the cold blackness of the night. "Stop her! She'll harm herself."

The two soldiers went charging out, leaving Ellen standing in the open door. How long she stood there, she could never afterwards remember. Somewhere off in the darkness she heard pounding feet and the troopers calling. A rooster honked a hoarse challenge and behind her she caught Marcia's faint moan. Far off, like a sound in a dream, she heard the faint wail of the forgotten baby.

Then one of the soldiers came back, his face pale and unhappy.

"Can't figure where she went," he said worriedly. "We've looked every place. Ed has gone to get some folks to help hunt."

"Thank you," said Ellen woodenly.

She turned back into the room and saw old Tom Findly's head sunk on his chest, where a crimson stain widened.

"Is he dead?" asked the soldier.

"He is dead," Ellen told him. "They are both dead."

She went to old Tom then and, overcoming her revulsion, touched his cooling face. No breath issued from his drooling mouth, his eyes were opaque, and she closed them mechanically. Then she bent over Tom and straightened his body, laid his hands on his breast. Bringing the damp cloth, she washed his smeared face and pushed back his sweated hair.

"I'll get somebody," offered the soldier, nervously. "I'll bring somebody to help you. I'll get Ranse Ridley."

"Thank you," Ellen said again in the same dead voice. "I shall need help."

Marcia came stumbling out then, weakly swaying. She clung to Ellen and stared dully at the sagging body of her husband.

"Harriet killed him," Ellen said. "She has run away. They've gone to find her."

"She had a right." Marcia shook her head and looked down dazedly at her hands. "I heard him. I heard what he said about my boy—about my Tom!"

She began to cry again then, shuddering all over, kneeling to press her palms on the dead boy's face, to croon maternal grief in incoherent moanings.

"He was my son too," Ellen said low. "He was my good son!"

Marcia straightened, listened. "I'd better fetch her." She hurried toward the stairs. "She's been crying a long time."

They found Harriet in the early morning when the autumn fog lifted.

Ranse Ridley found her in a cattle pond far back in one of old Tom Findly's fields, the rich fields he had slaved for, worshiped, that for him had come first always, before wife or child or God. She had been there all night.

The scarlet leaves fallen from a dogwood tree had caught in her heavy hair and made a little scarlet crown above her white dead face.

The two bereaved women moved like frozen statues in the Findly house.

Neighbors were there, people from town were there, somebody had brought Hessie and Hessie bustled and crooned and moaned in sympathy while she cooked food that no one ate. But for Ellen Harper and Marcia Findly all these were shadows. The minister and Mr. Merrill were shadows. So were Lennie Briscoe and her older daughters. All shadows. Only one thing was real any more. Hattie.

They passed her back and forth, one to the other, without jealousy. They wept into her yellow curls and the watching women sobbed in sympathy and turned their faces away.

"Leave them alone," advised gentle Lennie. "Leave them alone. I know!"

There was the strain and formality of burial, there were open graves again. Hattie, wrapped in a blanket, whimpered, and Marcia looked at Ellen and brought from a pocket in her black cloak the teething ring. Clods fell and solemn words met the desolate winds of autumn and were forever lost.

Mr. Merrill brought them back to the Findly house, hung about worriedly.

"This house is going to be mighty empty for you two," he said.

"We'll close up everything here. We'll go back to town," Ellen told him. "Marcia will go with me. Mr. Ridley says he'll take care of the place till she can find a renter. You needn't worry about us, Mr. Merrill. We'll get along. We have Hattie to think about."

"You've had a bad shock. I'll wait here and drive you back to town, when you've packed your things," Merrill offered.

"I—have a few things to do," Ellen told him. "We won't keep you waiting long."

In the upper room someone had closed Harriet's trunk and pushed it back against the wall. A little fire still burned in the grate and all Harriet's clothes had been put carefully out of sight by the solicitous women.

Ellen opened the trunk and brought out the taped bundles, the bonds that Harriet had gloated over almost in her last hour. Ellen studied them thoughtfully. Here was a fortune, here was wealth for little Hattie Findly. She opened a packet and shook out the stiff, green printed pieces of paper, sealed with the great Seal of the United States.

A fortune—but bought with too much blood. Too much blood, too much dishonor, too much evasion of what was decent and lawful. There was the blood of murder on these papers, the vengeful murder of six innocent men. Too much blood. No good could come of anything bought so dear.

Slowly, one by one, she laid the bonds on the fire. There were fifty of them and the stiff paper burned slowly, last to burn the scraggly signature of A. Lincoln, president of the United States.

She covered the charred scraps with ashes and then rose and gathered together her scattered possessions. Later they would come back and put the house in order. Later when the smell of blood had faded away.

Heavily she went downstairs. Marcia was holding little Hattie, warmly wrapped in a woolen shawl.

"You'd never believe I wore this shawl once," said Marcia Findly.

28

THE PEOPLE ON THE STREET STOOD VERY STILL.

It was spring and the sun filtered through the greening leaves with a soft, luminous, liquid light. Doves whirred about the cupola of the courthouse, their soft murmuring notes faintly audible above the slow thudding of solemn drums.

Past the bank, past the old Nesbitt house, moved the slow procession. Men in Union blue with arms reversed, flags bordered with crepe, sober citizens pacing in cadence with mourning bands on their sleeves and hats.

April again. April, 1865. A time of promise, a time of long-awaited peace. Appomattox was history. Richmond smoldered in ashes. But Abraham Lincoln was dead.

Somewhere to the north was moving now that black

shrouded funeral train bearing the body of the slain president of the United States to his ultimate resting place, but in every Kentucky city and town men and soldiers marched, drums muttered their hushed roll, flags hung at half-mast and people stood in silent reverence. The man they mourned had been flouted in Kentucky, misunderstood, even hated. But now there was quiet grief.

On the corner by the old Nesbitt house a group of women watched the mournful parade. Ellen Harper stood, holding restless little Hattie Findly by the hand. Hattie could walk and dance now, and the drums made her little feet tingle and she tugged at restraint and laughed. Marcia, less stooped, with a little youth come back into her patient face, bent and patted the small flushed cheek.

"Look, Hattie," she whispered, pointing. "Out there is your uncle. That's your Uncle William, marching there with all those sailors."

Ellen felt her throat cramp as her son went marching by, eyes straight ahead. William was still tall for his weight but he was no longer a gangling, awkward figure. He stood straight, with dignity, even in his faded uniform. A hand caught at her own and pressed it hard and she looked down into the shining eyes, the flushed happy face of Clemmy Briscoe.

"Isn't Willie wonderful?" breathed Clementine, raptly. "He looks like a man now."

A little way down the street, where the syringa bushes of the old Nesbitt place tossed petals of white bloom over the fence, stood Henri Nesbitt and Teresa, hand in hand. Ellen gave them a fond and happy smile. Henri was gaunt and ragged, worn with marching, sun-blackened and bearded, but he too stood tall and unafraid. There was still martial law in Kentucky, the writ of habeas corpus was still suspended—a club held over the state, men grumbled, to force Kentucky to ratify the Thirteenth Amendment abolishing slavery—but by an amazing reversal of public feeling the returned Confederate was now the hero.

He was still disfranchised, he had no rights of citizenship, but he was a Southerner, and for all the effort and control of the radicals, Kentucky would not forget that it was Southern too.

"What was the good of our winning the war, if these rebels are let to come back and take over again as though nothing had happened?" Mr. Merrill had complained to Ellen.

"They are ours. They have taken defeat with dignity," Ellen had argued.

She had seen Milo Nesbitt only the day before. He was prison-pale and half sick yet, but he was free. Free and lost and desolate. His mother, Milo told Ellen, had died in the winter in St. Louis. He had no idea what had become of Denise. He believed she had gone back to New Orleans. He had not heard from her in two years.

The drums beat on. The procession rounded a corner, disbanded in some confusion, then William came hurrying to where the women waited.

"I'm hungry, Mama," he said, getting a tight hold of Clemmy Nesbitt's hand. "Let's go home and eat."

Ellen looked down the street. "Go and get Henri, William," she said. "Henri and Little Tee—and, William, see if you can find Milo. He was standing alone over there by the bank a little while ago and he looked hungry too."

Hessie had a table bountifully spread when they returned to the Harper house.

"All these yere boys, they come home hungry," she grinned, "and you, Miss Baby, you always hungry!"

"If I had tried to eat food like this a week ago when I was

302

first released," Milo said with a wan smile, "it would have made me deathly sick."

Marcia put Hattie into a high chair and handed her a biscuit. "It's over," she said gently. "We have all seen dreadful times, we have all known terrible sorrow, but now it's peace in Kentucky and we can be thankful for it."

"You've still got General Palmer," Henri reminded her. "You've still got angry men who confuse victory with vengefulness."

William looked soberly around the familiar room. "And empty chairs," he said, reaching for his mother's hand. "It will take a little time, Mama. Give me time. I'll get used to it maybe."

"Lincoln would have done all he could to put down the idea of revenge," declared Henri. "But with men in power like Seward and Sumner and General Palmer anything can happen. I doubt if any repatriation act can pass soon. Those fellows in Washington will fight Andrew Johnson if he takes a stand for it."

"I saw Lincoln," said William, between hungry attacks on Hessie's fried chicken. "It was on the James, at City Point. The second of April, the Sunday the Confederates evacuated Richmond."

"And burned the city," said Henri.

"They didn't intend to burn it," William said. "They fired a lot of cotton in the warehouses to keep the Union from capturing it, and the fire got away from them and spread till half the city was destroyed. Lincoln was at City Point, on the *River Queen,* and Admiral Porter sent over his barge to take the president on board the *Malvern,* his flagship. I'd been on the *Malvern* all winter, and I went along to help row the barge. Afterwards, when Lincoln was bound to go up to Richmond, they got a tug to tow it. But I was close to Lincoln. He wore his tall silk hat and his face looked mighty sad and tired."

"We hated him," said Teresa. "Now it seems all wrong somehow, now that he is dead."

"Death," said Ellen gently, "is a great ennobler. We can see the good in all people, after they are dead."

William gave her a level, searching look, then his eyes went down to the end of the table, to that empty chair. Even his father, his taut young face conceded, could now be granted the nobility of death.

"It was a tricky business, getting the president up that river," he went on. "There were four big Confederate ironclads up there. After a little we heard a terrific explosion and Admiral Porter knew what it was. The rebels had blown up their boats. But the river was full of mines and sunken ships and there were still Confederate batteries in places, though luckily they had all been silenced and abandoned. But we all breathed a sigh of relief when finally we put Lincoln ashore with a Marine guard at Rockett's Landing. An old Negro man with white wool rushed out of the crowd then and fell down and kissed Lincoln's dusty shoes. I'm glad I saw him. It will be something to remember."

When the meal was over and they had all gone into the parlor, bright and sunny now and gay with the new flowered carpet, Ellen said, "Milo, you and Henri will stay here with us, till you can make some permanent arrangements."

"But Henri's going home with us, Mrs. Harper," said Teresa, flushing. "Henri and I are being married day after tomorrow."

"I'm glad for you, Little Tee." Ellen went and kissed her. "You too, Henri. Now perhaps you can paint again?"

"Clemmy and I," Henri grinned, "have a busy day tomorrow. We have to plant tobacco."

Marcia got up briskly. "I'd better put this young lady

down for a nap," she announced, gathering up small Hattie, who had been gaily dancing from one pattern to another on the carpet. "She's had an exciting morning."

"Hattie has saved us—Marcia and me," Ellen remarked. "She gave us something to live for after so much tragedy."

"She looks exactly like Tom," Teresa said. "William, if you're going to drive us home, we'd better start. Mama will want to hear all about the parade. She couldn't come because Ward and 'Ria both have the measles."

William returned at dusk, and found his mother sitting alone in the big downstairs bedroom. It was a little changed. There was no walnut chair, and no black coat hung upon it. There was brightness, and in his mother's face was a little of that brightness. Her son had come home. He perched on a hard chair and turned his faded cap in his hands.

"I'll have my discharge in a few days," he remarked. "Mama, do you think that a man twenty years old is too young to get married?"

A little pang of loss clutched briefly at Ellen's heart. She put it down firmly and smiled at her son.

"I think twenty is a very suitable age, son, especially when a man has served two years in a war and made himself into a real man. Of course you are not of age yet—"

"I know. I wanted to talk about that. About Pa's estate." William fiddled with his cap. "I don't know anything, you know—about what went on after he died—and Harriet," he reminded her.

"Mr. Merrill is your guardian until you are twenty-one," she told him. "And Hattie Findly's too. Hattie inherits her mother's share, as you know."

"That's all right, Mama. But there are a few things I'd like to have—for myself, when it's all legal. The mill—is it still operating?"

"Oh, yes, it has always been running, quite successfully," Ellen said. "We had army contracts to make spokes for wagon wheels and for caissons—lately we've been making wheels too, but not for the military. The farmers need everything now, so much has been destroyed."

"It would make a living, wouldn't it—for Clemmy and me?" he asked. "If they'd let me run it. Mama, I never want to go back to that bank again, even if they'd let me. But there is some banking I want to do—there is seven hundred dollars left of that money I borrowed from you. I banked it in St. Louis. They can draw a draft on it, can't they, so I can pay you back? I'll pay the rest too, as soon as I can. I spent some—and I gave Mrs. Nesbitt some money. She—things were not right in St. Louis, Mama. Denise—I'd rather not talk about it."

Ellen nodded. She had seen the graying of tragedy in Milo Nesbitt's face. She had asked no questions.

"There were—men," said William presently, looking down at the floor.

"William, I would like to give you that money. For a marriage gift. It was mine to give, you know. I do not need it."

He shook his head. "No. No, don't you see, I have to pay it back! I have to start right. I have to be honest and not ask favors. You see, don't you, Mama?"

"Yes, I see, my son. And I am humbly grateful that you feel that way," she said gently.

"Something else I wanted to ask about," he went on. "You know those mortgages Pa had—"

"The Briscoes? The Nesbitts?" she asked. "They were never foreclosed, William. I had the administrators withdraw all the papers after your father died."

He drew a deep breath. "I'm glad. I—knew somehow you'd do what was right, Mama. What was decent—anyway! I reckon Henri and Milo can pay off in time. Henri's going to run the Briscoe place. Clemmy will help him. Clemmy's got so much good sense, she'll help Henri this summer, but we want to get married in the fall."

"That will make me happy, William," Ellen said.

They went together out of the room. In the parlor, on the sofa, Milo Nesbitt lay sleeping, his thin arms dangling.

"Poor devil!" remarked William. "I hope they won't make it too hard on him if he wants to stay here and practice law again."

"Peace may come slowly, son," Ellen said. "But when it comes it will be forever, in Kentucky." Then she drew back a curtain abruptly. "William—look!"

He stared over her shoulder, gave a little excited exclamation.

"Wake up Milo!" he cried.

Ellen waked the sleeping man, pulled him, dazed and stumbling, to the window.

Out there in the street a single figure was making a slow way to the square. A bent and white-haired figure, with long beard flowing, cane tapping the pavement, but with chin up and pride denying the pitiful flapping garments that adorned a shrunken body.

Milo gave a shout and plunged out the door.

All alone, undefeated, Judge Horatio Nesbitt had come home!

(1)